For Lucy

CW00429169

The Chronicles of Harriet Shelley

Sarah Roux

Happy Birthday

Sarah Roux

2019

This book is a work of fiction. Any references to historical events, real people, or real places are used fictitiously. Other names, characters, places and events are products of the author's imagination, and any resemblance to actual events, places or persons, living or dead, is entirely coincidental

Copyright © 2019 Sarah Roux
Cover Design by Jill Rennie
All Rights Reserved
ISBN: 978-1-9997957-2-6

For Mike

Volume One
Harriet

~Prologue~

London, November 1816

She stood by the water's edge, dark in her cloak, darker still of mind. Night sounds came skimming like stones across the lake; a pair of water fowls flapping their wings as they bedded down in a nest of reeds, the shrill call of a fox to his vixen at the top of a grassy bank. A curricle drove by in the distance, its wheels rolling smoothly past on the way home from one of the pleasure gardens, the laughter of its occupants echoing faintly across the empty space of Hyde Park.

She lifted her head. She had been without companionship and laughter for so long she could acknowledge it in others without envy. Looking across the stretch of lake known as the Long Water, watching the wind blow and the water replying in gentle ripples, she remembered a time when she herself could evoke a meaningful response. A child's affection. A sisterly kiss. The look of horror in her husband's eyes as she had lurched towards him one final time, arms outstretched. Begging.

The wind blew a harsh breath dispersing the memories, making the flesh on the tops of her un-gloved hands pucker into goose bumps. Her gold and turquoise engagement ring, bereft now of the sentiment it had once contained, rolled restlessly around her wedding finger.

She shivered. Thrusting her hands into the pockets of her cloak searching for warmth, she found instead several heavy stones that she could not remember placing there.

Staring with unseeing eyes across the body of water, she tried to divine the significance of her actions and realised that of course, she was about to drown herself.

A distant bell chimed the early morning hour. Breath streamed from her mouth in misty vapours and she watched it rise into the air, surprised by the reminder that she was still alive.

She took a step forward. The curving banks of the lake veered away sinuously, the blackness of the winter waters shining in the moonlight.

She was ready.

∽One∾
Beginnings

London, 1800

She clutched her sister's hand as they walked out into the first stirrings of the fashionable hour. To the west lay the verdant sweep of Hyde Park where hordes of deer roamed the far reaches of the Serpentine, while to the east beckoned the glamour and luxury of the wide pavements of Bond Street; the glass plated shops waiting to be lit up like jewels at dusk when the lamp lighters would come, dragging their ladders as they made their rounds.

'It's a shame Mama couldn't come with us.'

Eliza nodded sagely. 'She is not feeling well today, Harriet. She needs to rest.'

A thin man, coming at a great pace from the opposite direction almost knocked her off her feet. He stopped short, raising his cap in apology.

'Beg pardon, Miss Harriet.'

Harriet recognised him as the man who had recently attended at their father's house with one of his apprentices, to fix a leak in the rain-water cistern.

Mr Alder bent down and ruffled Harriet's curls. She smiled up at him.

Recalling that Mr Alder owned a thriving plumbing business and that occasionally her father invited him to dine, Eliza nodded graciously. 'Good afternoon, Mr Alder. Come, Harriet.'

At the point where the road began to narrow, they halted at The Mount Coffee House, a striking building protruding at an odd angle onto Lower Grosvenor Street. A gentleman, his face enlivened with the effects of red wine, was passing through the door and with exaggerated courtesy he bowed as he held it open for them.

'This is no place for ladies,' he slurred. Harriet caught the man's grapey breath as he looked down at her.

'We are the Westbrooks.' Eliza's voice was cut-glass.

'Well now, John Westbrook certainly keeps a fine establishment here.'

Eliza smiled stiffly.

The door swung shut behind them. They edged around a group of swaggering young men who were debating the recent attempt on the King's life in Hyde Park. At a neighbouring table a father and his five sons squabbled over the proposed breed of a new pair of carriage horses; the Hackney Pony or the Cleveland Bay. Both evidently had their merits.

A cluster of older men, waving newspapers as they discussed Napoleon Bonaparte's march into Italy, registered them with curiosity as they passed by.

Harriet could feel her thoughts drowning in waves of masculine sound until they floated to the surface once more, borne away by the gentler susurration of verse as two poets composed couplets, the dregs of coffee, dark as night, caught at the bottom of their abandoned cups.

They journeyed further into the room. She pulled at Eliza's waist, hoping they could find a seat on the far side where a brightly coloured bird was whistling in a cage nailed to the wall, but Eliza led the way to a long wooden counter in the middle of the room, where several large copper urns stood by, kept constantly on the boil.

She closed her eyes, wanting to float away into the misty air, heavy with the aroma of ale, and the deep richness of roasted coffee beans.

Eliza shook her.

'Stand up straight, let me tie your sash.'

She bound the deep blue silk more firmly, imprisoning Harriet's slender waist.

Their father, alerted to their presence, appeared from the rooms upstairs where he conducted the day-to-day running of his business. He swung Harriet into his arms and lifted her onto the counter top.

Some of the regular customers clustered around, grinning.

'Here's little Harriet!'

'A beauty! You must be proud, John.'

'Indeed, I am.'

'And what age is she now?'

'She's five years old.'

'Ask her to dance a jig for us!'

'Or sing a verse or two!'

She stood there, merely looking beautiful.

The voices of the crowd faded. Enveloped in clouds of steam, she traced patterns with her eyes and thought she saw the tufts of a feathered quill floating beneath the fragments of a heart.

She shook herself out of her reverie, smiling politely as people admired her pale brown ringlets, and the blush of rose in her cheeks. She watched Eliza's eyes whip across the crowd, her father deferring to the audience with a sly smile.

Uneasy and lost in the whorls of vapour and admiration, she beseeched her sister with her eyes whose answering gaze she could not fathom; love and satisfaction beneath which lurked something uglier. Harriet recoiled, seeing Eliza as if for the first time, noticing her lank hair, her small eyes, the murky atmosphere of the coffee house casting sallow shadows across her face, highlighting her pock-marked complexion.

Later she spied Eliza taking a hopeless peek at her own reflection in the largest of the copper urns before giving a vicious shake of her head.

She wondered why it was considered a good thing to be pretty and whether her sister was disappointed at being so plain.

⁓ Two ⁓
Blushing Into Love

London, April 1811

At the northern edge of Clapham Common, the glissando notes of a harp flowed through the drawing room of the Church House School for Young Ladies.

At one end of the room, a makeshift stage had been erected. Against a backdrop of sky filled with silvered clouds, a canopy of paper trees framed the narrow steps leading up to a pedestal, adorned with a bower of flowers.

Harriet, in her long white gown, was dreading the climb. In rehearsals, she had stumbled each time. Last night, Mrs Fenning who ran the school with an iron rod, had wedged Harriet's satin slippers with paper at each end so that her feet wouldn't slip.

To allay her fears she began to speculate on matters more pleasant. Would she see him today? She trembled.

'Stand still, Harriet.'

Her room-mate, Hellen, wielding a brush in one hand and a mirror in the other was smoothing Harriet's hair into glossy rivulets that flowed down her back.

'I've finished.' She stepped back. 'Harriet, you have hair like a poet's dream.'

'What a thing to say,' said Harriet, her face growing hot.

'Mrs Fenning has been telling everybody that you were born to play the part of Venus.'

Harriet met her own gaze as she took the looking glass. Large, limpid eyes set in a blushed-rose complexion. The goddess of love and desire.

Her thoughts wandered once more into dangerous territory. 'Do you have any family coming to the performance today, Hellen?' She took care to avoid eye contact.

'Unfortunately not, my parents are visiting relatives in Wales.'

Harriet's shoulders drooped.

'However, my brother is planning to attend.' She paused. 'Harriet, I couldn't help noticing a copy of my brother's book was delivered to you the other day. Have you read it yet? Father has declared it quite unsuitable. I've always been an admirer of my brother's poetry and I'm disappointed I won't be able to read his latest work.'

Continuing to observe herself in the glass, Harriet saw the flush on her cheeks deepen. She took a few shallow breaths, trying to steady her voice.

'We've spent so much time rehearsing and learning lines, I haven't given the book a thought. I'm sure we can read a page or two together, before bed.'

Harriet was relieved to see Hellen accepting her falsehood. In reality, the gothic novel, *St Irvyne*, now lay covertly under Harriet's pillow, well-thumbed, its more thrilling passages already committed to memory.

'It was thoughtful of him to send you a copy. It seems as if he wishes to further your education. He complains endlessly about this school to father; it's his belief that learning music, sewing and dance is not sufficient for our needs.'

Harriet had left the stage area and withdrawn to the window overlooking the front drive, her eyes anxiously raking over the road.

She turned swiftly at Hellen's words.

'I think it's considerate that your brother would take the time and the trouble to think of me.'

'Yes. I suppose so. But sometimes he can go too far.'

'What do you mean?'

Hellen looked as if she wished she had not spoken. 'Perhaps I shouldn't have said anything.'

'What is it, Hellen?'

'Well…there have been some misdemeanours.'

'Please tell me. I would like to know.'

Hellen sighed. 'There was one time I remember, when he was home from school for the summer. He'd got up early one morning to roam the fields of our estate and to sail paper boats on the pond.

'We had a gardener, Mr Brockett, whose young granddaughter came to stay at his cottage. That morning she disappeared. The whole village turned out to look for little Meg, combing the woods and fields, dragging the pond. After a day of searching there was no sign of her. She had simply vanished. People began to speculate that she had been stolen away by the gypsies who had been camping nearby.'

'How terrible.'

'Late in the evening of Meg's disappearance, when we children were all asleep, Papa heard a noise from the schoolroom as he was passing down the corridor.

'He pushed open the door and was shocked to find poor little Meg weeping in a corner, surrounded by a great wall of books. It transpired that my brother had discovered her in the grounds that morning and had persuaded her to come back to the house.'

'But why?'

'He had hoped that by teaching her from his books he could make something of her. He had given it a lot of thought and had even mapped out a lesson plan. Of course, after coming down for supper he had completely forgotten about her and later that evening he had gone straight to bed and nobody had any idea she was there. He was about ten or eleven at the time. Papa was very angry.'

'I suppose your brother's intentions were good.'

'But the poor child was only three years old. She could barely talk, let alone read!'

As Harriet was about to reply, there were footsteps outside in the corridor and girlish laughter. The double doors were thrown open as their classmates arrived, followed by Mrs Fenning, imperious in flowing blue silk.

Harriet made her way back to the stage, her ears tuned to the sounds beyond the window, as visitors began to crunch along the gravel driveway, towards the stairs mounted beneath the iron gateway that led to the front door.

Mrs Fenning gathered the girls around her to deliver last minute instructions for the performance. 'Grace and beauty, girls. That's what your families wish to see today.'

The girls shuffled behind the curtains, quieter now. Peering through a chink in the drapes, Harriet watched the narrow figure of Eliza marching through the front door, making her way to the front row. Her heart careered wildly as she watched her heading for the neighbouring seat of one which had just been taken by a tall, thin young man with restless eyes and a dishevelled look, who sprang up eagerly at Eliza's arrival.

Percy.

Eliza had been cold and imperious at first when Mr Percy Bysshe Shelley had come calling at their house in Chapel Street, Mayfair, one frosty afternoon in January, with an introduction from his sister, Harriet's friend Hellen. Mr and Mrs Westbrook had been out but Eliza had said she would receive him.

He had presented himself in the drawing room, his tall thin frame fashionably clad in a dark cut away morning coat, pale pantaloons and long boots, unruly locks of curly hair flopping over his milky forehead.

He had bowed low, clutching a parcel tied with string and wrapped in paper, which he had presented to Harriet, scrutinising her from fascinating blue eyes. Two years younger than he and without his self-possession, her face had flamed. Her sister had immediately snatched and unwrapped the gift, and discovering some sheets of Greek poetry translated in Percy's own hand, had narrowed her eyes. Flicking through its pages for quite some time, she had closed it and transferred her chilly gaze to its author.

Upon learning that their guest was currently an Oxford scholar, the eldest son and heir of a Baronet and Member of Parliament, Eliza had swiftly settled a smile upon her face and sought to make him welcome.

He had been calling regularly at the house ever since.

Harriet had spent sleepless nights in her boarding school bed, overlooking the open plains of Clapham Common, wondering if they ever talked about her and if he thought about her as much as she did about him.

Mrs Fenning poked her head around the drapes. 'Young ladies, make yourselves ready.'

The girls took up their positions. The audience gave a sigh of admiration as the velvet curtains drew slowly back to reveal Harriet on her pedestal, her acolytes below fanned around her.

As the assembled guests gazed upon her, Harriet had to use all her powers of self-control not to stare at the chair in the front row that Percy Shelley occupied.

From far away she heard Mrs Fenning's voice intoning the introductory lines. 'We are pleased to welcome the families of our girls. Today, we would like to take you back in time to ancient Rome, where, in a wooded glade beneath the city, the gods have planned a sumptuous banquet to celebrate the coming of spring. But the goddess Venus is sad and pining away, for she has fallen in love...'

Harriet's gaze flickered towards Percy who caught her eye with his magnetic stare. Galvanised, she uttered her first lines.

The play had begun.

'Miss Westbrook, will you take a cup of tea?'

One of the junior girls pressed a porcelain cup into her unresisting hand as she stood to one side, school mistresses, parents and the younger girls approaching in a line to congratulate her on her performance. Stultified by all the praise, feeling it to be unwarranted, her eyes drifted to where she could see Mrs Fenning talking earnestly to Eliza. Every now and again one or the other would point in her direction, exchanging fond smiles as they cast a little of her glory over themselves.

After a while Eliza took leave of the headmistress and

approached.

'Harriet, I have suggested to Mrs Fenning that a walk in the fresh air may do you good after the excitement of the day. And as Mr Shelley is also going to take his sister for a turn on the common, we may as well accompany them.'

'I will go and fetch my shawl.'

It was warm in the afternoon sun. Hellen ran freely, holding her skirts above the fronds of lush spring grass, Eliza keeping pace, her watchful eye on the droves of swine snorting in the distance.

Harriet and Percy dropped behind.

'I enjoyed your performance, Miss Westbrook. You dazzled us from your lofty pedestal.'

'You are very kind, Mr Shelley. May I say I find you slightly less dazzling at this moment in time?'

Her mouth curved into a grin as Percy looked down at himself; smears of cream and a spattering of jam staining his jacket.

'You seem to have had quite a feast.'

'Not one of my better ideas.' He turned his pockets out to reveal the debris of several pastries which had spilled out across his clothing during the afternoon. 'I called at a tea shop on my way here, intent on bringing some treats for Hellen. Everything crumbled into pieces as soon as I sat down, of course.'

Percy gave his slightly high-pitched laugh. 'I resemble a street urchin. On the other hand, I would like to pay you a compliment: your dress, if I may say so, reminds me of hyacinths at midnight.'

It was her favourite gown, deep violet which Eliza had assured her, suited her well. She stole a glance at him and gave him a quick smile.

They had meandered slightly from the path that Eliza and Hellen were following. Percy looked around cautiously before stopping in his tracks. From an inner pocket, he drew out a tiny glass phial and presented it to her.

Terrified of the unbidden gift, Harriet faced him with wide eyes.

'The last time we met, I couldn't help noticing the sprinkling of freckles across your nose and so I took the liberty of preparing this lotion. You see, Miss Westbrook, you have very much been on my mind.'

She didn't know how to respond. She removed the stopper from the bottle, inhaling its scent. 'I can smell almonds.'

He nodded in approval. 'Almonds and soap of Venice which a cousin of mine brought back from his travels.'

'And you made this yourself?'

'My friend, Mr Hogg and I have recently begun to mix chemicals. Your potion was relatively simple to make but we are not always so lucky. The other night, one of our more ambitious experiments resulted in a small explosion which unfortunately set the drapes ablaze.'

She stared, imagining him beating back flames with a wild look in his eye, his mysterious conjurings turning out not the way he had expected. She wanted to draw him out further but he was intent on delivering instructions for the potion.

'Wash your face at night before applying the mixture. After only a few weeks the offending blemishes should fade.'

Harriet's face fell as she pondered her transgression. An image came to mind; of herself as some kind of hideous creature. 'We shall have to hope the experiment works', she said forlornly.

She turned her head to where Eliza was supervising Hellen picking wild flowers and remembered past summers when she had loved nothing more than to make daisy chains.

Those days suddenly seemed long gone.

She resumed walking towards the perimeter of Holy Trinity Church with its gold topped dome clock tower, the bell still echoing from the chiming of the hour moments earlier. She took a stride and then another before realising that Percy was no longer keeping pace. Once again he had stopped.

'Would you mind if we took another path? I should like to avoid the church.' He spoke softly but firmly. She looked at him in surprise but obediently turned her steps away from the churchyard. Percy's voice shook slightly as he turned towards her, his tall frame couched in his habitual stoop.

'I must confess something to you. You have, perhaps, heard I am no longer at university in Oxford?'

'I had not heard.'

'It has all been a lot of fuss about nothing. Aided by Mr Hogg, I wrote a pamphlet which I published anonymously and distributed in a couple of bookshops in Oxford. I thought nothing more of it until suddenly one day I was brought before the Master and the Fellows. They insisted I repudiate what I had written. When I refused, I found myself expelled. Mr Hogg was also sent down for his part in the incident.'

Harriet turned alarmed eyes upon him.

'What was the subject of this pamphlet?'

'The subject was the necessity of atheism.' He paused. 'I can see that you are shocked.'

She looked at him, trying to calculate his meaning, hoping she was wrong in her assumption. 'You are an atheist.' The awkward syllables ranged across her tongue like a warning bell. 'You don't believe in God?'

'That is correct. I believe that we should have proof of

his existence. Why bind ourselves in invisible slavery for no discernible reason?'

'Faith, perhaps, Mr Shelley?'

He gave a disarming shrug.

'Something I can at least say with certainty, is that the friendship you and your sister have lately offered me has been a bright lamp shining on a dark day. I hope you will not find it necessary to dim that light now that you have learned something of my philosophies?'

'I…I will endeavour not to.'

'Shall we continue our walk? Let's head towards that grove of poplar trees. I fancy they seem to be forming a cathedral all their own, with their boughs meeting skywards. Perhaps that is where a god, should there be one, would prefer to reside.'

She walked slowly, convinced that a bolt from the heavens must surely follow such blasphemy. The sky, containing nothing more threatening than a gathering of low clouds began to emit spots of rain which reluctantly broke up the outing. Percy turned to face her.

'I trust I may call on you sometime, Miss Westbrook?'

Their eyes met. Bolts of electricity shot through her as if she were coming to life for the first time.

She saw the world stretched before her, boundless.

She nodded.

∼Three∼
Chapel Street

London, July 1811

The chapel standing loftily at the head of the street that
had been named in its honour, was shrouded in night-time
solitude, its blue roof eclipsed by the darkness, the arched
windows overseeing the occupants of the neighbouring
streets.

At number twenty-three, newly arrived home for the
summer, Harriet's eyelids flickered in the mists of uneasy
dreams. In the parlour below, Eliza sat at her tapestry, the
draw of her needle unable to keep up with the rapidity of her
thoughts, which seemed always these days to return to Percy
Shelley.

Realising he was lonely in his lodgings in Poland Street
she had extended a welcome, carefully questioning him about
his home, Field Place in Sussex, his parents Sir Timothy and
Lady Shelley, his younger sisters and his schooling.

When he grew tired of conversation she had read his newly penned verses and commented on fragments of his prose, learning to keep pace with his abrupt turns of mood, his sudden bursts of joyful laughter. She appreciated his thoughtful glances in her direction, his solicitude when it was chilly, running to fetch her wrap.

He was an exceptionally charming man.

She checked herself, her sallow face sinking a little in the gloom of the late evening. It was the beautiful Harriet he was interested in, of course. Eliza knew herself to be merely in the shadows, observing the friendship. Manipulating. She was intrigued to see how far things might progress between her sister and the rebellious young heir.

During the summer term at the Church House School, Harriet had discovered her previous triumph as Venus had faded into obscurity in the light of the news of Percy's scandalous expulsion from Oxford. Sir Timothy had removed Hellen Shelley from the school, leaving the entire community, led by an indignant Mrs Fenning, free to spend the term endlessly gossiping and moralising about the dangerously unorthodox young man who had briefly walked in their midst.

Harriet had been unwavering in her defence of him, even as she had trembled in her bed at night, troubled by fears of the devil coming to claim her soul. Rising each troubled morning to face the derision of her classmates and teachers, she had spent the days ostracised by them all.

The fall from her pedestal had been ignominious.

Eliza clicked her tongue thoughtfully. Percy was away now, staying with relatives in Wales. But perhaps he should be made aware of the anguish Harriet had suffered as a consequence of her friendship with him.

Rising, she moved towards her bureau where a tied bundle of Harriet's letters, written at the height of her distress, lay like an unexploded firework. She sifted through the pages, finding several that contained passages where Harriet had written to her of suicide.

Eliza made a decision. She would write to Percy. Maybe she could include some of the more dramatic sections from Harriet's letters. A beautiful and innocent girl needing to be saved. What young man could resist such a lure? But Percy was impulsive. Like a child with a currently favoured toy, there was every danger that he would he soon tire of Harriet and seek a new diversion with which to amuse himself.

To ensure matters moved quickly she needed to speak to their father.

As it happened, gossip had reached the ears of John Westbrook at the coffee house. Returning to Chapel Street late one night, several days after Eliza had written to Percy, he returned home to find Eliza still up, lying in wait like a spider in the corner of the dimly lit parlour.

'Good evening, Papa. I hope you have had an enjoyable night.'

He grunted. Irritable in his tight knee breeches and silk stockings he flung himself into his chair. Eliza silently placed a glass of brandy on the side table beside him. She wondered how best to broach the subject but she needn't have worried. He looked up at her.

'Eliza, I have been hearing disagreeable things this evening, regarding Mr Shelley. I am no longer comfortable with him calling here. I really cannot see how you have allowed it.'

John Westbrook swirled the liquid around the glass, recognising resolve in Eliza's expression. His heart sank.

He wished he had thought to conduct the interview in the sanctuary of his library, where at least he would be able to puff on a cigar.

He heaved a sigh and continued.

'By all accounts, Mr Shelley is ungovernable. Since his removal from Oxford he has shown no remorse but seems to have spent his time running around spouting vague notions about atheism and revolution. All absolute nonsense! And certainly not a good influence for a girl like Harriet. I am dismayed that you have encouraged it, Eliza.'

'Sir Timothy Shelley, Percy's father is a Member of Parliament, is he not?' Eliza coaxed him, 'and I understand that the baronetcy will one day be passed down to Percy.'

John Westbrook lay back in his chair and briefly closed his eyes. A self-made man, his coffee house was so successful he could comfortably afford the Mayfair house where the family currently resided, and where he was gratified that his neighbours included an eminent surgeon, a Spanish ambassador and a Viscountess. But now he saw Harriet as Lady Shelley, dancing with jewels in her hair, all eyes upon her in a crowded ballroom.

There was no reason why his beautiful daughter shouldn't find herself in such a position. He could see Eliza thinking the same thing. But it would not do if the young man in question carried on in such a rebellious manner.

'Eliza, I am sure Mr Shelley will be a fine catch once his wild ways have subsided. In the meantime, Harriet will turn sixteen next week and although she seems to do nothing but mope, we should celebrate. I will buy her a new dress and arrange for oysters to be delivered and her favourite ices and we will enjoy a pleasant dinner and have no more talk of Mr Shelley.'

Eliza was almost satisfied.

'There remains one more matter. Do you intend sending her back to school next term?'

'Ordinarily, at sixteen one would not think of sending her back. But it would not be a bad thing for her to be out of harm's way for a year longer.

'I will let Harriet know my decision regarding the matter at the end of the summer; that will ensure we have a peaceful month. I will bid you goodnight, Eliza. It's very late.'

He made a mental note to speak to his wife, Ann of the dinner plans, retreating into the hall, making his slow way upstairs, feeling the smoothness of the wooden banisters curving confidently beneath his fingers, heaving a sigh as he reached the top of the landing.

He had not cared much for the gleam in Eliza's eye as he had got up and left the room. He wondered if he and Ann had made a mistake giving over so much of Harriet's care to her. But after Harriet had been born, Ann had been constantly ill and tired and it had seemed natural that thirteen-year old Eliza should have taken on some of the motherly tasks. Indeed, she had wanted to, had begged vehemently in fact, for the chance to help raise the baby that had so worn her mother out. When Ann failed to regain her health as quickly as he had hoped, Harriet had been left entirely in Eliza's care.

Maybe they had been wrong. He should have sought a suitable husband for his eldest daughter as soon as she had come of age instead of allowing her to be so involved, becoming possessive of her younger sister, even, dare he say it, controlling.

He sat down on his chair in the dressing room and divested himself of his uncomfortable garments. In the adjoining room he could hear Ann lightly snoring. Sitting in the dark he recalled the conversation with Eliza. She had been so quick to pour him that glass of brandy. His thoughts were spinning. As he sank back onto the pillows and drifted into sleep, he had the impression he had been managed in some way.

Too restless to sleep, Eliza went to the sideboard. Lifting the stopper once more from the neck of the silver-bordered decanter she poured a little of the brandy into a glass, draining the contents in a mirthless toast to herself, pondering the future.

After Harriet's birthday she would have to set the final scene. A casual comment, letting slip their father's intention of returning Harriet to school for the autumn term. After the anticipated storm of tears, Eliza would ensure paper and ink were at hand, pressing Harriet to her desk, making her comfortable, bringing her tea.

'*My dear Bysshe*,' Harriet would write imploringly,

'*I cannot believe that Father is still intent on returning me to that wretched school! Life is intolerable. How I long for my freedom!*

Sometimes I feel death would be the easiest solution for me. Then at least I would have peace.

Whatever should I do?

Please write me your reply at your earliest convenience.'
HW.

Eliza could imagine the letter down to the final full stop.

Already primed by her own letter, Percy would be outraged by yet more evidence of the injustice of Harriet's position. Seduced by her lustrous hair and the blank canvas of her mind, Eliza did not think it would be long before he would respond.

But could Mr Shelley be relied upon to provide a conventional mode of sanctuary? Would a gathering of like-minded people, sharing living space, reading and discussing philosophy and politics be a safe place for Harriet?

But surely Percy would treat Harriet with the utmost respect? She knew that Percy's philosophies were hidden within the folds of his thrilling fiction, their wild themes a young man's way of expressing himself, but there remained at their core a sense of natural justice. In Percy's fiction punishment was always meted out to the ungodly.

Besides which, his father, a pillar of the community, would surely not stand for the family name being dishonoured.

Her heart, tightly bound beneath her dress, beat a little in protestation as she contemplated the relinquishment of her authority over Harriet. But she would remain in the background, watching. Waiting for her cue. It wouldn't be long before Harriet discovered she still needed her.

And as for Eliza herself, who knew where her own fortune lay, once Harriet had opened the gateway of opportunity for them all?

∼Four∽
Flight

London, August 1811

It was strange, Harriet considered. She had received so many presents for her birthday; dresses, books and a watch chain from Mama and Papa but surely the most pertinent were the gifts from Eliza; a valise and a leather travel trunk, lined with grey silk

Eliza's prescience was troubling but Harriet was certain that she had not given herself away. She had made her preparations, obeying with the utmost care, Percy's demand for secrecy.

Harriet put the doubts to the back of her mind as she carefully closed the lid on her packing, her clothing and personal items piled within the depths of the new trunk lying at the side of her bed. She hoped it would not be too long before she would see it again; it would be sent for once she and Percy had announced to their families that they were husband and wife.

She moved to the looking glass, toying restlessly with the curls that brushed against her forehead, frowning at her new grown-up reflection. She had put up her hair for the first time that morning and she was unsure whether it suited her. Unable to solicit an opinion from Eliza or her mother, she was spending the day in her room pleading a headache, keeping out of sight.

Two o' clock. An hour remaining. Her thoughts hurtled out of control as once more, she read his letter.

'Dearest Harriet,

I have spoken to my cousin Charles and we have laid the final plans. We will be waiting for you in the coffee house at the end of Mount Street tomorrow afternoon at three. Charles has agreed to accompany us to Edinburgh as our chaperone.

Pack lightly dearest, for we will need to convey our belongings in an easy fashion.

Fear not, for by this time tomorrow, I will have liberated you!

Be sure to say nothing of our plans, for you can be sure that every attempt will be made to thwart us.

Yours in great haste,

P.B. Shelley

Percy was going to liberate her. It sounded so dramatic. She could hardly believe things had reached the stage they were at.

She and Percy had spent the first part of the summer exchanging letters daily. His writings to her had been full of the lush valleys resonating with birdsong, while she had sent him French verses in translation that she knew he would love.

But the tone of the letters had changed when her father had resolved to return her to school.

Percy had not seemed surprised; almost as if he had been expecting her news. He had written to her with a detailed plan. She had read of his notion to create a small egalitarian community and had been delighted at the thought. It was everything she had hoped for

After several more letters, she had become quietly alarmed when it became clear that Percy did not believe in marriage. She was aghast. To lie abed with Percy, unmarried, was unthinkable.

She had written asking him outright what he intended. In his reply to her, he had delicately side-stepped the question, choosing instead to reel off a list of names of possible friends who would join them in this adventure. Mr Hogg, she had read, possibly a cousin of Percy's and an unknown lady, previously unheard of, Miss Elizabeth Hitchener, to name but three.

She had gone to bed very early that night without writing. The following day, the pen and paper in her bureau remained untouched, and the next.

Finally, Percy had sent a scrawled missive, his sentences moving across the page in agitation at not having heard from her; a single paragraph at the end acquiescing with her plea for respectability.

…'Let me assure you that I understand your feelings. Of course we will marry! Even with my long-held theories about the tyranny of marriage I find myself persuaded, on your behalf that perhaps after all it is the pomp and ceremony that I most object to, rather than the marital state itself.'

Swiftly she had replied that under those circumstances, she would be happy to join him.

She was excited now and afraid in equal measure. As the clock ticked away the hour, she thought about unpacking her trunk and making her way downstairs to join her mother and sister in the parlour, savouring her safe and ordinary life.

But then an image of Percy, his eyes smiling, his hair tousled against his forehead as he waited for her, blew away her fears.

They were to take a coach to a tavern in the city from where the evening coach to Edinburgh would depart. Three days of travel and then, arriving at their destination, they would immediately apply for the marriage licence.

By the end of the week she would be Mrs Harriet Shelley.

It was too late for doubts. She was sixteen: too old for school, some would no doubt say too young for love, but she had made her decision. A vision of Eliza's tight smile as she had rung for the maid to take Harriet's last letter to Percy, slipped into her mind.

Had it been her decision?

She checked her watch again and swallowed as she realised it was time to leave. Taking up her valise she arranged her bonnet on top of her unaccustomed hair and was about to open the door when a thought struck her.

A careless remark Eliza had made, only a week or so ago, about how Scotland was often cold even in the summer months. From the depths of the linen press Harriet drew her thick pelisse and draped it around her shoulders.

Slipping out of her bedroom she trod carefully down the stairs into the hallway. The front door, usually locked, was to her surprise unbolted. She would not, after all, have to drag one of the hall chairs in front of the door and climb up to release the top catch.

She halted, feeling as she so often did, that her life was a performance, her actions dictated blindly by a script in an unknown hand. But surely now she was inscribing her own fate.

She turned the heavy handle and was out into the street before she could even register she had taken the final steps. Turning, she took a last lingering look upwards towards her bedroom window. For a moment, she thought she spied the dark dress of Eliza against the glass, then shook her head, obviously mistaken.

Eliza would not under any circumstances watch her leave the house with a valise, and allow her to go.

*

She gazed down at the unfamiliar ring on her finger. It had been an hour since Percy had surprised her, slipping it gently on in the briefest of ceremonies; chunks of turquoise set in elegant rose gold. His jeweller had designed it in a hurry and it was not yet paid for but Harriet loved it already.

With less affection, she looked upon the house on George Street which she and Percy now stood before, large and imposing in the grey drizzle of what Harriet feared was a typical Edinburgh summer.

The letting of the rooms had happened by chance, one of the witnesses, procured from the street to attend the short wedding ceremony, having a landlord friend with empty rooms in his town house.

As the newly-weds crossed the threshold of their first dwelling, Harriet felt her nerves fluttering as she faced her husband alone for the first time. For a moment, she wished Charles was still there with his easy manner, lightening the charged atmosphere, but he had been driven off on the midday coach heading back south, leaving them with his good wishes and several bank notes as a wedding gift.

The couple stood in the middle of the airy room entwined around each other, the rain pattering on the windowpanes making it an appealing fortress. Harriet felt she could have stayed in that pose forever; Percy's arms around her slim waist, her head tucked safely under his chin with her arms around his waist.

She smiled shyly as he broke away to take her hand and lead her into the bedroom.

'See how they have given us fresh white linen! If only I could have ordered roses to scatter their petals over your pillow, dearest Harriet. But I have at least, arranged a wedding feast for us.'

She realised how hungry she was; they had barely eaten since their arrival in the city the day before. She gazed at the foods spread atop the counterpane; a small plate of smoked meats, some cheese and a loaf of bread.

'We are going to be so happy together, my love.'

They sprawled across the bed, Percy tearing into great hunks of the bread and cheese, Harriet nibbling daintily at the meats. When the dishes were finally empty he placed them on the floor and pulled her towards him, his eyes ablaze.

With mounting emotion she responded.

'I did not know you were such a wild thing,' he murmured, covering her with kisses.

Afterwards, they whispered together, their bodies tangled between the twisted sheets, the air heavy with their lovemaking. Harriet, lying peacefully in his arms, felt she could stay in that position forever but then came the sound of the heavy front door knocker falling with a large crash, its sound reverberating along the hall. The couple pulled apart, their eyes meeting in dismay.

Harriet drew out a breath.

'Percy dear, it cannot be anybody come for us! Who do we know in these parts?'

'My father? Your father? Chasing up north to chastise us and plead for our return?'

'We are married now. They cannot part us.'

'Dearest, of course they cannot, calm yourself. The visitor must be seeking another guest in the house. Let's not waste a moment's more worry.'

He began to kiss her neck but her mind was on the approaching footsteps down the hall. A cautious rapping of knuckles sounded upon their door.

'It's only the landlord,' said Percy in a low voice. 'We'll pretend we are out.'

The knocking became more vigorous.

'Are you in there, Bysshe?'

The tenderness in the room evaporated as Percy turned to Harriet with delight.

'It's Hogg! He has come! At last!'

'Mr Hogg? What could he be doing here?'

Percy jumped down from the bed, straightening his clothes and smoothing his hair, hurrying from the bedchamber in his stockinged feet, through the adjoining sitting room to answer the door.

She heard the rumble of voices.

'My dear Bysshe, it's wonderful to see you again.'

'Come in, Thomas, you are most welcome.'

She brushed her hair and tried to soothe her lips, swollen from his kisses. When she entered the sitting room she found the two men seated companionably on the horsehair settle that dominated the room, loud bursts of laughter punctuating the conversation. Hogg had brought two flagons of wine and a tray of pastries. Crumbs were scattered everywhere, the flagons already half emptied.

Percy, halfway through an anecdote, didn't notice Harriet arriving with great dignity by his side. Hogg immediately sprang to his feet and bowed.

'Mrs Shelley! What a great pleasure it is to make your acquaintance at last.' He looked into her eyes and smiled his approval. Harriet blushed as she caught the spark of admiration flare in his look.

'Mr Hogg, I have heard much about you. I believe you are currently studying law at York? It is lovely to make your acquaintance.'

Percy, flushed with wine and the triumph of the moment pulled his bride upon his knee.

With delicacy Hogg removed himself to the armchair.

'And how are you finding Edinburgh, so far, Mrs Shelley?

Percy has been telling me how all the women seem to walk the streets barefoot, even in the rain, while still maintaining the usage of umbrellas and gloves.'

'Yes; I imagine they are rather hardened to the climate,' said Harriet, still shy.

Percy gave a shrill laugh. 'Don't think that will dissuade me from finding a woman for you, Hogg!'

'You needn't bother on my account,' Hogg grinned.

Percy was insistent. 'Why ever not? In my newly enlightened state I assert that everybody needs a mate. I have mine and as your friend, I intend to find you one. Even if we have to go down to the fish market to find a strapping lass, big-boned, and heavy-backed, we shall do it! In the meantime, let us pour more wine! I propose a toast.'

'To the bride and groom,' cut in Hogg but Percy turned upon him fiercely.

'To all of us! And to the beginnings of our perfect community.'

The two men banged their flagons together. Harriet sat quietly observing as they devoured the remaining wine and pastries.

After an hour, Percy turned to her and kissed her on the lips. 'My darling, Harriet, you look tired. Stay here and rest while I arrange a room for Hogg and settle him in.'

He kissed her again fiercely and for a moment she thought he would change his mind and stay.

Mr Hogg was heading towards the front door. 'Percy, I almost forgot. I bring tidings from your uncle and a purse of money. Enough for more wine.'

The two men left the room noisily.

Left alone in the startling quiet, Harriet pondered the meaning of marriage.

∼Five∽
Newly-weds

Edinburgh was divided into three separate entities; the shops and trades mostly to be found in the old town, the brash new town jostling for superiority, rising high over the ditch that divided them, and the port a mile away, nestled on the Firth of Forth.

Their early days were spent soberly picnicking atop Arthur's seat. After carousing with Hogg until dawn on that first night, Percy had sworn off wine forever. Harriet did not in the least mind as it would save them money which they could ill-afford.

Harriet tried to get them to make plans to find more permanent accommodation in the city, but their talking sooner or later switched to more searching questions. Could the people of the city be encouraged to seek different ways in which they lived their lives? And how could this be achieved?

Although keen to lead a revolt, Percy was unclear as to how to go about encouraging the good people of Edinburgh into enlightened thinking and after several hours, conversation would be abandoned to go in search of books or an outing to satisfy Percy's current craving for honey.

On Sundays Percy would drag them along to various gloomy kirks where they would slip in among the strait-laced congregations. At first people looked encouragingly upon the newcomers who gave the impression of listening intently to the sermons but then without warning Percy and Hogg would rise to shout aloud nonsense before childishly running out of the door with shrieks of laughter, leaving Harriet to follow apologetically in their wake.

Slowly the days fell into a pattern. Mornings were spent in study, Percy fetching books from the circulating library and guiding Harriet through the rudiments of Greek and Latin. During the afternoons Percy set Harriet transcribing an arduously long French moralising tract into English while Hogg sat beside her making copies. At the other end of the room, Percy composed long letters to the clergy of Edinburgh, the local MP and anyone of influence in the city, beseeching them to read the essay and seek to free the poor and downtrodden from their oppression.

One cooling afternoon, Harriet and Hogg set out to deliver these missives throughout the city. Shivering slightly under the setting sun, Harriet sighed. Her fingers ached from clutching the pen, her thoughts depressed by the stern words she had set down on the page. She could not quite see the difference between the hectoring clergymen Percy professed to despise so much and the delivery of his own deeply earnest, unsolicited missives.

Secretly she did not quite follow how the massed ranks of the working populace were to be saved in this manner.

Then came long days of waiting for something to happen. Sometimes, during the night hours, when Percy frequently found himself too wound up to sleep, the three would take to the streets and the fields beyond, stopping frequently to stare up into the sky, becoming lost in the stellar drifts as they stood below the late summer triangle slowly moving into its autumnal position, Deneb, Altair and Vega blazing overhead in their full glory.

On one such occasion, having craned his head at an awkward angle, Percy found himself in an agony of cramp back in their lodgings. Harriet placed her husband's head in her lap and massaged the throbbing ache in his neck.

She was learning to be a good wife. But she was still a daughter. A sister. And sometimes, she admitted to herself in the depths of the night, she longed to see her family again.

Harriet and Percy had heard various reports of the reaction to their elopement from Charles, who had visited both families upon his return to London.

The Shelley family had been furious. Upon hearing the news, Timothy Shelley had immediately made arrangements to withhold Percy's quarterly allowance hoping that his son would come to his senses and slink back to the fold.

John Westbrook had been quietly delighted at the news but as Harriet's mother had been hysterical and had taken to her bed with the shock, he had restrained himself and written the briefest of notes. He had been keen to settle an allowance on the pair but hearing of the Shelley family's fury he decided it would be best to wait awhile before signalling his approval and instead he had discreetly forwarded Harriet a sum of money that she had correctly taken to be a wedding present.

Delighted with the gift, Percy had immediately spent it all on books, ink and a large quantity of paper. He was beginning to write poetry in earnest. Harriet had said nothing, preferring not to think of their unpaid rent.

On a starry night, having spent hours tracking the flaming tail of a comet across the wide skies, Percy led the trio back to George Street, brooding upon what dark portents the visitation in the sky might bring.

Alone with Percy, settled in front of the fire Harriet, drowsy in the lateness of the hour, reached out towards her husband who rose abruptly and began to pace.

'There's something I need to tell you, Harriet. I had a quiet word with Hogg as he left us tonight. He is gathering his belongings together and we must do the same.'

Fully alert Harriet sat up from her reclining position.

'Dearest, why? Only this morning I heard a man at the fishmongers speaking of unrest on the street. The revolution has been slow to start but it may not be too long now.'

'The year is drawing on and it is time for Mr Hogg to return to his studies.'

'Oh, but maybe we could stay a while longer. It would be very pleasant, just the two of us.'

He came near and stroked her arm.

'We must face the truth. We've made no headway here. The people of Edinburgh have steadfastly refused to listen to our views on the danger of commercial enterprise. If we had truly lit a flame, the fire would be roaring by now. I suggest we go in search of a more deserving, more receptive audience. Besides, to tell the truth, this city makes too many inroads on our dwindling purse.'

'But -'

'There's nothing for it, Harriet, we must leave this house before dawn.'

'I see. Percy, if this is to do with the rent being due tomorrow I could write to Eliza ...'

'It's all arranged, my love. We are to catch the early morning coach and travel with Hogg to York. We can live more frugally there. And besides, Hogg is part of our community; we must stay together.'

She couldn't hide her disappointment. He drew her towards him.

'My darling, do not turn your mouth downwards.'

He kissed her. Adrift in the storm of his love she was mollified.

Their packing, done quickly, had been disorganised. Several hours after they had left and were jolting their way south, Harriet recalled she had left behind in one of the drawers of the sitting room bureau, a tiny pen and ink sketch that had been done of her on her wedding day by one of the witnesses, who had duly presented it to her as a wedding gift. Percy had not been fond of the portrait, finding it too amateurish to have captured her true likeness.

She was dismayed.

'Percy, could we not send for the picture once we are settled?'

'It would cost money that we do not have and anyway, the landlord will keep it in lieu of the money we owe.'

'But it is such a shame; my first portrait and it is lost forever. No-one will even remember it was of me.'

'My darling Harriet, you are so very beautiful that people will want to paint you a hundred times over in your lifetime! Do not be downhearted my love.'

He tried and failed to elicit a smile and presently turned his attention to Hogg who was in a happier frame of mind. Harriet continued to stare unseeingly out at the landscape beyond, each passing scene lost forever from her eyes as they journeyed on. The feeling of gloom stayed with her.

After an arduous journey they finally reached York, crossing the swollen river by way of a crude walkway, the famous Ouse Bridge having recently fallen into disrepair.

Alighting from the stage coach in Coney Street they found a place to stay at a dingy lodging run by a landlady who sent her dull-faced maid, wrapped in a shabby shawl, to frequent the coach stop whenever the next stage was due in.

With Hogg immediately caught up in his law studies,

Harriet and Percy set about exploring. They spent hours wandering the ruins of St Mary's Abbey, admiring the beauty of the swans upon the river, picnicking along its banks in the dying rays of summer.

'It must have been a fine building in its day', said Harriet, looking along the ruined cloister walls, 'it's sad to see it so diminished. Broken.'

The sun slipped behind a cloud as Percy broke into her dreamy admiration of past glories.

'You realise dear, these ruins are a symbol of man's inevitable fall when he becomes vain and powerful.'

'Oh, but the monks were kind to the poor, weren't they? And they tended the sick and the dying.'

'Power and wealth will corrupt all those who have it, eventually.'

Coney Street and the surrounding area was dark and cramped, with no sanitation, a far cry from the gentility of Edinburgh's George Street. As if to match their surroundings Percy's mood gradually deteriorated and he became withdrawn and listless. Harriet struggled to keep their domestic life in order as she waited for Percy's spirits to lift, for him to recover his hunger for their next political campaign or to complete the poems he was always half-composing.

On a brisk day, cold with an early autumnal breeze flitting through the alleys and streets of the city, Harriet was shaken awake at an early hour. It was a little after five. She rubbed the vestiges of sleep from her eyes to reveal Percy, standing fully dressed with a valise at his feet.

'Dearest? Where on earth are you going?'

'I'm going to Field Place to see my father. Hogg's father has now decided to only pay him the minimum allowance, at my own father's request. They wish to starve us out! I must have it out with him once and for all.'

Immediately she was up, gathering petticoats and grabbing

at clothing but Percy stopped her.

'You must stay here, my darling. We don't have enough money for two fares to Sussex, besides which, I am unsure as to the reception you may receive. Let me sort things first and then, of course, you must meet my family.'

He would not meet her eyes. Harriet went white.

'I cannot stay here alone, Percy without you! Not under the same roof as Mr Hogg, it's wholly improper. What will people think?'

'Harriet, we must learn not to care what others think of us. We are living life as we see fit, a community of like-minded spirits. We are bound to be deliberately misunderstood. People will always be quick to scent scandal where there is none. Be strong. I will write to you when I have news.'

At first, apart from sly comments from the landlady, all was well. Hogg, having previously spent far too much leisure time with the Shelleys was away in his office of law from dawn until dusk and was rarely to be seen.

As the long days passed Harriet felt without purpose. One evening, hearing the merry rumble of laughter in the street below, she was overwhelmed with loneliness. She had not seen or spoken to anyone for two days. Tentatively she knocked on Hogg's door. It opened immediately.

'Harriet! What a nice surprise! Come on in and tell me about your day. I don't suppose there is news from Bysshe? No, well no matter. We shall keep each other amused. As a matter of fact, I have rather a humorous tale to recount.'

She entered the door skirting carefully around him, settling her face into a neutral expression as she sat down in the armchair in his small sitting room.

Hogg smiled at her and she smiled back.

An entertaining talker, Hogg immediately launched into a

saga involving a legal case concerning ownership of a pair of piglets, and the evening passed pleasantly.

During the following weeks, the two drifted further together in Percy's absence; Hogg missing his friend's lively intelligence while Harriet longed for the reassuring feel of Percy's strong arms around her waist and the rush of his opinions, whispered into her ear as she drifted into sleep.

As the days passed without word from Percy, a change came over their relationship. Like white flesh turning a bruised purple Hogg began to colour their friendship with subtle declarations. Harriet endeavoured to ignore them but one morning she opened her door to find a sweet-smelling posy and a note from Hogg saying how much he was looking forward to seeing her that evening.

She did not visit him that night but he was back the next. Peering through a crack in the door she saw him standing there with chocolates and a little trinket he had picked up in the market on his way home. She did not answer.

The next day when they met out on the street, Harriet did her best to take him in hand, sternly chiding him for his inappropriate behaviour. He apologised but he could not stay away from her for long. Craving company they continued to meet, teetering on the bounds of respectability and unease.

One lunchtime, returning to the house after some errands she came upon the landlady with her ear pressed against Hogg's door. Seeing Harriet appear beside her in the corridor she jumped, a shifty look settling itself on her face.

'Ah, it's you, Mrs Shelley. I heard a sound from Mr Hogg's room as I was passing and knowing he must be at the law offices I assumed it was you inside. What could be making that blessed noise, I wonder? Maybe the cat has got in, somehow. No matter. Will you be wanting the key to the room, now you are here?'

'Indeed, I will not,' Harriet said with all the stiffness of character she could muster, making her way swiftly down the corridor, tears threatening to spring from her eyes.

Nasty, prying old woman she thought, safely within the bounds of her sitting room. But she was shaken, nonetheless.

That evening she rashly agreed to play a hand of cards with Hogg. Percy was quite correct, she comforted herself, this was the modern way of living and they were doing no harm. They played cards for an hour until lifting her head she saw the now-familiar longing drawing over Hogg. Instinctively she rose.

Something in his eyes hardened. He called out to her across the room.

'Harriet, I don't suppose Bysshe ever told you about a young cousin of his? An uncommonly pretty girl and very merry but sadly her father keeps her indoors most of the time. There was a time, early in our acquaintance, when Bysshe came up with the idea that I should seduce her, in order to free her from this tyranny. I dare say you recognise the familiarity of the plan?'

She went pale.

Hogg continued mercilessly.

'Oh yes, Bysshe had everything worked out. We three were all to live together under the same roof. Such a jolly life he had planned for us all. Sadly, the plan came to nothing but still, it was a good idea.'

She turned away from him, her hand on the doorknob. He was revelling in her discomfort.

'What I've always loved about Bysshe is his generosity of spirit. He simply doesn't believe in possessions or ownership; look at the way we've lived thus far. When he has money, he shares it with me and vice versa. And the plan with his cousin was equally generous. He certainly made it clear how her company would have been shared with me.'

He paused slyly. 'And I must confess, you are, as Percy once described you, a most amiable girl.'

Harriet found the strength to turn around and look him in the eye, forcing herself to laugh in the face of danger. 'This is a most interesting discussion, but alas, it is getting late and I must go as I have some letters to write before I go to sleep.'

But sleep did not come easy that night. She resorted, in the end, to moving a heavy chest in front of the bedroom door, just in case.

The next day was Saturday. Harriet awoke with a heavy heart, wondering how to avoid Hogg who she had no doubt would be skulking around the house all day. Dressing in the cold grey dawn she slipped out without breakfast and found herself wandering towards York Minster.

As she tripped through the quiet streets she allowed her thoughts to stray to her parents and Eliza at home in Chapel Street. She knew they must be wondering about her. Worrying.

She had not yet written to them, unwilling in those first enchanting weeks with Percy, to dilute the magic of the present with the sediments of her old life but now she found herself with a sudden longing for the familiar sensations of home.

She brought to mind the innocence of her bedroom, the softness of the rug against her bare feet as she rose from her bed, the vanity table at the window housing her feminine accoutrements; the lead and rose powder for her complexion, charcoal to accentuate the arch of her eyebrows, a jar of bear fat wax to smooth her curls.

Her hunger growing she thought with longing of breakfast, strong tea, hot rolls with creamy butter and moist plum cake, over which she and Eliza would plan their days; sometimes a stroll down to their favourite milliner in Conduit Street to pick out a new bonnet, stopping perhaps to collect Papa's new waistcoat, recently tailored at Weston's or a leisurely look through the bow windows of Hatchards, at the array of newly published novels.

She sighed for the lost days of simplicity but then shook herself, recalling how she had often felt confined beneath her sister's hooded gaze.

But she felt more trapped than ever now, within the suffocating walls of the boarding house, the looks of contempt from the landlady and the other lodgers and the growing arrogance of Hogg, who surely must have misunderstood Percy's intentions in having left her alone with him.

She brooded. There had been a day in Edinburgh, when Percy had one of his headaches and had opted out of the planned sketching party at the top of Arthur's Seat and he had insisted that Hogg accompany Harriet instead.

Hogg had been full of fun that day and attentive but there had been a moment, as she had risen from her seated position on a boulder, when she thought she had seen him sneaking a furtive glance at her ankles as the hem of her dress had risen with her movements.

Miserably, she wondered now if he had thought her action deliberately provocative.

Her aimless wandering had led to her arrival within the boundaries of the imposing Minster. She hesitated. It would be wrong to enter. She knew only too well, Percy's views on the vast amount of money it cost for its upkeep; money that could have gone to the poor and needy of the parish.

Somehow though, she found herself tiptoeing in, losing herself in the beauty of the intricate stone tracery and the dazzling stained glass windows, her soul soothed by the tranquillity embedded in its quiet corners.

It was in one such corner that she decided to send for Eliza.

∾Six∾
Trio

Harriet awoke to a stormy sky. Scraping together her last coins she wrapped her cloak around her and braved the heavy drizzle to fetch bread and milk for breakfast.

She was trudging back to Coney Street when with a shock, she saw a figure nudging his way along the gloomy street.

It was Percy.

'My love! You did not send word you were coming! Oh, this is the happiest day!'

'Harriet. I am so very weary. Let me hold you.'

The depressing news that Percy had argued with his father and that there was to be no financial support, could not dampen Harriet's blithe spirits as the two embraced on the rain-swept street.

A crack of lightening appeared overhead in the blackening sky. Overwrought from a night of hard travelling, Percy let out a demonic shriek. Sweat stood out on his brow and his eyes bulged as he held onto Harriet in the pouring rain.

Draping her cloak across his shivering form she led him back to their rooms where she arranged a nest of blankets across the bed where he fell asleep instantly.

She dried her hair in front of the fire, delighted to have him back, proud to have been the reassuring wife in his moment of need. As she sat dipping bread into milk she felt calm. But then came a sharp rap on their door.

Turning the door knob with her finger to her lip, ready to preserve the peace of Percy's slumber, she let out a breath of surprise.

There stood Eliza, sharply angular, with rain dripping from the closed folds of a silken umbrella, accompanied by a young boy in charge of an assortment of trunks and boxes at her feet.

'Well, sister, are you going to leave me standing out here in this dreary passageway?'

The landlady was smirking at the end of the hallway, a pile of linen in her arms.

'Is everything alright there, Mrs Shelley?'

'Perfectly fine, thank you.'

Harriet ushered Eliza inside and the boy followed, struggling with the myriad pieces of luggage. He disappeared as soon as Eliza had given him a couple of coins. Harriet closed the door behind him.

'It's good to see you, Eliza,' she said, offering a kiss on both cheeks. Her eyes came to rest on her own trunk that she had packed with such hope and optimism back in the summer.

'And I see you have brought my things for me. I am grateful to you.'

'Well, having received such a wretched letter as yours, obviously I came at once,' her sister boomed. 'Your husband is still away, I take it?'

Harriet gazed towards the door of the bedroom, shook her head and mimed a sleeping posture. Her eyes flitted around the sitting room desperately; she would have liked this first family visit to have taken place with fresh flowers on the table, the cups and plates washed and dried, the books she had been studying to have been stacked in an orderly pile.

Eliza made a face.

'Really Harriet, you should not be staying in a place like this. No wonder you have found yourself in such difficulties. And I find you extremely thin and pale. This will not do at all.'

It was impossible to feel like the mistress of her surroundings. She squirmed under the weight of scorn in Eliza's gaze.

But she had asked her to come. As she listened to Percy stirring in the adjoining room her heart sank. He wandered in, warm from sleep's embrace and seeing Eliza his face broke into a welcoming smile.

When it was not returned, he turned his curious pale blue eyes upon Harriet, seeking enlightenment. Eliza turned her fury upon him.

'You have done my sister a great wrong, Mr Shelley. Her reputation was put at risk by your removal from this house, leaving her under the same roof with another man.'

He opened his mouth to remonstrate and then closed it again. Having his sister-in-law's measure, he sensed there would be more important battles to fight. He held up his hands, conceding defeat gracefully.

'I do, of course, deeply regret my actions. But how can we seek to improve the situation? I will do all I can, of course, now that I have returned.'

Eliza barely acknowledged this.

'I have it in mind to find us different lodgings. If you would like to pack up your belongings, I will arrange somewhere more suitable.'

Like naughty school children the couple obediently left the room and within the space of an hour, without even having removed her gloves, Eliza had moved herself, Harriet and Percy into a greatly improved lodgings house in a smarter part of town.

Eliza had come with a full purse and the three enjoyed a substantial luncheon at their new landlady's refined table, although the atmosphere around the table was subdued. As Percy licked the last of the crumbs from his lips he pointed to the empty flagon.

'We really should have saved some of that for Hogg. He will be along later. I left a note to inform him where we are.'

Eliza fixed her eye coldly upon him and seemed surprised when he met her gaze without the slightest guile.

'Mr Hogg? I am surprised to hear you mention that name after all that has happened.'

Harriet fidgeted in her chair wishing that she had let matters concerning Mr Hogg slide away.

'As Percy returned only this morning, I have not had a chance to discuss matters with him. Perhaps if you allow us to have some time alone…'

'Harriet, you sent for me in some distress. I am not minded to leave you.'

'But Eliza –'

'Tell him immediately or I will have to do so myself.'

Percy's eyes swung from one sister to another. He rather admired his sister-in-law when she showed herself in such a fiery mood but he was damned if he knew what all the mystery was. Furthermore, it piqued him to see a docile expression slide onto Harriet's face which seemed to chime with her beauty.

Eliza sighed.

'Mr Shelley, when you journeyed south to your father's home you left my sister completely alone under the same roof as Mr Hogg.'

'It was not appropriate for my wife to accompany me at that time. I admitted earlier, that my actions were thoughtless. May we perhaps end this now?'

'We cannot. My sister is from a respectable household. By your actions, you placed her in an unfavourable light.'

'It certainly was not my intention to do so but you must understand that the plans we have for a new way of living are indeed different to what others may be used to. We intend to live as a community of kindred spirits, sharing common goals and a common purse.'

'Presumably this sharing does not extend to the sharing of wives with one's friends, Mr Shelley?'

Percy sprang up at this retort. Harriet thought she must have been mistaken when she caught the spark of satisfaction in his eyes.

'I beg your pardon, Miss Westbrook. I should like to speak to my wife alone.'

'Very well.' Eliza rose with a rustle of skirts and drifted into her bedchamber.

'Did something happen with Mr Hogg?'

Harriet explained, feeling in the aftermath that maybe she had acted foolishly after all. She looked carefully at him as he listened to her tale. The tell-tale spark was still in evidence. Her voice faltered.

'It unnerved me when Mr Hogg told me he loved me. And the other tenants were rather off-hand with me and so was the horrid landlady. I could sense the whispers. I sent for Eliza. Maybe I should not have been so hasty. Oh Percy, you could not have anticipated Mr Hogg's actions, surely? But where are you going?'

'To have it out with Hogg of course. I would like to hear his side of the story.'

'Do you not believe me? Is my story not enough to convince you?'

'There may still be some misunderstanding that can be cleared up.'

She could see he was hell bent on seeing Hogg. She thought he was perhaps looking forward to hearing it all over again.

'Please, Percy, let us keep our distance from him for a while, at least.'

'If my wife has been insulted then matters cannot wait.'

'Perhaps I should accompany you –'

The door slammed as he ran out into the late afternoon streets of York, bareheaded and quivering with impatience.

Upon his return, he refused to speak of what had happened, saying only that he was now officially estranged from his erstwhile friend, before calmly setting himself down with his books and papers, scribbling late into the night.

Harriet wisely said nothing, noting only from the mud on his cloak and boots that the two must have walked out into the fields beyond the city.

'At least they didn't get into a duel,' said Eliza with obvious relief as they discussed the matter privately that night.

'Percy does not believe in violence. I hope the matter can now be laid to rest. How long do you plan to stay?'

Harriet looked across at Eliza with some delicacy. With their fledgling community already fractured with Hogg's dismissal, she was eager for the commencement of their married life, alone as a couple.

'Oh, Papa is not expecting me back for some time and I plan to stay with you for a while to ensure everything is as it should be. You are very young to take on the duties of housekeeping Harriet and there is much I need to teach you. Tomorrow the three of us will sit down and draw up plans for how we are to live. Perhaps Percy can think of somewhere to make a fresh start. We will begin tomorrow.'

We, thought Harriet, as she lay restlessly under the heavy coverlet, sleep evading her, even as Percy snored gently at her side.

Once more, the young couple had become a trio.

*

The Lakes, Autumn 1811

At her first sight of Chestnut Cottage, sweet briar and dog rose winding their perfumed way around the front door, Harriet's spirits had lifted. Inside was clean and airy and at the back was a large garden from which could be enjoyed majestic views of Keswick and the surrounding fells.

Looking out towards the beautiful views of Derwent water, Harriet had felt a sense of happiness at having left behind the dark and narrow streets of York, its menacing atmosphere and unhappy memories replaced by the open beauty of the lakes.

Placing her possessions alongside those of Percy she had felt the welcome beginnings of a settled married life.

Except for the pervading presence of Eliza who insisted that as the cottage was so small she would run the household single-handedly. This would give Harriet time to study, she assured them and enable Percy to complete some of his poems and perhaps meet with the poet, Mr Southey that he so admired. It was a love of his poetry that had drawn Percy to choose this quiet part of the world.

Harriet was left with the distinct feeling of once again being put in her place.

She should not be so ungrateful, Harriet scolded herself as she took a solitary afternoon walk along the road to Borrowdale, the starkness of the trees a pleasing contrast to the snow-covered fields, a lone sheep almost invisible on a distant plain. There were a few villagers coming home from the woollen manufactory. Suspicious of the odd trio newly in residence on the brow of the hill, they sheered away off the path to avoid contact with her.

They had quickly become the topic of local gossip. Percy had experienced several prolonged bouts of sleepwalking, making forays into the fields under the stars, in his nightgown, frightening the shepherds and the bent-backed men on their way to the early shift at the slate mine.

His days were no less disturbing with chemical experiments in the garden going badly awry, wild explosions leaving a pall of black smoke hovering high above the lawns.

'What is it you are trying to create, dearest?' she had asked, rushing up after a particularly unnerving incident had caused the rafters in the cottage to shake. He had smiled sadly, blackened by his labours, gesturing to a smouldering mess on the singed lawn.

'I'm just randomly experimenting. Hopeless of course.' He had caught hold of her, deliberately smudging a trail of soot across her face. 'You are my most successful experiment. Which makes you forever mine,' he had added gripping her in his embrace.

She had freed herself but he had lunged with a roar, chasing her towards the cottage with wild screams of delight. Eliza's disapproving figure appearing immediately in the doorway had brought the horseplay to an end.

She took a pathway up to a hilltop that afforded a fine view of the lake of Derwent and its scattered collection of islands and bays. Finding a dry spot of moss, she sat for a while huddled into her cloak, sorting her thoughts.

She had left Percy hunched over the wooden table, scribbling yet more of his mad and furious letters, as Harriet secretly thought them. She allowed herself to hope that he would eventually find time to fashion a few lines of verse to take to Robert Southey who had at last extended an invitation for the following week.

She needed Percy to believe in his poetry, to take it seriously. The previous evening he had almost coyly shoved a creased notebook of ink-stained pages at her as they sat close to one another by the fire.

'For your eyes only,' he had whispered 'a collection of my scribblings over the years, Only my sisters have seen these poems. I'm not sure if they are any good.'

She had spent much of the night reading, excited at the promise the poetry had shown, struck by how much Percy revealed of himself in these early works. She resolved that when his political campaigning reached a conclusion she would speak to him. If he published his poetry it would be a source of income, which they sorely lacked. They would finally be able to make their own way without relying on parental allowances or Eliza.

Without Eliza, of course they would not have had the money to flee the awkwardness of Mr Hogg in York nor to afford the rent for Chestnut Cottage. There was no doubt that Eliza had made her presence felt, only not quite in the way that Harriet had anticipated. She had hoped that by being reunited with Eliza they would at last share confidences as sisters, after all Harriet was a married woman now and surely deserved some adult respect. But instead Eliza had slipped back immediately into her old role of substitute parent.

Harriet did not feel she needed a parent. She wanted a friend.

Percy, on the other hand, had plenty of friends. He had, for some time, been writing feverishly to 'a disciple' as he liked to call her, a lady by the name of Miss Elizabeth Hitchener, a school mistress who shared Percy's Utopian vision. Miss Hitchener seemed always on the brink of coming, it would seem, to live with them, to widen the egalitarian community which somehow never seemed to get underway.

She remembered when they had first talked about it in Edinburgh, on those starry nights when anything had seemed possible.

In the meantime, while Miss Hitchener procrastinated, Percy had acquired a new friend with whom he was busily exchanging letters, a Mr William Godwin, the radical thinker and writer whose work, *Political Justice*, Percy greatly admired. They appeared to share similar views on the theory of common property and political justice.

To read their letters, one would believe the whole world to be full of deserving causes.

Uneasy as to where these causes may lead them, she held in her heart a precious thought that she returned to, time and time again. Just a week previously she had taken great delight in whispering to Percy that his community looked set to have its numbers swelled by one, in nine months' time. Percy had looked incredulous at first and then a slow smile had appeared across his face.

She had delighted in such a grown-up achievement. Once

again, as in York, on the rain-sodden street, she had command of their relationship and she found it pleasing.

But she had been mistaken, the natural rhythms of her body disturbed perhaps by their unsettled life-style and before long the joyful expectancy had died away. Sad for a day, Harriet's sense of wellbeing soon returned. Feeling especially fecund in the lush surroundings she expected a happier result would follow before long.

Although it did occur to her to wonder what kind of a life they had to offer a baby. Theirs was an interesting household but perhaps they could do with a little stability.

Percy was convinced he was being followed and his letters tampered with. A suspected political agitator, leaving a trail of damaging letters and tracts in his wake, Percy had so far avoided being detained by the authorities. They were loathe to take conspicuous notice of the son of a Member of Parliament. But as Percy continued to speak and write of revolution, there was always a chance that steps would be taken against him one of these days.

A few nights ago they had encountered intruders in the cottage. Percy had fired his pistol into the air and fortunately they had retreated.

The low, autumnal sun was dropping steadily. For a moment, the great lake loomed before her like a watery grave. Harriet shivered, a sudden moment of gloom overtaking her as she allowed herself to imagine how it would feel if her head were to slide slowly under water to the sludge below, sinking down to the bottom in defeat.

Shaking herself she turned her steps towards the cottage.

*

'Mrs Shelley, I can't imagine how you keep this rascal of a husband of yours, in hand!'

Portly, clad in clashing shades of mauve and green, the Duke of Norfolk inadvertently sprayed the table cloth with gravy as he bellowed complacently down the table in her direction before turning his attention to another guest.

Greatly relieved that she was not expected to reply, Harriet took stock of the food currently being brought up to the table from the kitchen, eyeing an exotic display of pineapples with relish. Percy was seated a long way from her, halfway down the table of twenty guests, all of whom were of an age to be her parents. She glanced over at Eliza who was in her element beneath the castellated towers of Greystoke Castle, casting a regal smile while talking to a neighbouring land-owner.

The trio had been unexpectedly invited for a weekend house party at the Duke's estate which lay fifteen miles from Chestnut Cottage. The Duke was an old friend and patron of Percy's father. Percy had agreed to attend in the hope that perhaps the Duke might be persuaded to advise his father to resume paying his allowance.

'I am both alarmed and ecstatic that the Duke should bestow this invitation upon us', he had said when it had arrived. ' No doubt he will try his hardest to convince me to reconcile with my father, which is all well and good, as long as he does not think to persuade me to give you up and return home.'

Harriet, cutting delicately into a slice of game pie, reflected that the Duke had not done any such thing. Taking a turn around the rose garden before dinner he had been witty and charming to Harriet and Eliza and had spent an hour discussing political issues with Percy. Far from encouraging Percy to return to his parents at Field Place, he appeared to approve Percy's wandering lifestyle, seemingly encouraging it.

As the Duke called across to him now she had the feeling that the Duke saw something of his own legendary wildness in Percy.

'I have something to show you later, young Bysshe that may appeal to you; a letter from an acquaintance in Ireland.'

She watched her husband, noting his ease at the unfamiliar table laden with dozens of silver platters and crystal goblets of negus that shimmered in the candlelight, while she blushed beneath the gaze of the bewigged and liveried footmen hovering in the background.

She suddenly realised what a chameleon he could be. This was the lifestyle, after all, that he had vowed never to embrace and yet he was able to sit affably charming their host.

'This friend writes of a growing movement in Ireland calling for the repeal of the Act of Union. Imagine it! Catholic emancipation! Now there's a revolutionary cause a young man such as yourself could get his teeth into! What do you say? I find the idea rather fascinating.'

Harriet caught her breath. A new start in Ireland. The idea appealed to her. Somewhere different where they could make their mark, where they would have a purpose. And the Irish scenery, rumoured to be stunning, would inspire Percy's poetry. She looked at him, waiting for him to rise in excitement but he was sitting and staring silently. Maybe she should say something?

Throughout their stay with the Duke, his guests had praised Harriet to the skies for her bearing, her manners and her beauty, all the while Eliza preening herself in the background like a mother hen.

But there had to be more she could offer. She had her own thoughts.

'That does sound like something we could become

associated with.' She was aghast to hear the words, unbidden, springing from her lips into the swell of conversation.

The ladies at the table turned, bosoms heaving, their mouths forming scarlet circles of surprise. Eliza's eyes narrowed.

The Duke focussed his drunken eyes on her face and bared his teeth in surprise. Percy shook himself out of his daydream and gave a nod of encouragement.

The table was astir. Some of the younger ladies tittered.

Harriet bowed her head in confusion. When eventually she joined the ladies to retire, leaving the men conversing long after the candles had smouldered down to a fat pool of wax, she sat quietly alone, listening to their whispered derision.

'Revolutionaries? My dears, they are simply rebellious children playing a game of chase across the country.'

'I believe I heard Mr Shelley announcing earlier how much he considered the English manufacturing classes to be in need and yet suddenly, on a whim, they are running off to Ireland...'

She slunk away to bed amid more laughter.

Late in the night, Percy crept into their unfamiliar bedchamber, one of many sited along a freezing corridor and threw himself onto the bed.

'My darling! Tonight you surpassed yourself. Proclaiming yourself in that manner was inspired.'

Harriet smiled bravely in the dark, her face still aflame. She sat up.

'Perhaps, after all we should stay and achieve some good here. You said it yourself, dear, our workers are in an appalling position. They have no way of educating their children or paying for physicians, their homes are cramped and filthy and they undergo long, back-breaking hours of employment with low rates of pay. Tomorrow we could compose a letter to the factory owners, and perhaps plan a rally...'

He wasn't listening. Restlessly he jumped from the bed and began pacing. Listening to him Harriet's heart sank. It was clear that the Lakes had lost their charm and he was no longer able to appreciate their beauty, seeing only the ugly fissures of manufacture and commerce blighting the soil. The towns were too quiet for revolution, the people too slow-witted.

As soon as he could raise funds for a trip to Ireland, they would set sail.

Herding her thoughts in the dark, Harriet realised that at the mention of anything new and different, Percy was instantly captivated; with the idea if not the substance. She could not even blame herself in this instance as Percy had obviously been enthralled by the Duke's words from the moment they had been uttered. While she had been eagerly voicing her opinion he had been already been five paces ahead, planning.

As for Sir Timothy Shelley, he would no doubt, continue withholding the allowance once he heard of their latest plan.

She only hoped that the Irish would appreciate their presence.

∽Seven∾
Revolutionaries

Dublin, February 1812

It took several months to raise the funds for the Irish campaign and while the preparations were being made, Percy wrote with fierce absorption, for days on end. The result was a taut pamphlet, *Address to the Irish People*, focussing on the need for Catholic emancipation. Harriet thought it was excellent.

Finally, in early February, armed with rhetoric and money, they were ready to embark on the long journey.

Harriet, Percy and Eliza had never been to sea. Setting sail from the Isle of Man they endured long and miserable days on a heaving ship, tossed from side to side upon the waves of a relentless storm. Docking in the north of the country, their journey continued by land in a packed and filthy coach that finally deposited them in Dublin; a total of twelve exhausting days of travel.

After gaining lodgings in Sackville Street, not far from the River Liffey, Harriet, grimy with sea salt, her body thin from days of sea sickness, took to her bed.

Eliza, more robust, busied herself in their new surroundings, gathering provisions and bringing their furnished rooms into order. Percy had wasted no time and had found a printer who agreed to do business with him.

After the fourth day spent lying with her face against the wall, Harriet eased her stiff legs onto the bare floor boards and washed and dressed herself. In the sitting room, she took an apple from the bowl on the sideboard and a heel of cheese and sat down looking around appraisingly. The pamphlets, newly arrived off the press were piled in impressive towers along the edges of the walls. Looking at the crisp sheets of paper she felt invigorated. Having had misgivings about the trip, she was now ready to pour herself heart and soul into Percy's cause, as she always did. It was the only way to keep track of him.

She was glad when at last, she heard the welcome sound of voices as Percy and Eliza breezed in, Percy speaking rapidly.

'...I have a list of Irish patriots to target separately but we must also deliver to the ordinary people. Perhaps, Eliza, you could take the north of the city while I will take the south. Oh, but see, here is Harriet! It is so good to see you up and about again!'

Percy flung his arms around her, stealing a kiss as well as a morsel of cheese.

'Did you say there were pamphlets to deliver? I am ready to do all that is necessary,' she announced, 'let's go now, before the weather turns!'

She was sure there was a look of disappointment on Eliza's face as Percy hastily filled small sacks with bundles of paper. Hand in hand, leaving Eliza behind they stepped outside; a pair again, against the world.

Amidst the throng of Dublin's streets, she came alive, exhilarated by the broad streets, the smart public buildings and the lively atmosphere of College Green.

Finding a busy spot, at first they tried politely holding the pamphlets aloft, offering them to the thronging crowd. Percy, with his intense stare had far less luck than Harriet whose frank expression and warm smile endeared her to strangers who were happy to take one from her outstretched hand.

'What would I do without you, my love?' he whispered, reproved by a serious stare as Harriet continued with the task.

After a couple of hours, Percy's enthusiasm waned and before long he had begun to jest, enticing Harriet to slip the pamphlets into people's hoods or baskets as they walked past. With angry shouts ringing through the streets, he caught Harriet's hand and they ran down the street, hatless as usual with his mop of hair flying free in the wind.

They stopped on the corner of a grand terrace of houses, panting with exertion. Percy caught her in his arms. She pulled away gently.

'Percy! This printing must have cost a lot of money, dear. We must endeavour to do this correctly.'

'Actually, I haven't paid for them yet. I managed to persuade the printer to wait awhile until we receive funding. He believes in the cause as much as we do.'

'But surely that is even more reason not to squander the pages.'

In response, Percy covered her lips in kisses until it began to rain and soaked through the two returned to their rooms where their servant had lit a fire.

At a recent gathering in Dublin, Percy had met a young man named Dan Healy who he had taken a shine to and had brought him back to meet Harriet. Immediately, Dan had sworn allegiance to the young couple and had stepped into the role of servant in exchange for food.

While Harriet sat in the firelight and dried her frizzling

hair, Percy, unable to settle, stepped outside onto the dripping balcony and sent the remaining flocks of his folded pamphlets soaring through the air like doves, watching each one descend onto the rain-spattered streets below.

Harriet heard him laughing like a demon and came outside to calm his mood.

'I think I might have ordered too many of the wretched things,' he muttered. She stood close to him, stroking his arm until his body felt relaxed. They stood dreamily looking down upon the wide streets, their eyes following a path from the roof-tops of Trinity College to the high peaks of the mountains beyond.

Their tranquillity was broken by Dan who suddenly appeared, bowing as he offered up a letter to Percy.

'Aha,' said Percy, breaking from Harriet's grasp as he recognized the writing on the top envelope, 'news from Mr Godwin!'

His quick eyes perused the scrawled sheets.

'Is everything well in Skinner Street?' enquired Harriet.

Percy's friendship with William Godwin was deepening. The two households were on exceedingly cordial terms with compliments to wives and children carefully included in each missive.

The Godwins and the Shelleys had yet to meet but from the frequency and warmth of Godwin's letters, Percy was convinced that they would all become firm friends. Harriet, privately was unsure. The Godwin household seemed large and complicated; made up of Godwin and his second wife Mary Jane, her daughter and son from a previous marriage, Godwin's step-daughter Fanny and young William, the son of Godwin and Mary Jane. There was also Godwin's daughter, Mary from his first marriage to Mary Wollstonecraft.

In Godwin's letters, Harriet thought she detected an ebb and flow between the various children and parents that suggested things were not always cordial within the household.

'The Godwins are all well', Percy assured her, 'but here is the important part of the letter: Mr Godwin has been kind enough to include a note of introduction to John Philpot Curran.'

'Who is that gentleman? I have heard of him, I think.'

'Indeed, you will have; he is Master of the Rolls here in Ireland and is said to be extremely broad minded and sympathetic to Catholic emancipation and the repeal of the Union. If anyone can establish my reputation here, it will be him. I must send Dan to take a note around to him immediately. Now at last we can get things underway.'

With the pamphlets distributed and the note of introduction sent, the Shelleys entered a waiting period, attending gatherings, meeting people, trying to gain influence until they could finally meet with Mr Curran.

During this hiatus, with Eliza busy with household duties and Percy engaged in writing, Harriet found it pleasant to spend time with a recent acquaintance of whom she had become rather fond and was proud to call her friend, the first she had made in her married life. Catherine Nugent possessed a colourful and cultured past. She had been active in the Irish Rebellion of 1798 but nowadays led a more sedate life sewing furs in a shop in Grafton Street in order to eke out a living.

'It is for people such as yourself', Harriet had told her indignantly upon first meeting her 'that Percy has come to Dublin and for all those who toil for a pittance while advancing the comfort and status of the rich'.

One afternoon, Harriet, needing a walk, decided to call upon her. Pleased to receive her young friend but anxious not to invite her into her dingy basement, Catherine Nugent threw on a cloak and bonnet and stepped out into the street, linking arms with Harriet. After a while she drew her away from the fine streets, through the hidden back lanes and alleys where the wretched poor sprawled insensibly on the pavements, their daughters begging in rags, their sons slipping into the back yards of the rich hoping to steal a bread roll or two.

Harriet's sharp eyes took in every detail.

'And what news do you have today, my dear Harriet?'

'Nothing good to tell. Poor Percy has had a cool response from Mr Curran. He is rather bewildered. I have left him at home dashing off another letter, once again invoking the mutual friendship of William Godwin.'

They had left the dank odours of the alleyways and were now within sight of the railings of St Stephen's Green and its magnificent avenues of limes, the exclusive enclosed province of the rich and titled of the city.

'Let us sit and rest awhile,' suggested Catherine with a mischievous smile, pulling Harriet towards a gap in the railings that had been bent out of shape and could happily take the shape and form of the two slender women.

'Why should the rich have it all?' she murmured as they surreptitiously ducked through the gap and made their way to a bench bathed in the early spring sunshine.

'Regarding Mr Godwin,' said Catherine carefully, turning to face Harriet. 'How well do you know him?'

'By correspondence only,' said Harriet, 'Percy is a great admirer of his work.'

'My dear,' said Catherine, 'I am, I confess, living a far quieter life than those revolutionary days of my youth, when I was constantly fund-raising for the rebellion against British rule and visiting those who were in prison for their part in the uprisings.'

'You have earned the right to your rest.'

'Maybe. But I do envy you and Bysshe your youth and vitality. It seems to me that by far the bravest thing I must do, is to face growing old. But I can be useful in my own small way. I still know a great many people and I have heard things that it would be as well for you to know. Of course, it is up to you how you deal with such information.'

Harriet gazed at her.

'What is it you have heard?'

'Frankly, Mr Godwin may not be of as much use to your husband as he might have hoped. You see, Mr Godwin habitually 'begs' for money. Oh yes, my dear, you needn't look shocked, he is well known for it. He seems to believe that the world owes great intellectuals such as he, a living. No doubt the introduction to Mr Curran alerted that worthy gentleman that a letter requesting funds would be forthcoming, or worse, Mr Curran now believes poor Percy is here to collect on William Godwin's behalf.'

'I see,' said Harriet, thinking hard, her mind running over various missives from her husband to William Godwin that she had only recently come to realise were always directly linked to an unexplained lessening of the Shelley household coffers.

'Be careful of the Godwins. I am not at all sure they are your type of people. William Godwin will be quick to tell Percy what to read and how to think. I believe Mary was rather a precocious child, teaching herself philosophy at an early age from books in Godwin's library and writing stories while Fanny, her half-sister remained overlooked.'

'Goodness,' said Harriet.

'Mary has grown into rather an intellectual young woman, while Mrs Godwin's daughter, Claire is rather wild, I'm told.'

'Thank you, dear Catherine. I will consider all that you have told me.'

An hour later Harriet arrived back at their rooms to find Percy and Eliza chatting in the light of a single candle. Percy looked up with pleasure on his face at her return and she found herself enveloped in his embrace broken apart only by dint of Eliza's chastising.

'Harriet, you have been out late in such a thin cloak and gown. You'll catch cold. Come and sit by the fire.'

'Never mind that,' said Percy impatiently, 'let me tell you the most exciting news. Mr Curran has asked the three of us to dine with him tomorrow! What do you think to that?'

'That's wonderful news, Percy,' she said swallowing her surprise, relieved to think that perhaps Catherine Nugent had exaggerated William Godwin's faults and failings.

'I must put out my blue silk for pressing,' she mused aloud.

Percy looked up sharply.

'No, Harriet, not the blue, the pale grey is much more suitable. Now I must continue with this address so that it is in good shape for tomorrow for Mr Curran's perusal. Oh, and I must dash off a line to Mr Godwin too, thanking him.'

'I can do that,' said Harriet quickly.

'No dearest, you needn't trouble yourself worrying about my correspondence. If you need something to do, you may as well carry on with that Greek translation we were working on the other day.'

The dinner turned out to be a hopeless disappointment. At the last moment, Percy discovered that he had been invited alone. Upon arrival he was received casually and throughout the evening his host went to great lengths not to discuss William Godwin or engage in any political discussion. Percy, too young to change the tide of conversation, instead found himself being teased about his domestic life, in a ribald manner.

'You should have heard him,' he complained to Harriet as he undressed back at the cottage, 'he had no right to make insinuations about how I have chosen to live my life. What business is it of his? Why could he not have taken the time to give me the advice I sought? You know, Harriet, he didn't take me seriously at all.'

'Never mind,' said Harriet, staunchly, 'put him out of your mind and take up your pen. We don't need Mr Curran, we can move forward with our plans without him.'

Largely unsupported but undaunted, Percy continued to strive to win the attention of the Irish people. Finally, his labours culminated in an invitation to speak at a massed gathering of Catholics, alongside Daniel O' Connell, a politician who was campaigning hard for Catholic emancipation, in a theatre on Fishamble Street.

The night before the gathering, at two o' clock in the morning, Harriet awoke to find herself alone. Throwing back the covers she rushed out into the rain-washed street to find Percy in his night clothes, wandering by the side of the road.

She ran after him and coaxed him, shivering like a lamb, back inside.

'Where were you going?' she whispered, holding his hand as they sat warming themselves by the fire which Dan, rising from his bed, had hastily built.

Percy's eyes were wild. 'To the devil!' he shouted, 'to hell, where I will surely end my days.'

Refusing to return to bed he sat muttering under his breath while Harriet held his hand during the long hours before dawn.

That afternoon, following the course of the river Liffey, the trio made their way to the site of the theatre. Waiting in the wings for Percy to take the stand, they looked in bemusement at the members of the well-heeled audience chattering beneath the candlelit chandeliers, which included Catholics, Protestants, journalists and government spies.

'It doesn't feel right,' said Percy dismayed, 'it seems like more of an entertainment with the audience waiting for the act to begin. Am I supposed to drop onto my knees and fill the hall with a song?'

'Calm yourself, Percy.'

'Harriet, how can I find the right tone to address the notion of an independent Ireland in these frivolous surroundings?'

Before she could reply, one of the organisers came and led him onto the stage. He stood in the centre, his pale young face gazing anxiously upon the crowd.

Harriet and Eliza clutched each other. Percy darted a glance in Harriet's direction.

'Breathe,' she mouthed, motioning to the exaggerated rise and fall of her bosom.

He shuffled his papers and made a start. People seemed to listen, falling into silence as Percy's voice rang passionately clear, the words bubbling from his mouth with unalloyed enthusiasm.

'The poor among you should not feel like slaves! All men are free and make no mistake, you are all, first and foremost free men...'

'He is making his points well,' said Eliza approvingly.

It was Harriet who first noticed the traces of humour tugging at the mouths of the people and the sidelong winks and nudges as his speech came to its impassioned conclusion. He walked away from the stage to a smattering of applause but she perceived that nobody had taken his words to heart.

Afterwards, the assembly concluded with merriment and whisky, with scarcely a glance being aimed at Percy. The organisers politely shook his hand as he left with Harriet and Eliza to walk back to their lodgings. Even Dan's hearty turnip stew could not comfort the dejected rebels.

The truth was, Harriet acknowledged to herself, they were young and looked even younger. Maybe it was too early for their political lives to start in earnest. They might do better to wait awhile.

Over the following weeks, in an attempt to assess the reality of the situation Harriet took Percy on walks around Dublin, peering beyond the facades of the big houses into the large pockets of crowded streets and overflowing sewers, beggars on each corner, babies crying with hunger, their mothers half dead with the exhaustion of trying to stay alive.

Shocked, Percy realised that all the pretty speeches in the world would not help the desperate poor, who could barely focus on how to obtain their next morsel of food.

Percy's fervent admiration of William Godwin had also been dampened, the two having exchanged heated letters in the wake of Percy's failure to ignite the Dublin masses.

'I fear Godwin does not entirely understand me,' Percy confided to Harriet on what would turn out to be their final night in Dublin.

'It could be that Godwin does not understand Dublin,' she said firmly. Quietly she hoped that if Percy's admiration of Godwin were to wane, so might the health of their coffers begin to improve.

'Forget everything tonight, Percy. Write some verses, dear, it will calm you.'

After several hours of writing, Percy fell into a deep, untroubled sleep and awoke the next morning refreshed and calm. An hour after breakfast he announced that they were to set sail that afternoon, for Wales.

～Eight～
Haven

Wales, April 1812

'When will it end? Please, let it be soon.'

'The worst is over, in a matter of hours we will arrive at Holyhead. Shut your eyes and try to sleep. It will do you good.'

It was midnight. They had been at sea for over thirty hours in high winds and rough waters. Harriet, coping well this time with the vicissitudes of the Irish Sea, placed a comforting hand on Dan's brow.

As they had left their lodgings for the last time and had begun to make their way towards the port, Harriet had turned around to find the boy faithfully shadowing them. Percy had put his hand on his shoulder and told him they had no money to keep him on but this had not deterred the lad from silently reappearing beside their bags and baggage at Dublin harbour, having paid his own passage.

Percy came up alongside them. Eliza was taking a nap in a dark corner. Dan too had fallen into a light doze.

'Are you sad to be leaving, my love?'

Harriet took his hand. She knew how much Percy had hoped to achieve in Ireland, and for all his efforts to have come to nothing he was feeling downhearted. He had scarcely spoken since setting sail in Dublin.

To her surprise the light in his eyes was steady as he now turned to her.

'I am not sad, for I did my best, we all did. But now we must look to the future and the growth of our little community of equals'.

He looked to the sleeping form of Dan. 'All is not lost from this trip; we are returning with a follower, at least.'

She was thankful that he appeared sanguine. She took the time to wonder whether the proposal for living as complete equals meant that Percy would take a share in the household chores. He was messy and disorganised and if he had his way the household would eat nothing but vegetables. She spent the remainder of the voyage contemplating the new life they would achieve in Wales. A lodging house? A cottage? A ruined castle could lie ahead for all she could tell. She felt a surge of excitement for all that the future might hold.

Landing in Holyhead in the dead of night, sheets of rain cloaking the skies as they walked the mile to the nearest inn, Harriet's optimism never waned.

After a night's rest they began their travels, Percy keeping a sharp eye as he searched for a suitable dwelling place. They stopped at one or two places but were hindered by the fact that they possessed no money. A landlord who could be prevailed upon to grant them a lease on security seemed impossible to find.

They journeyed on cheaply, by boat to Aberystwyth and then, finding nothing there they headed east by road. At the point where the sea fell away unseen into the distance they began their descent into the lush valleys of Radnorshire.

Harriet glanced at Percy and noted the glint in his eye. He was familiar with this part of the world, it was here he had stayed with his cousin the previous summer, plotting the elopement to Scotland.

Harriet recalled how he had written with joy of the scenery; the high rocks and rushing rivers, the glades filled with birdsong. When they suddenly came upon Nantgwillt, a charming manor house near Rhayader, she fell immediately under its spell. The Shelley family were well-known in the area and to their delight, the landlord allowed them to take possession before finalising money arrangements.

As soon as they had gained entry, they left Eliza and Dan rearranging furniture and unpacking and hand in hand Harriet and Percy strolled outside to survey their land, across the undulating lawn towards the stream that ran down towards the River Claerwen. They halted at the sight of clumps of early bluebells in a shady grove.

Percy flung himself down onto the earth which was dry and warm in the spring air, pulling Harriet down beside him.

'Are you happy, dearest Harriet?'

'How could I be otherwise? To live here amongst all this...'

She gestured across the wide expanse; two hundred acres of land and wood, a vast space where Percy would be free to conduct his chemical experiments without causing disturbance to neighbours. They could farm and be self-sufficient. Most importantly, there was room for an embryonic community to grow and finally find its feet.

They fell in love with the place so passionately that within days they began to lay plans to buy it, once Percy came of age. With so much land they planned to let some of it to neighbouring farmers to assist the purchase.

In the meantime, Harriet began to busy herself for visitors. Word had come from London that the Godwins were planning a visit and also Miss Hitchener, whose devotion to Percy was progressing quite alarmingly, Harriet felt and who had taken to referring to herself in her letters as his 'eternal disciple.'

Helped by Dan, she and Eliza began to organise possible sleeping arrangements. She and Percy shared the largest bedroom, the room with a faded tapestry of the valleys on the wall and deep red velvet curtains which kept the harshest winds at bay. Eliza had her room at the end of the corridor and Dan slept downstairs in a dayroom with a bed in the corner. That left five further bedrooms upstairs.

'I think this one will do nicely for Miss Hitchener,' suggested Eliza. She and Harriet were standing in a sunny patch in a big bedroom on the opposite side of the corridor to that of Harriet and Percy.

Harriet paused delicately.

'I think not, Eliza. I am sure Miss Hitchener will be more comfortable further down the hallway, nearer to you. I had earmarked that bedroom for Mr and Mrs Godwin.'

'I see. Well, perhaps you are right.'

'And the room next to that I intend to keep for my dearest friend, Catherine Nugent. I know she always affirms that she does not wish to leave Ireland but I am ever optimistic that she may change her mind. I will tempt her to come once I have written her how beautiful it is here.'

'Now, what about the other Godwins? Are we to assume

they will all be descending on us?'

'Percy will write to Mr Godwin so that we can make the necessary arrangements. I have it in mind that as Fanny is the eldest she will require her own room. The younger girls, Claire and Mary will share. I am not sure about little William. We shall have to wait and see. Whoever wishes to come, we can accommodate them.'

Eliza, never happy when Harriet attempted to take command of her own household, raised her eyebrows. Saying nothing more, she swept Dan away to inspect the contents of the linen press.

Harriet, wandering the corridor, her head full of plans, heard thumping and dragging noises from one of the rooms downstairs. She pushed open a door to find Percy hard at work arranging what was to become the library. She stood amidst the chaos, hundreds of their books spilling out from boxes and decided to get Dan instantly to work, creating shelves. Seeing that Percy was perfectly content, she made her way outside.

Her pride and joy was the nascent growth of a huge vegetable patch. She hurried out into the warm spring afternoon and with a sense of achievement surveyed the newly dug earth. She and Dan had spent the previous day wielding their spades, turning over the soil and beginning to clear the weeds. She had no experience of gardening or growing things but Dan had shown her how to prepare the land and she was keen to learn, enjoying the sense of peace she got from communing with the earth.

Since leaving Dublin, Percy had formalised his loathing of meat believing that not consuming it would keep them free from disease and cure them of gluttony. He had urged them into a vegetarian lifestyle. Harriet envisaged a healthy harvest provided by her own hands, a way to cheaply feed a growing number of people.

But the idea for communal living collapsed before it could get started.

Like omens sent in the night to trouble those who dare to dream, first Harriet and then Percy fell ill with a mysterious fever leaving them much weakened and low in spirits for several weeks. Listless, they dragged themselves around the house without purpose.

And then on a misty day, when strangers would not normally be expected to be found venturing into the depths of the valleys, Harriet and Percy, feeling well once more, were taking the air in the grounds when Harriet, seeing two dark shapes up ahead, gave a scream.

'What is it ?'

'Up there, by those tall trees; two men in dark clothing, watching us!'

Percy raged inwardly that he had not thought to bring his pistol. He grabbed Harriet by the hand and the pair ran at a fair pace, back to the immediate boundaries of the manor house.

'Who are they? What do they want?'

'Maybe they are merely out for a stroll and have become lost. Nature lovers, perhaps?'

The couple looked at each other, not knowing what to believe.

Percy had recently had word that he had been put on a watch list. Ironically, his political rant in Dublin, although not reaching his desired audience, had struck at the heart of two government agents in the audience, who had sent Percy's name to the Home Office, citing subversive activity.

As a consequence, the Shelleys' movements and

whereabouts were likely to be recorded by the local authorities and the couple could be called in to answer questions at any time.

Shaken, the pair made their way back into the house and Harriet bid Dan close all the shutters. From that moment, she struggled to feel safe.

The inevitable expulsion from paradise, when it came, was not at the hands of government officials but due to the ever present crisis surrounding their lack of money.

The Welsh house had been taken on in the expectation that Timothy Shelley, relieved that his son was no longer causing trouble in Ireland, would be happy to help them put down solid roots and begin to lead a respectable life. However, rumours of the proposed community had re-ignited his anger and he began to backtrack. First he refused to pay for the furniture as he had promised and finally he refused to give them his promise that he would give assistance with the purchase of the property when Percy came of age.

With the dream of the charmed abode in ruins, they closed up the house and gathered their possessions.

Bitterly disappointed, Harriet, suffering a relapse of her recent fever, could only watch as Eliza packed her belongings into her trunk. Pale, convinced she could feel the pull of the tiny roots she had already began to put down, groan in protest as each step tore them to shreds, it was left to Percy to lift Harriet from the couch into the awaiting carriage.

'Where are we going?' asked Harriet dully.

'Mr Godwin has suggested Chepstow might be a good place for us. There is no harm in trying, after all none of us have been there before.'

As Eliza settled blankets around her and Percy gave final instructions to Dan to follow behind, Harriet could not help but feel that yet again, she was being managed.

~Nine~
Commune

Lynmouth, summer 1812

As they arrived at the edges of Chepstow, Percy looked morosely out of the carriage window and declared it to be wholly dull. They continued west only feeling relaxed once they were in the midst of the soft Devonshire countryside.

After a couple of hours Harriet, weak and ill as she was, raised her head when she spied a simple cottage on the roadside, with breath-taking sea views, picturesque cliffs rising sharply to the side and roses meandering along the cottage walls. It was obviously unoccupied. When the coach reached Lynmouth they dismounted and after making enquiries in the town, Percy managed to procure the lease.

Invigorated by the air and the growing unrest that hung across the land, Percy wrote for hours at a time. Back in May, the Prime Minister, Spencer Perceval had been assassinated and emboldened by the happenings in Westminster, Percy was inspired to set out his own political creed for equal rights.

Harriet, still delicate and confined indoors, read the pages as he completed them. When he had first sat down with his pen and paper she had hoped that he was writing poetry but he was fired up by his ideas and the hope that the country might be ready for revolt. He titled it *Declaration of Rights* and radical as it was, with its plea for the people's right of assembly, the political voting system to be made more inclusive and the necessity of a free press, Percy began to plot how to distribute it.

Harriet now up and about, taking regular walks along the shingle bay, was uneasy at the thought of the danger they might find themselves in for spreading such seditious ideas but then, casting an even larger cloud across the sky, Miss Elizabeth Hitchener suddenly arrived.

She was immediately shockingly intimate.

'Mrs Shelley; I have heard so much about you that I feel already acquainted with you! Bysshe (if I may, with your permission, call him so) has given such vivid descriptions of the life you lead together, I am anticipating happy times here! And indeed, I imagine there is much work to be done. There is no time like the present to begin sowing the seeds of revolution.

'If you would be so kind as to take me to my room and show me where I may put my things, I would really be most grateful. And I should like to wash before dinner.'

The speaker of these animated words gazed down at her from a lofty height; thin, dark haired and with a pock-marked complexion. Harriet directed Dan to take her bags to the littlest bedroom at the back of the house. Their commune had swelled to five.

Miss Hitchener quickly made it her duty to question

Harriet's every thought and feeling and once more feeling her lack of years, Harriet felt the shadow of intimidation wrap around her within her own home.

On a fine day in late July, Harriet and Eliza were seated on the garden bench enjoying a rare hour of peace and solitude.

The previous evening, Percy had finally hit upon a distribution plan and he and Harriet had spent much of the night making copies of the *Declaration of Rights*. After snatching a few hours of sleep he and Miss Hitchener, or Bessie, as she liked to style herself, had left the house, Percy casting a mysterious smile in Harriet's direction, and calling out instructions to meet him on the beach at six o' clock that evening.

Eliza poured lemonade from a pitcher as Harriet lounged opposite.

'This is nice,' Harriet said gesturing at the view, 'it's a fine antidote to feeling anxious. There seems little point in travelling all the way to Italy when we can find contentment here.'

'Italy?'

'Well, yes. A while back I had thought, with Percy despondent over the Irish business and with my health being so poor at that time, the warmth of the continent may have helped our spirits improve.'

'Oh Harriet, how I wish you and Percy would stand still once in a while. You cannot simply chase off across the continent on a whim.'

Harriet suppressed her annoyance. Across the lawn, in the distance, fishing boats were bobbing gently on turquoise shoals.

'Such a heavenly colour,' she said, hoping for peace, 'it reminds me of my betrothal ring.'

'I think it's rather garish,' said Eliza coldly.

Harriet gave an inward sigh. Sometimes Eliza could be almost spiteful. She wondered if it was because she did not have a man of her own.

Of course, her own man was at this moment spending a precious afternoon with another woman. It was just harmless Miss Hitchener of course, but Harriet would have liked to have been asked. She chided herself; he knew how tired she had been these past few days and he was being kind by allowing her time to rest.

She was being overly sensitive. She closed her eyes and tried to enjoy the warmth of the sun's rays on her face. Eliza was still talking mercilessly.

'Harriet, we must have a conversation about where we are to put the Godwin girls when they come; Fanny and Mary, isn't it? Percy knows so many people it's sometimes hard to keep all their names in one's head. I think the little box room at the front could be cleared temporarily of Percy's trunks and boxes, which would also have the happy effect of giving Dan something useful to do.'

Whenever Eliza spoke about their little community she managed to make it sound more like a house of correction than a happy, united little collective.

Harriet made a face.

'What is wrong?'

'If you must know, Percy and I are feeling rather insulted by the Godwins. Having been on such good terms these past long months and with all the letters that have been exchanged regarding the notion of them coming to stay, Mr Godwin has suddenly refused to allow Fanny and Mary to visit with us; he is concerned that he has not yet met us in person and it would be deemed inappropriate.'

'Well, I dare say he is entitled to feel like that, although why he has only just thought of this fact, I can't imagine. The Godwins have never sounded like particularly appropriate people to me, in any case. Fanny is his step-daughter is that correct? And Mary, the younger one, is his own child?'

'That's right. Mary's mother died giving birth to her. Mustn't it be awful to know that you are the reason your mother died?'

Eliza, who never entertained deep thoughts, looked surprised.

'It does not do to dwell on such things.'

'I wonder what kind of a girl she can be? Only two years separate us and I had hoped that we might meet one day and make friends. Well, but I even wonder whether we will bother with the Godwins again. You are probably right, and they are more trouble than they're worth.'

But Godwin's snub rankled and it was not until late afternoon when they were making their way down the winding path to the beach, that she was able to let it slip away.

At first, Harriet could only see Dan, kneeling at a distance further up the beach, engaged in building a miniature boat but as they drew nearer the shoreline Harriet saw a crowd of people gathering and pointing. Following their gaze, she peered into the distance towards a line of shingle and small rock pools where two figures could be seen picking their way across, their arms precariously full of bottles, filled with the carefully copied tracts from *Declaration of Rights*, ready to launch into the sea.

Percy and Miss Hitchener were balancing on the slippery rocks, tilting towards each other as they were caught in the passages of wind flying in from Avonmouth. As Miss Hitchener's skirts flew in the sea breezes, they screamed with laughter.

'Well really,' said Eliza brisk with embarrassment, 'what will the locals think of us? We must all appear quite mad. I'm sure half the King's men are watching Percy at this very moment, reporting back to the Government.'

Harriet, overcome with annoyance at the sight of her husband in such close and personal proximity to Miss Hitchener, ignored her. Bending down, she undid her shoes and rolled down her stockings, thrusting them into Eliza's arms. Dashing towards Percy she signalled for some bottles, ignoring Eliza's horrified shout.

They whooped as bottle after bottle was released into the waters of the Bristol Channel.

'Off they go!' Percy shouted, 'to Wales!'

'And Ireland!'

'And far and beyond. Across the Atlantic Ocean!'

Exhilarated by the successful launch, Percy caught her in his arms and kissed her. The crowd cheered and cackled. They kissed again.

It was Eliza who eventually waded in to rescue poor abandoned Bessie, who had been left with her ankle trapped in the depths of a rock pool, calling out in vain for Percy to save her.

'What are you working on now, dearest?' murmured Harriet. Percy had woken her several moments before, pushing back the sheets of their bed and half-sleepwalking towards a small table by the window where he was now burning a candle to light the words that were flowing from his quill.

'Hush. Back to sleep. It's not quite your birthday yet. A few hours more. Close your beautiful eyes.'

'Are you working on your balloon sonnet?' asked Harriet

sleepily.

The spread of Percy's propaganda had continued by even more outlandish means. Harriet, Eliza and Bessie had spent an entire day fashioning small pieces of silk into spirit-lit balloons. They had waited until dusk, and then, with a tiny sheet of Percy's tract tied beneath, they had sent them sailing across the Channel, lighting up the dusk like fireflies.

Harriet had been thrilled at the sight of the tiny balls of fire but what had pleased her even more was that Percy had been moved to begin a poem about them as soon as the launch had ended and the sparks had passed far into the night.

'Bright ball of flame,' she had heard him mutter that same night as he had sat down and prepared to write.

She swung her legs over the side of the bed and came up beside him. He was scribbling away in his notebook. Harriet was pleased to see he had made a few more entries since last she had looked in the book. She longed to read them. Sometimes it was difficult to keep pace with Percy's thoughts but when she read his poems it felt as though she was following a map of his mind.

He covered the page protectively with his arm. 'Don't look yet. It's a surprise. Go back to sleep, it's not your birthday until dawn.' He kissed her.

'Try not to spill ink over the pages, dearest.' As she drifted back to sleep Harriet could hear the scratch of the pen in her dreams.

The next morning on the pillow beside her lay the notebook, open at a new poem, entitled *'To Harriet'* and with the date: 1st *August 1812.*

She scanned the lines hungrily.

'May thy unwithering soul not cease to burn...And I must love thee even more than this.'

85

Her heart soared. This was the best birthday gift of all; an affirmation that after the turbulence and uncertainty of the year they had been together, his love for her was secure.

*

Late one afternoon, Harriet laughed to herself at the sight of Bessie Hitchener pantomiming the act of creeping around on tiptoe, as Percy took up his pen and began to scribble furiously in the corner designated as his writing spot.

Harriet caught her eye and Bessie came tripping over with the ingratiating grin that Harriet was beginning to find infuriating.

There was no doubt that communal living could be taxing. Not entirely secure in her fledgling married life, misunderstandings were rife.

The previous week she had been upset by a conversation she had overheard Percy having with Miss Hitchener, in which he had been expounding his view about the 'evils of marriage' and how a happy community could only thrive if the relationships within were not exclusive.

Harriet had found a quiet spot where she could let the tears fall. Afterwards, when she was calm, she realised that it was just Percy bandying words and could have laughed aloud but she could not help worrying about the hopeful gleam in Bessie's eye, whenever Percy looked at her.

Sometimes, she wondered why Percy could not chose his conversational words with more care, as he did in his poetry. Could he not see the effect his words were having on those around him?

She gritted her teeth and resolved to be kind to Miss Hitchener, who she sensed was heading for a fall. She gave a tired smile as Bessie gushed in her direction.

'Dear little Harriet, what do you think of *Queen Mab,*

Bysshe's latest poem? Seven hundred lines regarding the political atmosphere we find ourselves blanketed under; the constant threat of persecution for those depressed poor who dare to speak up for themselves. A political message delivered in a poetical style; what could be more harmonious for our little community to have produced such a masterpiece?'

'I am aware of my husband's work,' said Harriet patiently.

'Bessie,' called Eliza tartly from the kitchen, 'it is your turn to peel the potatoes.'

Miss Hitchener made a little grimace, turning it into a cough as she met Harriet's eye. She scuttled awkwardly away. Harriet wandered over to where Percy sat at the table, placing a loving hand on his shoulder as he scrawled final notes and instructions in the margins of his poem.

'Dearest,' he murmured looking up at her, 'the new publisher I have recently found is awaiting this in London. It is almost done!'

'That's wonderful news, Percy.'

He kissed her gently. 'I hope you realise I could never have achieved this without your unstinting patience and belief in me.'

With the poem on its way to completion they all felt that at last their community was on the brink of achieving something, but Percy was restless. He took to walking into town most mornings with Dan as company. One afternoon, Harriet was pegging out some washing on the line when Percy came rushing up through the fields.

'What is it?' she asked, alarmed at his sober expression.

'Dan has been arrested…it is my fault entirely.'

Haltingly he admitted that on their walks, he and Dan had been busily pasting unauthorised posters fashioned from *Declaration of Rights*. Having ventured further afield that day, Dan had been caught attempting to put up posters in Barnstaple and had been thrown into prison.

'But, we must do something. We cannot leave him there languishing.'

'There is absolutely nothing we can do. A £200 fine has been passed down for his crime. Without the money to pay he must stay in the cells until he has served a sufficient amount of time.'

They moved around the cottage in a haze of guilt. The next day unknown men began to lurk on the roadside, watching their movements through the windows and as the days went by it soon became clear that their post was being tampered with.

After an uncomfortable week, Percy stalked out indignantly to one of the men standing insolently by their gate. He returned moments later looking deflated.

'It seems we can do nothing to protect our privacy. They are here on the orders of the Home Office, to compile a dossier on our activities.'

He and Harriet exchanged a long look. The lovely little town had ceased to be a haven. Reluctantly, they decided to move on.

~Ten~
Family and Friends

Autumn 1812

'How intensely satisfying it is to be back in London,' said Eliza stretching across the chaise longue in front of the partially open window of Lewis's Hotel that looked out onto St James's Street. 'We have come home.'

Harriet rubbed her eyes tiredly, no longer sure where home was. In truth, she now feared the city and the traps she felt it might hold.

'Even with the Watchers somewhere out there?'

'They seem to have given up on us. Not a sighting for days. I'm sure they have far more important things to do than follow us around. Or if they haven't given up, they are at least lost in the crowd and so fail to bother us.'

Harriet came to stand beside her, the familiar stink of London slowly filling her nostrils. Tilting her head downwards she watched a press of carriages, brewers carts, and coal waggons making their way along the road, finely dressed ladies and gentlemen passing in lines along the raised pavements.

She craned her head further. In the distance, porters, market women, milk maids and bakers were making their way along a less refined street, picking through the mud and ashes and broken glass that lay underfoot. On the corner a stray dog growled at a shire horse pulling its load on the way to the wharves.

Her ears caught the sombre beat of drums as the guards marched to Hyde Park from the barracks nearby, an accompanying melody to the ever-present clanging and crashing reverberating from numerous building works strewn across the expanding city.

She closed her eyes searching for stillness, visualising the tumbling Welsh valley surrounding her beloved manor house, Nantgwillt.

'Harriet? You are always off in a daze. Are you listening to me? Wear something smart today. It will be the first time Mama and Papa have seen you as a married lady.'

Harriet sighed, wondering why Eliza always pointed out what was obvious. She turned her mind to more pressing matters.

'What are we to do with Miss Hitchener while we are at Chapel Street? Percy is at the publishers this afternoon.'

'Poor dear, she is like a limpet, clinging onto Percy for dear life as if only he can imbue her world with meaning. Percy will have to take her with him,' said Eliza thinking hard.

'But I have yet to meet the publisher myself,' protested Harriet, 'it would not be proper if she accompanied him on the first meeting.'

'Well she can't come with us and she won't stay here in the

hotel with nothing to do, so that leaves the publisher.'

'I know what to do. I will ask her to stay here and write a note to see how poor Dan is faring. If only she had been imprisoned in his place! Oh, of course, I don't really mean that but sometimes, when she talks to me in that patronising, school-mistress fashion, I want to scream.'

'There does seem to be very little point in carrying on with her now that we are back in London. She is certainly not the sort of person to take to see Mama and Papa. Or the Godwins when we finally meet them.'

Quashing further thoughts of the miserable Miss Hitchener, Eliza turned her attention to the small store of food they had amassed on the sideboard. Thickly buttering bread and slicing slivers of cheese she put a plate in front of Harriet and bade her eat breakfast.

Harriet ate slowly from her seat at the window, caught up in the October gloom of London. She missed spending time with Percy. Being much in demand, she had scarcely seen him. When he wasn't rushing around meeting people or writing letters to them, including still, William Godwin, he was either composing page after page of poetry or slumped in bed in the middle of the day, exhausted.

When they had first returned to London she had anticipated he would accompany her immediately to Chapel Street, fondly imagining her parents receiving them, herself on his arm like the bride she had so recently been, but John and Ann Westbrook had been away staying with relations in Somerset and so the homecoming had been rather flat.

With their parents finally back in residence in Chapel Street, Eliza had made the arrangements for this first visit but it was to be without Percy. There had been no real correspondence between Harriet and her parents since her elopement and

Eliza thought it best for Harriet to re-establish the familial links before bringing Percy formally into the fold.

Out on the cool street later that afternoon, wearing her best day dress, she shied away as Eliza attempted to link arms with her, feeling like a child being taken home at the end of a wonderful party.

Arriving at the front door she held her thoughts inward calming herself with a secret hope as she caressed her belly through the folds of her clothing. There would come a time, she told herself, when her sister and everybody else would have to look upon her as a grown woman.

Gazing at the familiar tea service spread out on the cloth before them, Harriet's throat contracted at the peacocks strutting around the rims of the saucers, nesting peahens in the centre of each tea plate, one or two of the matching blue cups damaged, their handles cracked. It had been in use since she was a small child. Her mother loving the set as she did, had never felt able to discard it for a new one.

She glanced around noticing changes in the parlour. A recent painting of John and Ann Westbrook posed inside the coffee house had been hung on the wall opposite and a new fire back had been fitted, patterned with an exotic landscape of flowers and fruit and coffee trees.

The subtle variations in the domestic landscape boded well. Perhaps her parents would be ready to acknowledge the newer version of herself.

'You look well, Harriet,' said her mother as she poured the weak china tea.

'No milk please, Mama,' said Harriet firmly.

Ann Westbrook raised her eyebrow, fighting the urge to comment. The conversation, stilted at first mellowed slowly into comfortable chatter as the family gradually drew back into its familiar shape. Eliza sat carefully monitoring the tone of the exchanges as they skirted around the circumstances surrounding Harriet's marriage.

'You have done a fair amount of travelling, I believe,' said John Westbrook.

'Yes, Papa. Edinburgh was most wondrous to behold.'

'Quite,' said her mother coolly, seeing in her mind's eye the lonely wedding service and plain dress of her best and beautiful daughter.

Harriet jumped forward hastily in her narrative.

'And then we were in York for a time, with its lovely cathedral. After a while, we tired of city living and we travelled onward to the Lakes. Mama you would have loved the views from the garden of our cottage. The weather was mostly fine and we enjoyed lots of walks into the foothills of the mountains.

'Early the following year we had an opportunity to travel by sea to Dublin; rather a thrilling adventure during which time Percy was an honorary speaker at a political rally.'

Seeing her father frown she continued before he had time to pose a question.

'Whilst in Dublin I made a very good friend, Mrs Catherine Nugent with whom I've been corresponding ever since we left. We were hoping she would come and stay with us during our summer in Lynmouth but she had so many engagements it was not possible. She is good company, I am sure you would take to her.

'After Ireland we travelled to Wales and all the time I remembered how much you both love that part of the country. Our dearest wish is to return there, as we feel that is where we belong.

'We also had a brief stay in Devon which was beautiful with the bluest summer skies full of gulls and swallows, and cornflowers in the fields beside the lane.'

'You are certainly well-travelled,' said Mr Westbrook, 'but tell me, has Percy thought about entering some kind of profession? Wandering up and down the country campaigning is not going to put money on the table.'

'He's writing poetry now, Papa. As we speak he is at the printing premises arranging copies.'

Her father looked unimpressed. 'Revolutionary tomes, no doubt. Nothing that will supply an income. And what about these Watchers that keep you in their sights? It is really a matter of grave concern, Harriet. These people can ruin your lives, you know.'

Her mother piped up. 'And living amongst all those strangers, Harriet! I don't mind telling you I had a most disturbing letter late last year from a woman named Mrs Hogg, in which she ranted about you and Percy and made all sorts of horrible insinuations.'

Ann Westbrook trembled with indignation. Eliza smoothly interjected.

'Dear Mama and Papa, Harriet and Percy like to have lots of friends around them, it is the modern way of living.'

'I don't recall any of our friends' children living in such a manner,' protested Ann Westbrook.

Eliza rolled onwards. 'As for Mrs Hogg, I really wouldn't worry about anything she has to say, she did not pay them a visit and therefore her information cannot be relied on. I do not think there is any need to worry about Percy's future; once he makes peace with his father matters will fall into place. There is a sizeable estate that he will eventually learn to manage, after all. Is there any more tea, Mama?'

Ann Westbrook looked unconvinced but she rang the little bell beside the table without further comment. Eliza skilfully changed the subject.

'Now, Percy and Harriet would like you both to come and dine at Lewis's Hotel tomorrow night. Isn't that so?'

Harriet nodded mutely.

John Westbrook beamed, her mother sat up even straighter, brushing imaginary dust from her skirts as she regarded Harriet with renewed fondness.

In truth, Ann Westbrook had often felt left-out over the years. Eliza had seemed to have Harriet in such a firm grip, fussing over her clothes and hair, supervising her deportment, buying her books, making her school arrangements. When the situation with Percy had first arisen she had thought at last it would be her turn to grab the reins and keep Harriet firmly in the fold. She was of the opinion that whatever game Eliza had been playing (for she knew Eliza's character well) she had overplayed her hand.

But her judgement had been wrong. Ignoring the first blow of elopement (and had she imagined it, but it had seemed to her at the time that both her husband and Eliza had taken the scandal remarkably well) she supposed things had turned out for the best.

Her thoughts shifted to what she might wear to Lewis's Hotel, when she would finally come face to face with her daughter's husband, the son of a baronet, as John had reminded her on numerous occasions. She wasn't sure that she had anything suitable. Turning to Harriet to ask her advice she was surprised to see a closed look on her daughter's face, so she said nothing.

On their way back to the hotel, Harriet and Eliza walked past the chapel. Its doors were open and Harriet glimpsed several solitary figures praying quietly, their heads bowed. She envied their moment of peace.

'Is everything quite well, Harriet? You are very quiet.'

Harriet regarded Eliza in silence.

She had felt a hot anger rise to the surface when the plan to dine at Lewis's Hotel had sallied forth from Eliza's lips. It had not been her place to issue the invitation.

Why did Eliza feel she had to control everything?

On impulse Harriet turned sharp right, the opposite way to the hotel.

'Where are you going?' Eliza's voice came, sounding uncertain.

'Father gave me some money as we left the house. All my gloves are either soiled, or unmatched; I can't go on wearing this pair for much longer. I will see you back at the hotel.'

She almost ran around the corner before Eliza could insist on accompanying her.

It was a relief to be alone.

*

The family dinner had been pleasant. Harriet was satisfied that she had managed to build some bridges between her old life and her newly married self. Percy had behaved perfectly towards her mother, regaling her with tales of his earlier life, describing his parents and sisters and life on the estate at Field Place.

Partway through the first course, Ann Westbrook had taken her arm and patted it gently in a way that Harriet knew meant she approved.

Percy had shared a few carefully chosen verses from *Queen Mab* with her father. It was likely that John Westbrook had not entirely understood them but nevertheless had been so impressed that he had insisted on paying for the lavish dinner and had even slid a few extra bank notes into Percy's pocket at the end of the evening.

Two nights later Harriet sat brushing her hair and reflected that making peace with her parents had been easy compared to what lay ahead that evening, when finally they were to make the acquaintance of the Godwins.

Patting an unruly curl into place she worried that after such a glorious correspondence, Percy and William Godwin would be disappointed with each other. And she was anxious for herself that she would feel foolish in such intellectual company.

When they alighted from their carriage outside the Godwins' bookshop in Skinner Street, Holborn, she saw that Percy was in a highly excitable state. A sheen of perspiration lay damp along his top lip. He jumped down first, holding out his hand to her. As she stepped down she was engulfed by a sensation of dread; her heart was racing like the wind.

'Wait.' She pulled at Percy's arm. 'I'm not sure we should go in.'

'Whatever is the matter, Harriet? It is perfectly fine, we are expected.'

'I just – I don't know. Can we leave? Please?'

In dismay she saw that Eliza was already on the pavement, rapping at the door.

Percy took her hand, reassuring her. When nobody answered their knock, Eliza gave the shop door an impatient push and it swung open to reveal a shabby interior; books on tilted shelves, journals piled on tables and columns of papers stretching high up to the ceiling, taking up half the floor space. Part of the old wooden unpolished counter was raised allowing access through to the back of the shop.

They made their upstairs, stepping into a room shaped

like two opposing semi-circles with a fireplace in one recess and book lined shelves and a door in the other. In the centre facing the leaping flames of the fire was a worn and patched leather armchair in which a man, his noble skull, large and bald, adrift at an angle sat snoozing with many sheets of paper scattered around him as if he had dropped them in his sleep. A thin snail's trail of saliva dribbled from his mouth.

Eliza made a moue of distaste before making one or two discreet coughs. The trio jumped in surprise as a dark-haired, bespectacled woman appeared from behind a curtained recess, a sycophantic smile spread across her face.

'My dears! We failed to answer your knock. I am so glad you found the door was on the latch and you let yourselves in. I would not like to think of you standing out on the street! Will, Will! The Shelleys and Miss Westbrook have arrived. Will!'

Eliza bowed to their hostess.

'How do you do, Mrs Godwin. How good it is for us all to meet at last.'

Harriet was unable to move. She breathed deeply, a technique she had developed in the past when similar inexplicable moods of panic had enveloped her. She stood close to Percy, smiling woodenly.

Awoken by his wife's raucous chatter, William Godwin opened his eyes and in one bounding movement jumped out of his chair, seized Percy by the arms and enfolded him in a bear hug.

At that moment, Mrs Godwin espied Harriet and giving a little scream of welcome she sent a shower of flowery phrases in her direction before announcing that dinner was served. They were led through to the dining room where the table was laid, candles were lit and a pleasing smell of freshly baked bread and vegetable and dumpling stew filled the room.

'Do not worry Mrs Shelley. Mr Godwin and I are sympathetic toward your vegetarian state and we have butchered no animals on your behalf. Indeed, we often go without meat for many weeks believing it to be a harmful substance to the body, but sometimes one does get a craving for a peppered mutton chop or a fowl broiled in the pot and so occasionally we do stray.'

Harriet glanced across at Eliza briefly. The Godwins were a little bit ridiculous, both of them in the habit of using twenty words when five would suffice. She couldn't imagine what she had been so worried about. She was glad however when Mrs Godwin announced that it would just be a small gathering at dinner as their various children were away, staying with assorted relatives. 'All except Fanny who will be along shortly, but we needn't wait for her'.

Mr Godwin frequently forgot his plate of food and Percy picked intermittently at the dishes as they sparred with their words vigorously, amid much laughter, Percy's voice becoming shriller with each hotly debated point. Mrs Godwin at the other end of the table spent much of her time muttering out of the side of her mouth to Eliza, which Harriet realised was a sign of furtive gossiping.

Harriet caught a movement in the doorway as a young woman arrived without fuss and slipped into the last seat at the table, folding her napkin onto her lap and helping herself to food with apologetic movements. Harriet decided that as nobody was going to introduce her she would take matters into her own hands.

'You must be Miss Fanny Imlay. How do you do? I am Mrs Shelley.'

Large eyes in a kind face gazed at her in gratitude.

'I am pleased to make your acquaintance, Mrs Shelley. I have so enjoyed reading your letters…and of course those of Mr Shelley.'

The large eyes grew rounder as they settled on Percy's animated countenance.

Harriet sighed. She was growing used to that look of adoration on the faces of women whenever they chanced across her husband. She looked fondly across at him, oblivious to the havoc he was so obviously wreaking in this poor, plain girl's heart.

For of course, she was so very plain, acknowledged Harriet, a hint of shame diluting her relief.

Later in the evening, leaving the men roaming the shelves of the bookstore and Eliza and Mrs Godwin to their chatter in the small parlour, Fanny took Harriet by the hand. They crossed reverently into William Godwin's study, an untidy shambles of papers and journals and half-written pages. Over the fireplace was a portrait of Mary Wollstonecraft, a most striking woman, with skin of alabaster, soft brown hair and piercing eyes that blazed with intelligence.

'Poor Mama,' said Fanny softly.

'I have of course, read her work but I not realised how beautiful she was,' said Harriet gently, 'You must miss her terribly.'

'I was very young when she died, and have only the vaguest memory of her. But I have missed growing up with her, all these years.'

'I'm sure Mrs Godwin is a most adequate step-mother for you.'

'Yes,' said Fanny doubtfully.

'And what of young Mary? When will she next be home? You must be looking forward to her return.'

'Yes,' said Fanny again in the same tone. 'When Mary is home, the house is sparkier somehow. Father of course dotes on her but Mrs Godwin often finds herself in disagreement with her. As for the two of us, we possess very different personalities. Mary is the sort of girl one can imagine adventures happening to whereas I will only ever hear about them second-hand. I sometimes imagine Mary flying away, with me holding onto the hem of her frock so as not to be left behind.'

'What type of person is she?'

'Clever. Amusing. Imaginative. As beautiful as our mother reportedly was.'

'Really?'

Harriet gazed again reflectively at the woman in the portrait and thought of the other Mary, her daughter.

She noticed that beyond admiration for her half-sister, Fanny had not once referred to her as being good or kind.

*

'What on earth –' Percy spluttered indignantly. Harriet showing her teeth in amusement clapped her hand gently over his mouth.

'Watch,' she whispered from the shadows of the doorway to their hotel room.

It was afterwards, when the shouting had died away that they finally pieced the events of the afternoon in place. It transpired that the idiotic Bessie Hitchener, having received a letter that morning from her hometown, had been delighted to learn that scandalous stories were being whispered about her being Percy's mistress.

Believing Eliza to be at home in Chapel Street and Percy and Harriet out walking, she had left her own small room in the hotel and had gained entrance to Harriet and Percy's rooms. Rummaging through Harriet's closet she had chosen a dress and Harriet's silk wrap and had dressed herself in the borrowed finery.

Harriet and Percy watched her take mincing steps across the floor, crooning softly to herself as she undertook a thrilling waltz with an imaginary dance partner. Clearly acting out some torrid daydream she slipped her unfastened dress down to display bony white shoulder blades to her invisible beau. The smile slipped from Harriet's face as she saw that Bessie had jammed Harriet's turquoise betrothal ring, left in haste on the dresser after bathing, onto her own wedding finger.

She saw that Percy too had realised that Miss Hitchener had gone too far.

He cleared his throat and ventured into the room, Harriet behind him. 'Bessie,' he said uncertainly.

The lone waltz came to an undignified end as Bessie jumped in fright, lost her footing and tumbled onto the rug. Percy leapt forward to help her. Harriet dropped to the floor seeking to retrieve her purloined ring which had gone flying from Miss Hitchener's finger in the mayhem.

'You startled me! I – I – did not perceive you to be there. Were you spying on me, Mrs Shelley?'

It was clear that Bessie was not going to concede that she had done anything wrong and at first did not understand when they firmly told her it was time to leave the hotel and their little group. Even as Harriet ran to Miss Hitchener's own room to pack up her belongings, Bessie refused to believe they really wanted her to go. She stood her ground, arguing with Percy, her tone becoming more truculent.

'This is all Godwin's fault,' she spat, 'ever since you met him, you have been under his spell with endless dinners and talks. Skinner Street is spinning its sinister little web, trapping you and Harriet and you have not the wit to realise! You allow Godwin to give you financial advice when he clearly has none worth imparting and he gives you reading lists as if you were a child, which you pore over for hours.

'You seem to have no time left for me at all. Oh Percy, what has happened to us that you should cease to regard me as the soul mate you once told me I was? What you need is someone to turn your mind away from the evil Godwin influence as your wife, this slip of a girl, is clearly unable to do this. I will be there for you when you need me, dearest Bysshe. Please, let go of my arm. Please…!'

After the hotel staff had finally seen Miss Hitchener off the premises, Harriet slipped away to write to Catherine Nugent, a wryly amusing letter of the departure, describing their great happiness of finally being free of her and the surprising fact that she had really believed Percy to be in love with her.

A chill ran up Harriet's spine as she put her pen down thoughtfully.

Miss Hitchener was doubtless irritating but she was not a fool; she had made some shrewd observations about Godwin. What had caused her to totally misunderstand her place in their community? She recalled hearing on more than one occasion, Percy telling Bessie that they were soul mates. Of course, he had not meant it in a romantic way. Miss Hitchener was old and unattractive. Their relationship had initially been as enthusiastic pen pals sharing the same ideals. It was unfortunate that as soon as she had joined them she had shown herself to be a woman of little intelligence.

Had Elizabeth Hitchener been in some way misled? Had Percy deceived her?

Harriet examined her conscience and admitted to herself that she was not entirely sure.

⁓Eleven⁓
A Pregnancy and a Poem

London, June 1813,

The sun hit the shutters, bathing the room and the city beyond in golden light. Harriet woke with a start. Heavy in the last weeks of pregnancy, she struggled to find a position of comfort.

She called out to Percy and Eliza, but her voice echoed in the stillness of the room. She sank back down on the banked pillows behind her head.

The last eight months had been frenetic. Discovering to her joy that she was expecting a child, her heart had been set on returning to Nantgwillt so the trio had travelled back to Wales. The journey had been particularly gruelling for Harriet, who had been nauseous throughout, the horses jolting the carriage pulling at great speeds over the rutted roads.

The only thing that had comforted her as she clung to Percy's arm and endured the long journey, had been the thought of settling back into the rooms they loved, making ready the smallest to become a nursery. To tread the familiar paths down to the banks of the river, where the blazing autumn trees were reflected in its clear water, breathing in the wood smoke that floated across the valley, was all she had desired.

But they had arrived to discover the manor house was unavailable, new tenants having recently signed an agreement for long-term residence. Her heart had plummeted at the thought of someone else filling the longed-for rooms with their own belongings and dreams.

Greatly disappointed, they had journeyed on, finally settling in Tremadoc, a wild and lonely valley in the shadow of Mount Snowdon, which had somehow suited their mood. Soon after they had arrived Percy had agreed to lend his support raising funds for a local project to repair a crumbling embankment. The proposed work would make the town commercially viable and give employment to the village labourers once the main road was eventually built.

Pleased to be involved in such virtuous work, their spirits had lifted. Once work had begun Percy's role was to make calls on the surrounding landowners and gentry and negotiate financial pledges to the cause. He got on well with them all until a few weeks later, he discovered that the workers were receiving their wages excessively late and sometimes not at all.

His natural sense of justice could not allow him to close his eyes. He began to encourage the workers to agitate for collective bargaining, supporting them in proposed strikes. The landowners in charge of the rebuilding project were enraged at this turn of events and much of the blame was placed upon Percy.

Nestled uncomfortably close to the gentry who now loathed them, the Shelleys' stay in the valley rapidly became unpleasant. Threats were made. The trio were ostracised. One dramatic night, believing the house had been broken into, Percy had fired shots at an alleged assailant. Their stay had been immediately terminated.

Unnerved and dejected, they had fled Wales and travelled back to Ireland. They needed to retrieve some of Percy's writing that had been left with the publisher in Dublin, and while they were there they hoped there might be another opportunity to help further the Irish cause. But that too, had come to nothing.

Downcast they had travelled back to London, arriving back in April, homeless, the unborn baby becoming more visible with each day. John Westbrook had insisted on paying for a set of rooms in Cooks Hotel as a temporary measure.

But somehow things always seemed to be temporary, thought Harriet. The baby kicked gently, reminding her that she should stop brooding on the past and look to the future, to contemplate herself as a mother.

She and Percy had been highly delighted at the idea of a baby. Eliza had been less so.

'Doing your duty by adding to our little community,' had been her only comment when Harriet had informed her that she was to be an aunt.

Hurt, Harriet had to concede that Eliza was jealous. Not for the first time, she had wondered whether she should ask Eliza to leave. Rather than make a fuss, she hoped that once the baby arrived, Eliza would feel out of place in the young family. Now that Dan had served his prison term and had found his way back to them in London, they would be able to manage.

Deciding she couldn't stay in bed a moment longer, she rose slowly from the depths of the bed and began wandering the rooms aimlessly. In the sitting room her eye was caught by something that had not been in evidence the previous evening. On the table, set apart from the assortment of scattered papers, was a nosegay of creamy yellow roses in a jar and a note addressed to her, Percy's words written at an even greater slant than usual.

'Harriet... Thou wert my purer mind, thou wert the inspiration of my song; Thine are these early wilding flowers... garlanded by me...'

Lines dedicated to her from *Queen Mab*, which was finally finished.

Percy had recently sent the poem to the printer and discarded pages lay around the room, randomly scattered, filled with his crossings out and accompanying notes.

She picked up a few sheets. Her happiness faded.

Percy's tart observations about marriage, scrawled in the margins of his work, stung.

'Love is free: to promise for ever to love the same woman, is not less absurd than to promise to believe the same creed: such a vow in both cases, excludes us from all enquiry. ...a system could not well have been devised more studiously hostile to human happiness than marriage...'

How could he write such things? Marriage as tyranny? She had assumed he shared her joy in the constancy of love, the excitement of stepping out onto an unknown road with a familiar and tender hand held close to ward off all dangers. It was disturbing that he considered affection to be a commodity that would naturally decay with the passage of time.

She shook away her thoughts. The poem, a philosophical work had been written like a fairy story, with Queen Mab's ethereal flight through the universe exposing the blackness at the root of monarchies and organised religions.

She was saddened that Percy had included marriage in his list of worldly evils. But she told herself she was being silly. The poem was written for effect, for the world to sit up and take notice of him; her ever-rebellious husband that only she really understood.

Harriet found a bag of cherry buns and took them back to bed where she gazed moodily across the room to the streets beyond the window. These rooms in the heart of fashionable London were worlds away from the places they had lived in before her pregnancy.

She held onto her hope that one day Nantgwillt might still be theirs. A place to bring up their child. And of course, to throw open the doors and invite the world.

Percy had gathered a new circle of sympathetic friends since their arrival back in the city; the bookseller, Hookham, a fellow poet named Peacock, a vegetarian and naturist by the name of John Newton, Godwin of course and surprisingly Mr Hogg, with whom they had finally resolved their problems from the Edinburgh days; kept rather at arm's length for the time being but who was by and large back in the fold.

Harriet had joked with Percy that he didn't seem to require her company as much as she needed his, noticing that whenever they found themselves blissfully alone, as she thought, he seemed to make some excuse either to go out or invite people around.

Feeling constrained and not merely by pregnancy, Harriet longed suddenly for more sky and less people.

She needed Percy.

She wondered if he would be back before the end of day. He had said he would be out for some time, organising a surprise for her, 'a special gift for his muse.'

She wondered what it could be and hoped fervently that it would not be expensive.

Eliza had been absent for much of the day, too. At the thought of her sister, Harriet's brow puckered. Eliza seemed to be making grand plans. For this, she blamed herself. She had been indiscreet.

A week ago Harriet had to her surprise received a letter from Percy's mother who had conveyed her pleasure that Harriet was with child and had expressed a desire to meet with her privately, 'away from the finances and the menfolk.' Lady Shelley had made it very clear that this should be kept from Percy but in the moment of happiness at the invitation, Harriet had told Eliza who had been delighted and was now firmly of the view that one day, in the not too distant future, Harriet's baby could be tucked up in Percy's old nursery in Field Place.

'Well, Harriet this is indeed good news that Lady Shelley is making friendly overtures and will surely pave the way to a reconciliation between Percy and Sir Timothy.

'And think of this: Percy will shortly reach his majority and I should imagine that the family will wish to officially mark the occasion in some way. I think maybe I should write to Sir Timothy myself and suggest a dinner.'

'Eliza! I forbid you to do such a thing. Leave things to happen by themselves, it is not right to force the issue. Percy's mother is being very cautious, and rightly so.'

She was not sure if Eliza would take heed; she had seen the look in her eye.

'With your child almost born, Harriet, everything has changed. One day it may inherit a title. You are within your rights to go to Field Place and be welcomed into the family.'

Harriet had kept the letter a secret from Percy; how she wished she had done the same with Eliza.

A tightening in her abdomen and a series of sharp little pains caused her to sit up abruptly.

Surely the babe was not coming now? Her mind contracted with fear. How to reach Percy if she needed him? He could be at Skinner Street, she supposed, where he seemed to spend far too much time. Lately she had made excuses not to accompany him. She really couldn't abide the company of Mrs Godwin. And Percy knew that, but still he would visit almost every day.

She must take herself in hand. She was merely being peevish as a result of the baby. Her mother had told her she should expect such heightened feelings.

There was that pain again. She sought frantically for the words the physician had intoned when it had happened previously.

In and out. In and out. After a few moments, it receded.

Percy's poem on the verge of being printed. And a summer baby. She hoped there would be a way for such divergent paths to cross with ease.

Volume Two
Matt

∼Twelve∽
Shock

December 2015

'Ten, nine, eight, seven...'

The customary New Year count-down was underway. Sitting on the stairs, tucked out of sight, Matt looked down on the crowd of party revellers blowing party streamers into the open space of the Ropers' L-shaped sitting room. The furniture, the floor and even the guests themselves were coated in a riotous shockwave of colour.

London cavorted, the great crowds gathered on the banks of the Thames whooping with delight at each new firework set ablaze. Matt and Gemma watched them on Gemma's new tablet, fizzing around Big Ben and the London Eye before exploding into the skies.

'Die, you numpty!' Gemma's younger brother, Davy and his friends were killing random targets via the games console in the family room, oblivious to the peace and goodwill of the season.

'Happy New Year!' the announcer shrieked and the heaving group of adults downstairs waved their arms in the air and swayed with delight.

Parents, thought Matt, they were just so uncool. But sweet in their own way. He fondly imagined his father and Jessie seeing in their first New Year in the new house, with a good bottle of red wine, a takeaway banquet from their favourite curry house, and each other.

He veered his mind away from his mother, Polly, bravely staying home like the divorced martyr she had recently become, stone-walling all attempts to drag her out on this unforgiving night of revelry, even though Gemma had assured her that she would be welcome at her parents' party.

From outside in the small gardens of the Victorian villas dotted around Ealing Broadway, smaller displays of pyrotechnics could be heard, banging and crackling through the darkness. Matt felt a surge of hope for all that the new year promised, flare within. He squeezed Gemma's hand. It lay unresponsive in his own.

'More fizz? Where's the other bottle gone? Have we finished it already?'

'Let's go onto cocktails! We've got some gin somewhere, haven't we, Tony?'

'I think your parents and their friends are having more fun than we are,' Matt grinned at Gemma and then lost the grin as he realised that was in fact, the truth.

'What's up Gem, you've been quiet all evening?' D'you want another drink? I'm going to grab myself a lager.'

'Just an orange juice.'

Matt eased his way through the crowd, most of whom were swaying and shuffling to an old eighties floor filler, and made his way to the table in the kitchen which was serving as the bar for the night.

All the ice had melted in the bucket leaving a cold watery pool at the bottom. Plunging his hand in, he came away with a soft drink and a bottle of lager, wiped his hand on a carelessly flung tea towel, picked up the last surviving bowl of crisps and returned to the stairs.

'Cheers!' he said in mock-merry fashion, trying to rally through the gloom. Gemma was still silent.

'Has something happened, Gem? I wish you'd tell me what's wrong.'

He took a gulp from the bottle. Alert in the silence on the staircase he looked at her. As he marked something unrecognisable in her eyes he knew, with a cold dread, what had happened.

He watched her face, watching him as he did some mental maths, Gemma's mood swings and snappiness of the past few weeks finally impacting on him in a great wave. Finally she spoke.

'It's more a case of what hasn't happened. We should have been more careful. I told you at the time…'

Gemma's voice trailed away in misery. Matt drained his lager bottle. They sat side by side, not touching, both reliving the night in late October when, drafted in by her parents to keep an eye on Davy while they went out to dinner, they had got carried away and had sex on the corner sofa in the sitting room.

Too late now, Matt thought, to kick yourself for having forgotten to bring condoms. They'd both realised the mood would be broken if one of them had to make a dash out to the corner shop. They hadn't stopped, lost as they were in the thrill of urgent, illicit lovemaking, eleven-year–old Davy in his bedroom above, obediently doing his guitar practice.

'Celebrate...!' called Gemma's parents with the remaining friends that were still standing.

In a daze Matt stared through the bannisters into the living room as if viewing a bad sit-com on the television. He found himself wondering how long Gemma's parents had been together. His parents had lasted nineteen years before his father had bailed out.

He couldn't imagine being with anyone that long but then, at seventeen it wasn't the kind of thing you thought about very often. He and Gemma had been seeing each other for ten months, a slow and comfortable, somewhat passive relationship which had suited them both.

Until now.

He was aware of their continuing silence. There were discussions to be had, decisions to be made. He didn't know where to begin. Someone had opened the front door and a cold breeze wafted in. It felt like freedom. He buried the thought.

'Are you sure? Did you do a test?'

'Three tests. All positive.'

'So what do you think we should do?' he said, as if she had all the answers filed away in a handy feminine drawer of instant remedies.

She shrugged almost casually. We should be hugging or holding each other, thought Matt, tiredly. He moved towards her but she leaned away from him.

'I think I want to keep it,' Gemma said and Matt heard the words rolling downwards as if from a great distance.

'Oh,' he said, shocked, stupidly, 'should we? I mean could we...?'

'Why not?'

115

'Well, we're so young. We haven't achieved anything yet. We haven't even done our 'A' levels. Would we move in together? How would we manage for money?'

He thought she looked at him with something like pity before clambering up from her position on the stair above him.

'I don't want to talk about it anymore. I'm going to bed now. You can see yourself out, can't you?'

'Gem, please! We need to talk about this. Sorry if I sounded negative, I was just so shocked. I need to get used to the idea. I'll come round tomorrow and we'll make some plans. I'm sure it will be fine, we can work it out somehow –'

She had gone. The bedroom door slammed. Downstairs the mood was turning mellow with couples intertwined, revolving in drunken happy circles on the parquet floor.

He picked up the empty bottle, collecting several other empties from the stairway as he brushed past the dancers.

Gemma's father raised an eyebrow and winked at him as he chucked rubbish into one of the randomly placed bin liners.

'Good lad,' he said distractedly with his face buried comfortably on his wife's shoulder.

Groping in the hallway through the mountain of coats to find his jacket, Matt was fairly sure that would be the last time those words would be applied to him for quite some time.

∼Thirteen∽
Parenthood

August 2016

The baby's eyes were a soft pale blue, fringed with curling lashes, unleashing an unwavering stare straight into his soul. He stroked her cheek gingerly, afraid he might hurt her with his lumbering hands, irrationally fearing he would infect her innocence with his sin.

His daughter.

He took a few pictures on his phone and then put it away as he heard the rustle of a dressing gown from behind and tired feet shuffling in slipper boots.

'Matt?'

He could scarcely tear his eyes away from the baby to face its mother. As his eyes finally roamed her exhausted pallor he could see the barest trace of the schoolgirl as he had last seen her.

His voice came out a couple of notches higher than normal.

'Your brother let me in. Sorry if it's not a good time. How are things?'

'Everything's fine.' She paused. 'Thank you for the beautiful roses you sent.'

Matt had planned not to reproach her but he saw her standing there with a wealth of experiences that he had hoped to have shared and his voice tightened.

'I kept hoping you'd change your mind and allow me to come to the hospital. I wanted to be there, you know?'

'I wanted my mum to be there and it would have been awkward with you there, too. You know what I mean.'

Remembering the last time he had seen Gemma's mother; the shrillness of her voice, her furious eyes signalling to Gemma's shocked and silent father as he and Gemma broke the news of the pregnancy, he nodded.

Over the following months, as Gemma's belly had swelled, the anger had dissipated. But still the families kept a pointedly polite distance. Rather than undergo the disappointed sighs from Matt's mother and simmering annoyance from Gemma's, the couple found it easier to meet in coffee shops and shopping malls; impersonal settings that fractured their strained relationship, the intimacy draining away in ceaseless rounds of cappuccinos and lattes.

'I tried texting you. I even rang you on the house phone hoping you'd pick up but your dad answered so I hung up. I just wanted to know how you both were.' He paused. 'Was the birth ok? I mean, I suppose it must have really hurt?'

He could have cursed his clumsy stupidity, venturing into territory that he knew nothing about. And neither should she, at her age he reminded himself.

But her voice was triumphant and somehow serene at the same time.

'It was fine. Quite quick, really. I was only in labour for about seven hours. The midwives were lovely.' She looked at his stricken face.

'It's ok now, I've forgotten it. They say that's what happens, otherwise nobody would ever have another baby.'

She gestured towards the slumbering baby in its low-hooded basket, as if to say, what does it all matter now that she's here.

'Well I'm sorry, but I couldn't stay away any longer, it was driving me mad, you know? I just wanted to see you. Both of you.'

He caught sight of his reflection in her dressing table mirror and blinked at the image of himself doing his best to masquerade as a father.

He noticed her eyes were softening. 'I went to Ealing Broadway and bought some stuff: nappies, some baby-grows and my mum bought some bits for you from the chemist that she said would be useful.'

He placed two big plastic carrier bags at her feet where she stood in the shadow of the night light. She half smiled at the sight of a small brown teddy bear which was stacked on top of several packets of cotton wool, a large container of baby lotion and a bumper packet of wet-wipes.

'Thank you. And please thank your mum too. How are things with the two of you?'

Matt ignored the vision of his stony-faced mother. 'A bit better.'

'Well that's good, isn't it?'

'Are your parents ok, now?'

Her mother's rants echoed in his mind.

'I'm not accusing you of wrong-doing', Gemma's mother had raged, 'we're not living in the dark ages. It's the stupidity of falling pregnant, when it should have been easily avoided, that I find unforgivable.'

But now the baby was here, the entire family was totally in love with her.

The baby began to stir restlessly, her legs beginning to kick, the signal that the first scream of the evening was imminent.

He watched Gemma take a deep breath before plunging into the basket and picking up the bundled baby, loosening it from its swaddling. She moved with it in her arms to a padded seat on wooden rockers, seating herself gently, wincing slightly as she lowered herself onto the cushioned base.

'Are you okay?'

'It's just my stitches pulling.'

He looked at her humbly.

As she began to fumble at her dressing gown to loosen it, leaning the baby in towards her breast, an overpowering need to flee overtook him. At the same time, he feared it might be rude if he abruptly took leave of her, cherry-picking his involvement.

She looked at him enquiringly, pausing before guiding the baby's mouth to her nipple.

Oh. Ok, he got it.

'Right then. I'll get off.'

He paused with his hand on the door knob. She was watching him impassively.

'So, shall I come again tomorrow?'

She dipped her head as the baby began to guzzle. Blink and he would have missed it, he thought she inclined it further forward for a second, as if in agreement.

When he arrived home, his mother was standing at the ironing board with her moody back turned towards him. He flung himself down on the sofa and put his legs up on the coffee table which he knew would annoy her. Surprisingly she refused to take the bait.

'Gemma said to say thanks for the stuff you bought,' he said eventually, knowing that someone had to break the silence. 'I've got some photos on my phone. Do you want to see them?'

She didn't turn. The soft swoosh of the iron and the hiss of steam permeated the air. After a while he sensed a small depression in the atmosphere. His mother placed an ironed blouse on a hanger and moved towards him.

He took her through the series of snapshots, provoking no reaction until he reached the close-up he had managed to catch when the baby had just opened her eyes.

'She looks the image of you,' she said eventually, her voice neutral. She stared at it in silence before returning to the ironing board but her back had softened.

'Your eyes are exactly the same shade of blue.'

She was still pushing the iron across the board with some force.

'So, what's going to happen now?'

'We didn't really talk about plans. Gemma was, you know, tired, distracted.'

If he was expecting a modicum of maternal sympathy from one mother to another none was forthcoming.

'I'm sure she was,' his mother said acidly. 'While you were out your father rang, he wants you to call him at seven. You had your mobile switched off, apparently.

That wouldn't have helped her mood, Matt realised. Ever since his father had left, eighteen months ago, his mother had been brittle at the best of times.

'Gemma said she'd bring the baby round to see you. Would you like that?'

She stopped ironing and reached for a box of tissues, dabbing her eyes fiercely.

'What I would really like, is not to be a grandmother at this present moment in time.'

She looked across at her son who was fiddling dejectedly with the television remote, not daring to switch on. 'Failing that, a cup of coffee would be nice.'

Sensing a thaw Matt got up, walked into the kitchen and filled the kettle.

'And a biscuit.'

When he returned with two mugs and a packet of chocolate chip cookies under his arm he discovered his mother had abandoned the ironing and was scrolling through the photos again.

'She is beautiful, Matt. How do you feel now that she's here?'

'It feels weird. I feel weird. But proud too. I want to see her again but I feel nervous about her at the same time.'

'You've got an important year coming up. Time to focus on the future.'

If his mother thought a change of subject would help, she was wrong.

'I don't want to think about school.'

His mother inhaled sharply.

'Well, you will have to, Matt, at some stage, think about school and beyond. You need to be thinking about your UCAS form for a start.'

'Gemma's not going back.'

'And?'

'I want to get a job so I can give Gemma some money every month.'

'There's no point throwing your life away, Matt. I don't

122

think the Ropers will expect or need your money.'

'I'm trying to do the right thing, here.'

He saw her biting back the words. The right thing would have been not to have had a baby.

'The baby is partly my responsibility, as you were all so quick to point out.'

His mother, knowing she had said enough, left the room with the ironed clothes, taking care not to let him hear her sigh.

*

He procrastinated for far too long and term had started by the time he made his way back to the school building.

School had finished for the day. Matt knew he would find Mrs Durbin, his art teacher, in the art rooms, cleaning up splodges of paint on the tables from the last lesson with the new, enthusiastic Year Sevens. She looked up at his approach, her face reflecting the rigours of the day, slowly morphing into a broad smile of welcome.

'It's nice to see you, Matt. I was concerned when you missed the start of term.'

She peered closely under his mop of fringed hair, noted the circles under his eyes and the perpetual worried frown he had worn ever since learning that Gemma was going to have his child.

'Sit.' Mrs Durbin scraped back one of the red, asteroid-embellished, chairs, a project from the previous summer term. Matt had dumped his messenger bag on the floor. It splayed open, revealing a brand new three-pack of pink baby pacifiers.

She leant to the far reaches of the table where sat a terracotta bowl of artistically arranged fruit and breaking off some stems from the bunched grapes shared them out.

There was a companionable silence. Matt sniffed the familiar, stale air, a heady mix of glue and paint and acrylics. The room was peaceful and after a while he felt he could speak.

'I'm having trouble getting my head around things.'

'I'm told that Gemma has had the baby. A girl, isn't it?'

Matt swallowed the lump in his throat. For a second he had been revelling in the normality of the familiar rooms, believing that he had stepped back into his old unencumbered life.

'Yep,' he said neutrally.

'I suspect with you two as parents, she must be very beautiful.'

'Yep,' he agreed again, this time with a spark of paternal pride in his eyes.

'In spite of everything, you did well last year, Matt. Time to get back to it, don't you think?

'I'm not really sure -'

'I do understand how difficult this is for all concerned but it's still early September and term has barely started. It's not too late to come back and pick up where you left off.'

'But it's too late for Gemma,' he burst out, frustration brimming over.

Mrs Durbin regarded him steadily. They had always got on well. 'That was Gemma's choice. You can't sit at home doing nothing because a baby's been born. You can sit your 'A' levels and still be a father. Gemma's choices are not wholly your responsibility.'

Mrs Durbin walked over to her desk and began to leaf through a folder. Matt watched her, his mind in turmoil. Was she saying that Gemma had been wrong to have the baby, he wondered. A week ago he would have agreed with her, like his mum and Gemma's parents. But now he'd seen his daughter he couldn't imagine her not being there.

'Go home, print out your timetable and get your books ready for tomorrow. I'll come and find you at some point in the day and we can talk some more.'

'Ok', he said, finally. It felt good that somebody was taking an interest in him again.

'Has your daughter been given a name, yet?' she asked, hoping she wasn't further disturbing deep water.

But he looked up and gave a great smile. 'Yes', he said with pride, 'Her name is Henrietta.'

'Unusual', murmured Mrs Durbin.

'We used some baby name dictionaries and we also spent time surfing the net. Henrietta was the name we both agreed on. It means 'The Ruler of the Home.''

'Indeed', said childless Mrs Durbin, imagining the power of a baby's cry.

'We thought at first we might want to use the shortened version, 'Halle.' Gemma tried it out a few times but she felt it didn't suit the baby. Apparently, it means 'an unexpected gift.''

Their eyes met in a single moment of mirth.

*

It was just a Saturday morning at the mall, Matt told himself, trying not to feel self-conscious as he strolled alongside Gemma and the buggy. Gemma had some shopping to do and afterwards they had arranged to meet a group of friends for coffee to show them the baby.

'I just need to get some formula for her and some more baby wipes.'

'Formula? I thought you were…I mean, I saw you feeding her yourself.' He watched her face tighten as if he was being judgemental.

'The Health Visitor thought I should introduce a bottle feed. She's a hungry baby and I haven't always got enough milk. Look, I'll be a lot quicker if I shop on my own. Why don't you go ahead and get a coffee and I'll meet you when I've finished?'

The bar of the buggy handle felt cold to the touch in the October breeze as she handed it over. He thought obscurely of the motor bike he had once planned to buy and the long-held wish of a road trip across Europe.

'There are nappies in that purple bag but you shouldn't need them, I changed her before she came out. Could you get me an iced vanilla latte? I won't be long.'

He watched her girlish figure almost galloping away, swinging her arms, free once more and sighed, remembering the weekends when Gemma would clothes-shop for hours before coming back to him laden with nothing more innocuous than a couple of dresses, a lipstick and a self-satisfied smile.

He headed over to the coffee shop. As he drew level with the doors he realised it was going to be tricky to negotiate his way in. He couldn't get the buggy through the single open door and as he tried to wedge the other door open with his body, his grip loosened on the handle of the buggy and it tilted away from him. In the end, a kindly woman held both doors apart whilst he puffed and panted his way in. The woman obviously thought her good deed had given her licence to coo and chat.

'Taking your baby sister, out are you? She looks like you with those beautiful eyes.'

Which, as Henrietta lay fast asleep with her features closed tight against the world, was a ridiculous statement for a stranger to make, Matt considered.

He preferred not to dwell on his silent denial of paternity.

Awkward in the queue, with the buggy rigidly in the way of customers, tables and staff, trying to deal with his wallet, two coffees and the buggy handle, he felt a slow frustration creeping up on him as he stood feeling utterly tethered. Finally, having first wheeled Henrietta over to an empty table, parked up the buggy and then returned for the coffee cups he sat down feeling exhausted and then felt guilty almost immediately, reminding himself that Gemma must feel like this most of the time.

He took a sip of reviving coffee savouring the smell. To his annoyance, a gang of younger teenagers had fanned ten chairs around the small table next to his. The girls' shrieks, the boys' joshing and the accompanying noise from various mobile phones was ear splitting. Instinctively he glanced into the buggy. To his surprise, Henrietta was awake and regarding him solemnly.

He looked at her in rising panic. Now he had sole command of her, he realised too late he didn't know what to do with her. The crowds, the buggy, the alien bag of baby paraphernalia closed in on him and he sat with an empty heart. Enraged he glared into the buggy. Henrietta continued to look at him before her cheeks dimpled and her mouth opened into a smile.

Don't do that, he thought. I'm not what you need. But she smiled on. Without realising what he was doing he bent down into the buggy, unstrapped her and lifted her into his arms.

The coffee implements hissed and ground, shook and steamed, their contrapuntal harmonies whirling above his head, as his daughter gathered up his heart. He couldn't remember experiencing such a deep moment of peace.

She was falling comfortably asleep in his arms when a small whirlwind gathered beside him, rustling bags dumped underneath the table, a coat flung on the back of a chair, Henrietta torn from his arms and flung onto the maternal lap.

'Hi Gem, you were quick. Did you get everything you need?'

'Yes. It was weird, though. I've been dreaming for weeks of the freedom to be on my own again, even just for half an hour but I guess I've got so used to her being with me all the time that I just felt empty. I couldn't wait to get back.'

She paused. 'About the bottle feeding. I mean, does it upset you?'

'Of course not. Why would I mind?'

'People can be so disapproving about formula feeding.'

'People?'

'Other mothers…you know, at the baby group and drop-in centres. Some of them really look down on you if you even whisper the word 'bottle.'

'Even if it's full of prosecco?'

She gave a tired grin.

Minutes later the door flew open once again and they looked up to see Alex, Rich, James, Kay and Jo, laughter reduced to silence as they encountered the spectacle of the new family for the first time.

This is awkward, thought Matt, his thoughts and eyes still firmly on his daughter. She gazed back he was sure, in voiceless agreement.

⟜Fourteen⟞
Struggling

He slammed the front door loudly behind him, knowing it would annoy his mother but unable to help himself. A rubbish day, he conceded silently to himself. The life he was trying to return to was frustrating. He didn't want or need to learn about the physical and mechanical properties of the various types of hardwood. Wilfred Owen's anthem for a very different kind of doomed youth, had broken his already fragile heart. And during Mr Jester's droning monologue about aperture as they had planned the final work for their photographic portfolios, he had sat and imagined Henrietta's dimpled cheeks appearing in focus, smiling at him.

And as for his friends, Rich, Alex and James spent a lot of time larking about. Comparing scores on endless shooting video games. Speculating about the next big movie to hit the screens. Pubs and clubs. Having fun. The teenage fun he should be having. He didn't know why he no longer cared about these things. Killing CGI characters or necking eight bottles of lager just seemed trite but…maybe one day he would wake one morning and not hear Henrietta's cry in his fading dreams, and his old self would return.

He noticed and ignored the fact that he had brought wet autumn leaves into the hallway that had clung onto his shoes from the walk across the park. That would give his mother something to moan about, he thought irritably.

Rooting around in kitchen cupboards for a snack he heard her steps coming down the stairs.

'Is everything alright? How was school? Did you give in your English assignment?'

'Mm.' He tried not to make it into a snarl.

'Come into the sitting room,' she called.

He dolloped chocolate spread indiscriminately onto several slices of bread and loped morosely into the front room. His mother was on her knees on the rug in front of the fire-place, surrounded by boxes and bags.

'Look! Remember this?' She held up a faded orange rabbit in a green spotted vest.

Matt gave a quick grin. 'I can't believe you've kept that all this time.'

'I know you were ready to throw it out all those years ago, but I just couldn't bear to get rid of it. It would have been getting rid of a little piece of you. You slept with this until you were eleven.'

Her voice had softened. The heat within him subsided. 'Henrietta would love it. Can I give it to her?'

'Of course you can.'

He gestured to the surrounding debris. 'What's all this?'

'I've been upstairs all afternoon clearing out the attic.'

'Why?'

'I thought we could think about having a loft conversion

next year.'

He looked at her.

'The third bedroom is really only a box-room. You can't get a bed in there. The loft would make a decent sized- bedroom for you and then Henrietta could have your current room as a nursery when she comes to stay. We could do it up for her nicely. Yellow, or maybe pink. Something girly.'

She meant well. He tried hard not to feel as if plans were being made over his head. Tried and failed. 'Don't rush into it Mum. Gemma and I might want to get our own place.'

She said nothing but he caught the hint of a frown.

He came and sat beside her on the rug and began to sift through sagging boxes and musty black sacks. Old school reports, scrapbooks from his car mania days, a football pennant, a few postcards, a stack of redundant text books, a wonky pottery tortoise from his third year of primary school.

'As well as all this lot, I found that old trunk that Granny left me but it was too heavy to lift. Let's leave it until the weekend and then we can get that down as well.'

'We've got Henrietta this weekend,' he reminded her.

'Well, some other time then. It's been up there for so long, another week won't hurt. I'll go and clean this and then you can give it to her on Saturday.'

She took the fur rabbit by its musty ears and headed into the kitchen. At the door, she turned.

'Is that likely?'

'What?'

'You and Gemma moving in together? How would that work?'

He put his head down, pretending interest in an old football calendar from 2009 and didn't look up again until the sound of the taps could be heard hissing over the kitchen sink, accompanied by the lemon fresh scent of detergent.

He'd been online and had found a few rental agencies and had saved several interesting possibilities. Rooting around in his desk drawers he found his building society passbook containing money his mother had managed to persuade him to squirrel away over the years; bits of birthday and Christmas money, in total the grand sum of £989.

God. Just enough to pay rent for a month on a studio flat. Not including the deposit. He kicked the desk in frustration. He had the sudden thought that he'd like some alcohol and debated sneaking a glass from his mother's sauvignon blanc chilling in the fridge door. Then thought better of it.

Changing tack, he logged on again and began to trawl again, this time employment websites. *Graduate. Higher Ed. Experienced. Graduate...*

What was the point? It was all useless. He was useless.

His mother's attic conversion began to sound a more attractive prospect.

When his mobile phone buzzed his spirits lifted a fraction. Perhaps his father would have some ideas.

*

'Listen, I was chatting to my dad last night. He went through a few things with me and I think I've come up with a plan for us to be able–'

'Hang on. Matt, I need to warm her bottle. Can I stick it in your mum's microwave? Where is your mum by the way? I thought she'd be here to see the baby.'

Unusually, Gemma had called round not long after he'd arrived back from school.

'She's had to go to Bristol to look after her sister. She's gone down with some kind of bug.'

While Gemma rattled around in the kitchen he lay beside Henrietta who was on her play-mat in the sitting room.

The mat was designed as a glade in an enchanted forest. A butterfly adorned one side, sporting white gauzy wings that made a crunching noise when touched. A heavily striped bee reclining on top of a small honey pot made a *zzz* each time it was pressed. Red and purple flowers sprouted from the corners of the mat, their leaves soft and velvet smooth. Henrietta was cocooned in a felt nest in the middle of the mat. She looked adorable. He guided her chubby little fingers towards the leaves so that she could feel the texture.

Henrietta was gurgling contentedly at Matt when Gemma came in wielding the bottle of feed. With a swooping motion she swept her up, sat down in an armchair and firmly put the bottle between the baby's lips. Henrietta cried and spluttered and choked on the milk.

'It doesn't look as though she wants it,' said Matt, sitting up.

'It's her three o' clock feed.'

'But what if she doesn't want it?'

'It's three o' clock,' Gemma repeated.

'My mum says I was a feed-on-demand baby.'

There was a slight atmosphere hovering above the magical glade. Matt raised his eyes to the ceiling and fought to stop his temper rising. At least with Gemma trapped in the armchair for half an hour, she would have to listen to him for a change.

He got up from the floor and left the room, returning a moment later with a folder under his arm and his laptop and settled himself down at the end of the sofa nearest to Gemma and Henrietta.

'So, as I was saying before, my Dad did this spreadsheet with me and if I got a part-time job and you could find one too, we could save enough money to –'

She wasn't listening. Not even pretending. He drummed his fingers along the back of the sofa waiting for her to finish tending to the baby.

Her head suddenly jerked towards him. 'Oh, Matt, you'll never guess…Kay's got a ticket for me for Glastonbury next year! You know I've always wanted to go. Her sister's boyfriend can't go so she's offering it to me. It'll be amazing! Henrietta will love it, won't you sweetheart?'

'Glastonbury?'

'She'll be fine. Loads of people take their babies and kids to the festival.'

'It's not that.' With a head full of figures and thoughts for their future, Matt was floundering at the thought of how much money would be spent on one weekend. Not to mention that Gemma seemed to be deliberately avoiding any talk of future plans.

Henrietta refused to take any more milk. Gemma put down the half-finished bottle and patted her lightly on the back.

'You'll have a good time won't you, my sweetheart?'

She jiggled the baby up and down on her knee humming softly.

The doorbell rang. Matt sighed and went to open it.

Kay and Rich were standing on the doorstep laughing hilariously. Rich high-fived him as Kay bounded ahead.

'Alright, mate?'

'S'pose.'

'Matt?' called Gemma, 'shall we go and see *Girl on a Train* tonight? My parents are at home and they'll babysit.'

He hated going out on a Monday, it made him feel tired for the rest of the week. And he had tons of reading to do for English, he was still trying to catch up from his late start. He'd only just started the assignment on *Frankenstein*.

He thought of his savings plan, his building society account dwindling daily pitched against the spiralling cost of baby essentials and Keeping-Gemma-Happy.

'Make up your mind, Kay's about to book it online.'

He capitulated. With so many battles lying ahead, this was one it was best to concede without a blow.

*

He let himself in with the new key his father and Jessie had both insisted he had. He hadn't fancied another evening on his own so he'd come straight from school. They were in the kitchen, his father washing mugs in the fancy butler sink, washing up solution rising in bubbles toward the high ceiling, Jessie beside him holding a tea towel.

He gazed around the kitchen; gadgets and crockery and mugs all in their places. A sun-coloured roller blind drew the eye outside towards a paved terrace where late autumn rust-coloured chrysanthemums still bloomed in stone pots.

His father playfully grabbed the tea towel from Jessie, rolled it up and aimed a loving swipe at her buttocks. She smiled and put her arms around him, nuzzling into his neck.

Matt watched the tableau, imagining himself and Gemma in a kitchen of their own, Henrietta in her highchair laughing along with them.

'Matt! Lovely to see you.' Jessie had caught sight of his reflection in one of the glass cabinets in the kitchen.

His father turned around and roared a welcome. 'Great to see you, Matt! Come in and sit down.'

'I'll finish up here, Ed, you take Matt into the front room.'

His father, Edward for nineteen years of marriage and now unaccountably Ed, sat down beside him on the soft leather sofa they had recently taken delivery of.

'Everything alright? Looking a bit tired there, lad. How are things? How's Henrietta?'

'I've got some photos here somewhere.' He fumbled in his bag for a plastic wallet.

'Don't tell me you've actually got real photographs?'

After a while, Jessie came to join them and admire Matt's photographic efforts. Matt had finished school early the previous day and had gone home to work on his photographic assignment, rigging up the sitting room as a studio with lights and props borrowed from the school and a tripod.

Keen to get some baby photographs done, Gemma had taken the opportunity to bring Henrietta around, who had been the perfect model, smiling when he waved a fluffy toy, kicking her arms and legs along to some nursery music he'd played on the speakers.

'They're good, Matt,' said his father. ' I was looking at courses the other day that you could think about after your 'A' levels. You don't have to go to university if you don't want to. You could study part time and work part time. Photography, for example. It might be a good option for you.'

'Well, I have been looking at courses in case I decide to go to uni. I'm thinking about journalism.'

'Journalism?' His father nodded thoughtfully.

Jessie put the photos down and stood up. 'Are you staying for supper, Matt?'

'If that's alright. I mean, if you've nothing already planned.'

'Great. I'll just pop out for half an hour and get some steaks and a bottle of wine. Won't be long.'

'Drive carefully, love.'

When Jessie had pulled out of the drive his father turned back to him. 'Is your mother still away?'

'Yeah, she stayed on a bit longer as Auntie Di was still not feeling right. I'm going up there tomorrow and we'll come back together on Sunday.'

He paused. 'To be honest, Dad, I've been glad to have some time on my own. Mum and I aren't getting along too well at the moment. I can't seem to do anything right.'

'Since the baby?'

'Because of the baby.'

'She's just worried about you, that's all. Give her time, she just needs to adjust to the situation. We all do.'

'I guess so.'

'What's Gemma up to tonight? Why don't you give her a call and invite her over, too? It would be nice to see her.'

'Nah. I'm happy as we are.'

His father switched on the television, fiddling with the sound controls for a while and flicking randomly through the programme menu.

Matt's eyes wandered over a set of photographs grouped on the sideboard; himself in various stages of childhood.

'I thought children were meant to bring couples closer together. I mean, did it with you and Mum? When I was born, I mean?'

His father gave a half smile. 'Well, of course, parenthood binds you for life. The shared pride in having created a new person. The fun you get when you recognize elements of yourself in your child; a look or a way of laughing.'

'So what went wrong?'

'Nothing specific. It was just a combination of factors. I worked long hours and I kind of just dipped in and out of the domestic scene. Your mother was so besotted with you, sometimes it didn't even register with her when I arrived home. And once she'd noticed I was there it felt like there was a drawbridge going up.

'At weekends, I felt like I was constantly playing catch-up. There were all kinds of rituals and an entire baby language that had evolved between the two of you that I just couldn't penetrate. I presumed it was some kind of baby phase but the divide seemed to grow over the years. Somehow your mother had become a completely different person. Maybe I had too. Whatever the reason, eventually there was nothing left of us.'

'Well that's depressing.'

'Like I said, it happens sometimes. Something on your mind? Henrietta? Gemma?'

'Kind of.'

'You and Gemma are both very young to be dealing with parenthood. And you're living in a kind of limbo and you don't know where you're going next. It's bound to be stressful but you'll find your way.'

There was a bit of a silence.

'Thanks, Dad,' said Matt eventually.

Moody violin notes from the speakers signalled the beginning of an old spy film, the kind they both really enjoyed.

'Hang on.' His father bounded out of the room, returning moments later with two bags of popcorn.

'You're sweet and I'm savoury.'

They were still watching and munching in the darkening room when Jessie came home to draw the curtains and keep the dusk at bay.

∽Fifteen∾
Family

'Ok everyone, settle down. I know it's Friday but we need to keep focussed. This part of the course is a practical investigation which needs to be supported by written material. The given topic is 'Deserted.' As you know, it can be interpreted in a variety of ways. I want you to spend this lesson harnessing your ideas and I'll call you up here individually so we can have a discussion about what you're thinking.'

The class began to glance at each other and murmur.

'Don't feel imprisoned by the title. You can be as broad or as abstract as you like using a variety of materials and mediums. As always, as you are planning your piece, pay close attention to texture and colour and how they inform the message you are trying to convey.'

Matt sighed. Since returning to school after Henrietta's birth, his creativity levels had been non-existent. No doubt his mum, with her usual acerbity, would be able to come up with some Freudian explanation for this fact.

He got a sheet of art paper and picking up a pencil began to sketch without thinking. After ten minutes the only thing he'd drawn resembled a baby. He rolled his eyes and sneaked a look around. The girl in front was trawling through images on her laptop of shadowy shopping malls late at night. His neighbour was making a preliminary sketch in varying shades of green.

'What's that?' Matt hissed at him.

'It's a road with figures walking away from scattered items of military uniform. Army deserters.'

'Matt?' Mrs Durbin called him over.

He flung the sheet of paper onto her desk.

'Calm down, Matt.' She looked at his sketch.

'It's a good start. Don't be so hard on yourself all the time. You've reacted to the topic in a positive way.'

He looked at her.

'I mean it. The guidelines state that you should be using ideas which are significant to your life. You'll obviously need to expand the idea but babyhood is a great way to have started. A baby must feel deserted all the time. Every time a mother leaves the room. When the baby's placed in the cot each night. Keep going. Broaden the theme. And well done.'

He returned to his desk and carried on sketching, still not convinced. He was fed up with himself. Everything he attempted to do seemed to come back to his own problems. Not that he would call his daughter a problem, exactly. He thought things would be made better if he could get Gemma to talk to him. He didn't even know if they were in a relationship any more. Were they simply bound together now, in parenthood?

He was drawing a baby reaching out to a pair of arms. Then, as an opposite frame of view he drew a baby and a figure walking away. For some reason, *Frankenstein* popped into his mind.

He sat thinking as his mind went round. Maybe there was something in these sketches after all. What about somebody who didn't love their child? Victor Frankenstein's abandonment of his creation? He quickly sketched a sad-looking depiction of the lonely monster and then started to write some notes.

'Mrs Durbin? Can I check this with you?'

She read swiftly and looked up with a smile.

'Matt, you now have the germ of something promising.'

He was taken by surprise when the bell rang signalling the end of the lesson and even more surprised to find that he felt good about himself. That hadn't happened for quite some time.

Late in the afternoon, Matt caught the train to Bristol Temple Meads. The train had been packed, he'd had to stand as far as Reading before a seat became available.

His mother and aunt were waiting at the station in his mother's car.

'It wasn't the best idea coming on a Friday night,' Matt said irritably as he closed the car boot on his rucksack and flung himself into the passenger seat.

'It's lovely that you could come', said his mother not rising to his biting tone, 'I missed you. And Di wanted to see you, too.'

'I had stuff to do at home,' muttered Matt in a gentler tone, refreshed somewhat by the change of scenery from town to pastoral on the short journey back through Stoke Gifford to a small hamlet just beyond, where his aunt had lived for the past thirty years.

Looking out of the window Matt felt an unexpected sense of peace wash over him, borrowed from the landscape beyond. He thought of London, that great caged animal, unpredictable, untameable; the lair where lay sleeping all the problems he was temporarily leaving behind for the weekend.

'I always forget how much I like the countryside around here,' he said, holding out an olive branch.

'It's not what I would call countryside,' his aunt said from the back seat where she was reclining, 'you should have seen it when I first came here; the village wasn't more than a main street then and a couple of lanes.'

'I'm a Londoner. This looks plenty rural enough to me.'

The sisters exchanged a conspiratorial look and smiled as Matt slowly unwound.

*

'Are you sure this isn't too much for her?' asked Matt anxiously. His aunt Di was walking slowly like a phantom, supported between himself and his mother.

'I'm not deaf you know.' His aunt cuffed him gently on the arm. They had driven out to Leigh Woods, somewhere Matt vaguely remembered, from childhood holidays at his grandparents' house in Clifton, riding a bike winding in and out of the trees. They walked on until his aunt admitted defeat, her lungs making sawing noises in the sharpness of the November air.

Glancing at her pale face, Matt guided them towards a bench and his aunt sank gratefully down. His mother fussed around her with car rugs until even she subsided, focussing on the spectacular view of the Suspension Bridge.

'The gateway to the west,' murmured his mother fixing her gaze upon the trails of traffic.

Matt looked at her. It always amused him how the soft roots

of her Bristolian accent re-emerged once she had crossed the county line.

'I suppose it is,' he said.

'Sounds so romantic, doesn't it?' said Di, 'until you smell the car fumes and see the queues.'

'I keep meaning to ask you, Di, if you are coming to us for Christmas,' said his mother, randomly going off-topic.

'That's nice of you, but a crowd of us have booked to go skiing. We'll be spending it in Chamonix.'

'We'll have a quiet one then. Matt has his mock 'A' levels straight after the holidays, anyway.'

'I imagine you might have Henrietta over on Christmas Day, though?'

'Obviously Henrietta will be at Gemma's for Christmas Day but I'm hoping to have her on Boxing Day,' Matt said brightly.

'I see. Do you have some kind of rota? Visitation rights or whatever they call them?'

'Not really,' said Matt, deliberately cool, 'we're just keeping things simple for now.'

Annoyed, he watched his mother suddenly become engrossed in the contents of a carrier bag, as if she wanted to evade the issue.

The previous week she had begun an unwanted debate about Matt needing to formalise matters concerning Henrietta. His mother disliked the way he seemed always content to take a back seat, as she had put it. The argument had grown quite heated and now it seemed as if she and Di had been discussing it too.

When his mother's rummaging proved to have a purpose after all, producing a flask of coffee and a packet of shortbread biscuits, he caught her eye and gave a half-smile which she returned.

'Pass the packet around. I wonder why biscuits are so comforting?'

'I think it's because we can always find a nice memory attached to them. Do you remember that time, Polly, when Mum had put a tray of ginger snaps on the counter to cool from the oven and the cat we had at the time, Inky, jumped up and boldly helped himself? We laughed so much...'

The sisters reminisced happily. Warmed by the heat of the drink, Matt sat with his eyes following the traffic heading west, wondering what everyone else was trying to escape from.

After a Sunday roast the following day, Matt left his mother finishing off in the kitchen and went upstairs to pack so they could leave before the traffic started to build up on the M4.

In the small back bedroom overlooking the long strip of garden he watched as two robins warily circled each other's movements around the stone bird table which housed a scattering of seeds. He was going to make sure that Henrietta grew up with an appreciation of wild life and nature. He hadn't seen much evidence of Gemma thinking this important. Maybe it wasn't exactly important, but he liked the idea of being able to open his daughter's eyes to the smallest of things, that she might otherwise miss.

He started to throw his belongings together. Retrieving his toothbrush from the bathroom, as he came back into the room his eye was caught by a flimsy carrying case protruding from under the bed, from which papers were spilling out. He must have caught it with his rucksack.

He bent down and tried to put the papers back into their plastic wallets which were hanging haphazardly from the carrying case, which he could see now was just a glorified filing system with a handle.

As he did his best to tidy the papers he realised they were copies of certificates; births, marriages and a few deaths; a fascinating mix of names and dates.

Certified Copy of an entry of Birth…Olive Jane Medley…1910 in the county of Gloucestershire…Certified Copy of an entry of Marriage…1931…Olive Jane Medley and Henry Simmonds. In the county of Bristol, he noticed.

So his roots lay deeply in the south west. He'd never considered it before. His mother thought she had escaped hers by moving to London.

He bounded down the stairs ready to confess his crime.

'Aunt Di, sorry but I dislodged some papers in a file under the bed.'

'I'm sure you haven't done any damage.'

'I tried to put them back in some kind of order.'

'Don't worry Matt. It's just a bit of family research I've been doing.'

His mother, giving the kitchen a final wipe down, frowned. 'Family research? You haven't mentioned this before. What are you searching for?'

Matt winced at his mother's tone. It betrayed her lack of imagination.

'I don't know. I suppose I'm on a bit of a quest into the past. We've already got a family tree from Dad's side of the family which one of his cousins did. I thought it would be nice to have Mum's side too.'

'It's very time consuming and it can be costly.'

'I enjoy the research. I like knowing the story of us.'

'I wonder what our own stories will look like one hundred years from now? Everything we managed to achieve shrunk down to a few words: born, married, divorced, died. Not exactly meaningful or riveting for those in the future who may search for us. Rather mundane, in fact.'

'Well, if you put it like that, it's bound to sound meaningless,' said Matt, indignant on his aunt's behalf.

Di looked crestfallen.

'I thought with Henrietta having come along, it would be a nice idea to produce a family tree. Illustrated maybe. I've got a friend who can transfer the information and photographs into beautiful charts; she draws them like blossom trees with great branches and the tiniest of twigs.'

His mother, bruised and betrayed by marital battles across the years said nothing. Her face grew dark.

'I think it's interesting,' said Matt, 'imagining all the complex stories and characters hidden behind a few lines on an official document.'

Like Henrietta's and mine he thought, remembering sitting silently with Gemma in the waiting room at Ealing Town Hall, preparing to register the birth.

'What have you discovered so far?' he asked.

His mother left the room. Overhead they heard her pulling open the chest of drawers, slamming items into her travel bag.

Matt rolled his eyes and looked over at his aunt, encouraging her.

'I'd only just started, really before I went down with that bug. I began with my grandmother, Olive –'

'Married to Henry.'

'That's right. I've got a photograph of them on their wedding day somewhere.'

As his aunt rose, the sounds of his mum's heavy feet and even heavier heart came clattering into the hallway.

He exchanged a glance with his aunt. His mouth turned

downwards.

'Don't be too hard on your mum. She's had a bad couple of years.'

'So have I.'

'Yes, you have,' she acknowledged. 'Are you alright, Matt? I haven't really had a chance to ask you about everything –'

'Matthew! Bags in the boot please. I don't want to be sitting in traffic for hours on end.'

'See you soon, Di.'

'Have we dropped the 'Auntie', then?'

'Well, I'm a father now, you know…'

'Look after yourself, Matt.'

'I will.'

He fumbled in his inner pockets for his headphones, relieved to find his phone was fully charged. He pressed shuffle on his favourite playlist and risked a glance towards his mother's impassive face. It was going to be a long ride home.

'I think I was rude to Diana, before we left.'

Matt looked at his mother. She'd been quiet in the car, calm not sullen. Arriving home at seven, after taking her things upstairs she'd come back down into the kitchen where he now sat doing a last-minute rushed piece of English course work.

'Uh huh.'

'I'm just a bit 'off' families at the moment, if you know what I mean.'

'I didn't realise that family was something you can opt out of when you feel like it.'

'I wish I bloody could. And maybe it would do you some good, too. Running around after that madam Gemma, when it's clear she doesn't want you.'

Shocked, he looked at her, slammed his books shut and rose.

'Oh God, no Matt. That's not what I meant to say. I'm just so worried about you.'

He sat down again. He was still hurt. 'That wasn't a nice thing to say.'

'You're right. I should keep my thoughts and worries to myself. I'll make us a drink, shall I?'

His mother moved around the kitchen, taking mugs from the cupboard, spooning in hot chocolate and sugar, delivering it to him in his favourite mug, topped with a cloud-like formation of cream.

He looked at her closely. She'd lost weight. He hadn't noticed before.

'What I said before, about family. I was talking about your dad. And…and Jessie.'

'He's my dad. I like visiting him. Them.'

'Of course you do and that's perfectly natural. I'm just saying it's hard for me that he left and found somebody else.'

'It's been nearly two years now, Mum; time to change.'

She looked at him in surprise, as if the thought had never occurred to her.

'Change? Why do I have to be the one to change? He was the one who initiated all the bloody changes around here.'

'Mum. You and Dad weren't happy or nice to each other, even when he was still here.'

'No. I know that. But you've got Gemma and Henrietta. I'm left feeling empty.'

'I'm still here. I haven't gone anywhere.'

He was irritated, not wanting to have to face his own future as well as cope with his mother's past. He kept trying.

'Join something. Find new friends. Or a partner.' Although

admittedly it was hard to imagine the man capable of breaking down his mother's defensive walls.

'Go out on dates again? I don't think so.'

'An activity or a club or something. I don't know. What do you like to do?'

Ever since he could remember, Matt had puzzled over the question of what his mother actually enjoyed. She was so passive, seeming resigned to life happening to her without the need for any input. He tried again. 'You know what I mean. I like photography and music. You need to like something too.'

'Well, your dad and I used to go to the opera, before you were born.'

'Organise with some of your friends to go to the opera, then.'

'I didn't really like opera, to be honest. It was more your dad that liked it and I went to keep him company.'

'A book club, then? You're always reading.'

'Well, I only read because I've got nothing else to do.'

He exhaled a great sigh. 'Why don't you do an internet search and get some ideas?'

'I'm not sure I can be bothered to go upstairs and get my laptop –' She stopped as she saw his face shut tight with annoyance. She drained her mug and left the room.

Later, he was in his room with his headphones clamped to his ears, listening to some music, the unfinished assignment laid out on his desk. She had probably knocked but he hadn't heard. He watched the door handle open and his heart sank.

'I didn't mean to disturb you, love.'

It was her way of apologising for what had been said before, without actually having to say the words. 'I'm going to be more proactive from now on. Sort myself out.

'I can't just go to work and come home again. You're right. And I'm going to call Diana and apologise to her. I know she enjoys family history and I shouldn't have been such a grouch to her.'

From beneath the scattered papers lying across Matt's desk, came the raucous outbreak of song as his mobile rang. He got up and looked at the number. Gemma. He swiped the green arrow across the screen.

'Hey. Tomorrow's good for me. Yep. Ok see you there. How's Henriet –'

'Short call,' said his mother softly, seeing his face as he closed his phone.

'I'd better get on with this assignment,' Matt said picking up his books again from his desk. He had his back turned to her and couldn't see her concerned face as she quietly left the room.

∼Sixteen∽
Detachment

January 2017

Christmas had been mostly enjoyable, Matt told himself as he walked alongside Gemma with the persistent hum of Central London traffic accompanying them.

It was the second day of the new year and they were walking through Hyde Park having travelled up on the Central Line from Ealing Broadway, to do some shopping in the sales. Packages from Hamleys were jostling together in the bottom of the buggy. At the other end of the park the lights of the Christmas fairground could be seen flickering in the distance, the screams of the riders on the rides echoing up into the skies.

His mother had made an effort over the Christmas period, allowing herself to be persuaded to buy a small tree, a huge step forward from the previous year, their first Christmas without Matt's father, when she had refused to even display the Christmas cards they had received, leaving them in a sad pile in a corner of the kitchen.

He had helped festoon the hall and stairs with sprigs of cut holly, cards and old fashioned paper chains; his mother not entirely joking when she declared she wasn't quite ready to deal with the sparkling jollity of tinsel.

On Christmas Eve, his mother had gone to a drinks party hosted by their next-door neighbour and Matt had gone out to the pub with Rich and Alex, where he had drunk far too much and struggled to get up at noon on Christmas Day after his mother had shouted up the stairs three times.

After the Christmas goose and accompanying vegetables they had settled in front of the television in the afternoon. Matt had been half asleep when the doorbell had rung and to his surprise his mother had brought Gemma and a smiling Henrietta into the room.

The baby's eyes had been glowing, all attention on her, as his mother had dived under the tree to retrieve the many Christmas presents that had been packaged and beribboned in her honour.

Gemma and Matt negotiated a handover in the middle of the room. Henrietta blew little wet bubbles into his face as he lifted her into his arms. His heart contracted.

'Thanks. I didn't realise we'd see her today.'

'It's her first Christmas. I thought you'd like to see her. And she had her nap early, so it seemed right to bring her over.'

'Well, great. Merry Christmas, Gemma. He kissed her cheek gently. She reddened slightly.

'Take Gemma's coat,' said his mother, 'you are staying, aren't you, Gemma?'

'Well, I…'

Matt knelt down in front of the pile of packages, balancing

Henrietta on his knee.

'What's Daddy bought you, my sweetheart?'

Grinning at her he began to tear away at the parcel he was most proud of. Silver wrapping paper fell in strips onto the floor to reveal penguins wearing scarves in the snow atop a wooden music box. He turned the handle slowly and the penguins began to sing and dance. Henrietta cooed.

Placing the baby on the floor he withdrew from under the tree, the small package he had wrapped for Gemma the previous week. A charm bracelet with a baby's rattle, and a love heart. He had remembered reading somewhere that it was customary to buy the mother of your child an eternity ring. The bracelet had been his nod to tradition. There were plenty of other charms to buy, as time went on and parenthood moved from stage to stage.

He smiled across at Gemma who met his look with empty eyes.

His heart gave a jolt as he realised all that was missing from her gaze; love, devotion, empathy. If those particular commodities could have been sent to her, gift- wrapped he would have done it in a heartbeat.

His smile disappeared. He put the package down, silently withholding it from her, meeting her impassive gaze with one of his own.

Sensing the vibe between them she turned towards the door.

'Not going already? His mother who had been absorbed in sorting Henrietta's gifts into an orderly pile, looked up at her movement.

Gemma gave a tight smile.

'I'm expected back for tea. My cousins are coming over. It's okay, keep Henrietta and bring her back at about six. She'll be ready for a feed then. I'll see myself out.'

Matt listened as the front door closed and the heels of Gemma's boots clicked sharply up the path. He looked sadly at the polite bunch of seasonal flowers with strands of glittery ribbon that Gemma had left on the table for Polly.

He slipped the wrapped bracelet into his pocket. He would get a refund in the new year.

After their spiky Christmas day encounter he had been surprised when Gemma had suggested the trip into London but he had agreed, reasoning that any time spent with his daughter would be worthwhile.

'Matt! Slow down, I can't keep up with you today. She's fallen asleep now. She won't wake for a while.'

He guided the buggy wheels over to a nearby bench, motioning for Gemma to join him. It was cold, too uncomfortable to sit without movement to keep the blood warmed but she joined him without argument.

The wind blew ripples across the emptiness of The Long Water. Too cold for boating, with just the odd duck skimming across its waters, the place was curiously unsettling. Sitting on the wooden slatted seat, an awkward silence settled across them. He folded his arms and looked across at her with his face a mask. Gemma cleared her throat.

'So, now would be a good time to tell you something. I wanted to make sure we both had an enjoyable Christmas before saying all this.'

'Saying all what?'

'My dad's firm want him to transfer to their New Zealand office for two years. He's flying out in a couple of weeks. Mum and Davy will wait until the break up for the Easter holidays and then they'll join him. She's found a school for him and he would be able to start at the beginning of the new term.'

She paused awkwardly.

Maybe, Matt thought, she wants us to move in together, after all. If his mother agreed to the loft conversion there would be plenty of space and maybe they could try and incorporate a shower room which he knew Gemma would appreciate. Matt's existing bedroom could then become the nursery.

He pushed away the disconcerting memory of her blank eyes, turning to reassure her, but she was carrying on the conversation.

'Henrietta and I would follow on later because my visa might be more complicated and I need to find a suitable course to apply for.'

He felt as if he'd plummeted into icy water.

'What? You mean you're going as well? You want to take Henrietta to the other side of the world?'

She was still talking.

'It will be great because Dad's sister is married to a New Zealander and lives out in Auckland where we'd be based. We've been having a few chats. She runs a restaurant and she thinks if I apply to do a cookery diploma I might be able to work part-time for her.'

Finally she ran out of steam. He pulled himself together although his voice shook slightly.

'But you could do cookery here, couldn't you?'

'New Zealand would be a great experience for all of us, Matt. Especially Henrietta.'

'But what about *me*?' He winced, aware that he sounded more like a petulant kid, than a father about to lose his child.

'I mean, what about us?' He gestured helplessly at the buggy, the packages, the sleeping child, London beneath the expanse of wintry sky. She stared at him, blank-faced.

'Come on, Gemma. I know we could make things work out here for us. We just need to try a bit harder…'

'Come on Matt, you know as well as I do; there's not really an us. Is there?'

He looked along the length of the bench; he at one end, she at the other, an entire world of grey planked wood stretched between them.

'The experience in New Zealand will give Henrietta a wonderful start in life. Better weather, a more relaxed way of life. I know it sounds harsh to put you out of the picture for that long but just imagine, for a moment, what it would mean for her?'

'But what the hell has all this been about?'

He drew a circle with his gloved fingers in the air, indicating the three of them.

Gemma shook her head, not meeting his eyes.

'It is what it is. I'm sorry.'

'What if I don't agree?'

'Oh Matt. Don't let's do this…it's for the best. For Henrietta.'

From the buggy came a low gurgle as Henrietta awoke, greedy for her bottle. Matt watched a lone Canada Goose come waddling up to them, also hungry.

'Come on, we need to get inside somewhere warm. Let's find a café so I can feed her.'

Wheeling the baby away she stopped as she realised Matt was still sitting on the bench.

'Are you coming?'

'I'm thinking.'

'I'll go on ahead. Catch us up?'

He watched her trim figure recede into the growing distance. Feeling a savage need to blot out his life, he felt for the tablet in his pocket and drew it out. It lit up at the part in *Frankenstein* where Victor paces the streets, filled with horror and loathing for his ill-fated creation.

Previously, Matt had held the opinion that he and Victor were quite similar in their own obsessive ways but now they appeared to be following very different paths; Victor, the mad creator, seeking to duck all responsibility for his conception while Matt stood on the brink of having his snatched away.

Love, hate and abandonment swirled around his mind like a drifting fog.

He read on until the cries from the fairground drifted towards him enticingly on the wind and he grew restless. Abruptly he rose and began to trudge towards the source of all the noise and laughter.

He reached the lurid entrance and paused, thinking of Gemma and Henrietta waiting for him. What was the point of being responsible now when he had lost everything?

He plunged in, losing himself in the lights and the music and the swelling crowd, his nostrils filled with the delicious sweetness of roasted chestnuts, hot chocolate with marshmallows, toffee apples and candy canes.

He gazed upwards. The urge to go on one of the terrifying rides was irresistible. He needed to feel lost in the plummet towards earth and the rush of wind heading upwards to the skies, to be whirled around, rolled and rocked and riding high, as if he were once more a baby in the cradle without a care in the world.

Standing in the long queue that stretched towards the booth selling tokens for rides he felt his phone vibrating in his pocket.

'*Where ru? H sick. W8ing at tube 4u.*'

He had reached the front of the queue, his ten-pound note

fluttering in front of the glass booth. Even as his phone beeped urgently again, he was walking away, stuffing the money back into his wallet, feeling old and tired. Defeated.

Volume Three
Harriet

∽Seventeen∾
A Daughter and some Debts

Bracknell, July 1813

The baby gurgled in his arms. He rocked her from side to side, experimentally. She seemed to laugh for a moment before her rosebud lips opened, issuing forth a series of high-pitched wails.

'Hush, hush, Ianthe,' implored Percy. His shoulders sagged with gloom as his daughter gave him a baleful stare.

He grimaced and entered the bedchamber. Harriet, exhausted, had fallen asleep with her plump, post-pregnancy chin resting on her collar bone. He shook her gently. When her response was to turn her face into the pillow, he took hold of her arm and pulled her into wakefulness.

'What is it? she muttered at him, stupid with lack of sleep.

'She's crying again. What a dark-tempered little fairy she is today.'

'Percy, could you keep her awhile? I'm so tired. I have been up three nights now and I cannot keep my eyes open or my wits about me.'

'I have to leave shortly. The Newtons are expecting me, we are going to listen to the orchestra and dine at Vauxhall.'

'Could you pass her over to Eliza, then? I just need another hour or so of sleep.'

'Eliza has temporarily departed, remember? She cannot stand the blessed crying any more than I can.'

'For pity's sake,' she murmured.

At her mother's voice, Ianthe stopped crying.

'There you see; it is you she wants. I am merely to be a source of money, no doubt, to this child.'

'Percy! What a thing to say in front of her!'

Harriet held her arms out and the babe nestled in cosily, closing her blue eyes, so like those of her father, instantly.

Percy began to dress, pulling on a clean linen shirt and a cravat.

'I'll be back later, dearest. The Newtons have promised a gift for Ianthe and I'm hopeful it may be a purse of coins.'

'That would be a most fortuitous gift at this time,' Harriet murmured, half mollified.

' I'll bring you back some treats. Cherries, perhaps, or strawberries to stain your precious lips.'

He kissed the top of her head, patted Ianthe's cheek and was gone.

By mid-morning the next day he had still not returned. Harriet, too tired to think straight, sent a note around to Chapel Street to summon Eliza.

Eliza had her supervisory face on, Harriet saw with dread, as she opened the door of their suite in the hotel.

'Well, what is all this, sister? You look simply dreadful, Harriet. Your hair is matted, your nightgown dishevelled and a little fusty. No wonder Percy has not returned if this is what he imagines will greet him! Come now, give me Ianthe and call for some hot water for a bath. You must make yourself presentable for your husband.'

Bathed and freshly dressed, Harriet looked little improved. Bruising crescents lay beneath her eyes, above which her brow lay furrowed with worry lines.

'We cannot have this,' said Eliza, peering closely at Harriet's face as if she were some badly painted portrait on display in a grand country house.

Harriet bit back a retort, blaming herself for yet again, involving her sister.

'I have been thinking,' said Harriet, looking down at the baby lying in her arms. 'Percy is greatly opposed to this plan but I would like to try to hire a wet-nurse for Ianthe.'

'I see. That is an exceedingly unusual proposal, Harriet. I am not sure you should go against your husband's wishes in this matter.'

'I am very tired, Eliza. I am not able to be up and about for very long, before Ianthe needs me again. I think it may suit our lifestyle better if I could be doing things for Percy as well as just the babe.'

'Well, if you are sure, I shall make some enquiries for you. But mark my words, Harriet, I would consider this very carefully if I were in your position.'

*

'I am sorry, Percy,' said Harriet, yet again. She had been apologising for a month now. She shut her lips tightly to preclude further conversation.

She knew of course, she was behaving in a fashion unlike her usual agreeable self, but since having Ianthe she had felt somehow different; as if there was an entirely new person trying to clamber out of her skin.

Percy's eyes were hot with anger. The door to their bedchamber was closed behind the wet-nurse and Ianthe, signalling that it was the afternoon feeding hour.

'It makes me shudder when I imagine that woman suckling our child!'

'She came with good recommendation. Please be calm, Percy.'

'It is not her I object to, I am sure she is perfectly nice. I would feel the same about any woman! Our baby should nurse on your milk alone, Harriet. Can you not see that?'

'It's not doing her any harm. I simply could not feed Ianthe hour upon hour. She was draining me and I was not giving her enough nourishment. With Martha here, I believe Ianthe is thriving and it is giving me the chance to recover.'

He continued the well-trodden argument, scowling as Eliza came into the room with a brisk smile and cold eyes.

'My thoughts remain the same: for you not to suckle Ianthe is a rejection of your own flesh and blood.'

Harriet shook her head, having nothing more to say, but Eliza had plenty. 'No more a rejection than a father and husband carousing into the small hours –'

'I'll thank you to keep your opinions to yourself, sister-in-law.'

'Certainly sir,' flashed back Eliza with malice.

'Do not speak harshly to Eliza,' implored Harriet, 'she has come today to help me with the packing.' She gestured at their belongings strewn across the bed and the couch, boxes and trunks lying empty on the floor.

The little community was moving the next day, to Bracknell. They were all looking forward to the move although to Percy's annoyance, Ianthe's wet nurse, Martha was to accompany them; that made four adults and the baby. Harriet had hoped that Dan would also accompany them but a few days previously, Percy and Dan had argued about wages, or rather the lack of them, and the young boy had taken his belongings and disappeared for good back to Ireland.

In Bracknell, they were to be the neighbours of the rather glamorous Mrs Boinville, a new addition to Percy's literary set. The recent widow of a French Revolutionary, Percy found her rather thrilling. Harriet privately considered her to be rather affected.

Percy and Harriet had met Mrs Boinville through their friendship with the Newtons; she was actually Mrs Newton's sister. White-haired but still beautiful with a sharp mind, good humour and charming manners, artists, writers and thinkers regularly flocked to her large welcoming house in Bracknell. Her married daughter, Cornelia was often in residence as her husband worked abroad for long periods.

When she had heard of Percy's plan to move, Mrs Boinville had arranged for them to rent an empty house that she owned and which was close by her own home. They would be able to see a lot of each other but still have their own hearth. Harriet, worried about the rocky path she and Percy had been walking since the birth of Ianthe, hoped that being part of Mrs Boinville's community would cheer Percy's spirits.

Percy gave Harriet a tight smile.

'I am going ahead to ensure High Elms has been made good and ready for us. Mrs Boinville is expecting me there at three. Now Harriet, I have ordered the carriage to be here tomorrow morning at ten, to collect you all. I shall gather a few of my things together now and be on my way.'

'Carriage,' snorted Eliza once Percy had left. At great expense, Percy had organised a carriage to be built, to his own design. With the bill not yet settled, Harriet feared how long it would be in their possession. Similarly she dared not wonder for how long Percy would be able to pay rent to Mrs Boinville.

'We may as well enjoy it, as long as we have it,' said Harriet tiredly, moving around the room slowly, collecting stray belongings.

The following day they arrived in Bracknell amid a thunderstorm. High Elms was judged to be pleasant enough. Percy had arranged logs for the fire but otherwise there was no sign of him. Ianthe was fractious from the moment they set foot in their new home, crying fitfully. Harriet could feel a dull headache approaching. Leaving Ianthe in Martha's arms she helped Eliza to unpack silently and with little joy, moving and arranging things with an air of detachment, as if she knew that it would only be a matter of time before they would be on the move again.

*

'Dear Mrs Shelley, you are looking rather radiant! I believe motherhood suits you.'

Harriet smiled at their most welcome visitor.

'And where is Bysshe? Have I travelled all this way, to be deprived of his company?'

The smile faded. Eliza rose from her chair and removed the teapot. 'I will fetch more hot water. Another slice of cake, Mr Peacock? Harriet, serve our guest.'

Harriet sliced through the fruited loaf with rather more intensity than necessary. Their visitor from London was a fellow poet of Percy's, Thomas Peacock. Harriet liked him very much. He caught her eye.

'Am I to infer that Percy is engaged elsewhere? Let me guess, he is currently spouting Petrarchan sonnets in an exaggerated Italian accent, with the simpering Cornelia and her mother?'

Harriet pealed with frank laughter. 'Percy has taken them into town today in our carriage, to see an exhibition. But I am sure the Italian accents are much in evidence.'

They smiled at each other in complicity. Thomas Peacock had visited them in Bracknell a number of times and was rather less enamoured of their neighbours, than Percy was.

She sighed. 'I should not mind only, I wanted to go out and buy myself a new gown. I have not purchased one for such a long time; look at me Mr Peacock, my sleeves are frayed and even my sister's needlework cannot save them. It really is too bad of Percy, for the third day in a row he has taken off directly after breakfast leaving me here without the means to get into town.'

'Well, that can be rectified. Allow me to escort you in my carriage after we have drunk another cup.'

Harriet smiled at him gratefully. 'I would like that very much.'

'I see you are surrounded by your books, dear Harriet. I must deduce that our dear Bysshe is continuing in his efforts to improve you. Although you have my assurances that amendments to your person are entirely unnecessary.'

Mr Peacock's lips twitched but Harriet, tracing his gaze to the pile of texts cluttering the table in the centre of the room, felt instantly dejected. Since their arrival several weeks ago, Percy had been nagging at her constantly to take up her Greek studies once more but her mind was jumbled through lack of sleep and baby worry. She had tried often, while Ianthe slept, taking up a book only to find her eyelids drooping within moments as the sentences swam before her eyes.

'I might get on better if Percy had more time to guide me.

But he is seldom here when I am awake. To be frank, I'm not sure if I am enjoying our life here.'

'How long do you expect to stay?' enquired Peacock.

'Percy thinks we will be here for three months which seems to me to be far too long. Our dearest wish is to be able to return to Wales permanently before the summer is out. We are still trying to secure our beloved Nantgwillt, you see. Percy is undertaking all sorts of schemes to try to raise the money. As you know, he recently came of age and since then he has been cautiously having talks with his father to try and mend some bridges.'

'I hope things progress happily for you, it would be much better to be settled now that you have Ianthe's needs to consider.'

'How right you are. I am beginning to detest all this packing and travelling, putting down roots only to have them ripped apart most abruptly. Dear Mr Peacock, you understand the position perfectly well.'

'Did I hear mention of a shopping expedition?' enquired Eliza sweeping in 'Harriet, you need new gloves as well as a new dress and I need some silks for my tapestry. We are very grateful to you, Mr Peacock. I am only sorry that Bysshe has missed the pleasure of your company.'

The time spent with Thomas Peacock was a much-needed diversion. With not much to do in the way of housekeeping and Percy ensconced daily at Mrs Boinville's house, Harriet often found herself with time on her hands as the summer slipped away with no sign of a move back to Wales.

On a day in early September, Harriet, having breakfasted, felt a spark of interest and energy for her book learning once more. If Percy could just take her through some of the passages she had been attempting before Ianthe's arrival, she calculated she would be back on course.

Ianthe was slumbering, Eliza was stitching in the parlour as Harriet lifted the latch and let herself out into the lane. The sun was high. Golden, tell-tale leaves, hinting at autumn, straddled the narrow pathway, as Harriet strolled the short distance to the Boinville residence, in search of Percy.

A maid let her into the hallway and led her to the door of Mrs Boinville's drawing room. The house felt quiet. Engaged in letter-writing, Mrs Boinville looked vaguely up at her and smiled. 'Harriet dear, how lovely to see you. You are seeking Bysshe, no doubt?'

Mrs Boinville favoured those who proffered loudly exclaimed opinions and lots of them, as opposed to Harriet's quietly measured thoughts and she had no interest in Harriet other than as Percy's wife. Harriet was well aware of this. She had once overheard Percy valiantly describing her to the Boinville set as his diamond, albeit an unpolished one, he had been quick to add. 'Oh, I much prefer the flash and vibrancy of a sapphire,' Cornelia Turner had trilled. 'Or the fire in the heart of a ruby,' Mrs Boinville had murmured.

Briefly they exchanged pleasantries and Mrs Boinville directed Harriet out towards the private patch of hedged garden beyond the wide immaculate lawns. She strolled from the house and rounded the corner to find a sight that caused a ripple across her heart.

Seated on a bench in the shade of the yew hedge was Cornelia Turner. Her pale tresses were displayed artfully across her shoulders where she absently teased a curl with a long, slender finger. On the ground, Percy sprawled at her feet, his clothes dusty from leaf fall, his eyes locked onto Cornelia's lips, tracing the passage of her words as they escaped into the air.

As Harriet came nearer, she recognised random words and phrases in Italian, their musical notes hovering above the tableau as Cornelia spoke softly, Percy repeating each word with great tenderness.

Somehow, she had imagined Percy safe within Mrs Boinville's large library on the first floor of the house, assorted members of Mrs Boinville's set in another corner earnestly debating the topic of the day and servants whisking in and out with trays of tea and pastries.

'Percy?'

Like a startled fawn, Cornelia twitched and recoiled.

'Mrs Shelley! Goodness, how you crept up on us.'

'Like an autumn breeze,' said Harriet, her tone cold and crisp as dried leaves.

Percy cast his blue eyes upon her appealingly.

'Cornelia was just leading me through some verses while Mrs Boinville is taking the air nearby in the rose garden –'

'Cornelia's mother is currently inside the house, dealing with her correspondence,' said Harriet, cutting through the subterfuge like butter, 'in fact, Cornelia, I believe she mentioned a letter from your husband has arrived.'

Cornelia Turner flinched and retrieved a book, which had fallen quite a time beforehand, from beneath the bench.

'Ah, yes. Alas, Mr Turner is obliged to work away for long periods.'

Harriet drew herself up to her full height and succeeded in delivering a scathing look.

'Perhaps he may feel the need, when he returns, to make enquiries about a posting nearer to home?'

Cornelia Turner, rose and fanned herself. Her scarlet cheeks looked charming, Harriet thought wretchedly.

'Please excuse me,' said Cornelia, taking her leave in great haste.

Harriet did not at all excuse her.

*

October, 1813

'Really Percy, this is just too much to bear. Are you saying that we need to pack up and leave today? Where do you propose we go this time? And why does it have to be this afternoon?'

Ianthe was cutting a tooth and had cried intermittently throughout the night. The mood in the house that morning was prickly. Percy had taken Harriet outside into the garden to speak privately to her away from their little community; Eliza, Martha who was tending to Ianthe and Thomas Peacock who had come from London the day before.

Harriet was plainly exasperated. 'Why can't we wait for news of Nantgwillt? It makes no sense to rush off again?'

'Harriet…we, that is I owe money which I do not have at this moment and unfortunately my creditors have discovered our whereabouts. We need to take the carriage and leave today.'

'The carriage that we cannot pay for. Like everything else.'

Percy nodded, seeming unrepentant. 'It is all a bit of a mess at the moment, I grant you, but yesterday, Mr Peacock managed to make an arrangement with a moneylender on my behalf. So, we are all set. But we must leave here today to make sure the London creditors do not pick up our trail.'

Harriet bit her lip.

Since coming of age in August, Percy was now legally responsible for his accumulated debts, which included printing costs, the fine carriage they had become used to and a trail of accumulated rent and household expenses that followed them across the country. The monthly allowance, which their fathers had been paying the couple over the last months, was not enough to cover their expenditure.

Worse still, Percy's inheritance was being obstructed by his father who remained outraged at his son's careless attitude to living. The whole affair had been put into Chancery. Percy was sure that he would receive his due one day but it looked likely to be a protracted process.

Harriet closed her eyes. For weeks, she had been dreaming of seeing the beloved Welsh manor house again; hoping that Percy's money would come through and the purchase of Nantgwillt could be realised. Behind closed lids she saw the solitude of the mountains, the sparkle of the river rushing through the lower valley of the River Claerwen and the enclosing comfort of the woods, sliding away from her.

'Where are we going?' she repeated tiredly.

Percy stood up and hooked his arms around her waist.

'Does it really matter? As long as we are all together? Another adventure...'

'Ianthe doesn't travel well, Percy.'

He pulled away.

'Mr Godwin has suggested a place to try in the Lakes; there is a rather fine inn in Ambleside, I believe which he used as a setting in his novel. Harriet, get ready, while I oversee the packing of my manuscript trunk.'

She sighed audibly. Godwin. Again.

In low spirits she went back into the house. Thomas Peacock looked across at her encouragingly.

'Mrs Shelley, rest awhile whilst Percy and I load up the carriage. It will be a fine, clear evening for travel and will afford us a marvellous view of the stars.'

She forced a small smile, happy that Mr Peacock was in their company. His good humour would sustain them.

As she sleepily settled into the plush seat, babe in arms, it was a long while, too late to rectify the mistake, before Harriet realised that Martha, the wet-nurse, had been left behind.

∾Eighteen∾
Discord

Edinburgh, November 1813

'Is it not nice to be back once more, in the city where it all began? We have come full circle, Harriet.'

Harriet watched her husband's face cautiously. As he gazed down onto the Edinburgh streets from their lodgings, she detected a dreamy cast across his delicate features which often heralded the birth of a new poem.

'Oh Percy, I would not like to think of our journey together as being circular, leastways not for many a year. We still have far to go, surely?'

She came to stand alongside him and began to stroke the curls at the back of his neck. He had always loved this endearment but today he arched his back impatiently at her touch. Hurt, she dropped her hands to her side.

'Look, there is Eliza.' They watched her tall frame weaving imperiously down Frederick Street, Peacock gallantly following in her wake, carrying parcels.

'But what has she been buying now?'

'Just a few skeins of wool, my love, that is all. Ianthe needs new clothing. She has grown much of late.'

Percy grumbled still not mollified.

'Why not write a little, while the baby sleeps?'

'I thought I might slip out for a while. There is a covert meeting I have heard about, being held in support of the striking weavers in Glasgow. I may be able to help in some way.'

'Oh my darling, don't go out at this hour. I shall fetch you a piece of fruit cake and you can settle at your desk and write for a bit. You will hear about the meeting soon enough.'

'Perhaps I will stay. I have not written anything in my notebook for a while. But what to write? I am uncertain these past days.'

'Maybe you could expand your recent musings upon Napoleon's defeat at Leipzig?'

'Godwin also thinks I should be diligently marking such points of history. Speaking of Godwin reminds me of something.'

Harriet stiffened at the mention of Godwin. Whenever his name was mentioned there seemed to be misunderstandings and trouble. Fleeing their creditors the previous month, they had charged up to the Lakes, seeking the place that Mr Godwin had endorsed in the most glowing terms, only to find a disappointingly small inn which had been unable to accommodate them.

And so, they had continued to Scotland. To what end, Harriet didn't know; other than to keep the creditors foxed as to their whereabouts.

Still, she was gratified to see that mention of Godwin had

caused Percy's spirits to rally.

He sprang over to the writing desk and immediately set to with a fresh sheet of paper, and before long was scribbling with his usual flourish.

She smiled proudly in anticipation of his next work. An hour later when Percy flung the paper and his pen down she automatically picked up the sheet to check his work as she usually did and her spirits plunged.

Reading it she realised, too late, as she raised her head, that danger had blown into the room as Eliza and Peacock returned.

'The packages in the corner, if you please, Mr Peacock. Harriet, call for the girl to fetch tea. But I see you two have been busy in our absence,' she remarked, boldly looking over Harriet's shoulder at Percy's handwritten page, 'it is about time you gave us another poem. But what is this?' Eliza's chill froze the air in the room.

Peacock removed himself to his chamber. Ianthe stirred restlessly in her crib.

'It need not concern you,' Harriet said desperately.

'Indeed, it does not,' Percy agreed coolly.

'But how could you contemplate such a thing?'

Percy stepped towards Eliza and reclaimed the offending piece of paper; long flowing paragraphs addressed to Godwin in which Percy had agreed to arrange a loan on his behalf.

'He wrote to say he was in dire financial straits. He is a friend and it is my duty to help.'

There was an aching silence in the room. Harriet's thoughts swam around her head. As usual, her opinion remained unsought.

'It is really none of your business, Miss Westbrook, what I choose to do with my money. If I choose to give some to Mr

Godwin then that is entirely my affair.'

'You have no money!' Eliza's shriek stretched to the corners of the cold room which they were unable to heat through lack of funds. Only the Shelleys' bedroom had any warmth, in deference to Ianthe.

'Percy, this is intolerable. We endeavour to live frugally yet Mr Godwin only has to snap his fingers and funds miraculously appear. I intend to pack my things and leave this instant.'

'Eliza, do not be hasty – '

'On the contrary,' Percy cut in, 'she should be as hasty as she wishes. In fact, I will help her to pack her belongings.'

'Percy, no!' said Harriet desperately, watching her sister's cheekbones turn a scalding red as she barged into her chamber and began noisily opening doors and drawers.

'You cannot leave like this.' Harriet followed Eliza into the hurricane of clothes and belongings that flew around her room.

'I cannot stay. I will not be insulted by your husband. He has been scratching around under my skin for weeks now. He even blames me for the wet-nurse, when in fact I told you employing her was not advisable. No matter. He shall have his way; all traces of me shall be gone as soon as my trunks can be moved.'

'Where will you go?'

'Back to Chapel Street, of course. It is still my home. I have had quite enough of this seemingly never ending adventure. Two years on and we are no nearer to achieving anything.'

'Eliza, do not leave in this manner.'

'For better or worse I have guided you thus far. As far as I can see, this marriage shows no signs of settling, nor Percy any inclination to behave like a responsible husband and father. You must cling to the hopes of a future title and the accompanying riches; Field Place, if you are very lucky. It will all be yours one day. You have charm and beauty, Harriet. Use the gifts that you have.'

'Percy and I married for love and we are happy as we are.'

'Are you happy? Can you honestly say it is as you thought it would be?

Harriet ignored this. 'Neither of us care about his title or the house in Sussex or the money. Why have you made such a drama, sister? Perhaps things are not as *you* thought they would be? Is it because the riches are not forthcoming?'

Harriet stared at her sister as if she was a stranger. Eliza dropped her gaze. But for a second, Harriet had seen exposure in her defeated eyes.

'Harriet! Ianthe is crying.'

Harriet looked sadly at her sister bent over her valise averting her face, before leaving the room in silence to join her husband and child.

*

In the weeks that followed Eliza's departure Harriet brooded. It was entirely true that she had married Percy for love. But remembering Hellen Shelley's tales about her privileged upbringing, the wonderful house, Field Place and how kind and gracious Lady Shelley was rumoured to be, she had always been curious about his origins.

She considered her own family ties. With Eliza having left her she felt strangely adrift. Often she picked up Lady Shelley's illicit letter and thought that it was time to explore the family she had yet to meet. Lady Shelley had a strong desire to meet her grandchild and was curious to know her daughter-in-law. And it might just be possible to tackle the unpleasantness that lay so deeply between Percy and his father, brokering a tentative mood towards peace.

To visit when Sir Timothy was there would be unthinkable. He would not receive her. Lady Shelley had written that should she wish to come, to write first and give warning. Sitting alone one afternoon with the light from the sky beginning to fade and Ianthe sleeping in her crib, Harriet put pen to paper and wrote a letter.

A fortnight later, she travelled down to London to visit her parents, accompanied by Mr Peacock who also needed to return to the capital. One morning she rose in the wintry dawn of Chapel Street and gathering a slumbering Ianthe into the depths of her shawl, set off to catch the coach to Sussex.

*

'Bysshe was a beautiful baby, you know. Great luminous eyes and the palest skin. And this little one takes after him, I think. Although rather more robust, I should imagine.'

'She is,' agreed Harriet relieved to have found some common ground with her rather grand hostess. Having arrived at Field Place after her six hour journey, she had been admitted without ceremony and immediately taken into the long dining room, set informally for the occasion. Lady Elizabeth Shelley, a striking woman, rising to greet her, had run her gaze thoughtfully over Harriet before succumbing to Ianthe's charms.

'Well, here is a pretty babe. My dear, you must be so proud. Tell me, is Bysshe greatly smitten with her? I suspect that is the case, for he was always very good with his younger sisters.'

She had smiled warmly at Harriet who, relieved, saw she had done the correct thing by instigating the visit. As they had dined on cold meats, salad, bread, cheese and a compote of pears, the baby had nestled comfortably against her grandmother's bosom while Harriet picked guiltily at snippets of meat and replied to her mother-in-law's gentle questioning about her son.

Now, Harriet, with Ianthe in her arms, was undergoing a tour of the manor house, conducted by her mother-in-law.

Lady Elizabeth Shelley led the way, in and out of the low-ceilinged rooms, whisking Harriet past the beautiful Jacobean bannisters, up and down narrow corridors, pointing out the delights of the marble fireplace in the drawing room, the extensive panelling in the Oak Room, the medieval hall in the east wing and a gallery of portraits featuring previous generations of Shelleys.

Finally, they settled in a much smaller, cosier room just off the drawing room where Harriet sat down feeling slightly breathless, disorientated to find herself in the place where Percy had been born and raised.

She smiled inwardly, imagining her husband as a young boy, his mop of hair bouncing as he ran in from the garden, clothing full of mud from the farmland he had been roaming all day, causing chaos as he weaved through the gaps in the bannisters, making a daring ascent of the stairs, dodging his nurse who was anxious to scrub him clean in the echoing bathroom.

Lady Shelley seemed at ease with Ianthe, Harriet thought, possessing a maternal air, although Harriet remembered Percy more than once saying how, once he had left Field Place as a ten-year-old to attend Syon Academy, his mother seemed not to be able to love him in the same way, and he had never managed to find his way back to her heart.

'And is our dear Bysshe managing to make a living?'

Harriet paused, unsure how best to answer the thorniest question of all.

'He is writing. He published a poem last summer.'

'Ah, yes. *Queen Mab*. Sir Timothy of course, would not allow it in the house, but I have seen it. And how is he generally? Is he eating well? Sleeping without nightmares?'

'More or less'. Harriet was glad to be able to confirm that her husband seemed settled.

'And how exactly do you live? I have been told you move around the country rather a lot. That must be difficult now you have a child.'

'Yes. It is.'

'Do you plan to settle?'

'Well…' Harriet told her mother-in-law about Nangtgwillt. 'I think if you saw the place you would be as much in love with it as we are. It is the most perfect place for a family to settle in peace. Of course, Lady Shelley, the success of the plan depends on whether Percy and his father can agree on the terms of his inheritance.'

Lady Shelley frowned. 'The problem, my dear, is that Percy does insist on this rather chaotic mode of living that his father simply cannot condone. It might be best to prepare yourself for disappointment. Does Bysshe know you have come to see me?'

'I thought it best to keep it between ourselves.'

'Ah.' Her hostess drew out a long sigh.

Lady Shelley rang a little bell and a servant appeared.

'Please fetch the packaged item for Mrs Shelley.'

When it was placed before Harriet she carefully unfurled the wrapping and drew from its depths a tiny wooden box containing a miniature dinner service; twelve china plates, bowls, wine goblets and platters, in a pale blue pattern edged in gold.

'I was given these by my mother on my wedding day. They came from her baby house which was passed down to my children and which lives still in the nursery upstairs. Perhaps I will keep the house for Ianthe for when she is grown but for now, please keep these for her.'

'They are beautiful. Thank you, Lady Shelley.'

'They were to be a christening gift. But I suppose Bysshe has not allowed this child to be christened?'

Harriet shook her head. 'I still hope he can be persuaded.'

'Such a great pity. Dear Bysshe has always had rather fanciful notions. I suppose one must blame his grandfather, Sir Timothy's father, an unconventional man from whom he seems to have inherited rather a wild streak. It will prove to be his downfall, Sir Timothy says. There again, dear Percy will also inherit most of his grandfather's money which again, Sir Timothy is unhappy about.' She sighed.' Families can be so complicated, don't you agree?'

She smiled at Harriet sadly. 'When she gets older, please be sure to let Ianthe know the gift came from her grandmother, with fondest regards.'

'I will do. It is extraordinarily kind of you.'

The little box was tucked discreetly away into Harriet's bag. She would have to find a hiding place for it, until she found a good time to tell Percy about her visit to his mother.

It was late afternoon and already darkness had fallen. The last coach would be leaving shortly. Even at the last minute she hoped she may be asked to stay and meet Sir Timothy.

As if sensing her thoughts, Lady Shelley, reached for the bell once more.

'It has been so lovely to meet you, my dear. And your dear precious babe, Ianthe. I think, given the circumstances, we have done rather well today. And I think Bysshe has done rather well for himself too.'

She gave Harriet a sudden warm smile which departed as

quickly as it came.

'I will not detain you any longer…one never knows when my husband will return, you see.'

The old family butler arrived discreetly at Harriet's side. She gathered up her belongings and swooped Ianthe into her arms. The baby cooed over her shoulder at Lady Shelley's departing wave.

The visit was over.

*

London, January 1814

It was the coldest winter anyone could remember. The warmest furs could not guard against the blunt chill in the air, a biting wind that froze the ink in Percy's pot and the silk tassels on Harriet's dress left airing outside the scullery.

Icicles, half a yard long, hung from the roof top of 23 Chapel Street; inside a frosty atmosphere, that had little to do with the outdoor elements, curled around the edges of each room where Harriet, Percy and Ianthe had found themselves living with Harriet's parents since the beginning of the new year.

The Shelleys' finances were, as ever, precarious. Under John Westbrook's comfortable roof, naturally the couple's needs were taken care of. But relations were strained between Percy and his in-laws, not least because Ann Westbrook had overheard Percy, in a great temper, describing Eliza as a 'loathsome worm.'

Harriet had done all within her power to smooth things over, relying heavily on Ianthe's dimpled charm but she knew their days at Chapel Street were numbered.

It had been snowing heavily for days and the sounds from the normally active London streets beyond the drawing room windows were eerily muffled. Tea was being served in a chilly silence when John Westbrook entered the house. Semi-retired now, he had taken to calling into his coffee house once a day to check things were still running to his satisfaction.

As Harriet's mother reached for the teapot her husband entered in a flurry from the hallway. His cloak was damp with melting snow as he made for the fire to warm his hands.

'Tea, John?'

'A quick cup, my dear and then you must all put on your warmest things and come out.'

'Come out? Really, John, what has happened to make you so giddy?'

'And this little miss will be coming too! Harriet, tuck her into her warmest shawl. We can take it in turns to carry her.'

'Carry her where, Sir, if I may ask?'

John Westbrook's eyes were glowing as he looked across at his son-in-law. 'The Thames has frozen! Already the river is packed with stalls and people. I've just supervised the closing of the coffee house and Jacob is going to set up a stall on the ice. There's nothing people will enjoy better than our finest hot chocolate and marshmallows sipped outside in the frosty air.'

'A Frost Fair! Oh, John, there hasn't been one for many a year, not since Eliza was a small child. I remember her clutching your hand as you showed her how to skate. How we enjoyed ourselves on the ice of the Thames! Shall we really go again?'

'Yes, yes, my dear, hurry, go and make yourself ready.'

'It is most unfortunate that Eliza is not here with us to enjoy the revels,' called Mrs Westbrook over her shoulder, a swipe aimed at Percy no doubt. Eliza had decamped to relatives in Bath, not wishing to make the situation more awkward than it already was for her parents.

Harriet had on her new, peacock-blue pelisse. She huddled into its depths as her father paid the fee to the watermen who had been quick to set up admission booths for entry onto the ice.

'You look ravishing against the whiteness,' Percy whispered into her ear.

'I wish we could have treated Mama and Papa. I hate having to take Papa's money all the time.'

'What of it?' Percy asked, pulling away from her. 'Your father is more than happy to pay for us. For goodness sake, Harriet, let us just enjoy the fun.'

Percy's eyes glittered at the spectacle before them. Tents and stalls fashioned from sails and supported by a framework of oars had been set up as far as the eye could see, from London Bridge to Blackfriars. Fires had been lit and the smell of roasting ox and mutton hung in the air; a pall of smoke floated towards the far dome of St Paul's Cathedral. Cauldrons of hot ale laced with spices, baskets of baked apples and liberal cups of gin were on sale everywhere.

Harriet smiled wanly as her father came upon them, pressing a generous slab of gingerbread into her hand and another for Percy. She crammed small pieces into her mouth, enjoying the sensation of the rich spice warming the back of her throat

She did her best to emulate Percy's excitement as they moved with the crowd but she was anxious about Ianthe, checking to be sure the baby's bonnet was tightly laced against the cold air and her tiny mittens covered each finger. She failed to take in many of the sights; random bookstalls, a group of boys bunched around a set of wooden skittles, pedlars selling children's toys, a donkey race, a man with a wooden leg trapped in the ice.

She even managed to miss the most extraordinary spectacle of all: the dark massed shape of an elephant as it was paraded onto the ice with great majesty. She lifted her head at the roar of the awestruck crowd but the mass of people obscured the sight of the disgruntled creature being led away towards Blackfriars Bridge.

Percy was cross. 'Dearest, you are not taking anything in. Look over there, see that crowd of fellows by that printing press. Let us go over and see what is being produced.'

'One moment, Percy, Ianthe's nose feels very cold. I have to keep rubbing it with my hands to warm her up a little.'

'We should have left her with the servants, Harriet.'

'I wanted us to enjoy the experience, as a family.'

'Very well. Let's take her onto the swings, you'd like that, wouldn't you sweetheart?'

His daughter gazed up at him, gurgling happily. 'She will enjoy rushing upwards to the great bank of stars that have just begun to break through the gloom.'

'Percy, no, I don't think so. She is too little and some of the people seem a little rough.'

A band of musicians had congregated on a makeshift stage and Harriet and Percy were unable to continue the conversation as drum and fiddle notes pierced the air. A ragged boy tugged at Percy's coat tails. He was holding a bunch of strap-on skates tied together with a rope.

'Skates for hire, mister? Missus?'

'Shall we?' Percy said hopefully, looking after the young couples sloshing around on the ice, attempting to stay upright. Their carefree laughter echoed into the skies. Harriet saw him glance at Ianthe and sigh and shake his head, sending the boy on his way.

'My head is quite in a whirl,' said Ann Westbrook, coming up behind the young couple. She and John had spent quite some time at his refreshment tent. From the giddy look in her mother's eyes, Harriet suspected that a fair amount of gin had been imbibed.

'I think we are ready to return home, aren't we John? Harriet, Percy, are you coming too?'

'Yes, Ianthe is so very cold,' said Harriet. 'You could stay awhile,' she said to her husband who was standing slightly apart, staring out at the dreamlike spectacle of London on ice.

She expected him to dash away eagerly as he was always so ready to do these days and she prepared herself for the familiar jolt of her heart. For some reason, she felt more worried when he gave a small smile, shook his head and joined them for the slippery walk home, without a murmur.

The weeks passed quickly, along with the frost and snow. On a spring afternoon in early March, Harriet and Percy were taking the air in Green Park, soft rays of sunshine falling on the spires of Westminster in the distance.

They were spending rare time together without Ianthe who was being cooed over by some old friends of the Westbrooks who had called at Chapel Street. After a dull luncheon party Harriet had seen Percy looking restlessly out of the window and she had quickly devised the impromptu outing.

'Harriet, I've been trying to find a quiet moment to talk to you. I have been advised by my father's solicitors that we need to remarry.'

'As you have asked me so nicely, it will be my pleasure, Sir,' she said with a solemn little curtsey and a flourish of skirts. She had thought to make him laugh, but he stared unsmiling at her. She adopted a serious tone. 'Why is it necessary?'

'There may be some legal difficulties arising from the Edinburgh ceremony. We need to iron out any uncertainties, now that I have come of age and I have a child.'

'I see.' She bit her lip at his listless tone. He sounded as if he were discussing a business venture.

'The earliest we can be married is the 24th of this month. I have already spoken to the rector at St George's. It will be for the best if we do it with speed and simplicity.'

'I understand. It will be a wonderful day for Papa and Mama; after all they were not present in Edinburgh and I am sure Father would give us a luncheon afterwards.'

'Godwin I'm sure will offer the same.'

'But Percy –'

'If we cannot agree on festivities then we should dispense with them. The ceremony is merely a formality after all. I have no desire to sit at a table with your sister. You obviously feel the same about Godwin.'

What is happening to us, she thought bleakly. The feud with Eliza was sucking all the love and tenderness down into a black hole. Rather than try and rectify things, Percy seemed to want to run away from it all, to the Godwins where he spent most of his time.

She took his arm. 'Maybe if it's a fine day we could come here again to the park. Just you and I and our babe. We could wrap up warmly and bring a hamper of food such as we had in Scotland. Do you remember, my love?'

The bitterness in his eyes broke as he looked at his still young and beautiful bride.

'A picnic would be very fitting.'

He kissed her hand in a placatory manner.

It was a brittle armistice in the face of the broadsides that had been fired across the marital threshold in recent months, but Harriet accepted it gratefully.

⌒Nineteen⌒
Unravelling

Spring, 1814

The day after the marriage ceremony they left London and all its distractions behind, Harriet desperate to try and regain the rhythms of family life. Having to leave Godwin's influence was a blow to Percy but he had assented to the move provided they could live close to Mrs Boinville.

As there was still no news of Percy's settlement, they had to take whatever accommodation was on offer. Reeds Hill Farm Cottage was a pretty timber-framed building, perched on top of a slight incline near the church in East Hampstead. It had light, airy rooms, well-appointed bedchambers and walled grounds with a kitchen garden to the side and banks of daffodils, just beginning to unfurl their golden trumpets as the family took up residence.

Harriet, her thoughts always drifting back to the manor house in Wales, did not think much of the house or its surroundings.

Eliza was back with them. As Mr Westbrook was paying the rent on the cottage, Percy had little say in the matter but Harriet realised he was doing his best to exclude Eliza at every opportunity; persuading Harriet out on her own for long rambles down the pathways of the forest, where they walked and enjoyed moments like the young lovers they had once been, putting aside their debts and quarrels and choosing to discuss poetry and philosophy. Inside the cottage, he would refuse a look of welcome and a space for Eliza as the little family sat beside the fire, watching Ianthe drift into sleep.

The household was full of niggles and regrets. Percy was disappointed when Harriet spent time singing lullabies to Ianthe or knitting bootees instead of focussing her mind on the texts he had provided for her. Harriet could never escape the hurt sensation that crept over her each time Percy lifted the latch on the door and walked across the field to Mrs Boinville's house, with great quantities of books tied up with string and an expression of relief on his face, as if he had been sprung from a trap.

And then there was the darkness of the ever-present Eliza. Once the weaver of their love story, she now seemed intent on pulling at its loose ends to see how far the yarn would stretch.

On a typical morning of domestic duties, Percy as usual at Mrs Boinville's house and Harriet picking herbs from the garden, Eliza, flicking her feather duster into dim corners, discovered a sheet of paper that had fallen beneath Percy's writing desk.

Retrieving it, she half-glanced at the words. She did not particularly care for her brother-in-law's poetry; it left her unmoved. She was of the opinion that it was time he put his mind to more serious moneymaking opportunities, or better still, give up his revolutionary ideas, work harder to heal the rift with his father and agree his settlement.

Her blood began to race as she read. 'Harriet!' she called, her voice shrill.

Harriet came in from the cool spring sunshine. Wrapped in a cloak of scarlet and carrying a basket filled with small sprigs of spring parsley, thyme and wild garlic for soup that evening, she was full of tender thoughts. She had a suspicion that she might be carrying another child and she was imagining Percy's joy at the news.

She almost dropped her gatherings when she caught sight of Eliza's face. 'Eliza? What on earth is the matter?'

'*Thy gentle words stir poison…Duty's hard control…*' This is how your husband views family life, is it?' She waved the paper in Harriet's face, sneering.

Harriet's spirits plummeted but she fought bravely against it. 'I think you are misunderstanding something you were not meant to have read in its current form. Percy always writes such beautiful things about me and our dear little babe, too.'

She took Percy's notebook away from Eliza and sat down to read. Rifling through the pages she tried inwardly to calm herself. Percy was simply tired, down-hearted that Eliza was there with them all the time, taking control of her as she had always done. '*Duty's hard control*'. That is what those words referred to. They were not about her.

She found some happier lines and read aloud.

'*I love thee, baby for thine own sweet sake…*and this…*O Harriet, love like mine that glows, what rolling years can e'er destroy?*' You see? He is happy. With his wife and child, at least.'

'When were those poems written, Harriet? Last year,

sometime? These lines I am talking about are fresh!'

Harriet drew a breath. It was time to draw the circle closer. 'Eliza.' Her voice was cool. 'You should not be snooping around among Percy's things. What he writes is his business. I would have thought you would have learnt from what happened last time.'

'You're not listening, Harriet. Percy has all kinds of black thoughts flying through his heart and mind. You should be worried.' She paused. 'It may well be, that he seeks to call time on his experiment with you.'

Harriet's eyes blazed. 'Our marriage is a commitment not an experiment! You have no idea what you are talking about. I think you should go back to London for a while. Mama has been out of sorts for a while and I am sure she would welcome your company.'

Eliza glared at Harriet. 'The impertinence! And the ingratitude! The dolly thinks she can play at being an adult, now?'

The cruel retort stung but Harriet held onto her temper. 'Don't be like this, please. Let's enjoy a peaceful break from one another. It's hard to live so close together like this. I will return in the late spring when the lease ends on this place. We may well settle in London, nearby. I would be very grateful if you could look around for suitable rooms for us?'

Still deeply offended, Eliza left an hour later, without waiting for Percy's return. That evening, Harriet cooked supper, taking control of her domestic hearth, at peace with herself, ready to open a new chapter in their married life.

*

'Good morning, Mrs Boinville. Forgive my dishevelled state, I am running behind with my chores today. Please come in.'

Harriet tried to shake herself from her inertia as Mrs

Boinville swept into the small cottage filling it with the aroma of her expensive scent, and settled herself by the unlit hearth.

Harriet, holding Ianthe with one hand, went towards the tea caddy, a present from her father, high on the shelf, but Mrs Boinville stopped her.

'It's a little early for tea, my dear. Perhaps a glass of lemonade?'

Harriet moved to the stone pitcher on the dresser and poured two glasses, tidying her curls and smoothing her old day dress discreetly, before sitting down to join her guest.

Mrs Boinville looked at her expectantly. 'Have you heard from our dear Mr Shelley? I understand he has gone up to London, quite suddenly?'

Harriet's heart froze. The memory of the previous day was still too fresh to contemplate. She had gone to a lot of trouble with the Sunday dinner; carefully rolling pastry while Percy wrote letters by the fire. She and Percy were still committed vegetarians and with limited produce and the smallest of kitchens, she strove to produce creative dishes.

The vegetable pasties on Sunday had been the first unburnt offerings she had made since Eliza's departure. She had served them with buttered carrots and potatoes flavoured with rosemary from the kitchen garden, proudly bringing the dishes to the table, calling her husband to sit.

Percy, ravenous as always, had torn into the food, barely noticing its merits. Hurt, she had said nothing, hoping instead, to impress him with her lemon syllabub. She had even walked up to the farm on the brow of the hill, to get a basin of fresh cream as an extra treat.

As she had poured the rich cream over the dessert she had cleared her throat.

'Percy, I have some news.'

193

'I do hope it is not Eliza returning.'

He was obviously in a churlish mood. She had tried again. 'My darling, no.'

He was scraping up the remains of his syllabub with his spoon. Harriet, sensing his impatience, had rushed her words. 'I am pregnant, Percy!'

Something flickered in his pale blue eyes. He slumped back in his chair. He couldn't quite meet her gaze. 'Darling, Harriet, that is a surprise.'

Harriet wondered why it should be. She noted with dismay that Percy seemed underwhelmed. Nothing could have prepared her for the blade-like slash through the heart when he had abruptly got up from his place at the table, kissed her perfunctorily, and dashed up the narrow staircase to pack a case before reappearing.

'Harriet I am expected at Mrs Boinville's and then I shall head straight to London.'

'London? I thought you wanted to work on your essays.'

Percy was in the middle of writing a number of philosophical essays dealing with such varied topics as the vegetable diet, animal rights and a refutation of deism. Harriet had thought they could spend a few days making amendments together, she was toying with the idea of making them into a single small volume.

He had avoided her eye. 'I just need a few days away.'

From what he hadn't said, and she had been too afraid to ask.

Harriet stared thoughtfully across at her guest. Did Mrs Boinville know about the baby? Had she come to stir a pot of discord which Percy had lain on her table the previous day? Or was she genuinely concerned, as she herself was, for Percy's state of mind?

'My dear; I wondered if perhaps you and Ianthe would like to accompany me to the May dance in the town, this afternoon? As Percy is away and Eliza too, I thought you may like some company. Cornelia is abroad with her husband and I too, am alone today.'

Harriet immediately felt ashamed. Mrs Boinville was merely being kind. They were after all, friends and neighbours. Her spirits rallied at the thought of an outing.

'I would like that very much.'

'Dress Ianthe in her outdoor clothes while I finish my drink. There is no hurry.'

The sky was dotted with pale grey clouds but Mrs Boinville was confident the rain would hold off. Harriet felt the tension roll away as the pleasures of late spring were laid out before her eyes. The woodlands were strewn with a canopy of bluebells, the overhead branches vibrating with bird song. Along the lanes purple orchids bloomed intertwined with violets and vibrant red campion and the hedgerows were humming with activity; yellow hammers and linnets rustling in their nests and on the ground the foraging sounds of hedgehogs and mice.

Outside the Red Lion Inn, a maypole under a bower of green boughs and garlanded flowers had been erected. A pipe and fiddle ensemble was playing loudly, people's rowdy chatter rising above the melody as couples, dressed in their best gay colours danced in the sunshine, hands joined as they whirled around the pole.

Harriet's cheeks were flushed. Defiantly she accepted a glass of mead and fixed her eyes on the dancers. A couple of workers dared ask her to dance and of course, she refused them charmingly.

She wondered what Percy was doing amid the thronging

streets of London.

Heading home several hours later, brooding along the way, she let out a sigh.

'Are you feeling alright, Harriet?'

'I…I sometimes feel my husband is bored of me.' The words were out before she could suppress them.

'Nonsense.' Mrs Boinville's eyes filled with unexpected pity. Her voice wavered. 'I am sure something of urgency is keeping Bysshe away from you.'

'Something that undoubtedly involves Mr Godwin.'

Mrs Boinville looked at her sharply. 'My dear, I have tried to speak to Bysshe about my views on his devotion to the Godwins. I believe Mr Godwin's rather seditious views have inculcated Percy to act rashly. *Queen Mab* was a fine poem but it could perhaps have been written in a more subtle way, so as not to offend the public. In that manner, it would have been able to be published and Percy would have made some money from his work instead of having to pay for it to be privately printed and not circulated widely.'

Harriet acknowledged this with a nod. 'Mr Godwin merely has to hold out his palm and my husband is ready to pour whatever money we have or have borrowed, into its grasp. It is too bad,' she concluded, 'Percy is supposed to be negotiating the purchase of Nantgwillt and instead he is constantly distracted by the least little drama in Skinner Street.'

'Perhaps a firmer wifely hand is required; a suggestion to Percy that he leave the Godwins to their own devices.'

They had reached the gate that enclosed the cottage garden. Harriet placed a gloved hand on the latch. 'I am sure you are right.'

But I hope I am not too late to change, she thought silently, as Mrs Boinville waved and glided elegantly back down the lane.

Late in the evening Ianthe was slumbering heavily, worn out from the unusual excitement of the day. Before Percy had left for London he had charged around the bedroom, opening drawers and cupboards, collecting belongings in his usual haphazard fashion and now Harriet sought to restore calm and order to the room. She wandered across the floorboards picking up stray items that Percy had left lying in his wake.

With a dart of alarm her eyes spied her silken scarf in which she had wrapped Lady Shelley's secret gift for Ianthe, lying in a heap underneath the bureau.

The miniature dinner service was gone.

She sat down, her thoughts sinking into horror. Their household had not seen an influx of funds. She surmised, therefore, that Percy had sold it to add to the coffers of Godwin.

His mother's childhood treasure; Percy must have recognised it. But it had evidently meant nothing to him.

As she had kept secrets from him, she could not now upbraid him.

But how, in all conscience, could he have sold it? He must have realised its significance; that his mother had been happy to welcome Harriet and Ianthe into the Shelley household. Why had he not spoken to her of his discovery so that she could have confessed her visit? They could have made plans to return to Field Place together.

This desire to constantly please William Godwin was perplexing indeed. Was there nothing he would not do to gratify that man?

A thought occurred to her. She would not like Percy to go snooping further for more items to sell. She always wore her watch chain from her parents and of course her betrothal ring but the special gift he had presented to her upon the publication of *Queen Mab*, she had always considered far too ornate and valuable to wear. Thinking hard, she tucked it into a bundle of Ianthe's small gowns.

She was confident that when he finally chose to return, he would not find it.

*

Summer, 1814

'My dear Mrs Nugent, as you can see from the address, I am currently in Bath with Eliza and my dear sweet Babe. We have come to stay with Papa's relatives in Queen Square in a wonderful house. The rooms are spacious and grand and Ianthe and I have a view from our bedroom window of the Egyptian obelisk; how Ianthe's eyes open wide as she gazes up at its peak.

We can walk with ease to the Pump Room and the Baths and to the Abbey and as the maids of the house are happy to take care of Ianthe, Eliza and I have enjoyed walks, carriage rides, and shopping since my arrival last week.

I cannot tell you how good it feels to be back among family and friends, for as you know, the past months were lonely for me in Bracknell.

As for Mr Shelley, he is still in London, in lodgings in Fleet Street but spends much time with the Godwins. He writes me often so I at least know he has not been caught by bailiffs, although he has written that on occasion he has been followed in the streets.

My dear friend, if you would like some respite from your labours, there is room for you to stay with us here in this ever-changing city; the streets filled with sunshine on one day and the next full of mist and shadows.

Or perhaps you would care to wait until August? I am

planning a celebration dinner for my 19th birthday and our third wedding anniversary. How the time has flown. Although perhaps these past few months have dragged a little.

At any rate, I shall be glad to return to Percy in London as soon as he has concluded his financial dealings on Mr Godwin's behalf. How you warned me of that man; but I have been unable to make Percy see things the way they truly are.

Write in haste and let me know if you plan to join us.

Yours affectionately

H.S'

'Harriet, come get yourself ready. We are invited to the Barretts in Milsom Street. They wish to meet you and Ianthe. Mr Barrett recently acquired a copy of *Queen Mab* and Papa whispered to him discreetly that the anonymous author was in fact, Percy. You must bring Percy's note-book; I am sure the Barretts would be interested in his work.'

Harriet looked, unseeing in her sister's direction.

'I cannot,' she whispered.

'Very well, leave the note-book behind if you must, I know how you are possessive of it. Why, whatever is the matter, Harriet?'

Harriet was standing in a daze, her face flushing vermilion before turning the colour of ash. 'Eliza...we must leave for London immediately. Percy has urgently written that I join him.'

'We will most certainly not go tearing off now. Mr Barrett is an old friend of Papa's and it would be very rude to cancel at the very last moment. And besides, Mr Farthing Beauchamp, the banker whom we were introduced to last week will also be there. I rather liked him; he is an interesting man.'

'Please, Eliza, I implore you. Pack a few items for yourself while I awaken Ianthe. There is a coach that leaves at two.'

Eliza watched, perplexed, as Harriet hastened around her bedroom, folding items of clothing and putting them into her portmanteau.

'I suppose you would go alone if I did not consent to accompany you? Very well, Harriet, I cannot allow you and Ianthe to travel all that way by yourself, but it is extremely tiresome not be told why we must leave in such haste.'

Harriet turned her strained face towards her sister.

'I didn't say anything as I did not want to worry you but I hadn't heard from Percy for several days. He simply ceased writing to me, which is why I have been a little on edge. I haven't known what to think; was he ill or in trouble with the debt collectors? Finally, I have just received word from him that he wishes to meet me today at his lodgings. But I feel a certain concern as it was a note of a most sombre tone.

'Come sister, let us not be late. I will meet you downstairs at the front steps.'

Within the hour, they were boxed into a dusty carriage and jolting along the road to London, Harriet pale with excitement, her restless eyes following the broad sweep of the River Avon, her thoughts flying to the reunion with her husband. She had grown in maturity during his absence and now she was returning to him as a more self-assured wife.

Whatever was wrong with Percy she could help fix it. She was more than ready for a new beginning.

∼Twenty∼
Estrangement

He held on to her hand tightly, as if she were an errant child about to run into the streets beyond and become lost forever.

'Harriet. I'm so very sorry but I must make you listen.'

Fear roared like faraway waves in the seashells that Percy had once held close to her ear in Lynmouth. Percy's face was closed to her, his eyes distant.

'Husband?'

He shied away from the word. From her.

Her legs buckled beneath her. She could barely make it to the chair which he offered her, a frown playing above his eyes. Harriet's throat tightened. She scrabbled for breath like a person half-drowned.

'Let me fetch you some water.'

She ached for him to hold her like his lover, his wife. Instead, he fussed around her as if she was an invalid, not meeting her eyes, compassion blazing like a fever. At last he spoke. Half an hour of incoherent rambling and terrible words, one word above all others, repeated often.

Mary. The name flew through her head like an arrow.

She closed her eyes, shivering, trying to steady her thoughts which ran violently in appalling sequence.

Mary Godwin, newly returned to London, meeting Percy's eyes across the bookshop counter for the first time. Mary, rushing down the rickety stairway into the shabby shop at the sound of Percy's voice. Mary and Percy at her mother's grave, reading poetry and declaring undying love for each other.

It was a long while before she found her voice.

'Percy; I know there have been difficulties of late. Ianthe is demanding and I should have paid you more attention. And Eliza: well, I will admit it was a mistake to have her back in our home. But all can be well again. We must forge ahead with our move to Wales. We can start again in the mountain air that you loved so much. You, me, Ianthe and our new-born when it arrives. You must forget this dalliance and let us start afresh. I will forgive you, if you put it behind you.'

He shook his head slowly.

'I want to be with Mary…I have to be with Mary! I love you, Harriet, like my sister. But Mary is my other half. My twin soul.'

He was ripping her heart into fragments.

There was a long silence during which neither met the other's eye. She gathered herself together. 'And what has Godwin to say about you seducing his precious daughter?' Her voice strengthened. 'Oh, but I suppose he is all in favour! He has finally captured the man who holds the purse strings and forced his feet firmly under the table…how he must be rejoicing!'

Percy looked over at her wretchedly. 'But he is not! He is incandescent with rage. He calls our love affair inconvenient

He is threatening to lock Mary in the house. For her own safety, he says, away from me. He is behaving like a tyrant towards her!'

Harriet went cold. A young, attractive girl, a father curtailing her freedom; she was almost disappointed that her husband, creative genius and thinker that he was, had proved to be so unimaginative.

Three years gone by in a flash and already history was repeating itself.

She rose from the chair with momentary self-possession. Her husband had the grace to look ashamed as she swept past him, out of the lodging house, without a look.

The poise stayed with her as she pounded the streets, her heart beating wildly, desperate to get to Chapel Street as quickly as possible. It disappeared as soon as she reached the sanctuary of the parlour.

Eliza discovered her lying pale and silent as a corpse on the chaise-longue.

'Harriet? What on earth has happened? Here, drink this.'

For the second time that afternoon she was handed a tumbler. This time it was filled with brandy. She took a long draught. The spirit coursed through her blood and after a while she was able to convey all to Eliza.

Her sister's countenance wilted; like one who has lost an important cribbage game.

'What do you propose to do, Harriet?'

Harriet stared at her with empty eyes. Eliza, the spinner of the tale, had no great ending planned, it seemed. The maid knocked quietly and brought in a letter addressed to Harriet. She turned it over delicately, blanching when she spied the handwriting.

'Godwin! The cause of all my sorrows and he has the

audacity to write to me!'

'Godwin is most certainly not the cause, Harriet…'

Ignoring her, Harriet read the short letter quickly and raised her head.

'There is hope! Godwin wishes to meet with me immediately after breakfast tomorrow morning. It would seem he is doing all he can to contain the storm that is beating around both our doors. If we act together we may yet save two worlds from colliding.'

In the event, Harriet fell ill with a severe headache and was unable to keep the appointment, so Eliza went in her place. She returned two hours later, red in the face, her hair springing out of place. Harriet had never seen her look so sour.

'Tell me all.' She clutched at her sister's sleeve across the quilt.

'I am not sure you are well enough, Harriet. When you are better we can discuss the matter.'

Harriet thrashed wildly in the bedclothes and struggled to sit up. 'I insist on knowing, now.'

'Very well. I arrived to find Godwin's shop was closed, even though it was a normal working day. Mrs Godwin let me in. She was even worse than usual; her excitable arms were waving all over the place and her eyes were darting wildly. Although I did not care to hear the answer, I politely enquired as to her health. She had the audacity to proclaim that the sorry state of affairs was making her feel wretched! She seemed not to grasp the gravity of our case, at all!

'She was chiefly concerned about the fact that Percy has yet to complete loan arrangements on behalf of Mr Godwin and that the situation with Mary was making matters very awkward! Words failed me. Presently she realised she would get no further conversation from me and she led me to a room at the top of the house where Godwin was waiting in an upright chair, with Mary standing beside him.'

'Mary! Mary was there? What right has she, to meet with you?' Harriet paused. She couldn't help herself. 'Is she…is she very beautiful?'

Eliza ignored this. 'Mary and I exchanged no pleasantries. The moment we met she launched into conversation, informing me in a rather measured way, that last night, Percy attempted to take an overdose of laudanum. Mary found him wandering, muttering and deluded, clutching the bottle to his breast, not far from Skinner Street. Mary says you are to blame.'

Harriet gasped. 'Where is Percy now? How is he? I must go to him.'

'He is resting in his rooms at this present time. I have sent word that you will call on him presently. Take Ianthe with you, make him see what his is turning his back on.'

'I do not wish to make Ianthe a possession to be bartered over.'

Eliza sighed. 'I made it very clear to Mary Godwin that she should sever all ties and attachments to Percy who is, after all, a married man. But her view was that matrimonial bonds are of no importance for a poet and free-thinker such as Percy. She said that, as much as Percy has enjoyed your amiability, it is her intellect that now acts as the light to his creative fuse.' She hesitated. 'In answer to your question; I found her rather plain-looking.'

Harriet threw herself back upon her pillows.

'It is no good becoming hysterical again, Harriet. You must bathe and dress and present yourself to your husband.'

*

'How are you feeling, Percy?' Harriet peered anxiously at his pale face.

'I am recovered now.'

'But Percy, what on earth were you thinking to do such a thing?'

'I was tired…confused…not thinking straight. This mess has got my head spinning and I couldn't see a way out of it.'

'I see.'

'Thank you for bringing my sweet babe to me. Her peaceful innocence is balm to my soul.'

'*Our* sweet babe,' said Harriet tightly. 'And, lest you forget, another on the way,' she added.

Percy looked at her as if she had slapped him. 'Harriet.' He stopped. 'Perhaps I have not been clear… I am not forsaking you; merely proposing a new way in which to continue sharing our lives. Mary and I are hoping to travel abroad soon, her father is creating such a rumpus there is no point in staying in England. We thought we might journey to France.'

She snorted. 'France? You would go there, at this time?'

'Napoleon has been banished and the war is over. I think it would be interesting to observe the aftermath of his reign. You are my dearest friend…come with us! How often have we spoken of travelling to the Continent? There would be a beautiful simplicity in us all being together as one big family. I will write my poetry, you will tend the house and care for the children and Mary – well – for some time now, she has been considering writing…a novel, she thought, if she was sufficiently inspired.'

Harriet was rendered temporarily speechless, grappling for words. They arrived in a torrent. 'You wish me to bring our baby to war-ravaged France and play housekeeper for you, while Mary writes a novel? And you think that would make me happy, Percy? How deluded are you? And for pity's sake, what experiences could Mary ever hope to impart in a novel? She is sixteen years old! The only thing she seems to have done, thus far, is to ruin my life. Our lives. But wait, I suppose you were planning to write a novel together…it's all part of your plan, is it not?'

'Harriet, I don't wish to quarrel…'

'And your expectation is for us to live together as part of the same community?'

'I see you are displeased with the idea. But it is of course, what we have been striving for all these years; for everyone to be welcome in our community of equals.'

'It sounds neither welcoming or equal. I am your wife, Percy, yet you seek to position another above me. It seems to me that you wish only for me to know my place in your newly shuffled pack.'

Ianthe began to move restlessly in Percy's arms. He handed her back to Harriet. 'We must also discuss money, Harriet.'

'I am not discussing anything else with you now. Let's meet again tomorrow. I hope that you will have seen sense by the morning.'

She only just made it back to Chapel Street before she collapsed and took to her bed with nervous exhaustion.

Listlessly, Harriet picked at a morsel of boiled fowl. Her mother had brought up a plate of food and had spent half an hour trying to tempt her to eat before finally giving up. Now, left alone, she conceded that with the baby growing every day in her womb, she had to eat. She had cleared the plate when Eliza came in with Ianthe who waved her plump arms in delight at seeing her mother.

'Have you any news?'

Eliza looked slyly pleased.

'I happened to see that girl, the one who washes the clothes at Skinner Street. She told me Godwin has Mary under lock and key! Neither Mary nor Claire, her step-sister are allowed to set foot out of the house!'

Harriet let out a horrified gasp.

Eliza blithely continued. 'Now there is every hope that cut off from the source, this madness of Percy's will blow itself cold. Perhaps it is time to visit him again, Harriet. Let me comb your hair free from those tangles.'

Eliza picked up Harriet's hairbrush and mirror set and advanced towards her but Harriet, using Ianthe as a shield, waved her away.

Eliza stiffened. 'You cannot lie there refusing to accept your position, Harriet, waiting for things to work themselves out. Life is a series of movements and game-playing and now it is your turn to make a move. As usual, I suppose you are waiting for me to reposition the pieces.'

Beneath the scorn, curling like the frost above the rosebud, Harriet refused to shrivel.

After Eliza had closed the door with a short bang of disapproval, Harriet lay staring at the wallpaper, her eyes chasing the stripes and flowers restlessly.

What would happen to her, if the game was finally over?

For the past three years, her thoughts, words and deeds had been prescribed by Percy. Placing herself like clay in his capable hands, clearly, he had, in the end, been displeased with his fabrication. But surely that was not her fault. She stroked Ianthe's curls, protectively and cast her mind back to her haven of Nantgwillt.

She could see the mist coming down from the mountain and she was afraid.

The next day, a single sentence arrived from Skinner Street containing an echo from down the years. In the early hours of dawn, Percy had turned the key in the locked door and had eloped with Mary and her wild and unpredictable step-sister, Claire.

*

August 1814

It was Harriet's birthday, her nineteenth. As she rose that morning, she lacked the joy of her young years, feeling like a much older woman, drab and heavy, the baby weight spreading around her abdomen. Anticipating Eliza's arrival, she draped her gown around her and headed for her dressing table.

Eliza found her seated, looking at her reflection with some distress.

'On this day of days, you would sit looking miserable in front of the glass, frowning? Come now, I will pick out your prettiest gown and we shall go downstairs for breakfast. Ianthe and Mama are waiting for you.'

'I do not have a best dress or any dress in fact; nothing fits me.'

'Sara sewed some extra panels in a couple of dresses for you last night. Look, she has hung them up for you and you have not even noticed.'

'I do not care.'

'I will see you downstairs in twenty minutes. Don't keep Ianthe waiting, she longs to see you this morning.'

Harriet rose with a determined air. The previous day she had given in to temptation and remained in her bed the whole day, seeing nobody save her mother who came several times, in an attempt to get her to eat something.

'Very well.'

Dressed in a pretty blue gown, Harriet sat in the parlour in a patch of warm sunshine, singing to Ianthe who was curled in her lap. The child gazed up at her beloved Mama with pure love. Drawing strength from her child's faith in her Harriet felt stronger. She determined not to let hopeless thoughts of Percy spoil the day. And besides, each day that passed, brought hope that he would soon grow tired of Mary and return home to her.

The summer's day was bright with promise. They were to picnic in the early afternoon in St James' Park beside the brightly coloured bridge and Chinese pagoda rising seven stories high above the canal. It was to be a summer of celebrations in London; victory over Napoleon had finally been achieved and the House of Hanover was also celebrating one hundred years of rule.

In Green Park that evening there was to be a balloon ascent followed by a display of fireworks. The whole household was looking forward to the spectacle.

Before their picnic, they took Ianthe into Hyde Park which was festooned with tents and stalls, pavilions and sideshows. Ianthe clapped her hands with a toothy grin at the jugglers and acrobats as the trio made their way through the crowds, mingling with the hordes of people, strolling and laughing uproariously at the least little thing, dandies preening themselves in the new clothes brought especially for this day, women in silks and feathers, some boating on the water, others feeding the swans. Everywhere flags and pennants fluttered in the gentle breeze.

London was at her finest. Harriet thought wryly that she herself was far less so. The shock of Percy's dalliance with Mary had wrought a change in her features; her eyes were smaller, dulled from lack of sleep and sore from weeping, tiny frown lines had appeared on her white forehead and there was permanent tension around her mouth.

Holding Ianthe's hand as the tiny child skipped alongside, she quashed thoughts of Percy arm-in-arm with Mary, boldly traversing France. But it was not easy.

Still, she dared to hope that Percy would write to her today on her birthday.

She sighed. Eliza was asking her a question.

'Sorry, sister, I was daydreaming. What is it you asked?'

'I said, should we take Ianthe to the fireworks this evening? I know she is very young but I am sure she would enjoy them.'

Harriet opened her mouth to protest. It would be too late an hour for Ianthe to be up, the noise may frighten her, the crowds close in and oppress her. She caught herself. They were fears pertaining to herself. A child should feel happy and buoyant with the promise of the future.

'If we go back home and rest I am sure we will be able to venture out again this evening.'

When the three arrived back at Chapel Place they found a letter had arrived. Recognising the seal, Harriet snatched it from the salver and rushed upstairs to her bedroom. She knew he would not have forgotten her on this day.

She perused the lines eagerly.

...Dearest, having travelled hard through France I write from the lush pastures of Switzerland, where I am still hoping you will come and join us. The weather is fine and the mountain peaks are majestic...I hope this letter finds you in good spirits and good heart......I cling to the hope that I will see you and our babe very soon. There was no mention of her birthday. Saddened, her eyes jumped to the final line.

...Also, Harriet, there are some papers that have been drawn

up which need to be signed by both of us; if you were to come to Switzerland and bring them with you, this would greatly enable matters to proceed smoothly, for both our sakes...

She caught her breath. He was hoping she would come and visit so she could bring him the papers regarding their legal separation.

*

'I am happy to see you, Mr Peacock. It was thoughtful of you to come today.'

Neither she nor Thomas Love Peacock alluded further to the significance of the date: 29th August, her third wedding anniversary.

But the pain of her situation was unavoidable.

'Have you further news?' asked Thomas in a low voice.

'Nothing. My husband is obviously far too busy to bother to write to me and there was nothing more to say, once he realised I would not be joining his entourage.'

She was too well-mannered to spit the last word but there was an inflexion in her tone. She looked at Thomas with a frankness that melted his heart.

'How could he? If he thinks so little of me I can and must bear it, but what of Ianthe? And our babe not yet born? It is just intolerable...'

Her voice tailed away. She looked downwards; he could count the lashes beneath her wonderful eyes. He shook the thought away sternly.

'This attraction to Mary...it is connected to his obsession with Godwin in some way. Mary is the idealism, the Godwin philosophy in feminine form. It will burn itself out. It must.'

He looked at Harriet's swelling stomach. 'She may have the intellect that Percy requires but you are his wife and the mother of his child. Children,' he amended. 'In a matter of months, you may be presenting him with a son and heir.'

'I hope you are not implying I am stupid.'

'My dear Harriet you are anything but stupid. You are bright and articulate with a quick mind. Mary's other asset, apart from being Godwin's daughter is that she offers Percy the chance of the unknown…You must own that Percy does crave change. But I believe that it will always be you who will have his heart.'

He did his best to look optimistic.

'Did you go to the celebrations, Mr Peacock?' Harriet wished to change the subject.

'Yes. It seemed as if the whole of London had gathered to watch. Such a splendid display of fireworks. Magnificent.'

'We could hear them from here. The servants assembled in the garden to catch a glimpse. The sky was quite lit up, so they said. Orange, yellow and violet flashes exploding in the sky. It sounded like fun.'

Her face did not look as if it had seen fun for quite some time.

'Well, I must go, but I will call again if I may. And Harriet… please take heart. He will be back again soon, I am sure.'

'Yes, of course he will. When the money has run out, no doubt.'

She decided to pay a visit to the bank the next day.

∼Twenty One∼
Tension and Lies

September, 1814

'Harriet! Come quickly! Percy is here!'

She had known he would eventually come. She had said all along, it would merely be a matter of time before he grew tired of Mary. She cast an eye over her complexion, plunging liberally into her pots and potions on the dressing table, dabbing at her face.

The trouble with Percy was he needed to take ownership of people; the thrill was in the chase. She was relieved that she had not followed them abroad, no doubt the young girl had run out of charm and novelty somewhere on the Continent and Percy's thoughts had turned longingly towards home.

Sara the maid was admitting Percy into the entrance hall. Harriet could hear him commenting on how cold it was for September. Regally she descended the steps and appeared in front of him, unruffled at the foot of the stairs.

John Westbrook, hearing voices, came out of the library and then, seeing his estranged son-in-law, ducked back inside.

'Well, Percy,' she said in a measured voice.

'Harriet. It is good to see you.'

'I'll ask Sara to bring some refreshments, I'm sure you are hungry.'

'Always,' he allowed with a wry smile.

She led him into the empty parlour, two chairs and a pack of playing cards left scattered, her mother having rapidly withdrawn to the nursery with Eliza, to keep Ianthe occupied.

Once they had settled into armchairs, tea and a platter of tarts placed on a small table before them, Harriet inclined her head politely, like a society hostess making small talk with an acquaintance.

'How was your tour?'

She was looking bonny, he thought, in the late stages of pregnancy. Although, if he looked closely he could see a heavy smattering of powder and was that rouge? Hastily applied, he surmised. It was not like Harriet to adorn herself in such a fashion.

A feeling of foreboding began to surface.

'France did not quite work out as anticipated so we moved on fairly quickly to Switzerland. The scenery was beautiful and Mary and I -'

'I'm so glad,' interjected Harriet swiftly, 'that you enjoyed your little holiday and I am sure that it did you much good. I hope you have returned with a clear head and a good heart. Did you leave your baggage in the hall? I will ring for Sara to take it upstairs.'

Her excitement rose. 'It's wonderful to have you back again, Percy. I hope we can put this whole episode behind us and make some plans.'

Love blazed from her eyes. His heart dropped like a stone. She thought he had come back to her. He swallowed.

'Harriet...I have come to cast myself on your mercy.'

After six weeks of pleasure, Percy, Mary and Claire had arrived back in London to the unhappy discovery that Harriet had withdrawn from the bank all the money that she and Percy owned. Their situation had worsened after they had driven round to Skinner Street. William Godwin, still outraged by their conduct, had refused to speak to them or admit them to the house. Mary, tired and nervy had broken out into a rash accompanied by a bout of sickness in the middle of the street.

Without money and with nowhere to stay, Percy had been persuaded to drive the trio to Chapel Street to pull upon Harriet's purse strings.

Percy stood up awkwardly, hands behind his back like a school boy in the headmaster's study.

'I was wondering if you could give me some money, Harriet. I have none, you see.'

'Money? You have come here for money?'

Her smile faded; beneath the cosmetic mask she turned white. Slowly, she rose from her chair and made her way to the window arch that overlooked the street.

She noted the waiting carriage below, the horse tossing its head impatiently. She peered inside, her sharp eyes glimpsing within, a puffed silk sleeve and the sheen of black hair across delicate shoulders.

'All spent in Switzerland?' Harriet suggested, turning from the window in anger.

There was a long pause.

Hearing the pitter-patter of Ianthe's footsteps overhead in the nursery, Percy remembered something. 'How is our darling babe? I brought her something from my travels.' He handed over a pretty wooden cow bell, tied with a green and gold ribbon, engraved with mountain peaks and edelweiss.

Harriet's mind began to work. Perhaps the sight of Ianthe would shake him from this monstrous obsession. 'I will call her downstairs presently and you may give her the gift yourself. I am sure she would be very happy to see you.'

'And I her. And forgive me, I have not yet asked how you are, Harriet? I mean -?' He gestured unhappily at her sizeable bump.

'All is well, thank you, Percy. In six weeks or less our second child will be with us.'

She gazed at him expressionless. 'I have a strong notion it will be a boy.'

'Do you think so? Really?'

In his sudden eagerness at the thought of an heir, he looked little more than a boy himself. Then he remembered his situation and his smile slipped.

'I can let you have thirty pounds,' said Harriet eventually, 'that will leave enough for Ianthe's needs, for the time being.'

'Thank you,' he said humbly, 'We…I am grateful.'

Gratitude, thought Harriet in despair. Was that all that was left between them?

October came and along with the cooling air came a distinctly chillier aspect to Harriet and Percy's relationship.

Harriet, clinging to the notion that Percy intended to free himself from Mary's enchantments, did everything she could to coax him from his entanglement.

Percy was sure that Harriet would eventually be persuaded to live alongside Mary and Claire and took every opportunity to impress on her how mutually rewarding the proposed living arrangements could be; languages to be learnt, poetry and philosophy to be debated; a creative circle in which she could learn to thrive. Apparently, Mary was beginning to show great promise as a writer and he thought perhaps Harriet could try her hand at a novel, too.

But always, Harriet dismissed him with hurt, pleading eyes.

With Harriet near to giving birth again, John Westbrook persuaded her to consult a lawyer with a view to forcing Percy to make financial arrangements. Percy was furious at this interference and he and Harriet had several heated arguments over her father's involvement.

After receiving several letters from Percy in which he grew ever more condescending towards the Westbrook family, Harriet was left with no choice than to break all contact and instruct Sara to say she was out, whenever Percy came to call.

Her pregnancy progressed peacefully into its last stages until one morning when she received a short letter from Percy. It had been several weeks since she had last heard from him and she was able to open it with a sense of calm.

The first few lines seemed to herald the promise of a more stable future. He began by acknowledging that Ianthe and his unborn child would always need a father figure, a protector by their side. Harriet experienced a surge of hope. Was it possible that finally he was coming to his senses? She read on.

Apparently, her husband hoped very much, that as Harriet did not wish to join him in his little community, she would have the sense to go and find herself a lover.

Presumably one who would provide for her and save him the trouble.

She thought he must be mad. She tore up the letter into tiny pieces, hurt beyond words that he should think so little of her.

'It is Mary, poisoning his mind against me,' she said to Eliza, 'but I will remain hopeful. Once the baby is born he will return. Mary may be counting on her intellect but I am the mother of his children.'

Several days later, Harriet's mother alarmed the household with a shriek that summoned them all. Gossip had travelled the half mile between Chapel Street and the lodging house where Percy and Mary had taken refuge; a torturous route via the servants, who had whispered amongst themselves across the fences and beneath the laundry lines. Finally, it had reached Ann Westbrook's ears.

Mary was expecting Percy's child.

*

Winter, 1815

Amid the grey gloom of January, Percy's irascible old grandfather, Sir Bysshe Shelley, who had collected a variety of wives, mistresses and children in his time, died and at last, Percy had the legal promise of money to ward off poverty's cold mantle.

Harriet and Percy now had two children. Charles had been born on the last day of November; a son and heir to the Shelley name and fortune. He was a sickly child and for the first month, Harriet was constantly by his side, nursing him until he began to show signs of improving health.

With Percy's departure, Harriet's life had shrunk to the four walls of her father's house, where she flitted uncertainly like a ghost in her own life.

As a deserted wife, she had brought a modicum of shame and uncertainty upon her family; her father, preoccupied with business affairs, avoided his club, her mother received no-one, preferring to stay safely in her drawing room with her books and embroidery. Only Eliza, the author of Harriet's existence, went about as normal, her head held as high as it had ever been.

On a wintry afternoon, with no snow but a lingering frost on the ground, Eliza persuaded Harriet to leave the house and accompany her on a walk. As of old, they gravitated towards Gunter's Tea Shop and slipped inside. Too cold for ices, Eliza ordered tea and pastries for them both.

An acquaintance of their mother passed by their table and nodded at Eliza, quickly averting her gaze when she recognized Harriet.

'It's lovely to be out,' Harriet ventured bravely to her sister.

Eliza planted her hands firmly on the table and looked at Harriet with a business-like air.

'Father tells me that legal proceedings are underway, regarding Percy's grandfather's settlement. In due course, you can expect to have a sum settled upon you with provision for the children, too, no doubt.' She paused delicately. 'And Father is also to give you an allowance. So, you see, Harriet, your financial woes at least, have been taken away.'

The waiter interrupted the conversation, bringing to the table a tower of pastries. Harriet felt faint at the thought of such sugared richness but Eliza boldly plunged her fork into a rich concoction. When she had finished her portion, she twirled her fork combatively in the air. A smear of cream adorned her bottom lip.

'Eat something Harriet, you are far too thin. Scrawny, almost.'

It was true, thought Harriet, observing her thin white wrists guiding her hands towards a plump fruit tart, glistening with syrup. Whatever she ate, and that was little of late she suddenly realised, was never enough to coax back the womanly curves of which she once had been so proud, and her estranged husband so greedy.

'I am trying to reconcile you, Harriet to your future. You must face it sooner or later. Do you have any plans?'

In truth, her one and only plan was to recover her husband. 'When I next see Percy, I will speak to him.'

'Speaking to Percy is not going to get you very far. The two of you have done nothing but speak. Mainly acrimoniously, it should be said.'

'Yes, but now things are different. Ianthe and Charles are to be christened at the end of the month and Mama has been persuaded to hold a dinner party which Percy has promised he will attend. The importance of the day might persuade him, once and for all, to return to the family fold.

'And then of course, his inheritance will make so much difference now. We always dreamed that when the money eventually came we would be able to purchase Nangtgwillt.'

At the mention of her Welsh paradise, Harriet's thoughts drifted to where her beloved house lay nestled amid oak, larch and fir, the melodic notes of the river splashing the banks with peaceful sighs.

Eliza's ugly tone cut brutally across her valley of dreams. 'Harriet, that was before the arrival of Mary Godwin.'

'Mary is a temporary confusion, I grant you. But –'

'No buts, my dear sister. Mary and Percy live together, for all the world to see, as man and wife and the best thing you can do is to take yourself and the children away. The countryside in Warwickshire is peaceful; Father knows a couple who would happily give you lodgings. It would be the ideal place; quiet and peaceful, somewhere to escape with Ianthe and Charles, away from the disgrace.

'With your husband running around with Mary and that

wretched Claire and now a baby on the way, surely you can see it would be for the best.'

Harriet could have sworn there was almost a note of self-satisfaction in her sister's voice. She looked closely at Eliza, discerning a sudden pleasing fattening of the cheeks, noticing her hair was curled into a softer style. It even looked as if she had attended to her complexion, resulting in a pearly-blushed appearance.

Harriet was thoughtful. All of Eliza's time and energy, previously spent on her, was now seemingly applied to herself. She looked again, noting the sparkle in her eyes. And now she recalled Eliza's frequent trips to Bath, and an occasion just before Christmas Day when a gentleman had called at Chapel Street and had been received by John and Ann Westbrook. Harriet had not been invited downstairs.

Harriet's thoughts sped rapidly. There had been a gentleman in Bath; in the background, hovering. He had been a dinner guest a few times and Eliza had also, by chance, she had always claimed, bumped into him at an exhibition. What had been his name?

'Mr Farthing Beauchamp,' she said, softly under her breath.

Eliza, her mouth filled with a second helping of pastry, almost choked.

'Really, Harriet, I can't think what you mean.'

But Harriet had seen the truth. Eliza had found herself an admirer. With a golden ladder of her own to ascend, she was now afraid Harriet would impede her progress.

*

Summer, 1815

Harriet paced the nursery relentlessly. The year seemed to be slipping from her grasp, When she looked back it seemed to her that throughout most of it, she had been plunged daily into emotional peaks and troughs as her hope for a future with Percy ebbed and flowed with each passing month.

The much-anticipated christening day of Ianthe and Charles had been disappointingly low-key. Percy had obediently attended the service at St George's in Hanover Square but had disappeared shortly after and the family dinner party had fizzled out in the face of Harriet's gloom.

Four weeks later Mary had given birth to a baby girl.

Harriet had barely had time to assimilate her feelings before the sad tidings had come that the child, weak and sickly had died.

As cautiously as winter had evolved into spring, Harriet and Percy had begun a ritual of afternoon meetings; sometimes walking in one of the parks, often meeting at Chapel Street so that Percy could spend time with Ianthe and Charles.

Eliza and her parents positively encouraged these meetings, believing that when the time came for issues dealing with custody and annuities to be settled, a friendly relationship between the estranged couple would be conducive to a smoother settlement.

For Harriet, their meetings had evolved into something quite different.

The meetings had begun a few weeks after the death of Mary and Percy's child. Harriet's company was balm to Percy's sorrow and the shadows that followed him from his new household in Windsor

Learning that Mary was quiet and withdrawn, she surmised Percy was lacking in creature comforts and ensured that in Chapel Street, plates of Percy's favourite nibbles were always available. She stopped chiding him for the way he was living his life and kept the tone of conversation neutral. She sought to amuse him, taking him back fondly to memories of their shared past and travels. Ianthe and Charles were also a great source of love and comfort to him at this time.

Percy confided in her. He told her that Mary's stepsister, Claire had left the household, seeking adventures of her own. Mr Hogg had recently arrived and was apparently smitten with Mary, seeking to distract her from her sorrows.

'He is busily wooing her with his efforts at love poetry,' Percy had said, smiling.

'And you are happy with this arrangement?' she had asked him, secretly aghast at how history seemed to repeat itself within Percy's circle, over and over.

'Poor Hogg, how he tries but his poetry is weak compared to mine.'

As the weeks wore on, Harriet and Percy found themselves bound closer together by the forthcoming publication of *Queen Mab* in a new monthly journal. The rejuvenation of his work, forged when they had enjoyed their happiest times, soothed the turbulence of the present.

Harriet almost forgot that when Percy left her he was returning to Mary; indeed, sometimes she was sure he stifled a tiny sigh when he realised the lateness of the hour and rose reluctantly to leave.

Now it was the day of publication and it was half past two when, checking her watch again, she heard the door knocker raised, letting fall the happiest sound, she thought. Moments later, Percy was climbing the stairs to the nursery, his eagerness surging with each footstep. He burst in, his eyes wild, his hair dishevelled. It was all she could do not to smooth away the lock that flopped over his forehead.

'I have it, Harriet!'

He waved a freshly-printed journal in her face.

'How you tease me, Percy. Let me see!'

She danced around, trying to wrest it from Percy's hold who held it aloft, laughing. The nursery was filled with the unfamiliar sound of adult laughter. Ianthe gazed at her parents solemnly.

'Come, sit at my feet, Harriet and I will read to you aloud. Like I used to,' said Percy softly.

It was the happiest hour she could remember for many a month. Charles was asleep in his crib but she drew Ianthe upon her knee and Harriet repeated some of the verses into the little girl's ear. '*Ianthe doth not sleep*…that is you, our darling girl.'

Not understanding but catching the swelling emotion in the nursery, Ianthe reached for her parents and they found themselves drawn into a long embrace. Harriet broke away first and gazed with longing at Percy. She was dismayed when he took a step back.

'I have been meaning to tell you, Harriet,' he said, in formal tones. The blaze of lightness had left him. He looked pallid.

'What is it, Percy? Are you ill?'

'Ill? No, not I…that is…'

Mary was ill. It was natural for him to be upset. But she could comfort him in this worrying time.

'Mary is again, with child,' he said, gazing at a speck of dust in the far reaches of the ceiling.

A long silence settled upon the room. From a long way off, she heard the door bang in the hallway behind him.

∽Twenty Two∾
Despair

January, 1816

'Mary has been delivered of a son,' said Percy, standing awkwardly on the threshold of the house in Chapel Street. He had been refused entry since the previous summer, when he had announced that Mary was pregnant once more.

Harriet stood by the front door in utter misery.

'Thank you for telling me,' she said tautly.

'I thought perhaps I could take Ianthe to see her brother –'

'Harriet?' called John Westbrook from the upstairs landing, 'is everything quite alright?'

'Yes, Papa, all is well. I am coming now.'

She shut the door on Percy with a heavy sigh. The confusing marital games that Percy insisted on playing, would be the death of her, she thought tiredly.

Even so, she was gladdened to hear him shouting from the steps outside, that he would call again tomorrow and in spite of her anger and humiliation, still her mind reached for an image of a gown in her wardrobe that he might find appealing.

She may not let him in tomorrow, or the next. But the threads that bound them together were strong and she knew she would not resist for long.

It took Harriet a month before she relented. With Mary busy with the baby, Percy had been left to his own devices so finally Harriet had taken pity on him and allowed him access to Ianthe and Charles in the nursery.

On a day in March he bounded in enthusiastically, clutching a bound copy of his latest poetry compilation which he presented to Harriet.

'*Alastor or The Spirit of Solitude*,' read Harriet, slowly. 'It does not much sound like you, Percy.'

Proud that he still solicited her opinion, she read on. The poem was the first long piece he had worked on since their separation and she thought she could detect a self-absorbed tone to this new work. Percy, the would-be-reformer, concerned with the suffering of his fellow human beings, seemed now to be pleading more for pity and understanding of himself than on behalf of others. He had moved from the political to the personal sphere.

Percy was watching her closely as she read.

'What do you think?'

'There are some lovely lyrical lines.'

She knew he was disappointed by her reaction. In truth, she was a little concerned. The poem sounded melancholy, without hope.

Percy was bouncing Charles on his knee robustly but the little boy, pale and thin, did not seem to be deriving any pleasure from his father's playfulness.

'Percy, Charles was sick this morning, please let him be.'

Disappointed, Percy handed him over. His eyes roamed the room distractedly. He coughed.

'Harriet, Mary and I –'

'Yes?' Her tone was wintry, like the frost and snow that lay outside beyond the windowpane, covering London in a pale, shimmering cloak. She set her shoulders firmly, expecting him to plead with her, once more, to sign the formal deed of separation which was something she still could not bring herself to do. Everybody thought she should have done it months ago; her father and Eliza simply couldn't understand what she was waiting for.

But it was something else he wanted that day.

'I was telling Mary about my early poems contained in the notebook you have. She has plans to put them into some kind of order, edit them perhaps to create an anthology.'

'The notebook is mine, Percy. You gave it to me.'

'Yes, but it is, after all, a body of my work.'

'It is mine,' she echoed, flatly, 'you owe me that much at least.'

The room filled with silence.

When the door knocker sounded below and Eliza's voice could be heard archly calling, Percy raised a spiteful smile.

'She is still being courted, then?'

Despite the tension in the room, Harriet smiled. Only Percy could have appreciated the rapid change that Eliza had undergone; the constant preening, the simpering voice and the silly, unbecoming giggle she had recently cultivated. He and Harriet had enjoyed many a wry laugh over the past months.

What Harriet had not divulged to Percy was how she and

the children were rarely allowed to meet with Eliza's beau and when they did, Mr Farthing Beachamp's eyes were generally full of embarrassment and unease.

'I must be off,' said Percy, enfolding Ianthe in a huge bear-hug. She squealed with pleasure.

'Not much wrong with this one, she has the constitution of an ox.'

Little Charles however had withdrawn to the chaise-longue and he turned his face away disinterestedly when Percy gently cuffed him on the chin to say goodbye.

'When are you next in town?' enquired Harriet as she put a gentle hand on Charles's forehead to reassure him.

'I will be back within a week. Another date has been set for the court hearing, for the matters relating to Grandfather's estate and Charles's inheritance.'

'And will you stay at Skinner Street, this time?' Harriet knew full well that he was still unwelcome at the Godwins.

'I shall be in my usual lodgings no doubt.'

'I may not see you,' said Harriet briskly, 'As you can see, Charles is not thriving as he should in the town air. We are going to stay with acquaintances in the countryside for a while.'

Percy's eyes glittered.

'But Harriet, you cannot be leaving town. Did you not receive a letter asking you to bring Charles to court?'

Harriet's father had finally organised lawyers to push for Percy to pay for the children's support. In retaliation, Percy had ordered his lawyers to counter sue for custody. Matters were further complicated due to Charles being Shelley's heir to his late grandfather's estate and title.

She frowned and dropped her eyes.

'I – well I did receive something. However, it is obvious

how poorly Charles is. How can he possibly attend in his condition?'

'Harriet, I am not the one that is asking. If you do not attend the hearing, the court will send round an official to bring Charles to the court. You will have to bring him.'

'Very well,' said Harriet after a long pause, 'but as soon as this matter is settled I must go to Warwickshire. Father and Eliza are most insistent.'

'Really?' said Percy, his eyebrow raised.

Harriet knew what he was thinking. Eliza, managing things yet again. But really, he was annoyed that he no longer had the power to manage her himself. But it would take just a few words from him and all that could be changed.

She knew only too well, that she and Percy were dancing around each other in dangerous circles. He was desperate to formalise their separation and she was anxious to prevent it. But sometimes, in the nursery hours, when the children took hold of Percy's heart and the family came together, she hoped and prayed that Percy would see sense and return to her.

*

Spring, 1816

In the cold misty aftermath of morning rain, Warwick Castle loomed over the River Avon. Through the window pane of the parlour, Harriet could see the sky lightening behind the turrets, bringing hope of a drier afternoon.

The Lavingtons' house was not as well-appointed as Chapel Street but it was comfortable, with fires in every room, a good plain-cook in residence and a housemaid. Mrs Lavington had not hired a nurse for the children; having none of her own, she was delighted to be able to attend to their needs herself.

Ianthe was seated on a rug in front of the fire and Mrs

Lavington was playing cat's cradle with the little girl, skeins of red wool looped between her fingers. Charles was playing methodically with wooden bricks, building a tower in the corner of the room. Harriet had to admit he was looking less pasty and with his newly found appetite for fresh milk, best bacon and farm eggs he was more robust, less prone to bouts of sickness than he had been in London.

She wondered if it was only the change in air that he was responding to, content and settled as he seemed in this non-combative household.

She pushed away the recent memory of little Charles in court, frightened by the strangers and their booming voices and sombre dress, not understanding the questions that were parried over his head, his eyes filling with tears at the air of spitefulness that pervaded the courtroom.

She shivered, watching her children with the Lavingtons, shaking away the feeling of doom that swept over her.

'Mama, goats!'

'Yes, dearest, we shall see them presently.'

'I want to feed them!'

'Yes, we shall feed them.'

She smiled at Ianthe distractedly. She had received a letter from Eliza that morning in which she had written that their mother was ill, demanding that Harriet return to Chapel Street to help nurse her. Without the children, of course.

Harriet took this to mean that Eliza was too busy gadding about with her beau to deal with household matters.

Summoning me as if I were a servant, thought Harriet. I can't leave the children. She ran her fingers through her hair. She had not bothered much with it since leaving London, it felt brittle to the touch.

Mr Lavington came in cheerily with a bundle of envelopes.

'The second post has arrived. I am sure it gets later every day. Let me see; two letters for me, one for you my dear and there is also one for you, Mrs Shelley.'

Her heart jumped when she recognized Percy's handwriting. She opened the sheet of paper eagerly, scanning the contents quickly.

He was at a loose end in London, the matters relating to his grandfather's estate were taking far longer than he had envisaged. His lodgings were dismal and everybody was away from the city. Mary was ensconced in Windsor.

He was lonely.

Percy. She had not seen him for five weeks since the time they had left London and now, more than ever she felt the magnet pull of his attraction.

'Is there bad news, Mrs Shelley?'

'As I mentioned this morning, my mother is rather unwell and Eliza feels I should return and lend a hand.'

'Oh, poor dear Ann, how dreadful.'

'Yes, she has the fever, Eliza says. I think I must pack and leave immediately. But the children...'

'Ianthe and Charles are fine with us,' said Mrs Lavington firmly.

'I could bring Ianthe and leave Charles,' said Harriet doubtfully.

'The children will stay here.' Mrs Lavington rose and clapped her hands. 'Let's all wrap up in our warm things and go and see the goats.'

Both children clustered around Mrs Lavington, Harriet quite forgotten. She went to pack, worriedly and a little guiltily. The Lavingtons were good and kind. Ianthe and Charles seemed to have settled well. And she need not be away from them for too long.

Eliza would be cross if she did not return to London. Her letter had been full of how their mother needed her fever kept at bay, cold cloths and cool drinks, her bedding changed daily. Harriet would certainly be able to lend a hand if she returned.

And once she had seen to her mother, there would be plenty of time to see Percy.

*

Stepping out of the coach, Harriet was surprised to see the return of snow on the rooftops. A cold flurry whirled around her as she hurried home. In Chapel Street, Harriet's mother greeted her wanly. She was in her bed, sitting propped up with half a dozen pillows, an opened book lying face down by her side, a fire roaring in the hearth.

There was no sign of fever.

'Mama. How are you?' Harriet dropped her cheek for a dry kiss.

'I am much better. It was good of you to come. You are looking bonnier than I have seen you for some time; the country air has had a happy effect. Do sit and read to me a while, it is tiresome sitting here all day.'

'Where is Eliza?' asked Harriet as she shrugged off her cloak and laid it across a chair.

'She is calling on Lady Brestwell.'

'I see.'

'She cannot be expected to stay here with me all day,' her mother said curtly, catching something in Harriet's tone. 'Tell me, dear, how are the little ones liking Warwick? Margaret Lavington will be spoiling them no doubt, but I dare say they deserve some treats and a little fun. How does Charles fare? Has his sickness improved?'

'Ianthe and Charles are very well,' said Harriet tiredly, picking up her mother's book.

As she read the text aloud, her thoughts darted wildly. If her mother was on the mend it would mean more time to spend with Percy. If she could just recreate some of the earlier happiness they had shared before the children had arrived, perhaps Percy would finally realise that the business with Mary was just an interlude, a mistake.

Later, after her mother had fallen asleep through the second chapter, she tiptoed from the chamber, back into her bedroom and unpacked her belongings. Snatching pen and paper, she sat down to write a hasty note to Percy telling him she had arrived back in London and to call upon her tomorrow.

He came eagerly the next morning. The household was quiet. Eliza, tired from the previous day's engagement was abed, as was Ann Westbrook. John Westbrook was attending a meeting at his bank. It was wash day and the servants were busy with the extra bed linen that had been required during Mrs Westbrook's illness.

Harriet received Percy in the parlour where he threw himself onto a chair with a petulant look upon his face.

'At long last, spring has seen fit to spread her cloak all around but still I feel nothing but a wintry discontent in my heart.'

'Really Percy, it is not even eleven o' clock and yet you seem already to have written off the entire day, or perhaps the whole season itself.'

Harriet's eyes were alight with mischief and Percy caught hold of himself and grinned.

'You are right, sweet girl. Why should I let one or two indifferent reviews of *Alastor* spoil the entire day. You were ever the most sensible part of me, Harriet. Come, let's take a walk so that we may feel cheered in each other's company.'

She had changed into an old gown found languishing in the back of the closet. It was violet, her favourite colour. Percy had once loved it, she remembered. She smoothed it over her figure; it still fitted her, even after the birth of the children.

'Harriet, let us not fight any more. Can we make a vow to put aside our differences; the battles over the children, the poetry notebook, money and Mary? Let us be friends. True friends.'

The spring air was sharp, enlivening. She felt herself unfolding like the flowers from their winter sleep. The trees were heavy with blossom, the young grass shoots standing proud on the lawns as they strolled along the pathway, like any husband and wife, she thought. For in law, that is what they were. She stole a glance at him and her heart melted with love.

Percy must have discerned her feelings. He slowed his habitual bouncing gait, and took her arm.

'I told my landlady that my wife may be visiting today,' her murmured softly into her ear.

She stiffened. Was that how he referred to Mary, these days?

He looked at her intently. 'My wife,' he repeated. He took her hand. His touch was electric. Her breath came in shallow gasps.

'Shall we?'

She realised their steps had changed direction. She held her head high, blushing as they walked with some urgency toward Percy's lodging house.

*

June 1816

'Eliza,' Harriet began, quietly.

235

'Ah, Harriet, there you are. How do you like my new frock? Is it not becoming? It is quite the latest thing.'

Her sister twirled her satin skirts in a girlish fashion. She looked faintly ridiculous thought Harriet. 'You look lovely,' she said.

'There is a ball tonight at Mrs Radford's in Piccadilly. I am to attend with Mr Farthing Beauchamp and his cousins who are visiting from Somerset.'

'It sounds lovely, Eliza. I am sure you will have the most marvellous time.'

'Did I tell you, I have been invited to their country estate? There is to be a house party at the end of the summer. Mother and Papa are most happy for me to go. I think Mama hopes…'

She stopped coyly.

'Sara!' she boomed imperiously. 'Where is that girl? She promised to fix my hair.'

'Mama has her mending a tear in one of the tablecloths. I could do it,' said Harriet humbly.

Eliza seated herself in front of the glass and Harriet gathered up a collection of combs and Eliza's hard-backed brush and began to work through her hair.

'Eliza, would you be able to speak to Papa on my behalf? He does not seem to fully comprehend what I need.'

'What you need?' said Eliza. She was not really listening, Harriet could tell, there was a faraway look in her eyes.

Harriet tried again in a firmer voice. 'I need a place to live, Eliza. I would like once more, to have my own home.'

'Why? Here you are, with a roof over your head, good meals and books to read. What more do you desire?' Eliza was perplexed.

'Well…' Harriet stopped. Percy of course was still viewed with great disfavour. It was too early to explain to her family that she and Percy were once more intimate and she wanted to be able to entertain him once more, as a wife. She had no words to make them understand how much she hoped that if she had her own rooms, when Ianthe and Charles eventually returned to London, she had every hope that they would be a family again.

'Harriet, as Percy will not pay anything, Papa is having to provide for the children's board with the Lavingtons. He cannot be expected to provide you with a home as well.'

'Why can't the children come back here to be with me? I am sure Papa could find somewhere small for us to live?' Harriet's lip began to quiver as she spoke of her children. Daily she yearned for them and daily she was told to leave them be, they were perfectly happy where they were.

'Charles is too sickly to live here in town, you know that. And you could not move away from us to live with them alone.'

'Why not?'

'It will not do, Harriet; a single woman living alone with two children. What will people think of that arrangement? The family is making the best of a bad situation. Please don't go upsetting everything again.'

'But what am I to do here, Eliza?'

With her hair finally looking as she wished, Eliza rose.

'I really don't know, Harriet. I suppose you must simply endeavour to make the best of things. Now I must dress so please leave, if you would be so kind.'

She swept past Harriet as if she were dismissing a maid.

Harriet took a deep breath. She would wait and bide her time. She would be twenty-one in August; an age when finally, she would be allowed to manage her own financial affairs. She swallowed, feeling, without warning, faint and a little sick from the unpleasant exchange with Eliza. She dashed to the cool depths of the bathroom and vomited.

～Twenty Three～
Drowning

London, summer 1816

Harriet prowled her bedroom restlessly. She had tidied everything she possibly could; her dresses and shoes were neatly ordered, the jars and bottles on her dressing table were standing in rows; she had even picked the hair and fluff free from her brushes.

She had written her daily letters to the children and they lay waiting to be taken downstairs in the hall, in readiness for the mail coach.

It was half past ten and she had nothing left to do. Her only hope was that Percy would call for her and they would go walking and then maybe afterwards…

She swallowed. Her mouth was dry all the time these days with a nasty lingering taste. She hoped she was not coming down with a summer cold.

Please come today, Percy she murmured under her breath.

It was over a week since she had last seen him. The previous weekend he had returned to Windsor to see Mary and baby William.

Most of the time, Harriet tried not to think of Mary. She wondered when Percy would end the dalliance and tell Mary that he had fallen back in love with his wife. Maybe he already had. It would not be too long before the community in Windsor was dismantled.

She hoped that Percy would be gentle with Mary; after all that had happened, she bore her no malice and she knew first-hand, how difficult it all was, especially when there were children to be considered. The madness with Mary had been one of Percy's experiments, Harriet concluded, and it had finally run its course.

Hearing the door-knocker she sprang up and took the stairs two at a time in her eagerness.

'Percy!'

'Harriet.'

She giggled up at him and then took a step back in response to his unbending stance.

'My, you look serious today.'

'Shall we walk for a while?'

She looked doubtfully up at the gloomy skies which threatened rain. 'Very well, but I must fetch my wrap. Considering it is summer, the day feels unpleasantly cool.'

They walked for a while in Green Park. The ground was wet from a recent downpour. Under the branched canopy of a chestnut tree, its leaves glossy with raindrops, they lingered. Harriet closed her eyes, awaiting his kiss.

Percy cleared his throat for what seemed like a long time. She felt his tension and a wave of expectation engulfed her. He was going to ask her to take him back.

'Oh Percy, my dearest, you know I will!'

There was a silence. Harriet wrenched her eyes open and looked into the depths of him. He looked confounded.

'Harriet, I was going to ask you not to miss me, when I leave tomorrow, rather, remain your former, happy self. It has been pleasant to see that side of you, these past weeks.'

She began to shiver violently. 'I'm not sure I understand, Percy. You are leaving?'

'Mary and I have decided we need a change of scenery. We leave for Switzerland tomorrow morning. Claire will travel with us as well, to help out with William.

'We have taken a villa just outside Geneva, on the shores of the lake, not far from where Lord Byron is staying. I am bound to be motivated to write more in his company, I have been very slack of late. I cannot think what I have been doing these past few months; dawdling here in town, not writing anything of note.

'Mary has noticed it of me also; a lack of appetite she has called it. Switzerland will be very fine at this time of year. If we are lucky we will be able to work in the mornings and we should be able to swim and sail after lunch.'

He noticed how quiet she was.

'Have you plans for the summer?' he asked politely after a while, 'I thought you may travel to Warwick to see the little ones.'

There was a rushing sound in her ears. She felt faint.

'I must not tarry today, Harriet, Mary has a list of things for me to fetch from the shops here in town, before we leave.'

He paused. 'Harriet…I do not like to keep asking but if you could think about signing the deed while we are away…?'

He had not even noticed her stricken face. But that was because he was not looking at her.

She struggled to find her voice. 'You obviously have a great deal to do. I won't trouble you any further, Percy.'

'Allow me to walk you back to Chapel Street.'

'If you must.'

All around beat the steady heart of the city; its streets full of horses, carriages, people, pedlars, paupers. A gang of urchins, no older than Ianthe, were weaving their way between the railings of the grand houses. Harriet watched glassy-eyed, wondering that her own heart continued to beat. Percy was rattling on beside her, excited at the prospect of travel.

It had all meant nothing to him. She meant nothing to him.

They had reached Chapel Street. She ran up the stairs to the front door and then turned but he had already walked on, reading from a piece of paper in his hand, absorbing Mary's requirements.

It took all of Harriet's strength to lift the door knocker before the world shimmered before her eyes. Sara had barely opened the door before Harriet tumbled inside, sliding to the floor with a muted sigh.

*

Her twenty-first birthday had come and gone, in an almost apologetic whisper, lost in the busy Westbrook household where the focus was now on Eliza's hopes and dreams. Ianthe and Charles had sent Harriet a birthday letter with colourful scrawls, flowers, hearts and kisses. Mrs Nugent had dispatched a charming letter from Dublin. Her parents and Eliza had presented her with a leather-bound journal and a velvet wrap strung with beads, amidst muted congratulations.

Sorrow lay like a shroud across her shoulders. The shock of Percy's departure at the height of summer had laid her low for a week. Her sickness had continued even after she had eventually risen from her bed and gone about what little daily business was still required of her. She made half-hearted attempts to visit the children in Warwick but the thought of the endless journey brought on more nausea; she took to writing regularly with promises of an autumn visit.

Tittle-tattle from Percy and Mary's villa in Switzerland had inevitably reached 23 Chapel Street, describing a rather more luxurious life than she would have expected, given their perennial lack of funds. Percy's idea of an egalitarian community these days, seemed to include a cook and servants. She thought back to their more honest, humble days in Edinburgh and York and felt once again, how Percy was betraying not just her but the better part of himself, the side of him that felt the need to champion the poor and downtrodden.

In the cooling month of September, Harriet was subjected to further shocks.

She heard, entirely innocently from Thomas Peacock, that Percy had been in England briefly, securing a pretty cottage in Marlow for himself and Mary for the autumn. She was shocked that he had not made any attempt to contact her or enquire about his children.

'Percy had written to me from Switzerland and asked me to look around for a suitable house for rent, near where I am staying,' Mr Peacock explained to Harriet, 'he and Mary seemed keen on the area when they last came to visit me. I must say I look forward to being able to spend some time with him when they return. Keep an eye on the old rascal,' he said awkwardly seeing Harriet's woebegone look.

'And you,' he said kindly, 'we must think about you. Get you started back on your studies. Maybe you could think about writing some poetry of your own? Or a novel? I gather

Mary is busy writing and there is absolutely no reason for you not to do likewise. I would be very happy to assist you, dear Harriet.'

She gave him an empty smile.

It had been two years since Percy's desertion and everyone expected her to be reconciled to the new order of things. But nobody knew of those recent private days in the early summer, when she and Percy had rekindled everything that had once been joyous between them. And now that he had once again cast her aside, she could not further humiliate herself by telling people. Besides, they simply would not believe her. They would accuse her of fantasising.

Almost as an afterthought, Thomas Peacock relayed some information. Harriet had, after all, been in Percy's thoughts; he had apparently signed his will whilst he was concluding the rental on the cottage, and he had left her a small legacy.

A small legacy.

When Thomas Peacock had left she let out a sigh. Percy had indeed left her a small legacy; one she had only come to realise in the past weeks.

She was pregnant again.

She had not the faintest idea how to explain it to her family and the rest of the world but something would have to be done very soon.

Before she could decide how to broach the delicate subject, matters came to the fore when Eliza came home unexpectedly early from a gathering one evening, to find Harriet being sick. Her face was one of abject horror when she divined the cause. Refusing to discuss it with Harriet, Eliza stalked downstairs into the parlour where her parents were sitting enjoying a quiet evening together.

Harriet shrank as she cowered on the stairs listening to

the raised voices, her father shouting, her mother shrieking before bursting into tears.

'Oh no…how could she?'

'To think that a daughter of mine can have been so stupid! And who on earth -?'

'Papa, she claims that Percy is the father.'

'Percy?' The girl is totally deluded. How can it possibly be Percy's?'

'Harriet insists it is Percy's.'

'John, you must demand he come and explain himself.'

'Mama, Harriet says he will deny it as he still infatuated with the blasted Godwin girl.'

'Of course it is not Percy's!'

'But he has called here rather often -'

'To enquire about his children, Ann! It's obvious he no longer has any regard for poor Harriet.'

Ann Westbrook let out a sob. 'In that case, things are far more serious with Harriet than we have realised. If she can possibly think it is Percy's baby, her mind must be going. Maybe it was caused by the shock of Percy having left her in the first place. Thank goodness poor dear Ianthe and Charles are no longer in her care.'

'You don't suppose Percy left her because she was showing signs of delusion?'

'I suppose it's possible. None of us have ever really understood what went on in that travesty of a marriage. Nor why he chose to leave her for somebody else.'

'What are we to do?'

'Mama, this puts us all in a terrible position…'

The voices dropped lower. She guessed they were discussing the implications of her situation with regard to Eliza's beau. Harriet sank onto the floor in misery.

Hearing footsteps eventually beating a path to her door she locked herself into her bedroom for the rest of the evening refusing both entry and reply to Eliza's persistent questions and demands.

On the following morning, she awoke to find her room bathed in the warm glow of sunshine. She realised she had not been out of the house for several days. She sat up cautiously. No nausea.

She dressed, rummaging at the back of the closet to find one of the loose dresses she had worn whilst pregnant with Charles, then let herself out of the front door as the servants began to fill the house with the muted sounds of early morning activity.

London was beautiful in the autumn light, a chilly nip in the air but the cobalt sky augured well for the day. Harriet walked with purpose determined not to waste time. She was so engrossed in her thoughts that she almost ran into a man walking in the opposite direction. She was at fault but he doffed his cap politely as he apologised. She looked closely at him.

'Why, Mr Alder, it is you! I have not seen you for many a year now, but still I would know you anywhere.'

'Miss Westbrook…begging your pardon, Mrs Shelley. You are up and about early this fine day. How are those beautiful children; Miss Ianthe and Master Charles?'

Suddenly she had tears in her eyes, remembering her untroubled days as a child, when Mr Alder had often been called to the house to attend to the old plumbing system and she had followed him around the house, chattering. He had always had time to listen. Over the years she had heard he had prospered, taking on apprentices, gradually overseeing a sizeable band of workers, becoming a successful business man who often dined with Mr Westbrook. He was a family friend, she considered and he had always had a soft spot for her.

She decided.

Mr Alder, realising he had stumbled into a situation, had drawn her to the side of the pavement by some railings and was handing her a laundered handkerchief.

She wiped her eyes.

'May I assist you in some way, Mrs Shelley? It pains me to see you distressed.'

'I need a place to stay, Mr Alder.'

He looked surprised but directed his thoughts to the problem without comment. 'Will you be staying alone? I understand that Mr Shelley is no longer around.'

'For now, yes. I am hoping that the children will eventually join me. But not yet. And I'm afraid I have little money.' Unconsciously she stroked her stomach.

He followed her gaze downwards and swallowed the lump that had formed in his throat.

'I might know of somewhere, I will make some enquiries. Could you meet with me this afternoon? I will write down the address.' He searched his pockets, finding a pencil stub and a scrap of paper, scribbled a couple of lines and folded it carefully as he passed it to her.

'I will be discreet,' he promised.

She managed to avoid Eliza and her mother by returning to the house before they were even bathed and dressed. She took a light luncheon in her bedroom, and while Eliza was entertaining in the drawing room that afternoon, she slipped out of the house once again.

Elizabeth Street was an unassuming backwater not far from Hyde Park, the house was quiet, just the landlady and the serving girl in residence. Harriet thought it was far enough away from Chapel Street to be able to give her parents back their dignity and good name. With the small allowance from her father, she would be able to manage the rent for a while. With this in mind she agreed terms and signed the register as Mrs Harriet Smith.

She set her jaw. Now she had somewhere to live quietly as her pregnancy advanced. Beyond that she had no plans for herself. Harriet and Mr Alder shook hands with the landlady and it was arranged that she would move the next day.

Having told the family her plans she went quietly upstairs to pack her things. The Westbrooks were bemused.

'Maybe it's for the best that she will no longer be under our roof. We do not have to worry about further explanations,' Eliza said delicately. 'I imagine that's her intention.'

'But surely, somebody will realise who she is?'

'Papa, she has had the sense to register under a false name. Nobody will know. She has told the landlady that her husband is abroad.'

'But is it entirely respectable?'

'I am sure the landlady keeps a decent enough house. Harriet will have ascertained that the room is clean and comfortable and she says she will have her meals prepared for her. If she keeps to herself then there will be no scandal.'

'But what to do about her state of mind? What if she is going mad?'

'I think she may be under a temporary delusion regarding Percy. As time goes on, she will come to her senses. I will ask Mr Alder to keep an eye on her,' her father said with a sigh, 'he has handled the situation well, I feel.'

'And of course, she can always visit here,' said Ann Westbrook.

'Under cover of darkness,' said Eliza tartly. 'We do have to consider what people will say as her pregnancy begins to show.'

'What have you said to Mr Farthing Beauchamp?' said her father anxiously.

'Merely that Harriet has gone to Warwick to spend time with the children. Later on, I will say that she has journeyed to friends in Wales. He will never know.'

'But what of the child when it is born?' said Ann Westbrook in despair.

'Perhaps,' said Eliza thoughtfully, 'it may not come to anything…Harriet is after all depressed and not in the best of health…sometimes these things can go wrong.'

'Harriet has had two safe and healthy pregnancies,' protested her mother, 'There is no reason to suppose this one should be any different. I should not like to think of anything bad befalling her.'

'That's as may be, but it does not answer the question about what to do with the pair of them after the birth.'

Nobody knew what else to say and presently the family drifted into dinner.

Harriet settled meekly into her new lodgings, doing her best not to become down-hearted. She walked on fine days in the parks and window-shopped when she was bored, doing her best to suppress thoughts of Ianthe's arms clinging to her waist and Charles staring up at her with his wide serious eyes.

It was several weeks before she felt brave enough to venture home. After thinking about it all morning, she thought perhaps she would walk to Chapel Street and visit Eliza and her mother for tea. Her sister had called on her regularly in the first week but it had been several days since she had last seen her; she seemed always to be busy.

She washed in the basin of warm water provided for her each day, dressed and did her hair carefully. It would not do to turn up looking dishevelled, the last time Eliza had come to her rooms, she had turned her nose up and had proclaimed her to be a real fright.

It was pleasant in the late summer breeze. She bought a bag of cherry buns from the baker across the road knowing they were Eliza's favourite and, ravenous in the open air, she couldn't help dipping into the bag and taking a bite, the delicious flavour flooding her mouth. Arriving at the top of Chapel Street, she was about to cross the road when a grand carriage pulled up outside the Westbrook residence.

She lowered her head and tried to peer from under her bonnet as she scurried past. Two over-dressed ladies were seated side-by-side, talking earnestly. Guests of Eliza's. Possibly some relatives of Mr Farthing Beauchamp, she guessed. Whoever they were, Eliza would not welcome her presence now. The front door of number 23 swung open and she ducked into the shadows.

Eliza swept down the stairs like an aging swan, in feathers and ridiculous over-puffed sleeves, followed by her mother, less mousy these days with her hair freshly done and powder on her cheeks. The footman jumped down and opened the carriage doors to admit them and then they were away, leaving the street quiet once more after their echoing laughter had died away.

Harriet wondered if Eliza would be getting married soon. She looked around, remembering how only five years ago she herself had skipped down those perfectly scrubbed stairs and practically flown around the corner to where Percy had been waiting, carriage at the ready. How adoringly he had looked at her as she had arrived, breathless and laughing, to whisk her away to a new life.

For we were always laughing, in the beginning, she thought, her heart so heavy she thought it might burst.

*

London, October 1816

'Mrs Smith? Are you in there? Is everything alright?'

Harriet stirred under the blankets. She had slept in again and had missed breakfast. The landlady, a kindly soul, had climbed the two flights of stairs to her attic room, with a bowl of soup, hoping to tempt her quiet and unassuming lodger to eat some lunch.

'Just one moment.'

She swung her legs awkwardly out of bed and fumbled around for her gown, wrapping it loosely around her body to disguise her protruding stomach.

'Can I get you some bread to go with that, Mrs Smith?'

'No thank you' said Harriet tiredly. She had barely any appetite.

'You should be eating more,' said the landlady kindly. Having had five children, she was not easily fooled.

'I suppose I should be,' Harriet, said defeated.

'A gentleman called for you at about ten o 'clock. Said he'd come by later.'

Even though Percy did not know where she was, Harriet never gave up hoping that one day he would knock on the door, break it down if he had to and rescue her once more. She had written to him after she had moved from Chapel Street, guardedly saying she was no longer under her father's roof but not disclosing her whereabouts. She told herself that if he wanted her he would find her.

During the autumn months, her spirits had been at their lowest. Daily, she tortured herself with imagined scenes from Percy's new life with Mary; their latest residence in Bath that Eliza had heard he and Mary had taken, where she imagined them both writing furiously, their son William playing contentedly at their feet. She sighed, feeling herself despised and hated.

'It was your friend, Mr Alder, I believe.'

Dear Mr Alder, he had not given up on her.

'Still no word from your husband?' said the landlady sympathetically. Mr Alder had told her that Harriet's husband was a soldier with the British East India Company, away overseas.

Harriet shook her head mutely.

'How about taking the air, Mrs Smith? It's fresh out but if you wrap up nice and warm it would do you good to get out and about.'

Sooty drifts of smoke clung like wet wool to the roof tops, obscuring the daylight as she stepped out into the gloom of Elizabeth Street. Along the way the chophouses gave forth heavy scents in the air that made her stomach churn. She turned her steps towards Green Park, a place she would always associate with the happier times she had known with Percy. She stroked her stomach, caressing her swollen belly, hidden in the folds of her cloak. She remembered a particular tree they had always been drawn to, chasing around its enormous trunk, ducking beneath the gnarled branches to kiss and hold each other.

Almost without realising it, her steps had led her to its shade.

And then she looked up and saw them.

Walking past her tree, *their* tree, were Percy and Mary, arm in arm. He was whispering into her ear and she was laughing, a rather deep, unattractive bellow. Just behind them trailed a nursemaid tending to William who was running unsteadily, giggling, his face lit up to be outside.

The picture of perfect family happiness. And then it was shattered by a monstrous cry which belatedly, Harriet realised came from her own mouth.

Percy and Mary stopped and turned, Percy locking his gaze onto hers. Mary's eyes filled with shame and then horror as the raging sound climbed to a crescendo.

Percy took an uncertain step towards her. 'Harriet?' he said, 'are you quite well?'

She had no words. She simply stood there, her wrath coursing through her body, her eyes wide and staring, baring her teeth, pulling her black cloak around her.

'What are you doing here?' she hissed.

'We have come down to London for a few days to try and see Mary's father. Harriet, I understand that you have left Chapel Street and are living on your own. Is that correct?'

She gave a shrieking laugh. 'Yes, Percy, I am all alone.'

Mary pulled Percy back into the family circle and took hold of William protectively.

'Mama,' whimpered the child, 'I'm scared.'

Harriet's face dropped. To think that she had frightened an innocent child. 'I'm sorry,' she whispered, 'I won't hurt you.'

But the little family was turning away in disgust.

'Please, Percy,' she said pleading with him to understand, 'I didn't mean any harm.'

He turned back for a moment but at the sight of her outstretched arms reaching towards him, he quickened the family's pace and they retreated into the distance.

London, November 1816

Mrs Smith had been distracted for weeks, thought the landlady. She came down each day even paler than usual. And there was something in Harriet's eyes that bothered her, a glassy element. She shook her head. She'd take her up a cup of tea before she got started on the meal.

An early supper was served late in the afternoon. Harriet took her seat by the fireside where she seemed to enjoy the pot roast prepared for her and even took a little sip of gin, the landlady noted approvingly. When she came back from the kitchen to refill her glass, Harriet had disappeared up to her room.

By ten o 'clock the house was quiet, the landlady falling asleep the moment her head touched the pillow, worn out from the rigours of the daily grind.

But beneath the sheets, Harriet was restless, her thoughts spiralling. She rose and sat on the side of the bed feeling giddy. Feeling the walls closing in on her she began to pull her clothes on.

The moon glided from behind the cloud, bathing the mean little room in light. She looked around dispassionately at the few possessions that allowed her to call it home. Her few gowns hung on the back of the door. A single pair of shoes. Her shawl. Hair brush, pins, powder and looking-glass placed carefully on the bureau beside her writing things. A few hair ribbons. In the cupboard, her most precious items; Percy's notebook filled with poems that she read each morning and her jewellery box, almost empty now; just one precious item wrapped carefully at the bottom.

She had sold nearly all the belongings she had originally brought with her from Chapel Street. Her father's allowance covered the rent but she paid extra for her meals and her washing. With the baby coming she had been doing what little she could to raise money for the future. Wherever that may be.

With a heavy heart, she forced her fears away, stood up and wrapped her cloak around her. Although the hour was late, she had it in mind to go into Hyde Park and take the air around the lake. She had done that often since that fateful day in Green Park, her days spent finding solace in watching other people's lives lived far more successfully than her own.

She hoped that by the time she reached the water, the bad thoughts would recede; they almost always did.

Unheard, she crept down the stairs, slipped the latch on the front door and let herself out into the dead of night.

∼Twenty Four∽
Guilt

Bath, December 1816

'What? WHAT? No, no, no.'

'Percy! Calm yourself, my love. What has happened?'

He stared at Mary wildly.

'Harriet,' he whispered.

'What now? She is demanding more money, I suppose in that pitiful way she has when she writes. As if you owe her anything. She is the one being difficult about the children. She is the one who made such a scene in the park and terrified William...'

'Quiet!' Percy said ferociously, brandishing a letter in her face.

'Please calm down, Percy, I implore you. That is Mr Hookham's handwriting, if I am not mistaken?'

'Yes', whispered Percy, his face draining. 'After that strange incident in the park I asked him to discover Harriet's whereabouts and to find out how Ianthe and Charles are. All I knew was that she had set up on her own, living under the name of Harriet Smith.

'For the life of me I could not understand why but I made no enquiries, thinking she was perhaps, simply seeking to gain my attention by these strange actions. But Mary, this is simply awful…'

He could not bring himself to say it.

Mary, receiving no sense from his words, snatched the sheet of paper and read for herself the lines contained therein. Not once but twice, being sure to divine their correct meaning.

A woman's body had been pulled from the Serpentine having apparently committed suicide. The body, which had been wearing a valuable turquoise ring on its finger, had been identified by a family friend, as being that of Mrs Harriet Smith.

Percy could scarcely breathe, remembering how he had given Harriet that ring, filled with love and hope for their future together. 'But why, why, why?' Percy muttered over and over, taking back the letter, his eyes wild. He read on.

'Apparently, her room had contained very little. She had left a letter addressed to Eliza, saying that she could no longer bear to live, along with the notebook of my poems that she would never be parted from.'

'Percy,' Mary said sharply, 'read the letter again. It says that Harriet was with child. She had lost her honour.'

Percy drew in his breath. Mary watched him closely. He seemed to be concentrating on some mysterious inner workings.

'With child?' He looked as if he might faint.

'Percy?'

'It's my fault.'

'What do you mean? The foolish girl got herself pregnant and whoever he is refused to stand by her. I can't understand how you can blame yourself for this tragic outcome.'

He could not utter the words that would damn him forever in her eyes.

'I abandoned her,' he said, finally.

'Dearest, that was two years ago. You cannot be blamed.'

'Drowned…in the Serpentine…poor, poor Harriet.'

He remembered back to five years previously, when he had rescued her from the school she had hated, the family who had not understood her. She had written of suicide then. But he had thought she had become a different person under his tutelage.

Saying nothing more he went upstairs to pack, his thoughts spinning out of control. Harriet. Pregnant. Drowned. What a confusion. He tried his best not to recall the heartbreak written on her face the last time he had seen her.

His unborn child…He told himself not to think of it.

He tried to clear his head. He needed to get to London, to wade through the tidal wave of lies and gossip and accusations, to concentrate solely on what was most important now: to ensure Ianthe and Charles, his children, would be handed over to him at the earliest possible time.

Percy woke from the nightmare, screaming. It had been the third time that week, the same dream. His entire body sinking like lead, his arms thrashing against the force of water that was slowly covering his head.

Emerging from underneath the sheets he pulled back the covers, at first unsure as to where he was. It was only when Mary sighed beside him that he realised he was in Bath. He soothed her back to sleep. He needed to be alone in the darkness to assemble his thoughts.

It had been two weeks since that terrible day he had learnt the news about Harriet, but the shock still engulfed him like the slap of a wave every time he thought about what had happened.

He had spent the time shuttling backwards and forwards between Bath and London. The fight for his children had begun as soon as he had learnt of Harriet's death and he had been informed that Eliza had in her possession a letter from Harriet, in which she expressed her firmest wish that Ianthe at least, should remain with her.

Barred from entering 23 Chapel Street, Percy had been reduced to bartering on the doorstep with his sister-in-law.

'I demand to see the letter, Eliza! Why should I believe you if you will not allow me that, at least?'

'If I show you the letter, will you agree to her request?'

'I will not. Ianthe is my daughter and belongs to me.'

'Then we shall meet in court, shall we not?'

He had grabbed at her arm.

'Just tell me, Eliza, why would Harriet not wish Ianthe to live with her own father? Why?'

'Percy, she did not go into detail. Obviously, Ianthe and I are close, I have cared for her during her short life whenever Harriet was indisposed or ill with all the worry you caused her.'

He had flinched.

'But if you were to ask me, I would imagine she would be reluctant to submit her daughter to a wandering life with Mary who no doubt she would be expected to call 'Mama,' alongside Mary's step-sister who seems to be quite happy to offer herself to any wandering poet who should chance across her path; yourself included, if the rumours are true.'

'You should be careful that I am not pressing a charge against you for slander.'

'That's as maybe. But you will not win the custody case. All we have to do is produce *Queen Mab* for the judge's edification and your ungodly beliefs and revolutionary way of life will be laid bare for all to see how you are completely unsuitable to bring up these children.'

'I will see you in court, Madam. I would like to meet the judge who believes a father has no right to raise his children.'

But the wobble in his voice had weakened the argument.

In limbo with regard to his children, other areas of his life were moving forward at a frenzied pace. Earlier that evening, he and Mary had taken an evening stroll around Bath, while the nursemaid put William to bed.

He had put his arm around her. 'Did you know of these rumours that surround us?'

'Well, yes. Apart from our own scandalous beginnings of course, Claire's behaviour has also been shameless; all that summer love with Byron and now she is hiding herself in lodgings almost on our doorstep, because she is with child.'

'Some people are saying it is my child.'

He saw Mary look at him, remembering nights on their sojourn abroad, when she had woken up in an empty bed with doors quietly closing along the corridor, muffled footsteps and laughter.

'Dear Mary,' he pressed on, 'I would like you very much, to be my wife.'

She had given a happy cry, stopping on the street to kiss him under cover of darkness.

'It will stop all the rumours if we are legally bound in matrimony. I cannot have clouds of gossip and bad feeling following me around if I am to go the courts for Ianthe and

Charles.'

He had stopped, searching his tired heart for flowers and romance. He saw her doing her best to smile up at him.

'I will happily be your wife, Percy. Let us not delay, dearest. I will come to London with you next week, to arrange things. A small wedding at St Mildred's, I think. I will sew something fine to wear; mauve perhaps. How I hope my father can be prevailed upon to attend. I will write to him tomorrow.

'Dearest, we will be married by the end of the year! And as the building work on the house in Marlow is almost finished, we can begin our lives afresh.'

They had kissed once more.

Marriage! Again! As the darkness of the night began to pale into a wintry dawn, Percy wrapped himself in a blanket and sat beneath the window seat looking out at the rooftops, wondering what kind of peaceful lives were lived beneath. He envied them. He did not believe he would ever find it for himself. Perhaps it was because he did not really know what it was he wanted.

He wondered if Harriet had at last found tranquillity. She had always craved it; even in the midst of their chaotic travels across the country, she had always been the one to pull him away from the centre of the storm into a calmer corner. He doubted if there were any such corners left in the world for him, now.

He thought of Harriet, her beauty washed away under the cold water, her exquisite eyes closed forever, her lustrous hair curling away like snakes. He needed to honour her. He moved to the table, dipped his pen and began to write.

In the bedchamber Mary stirred, awakened by the scratch of the nib on paper. She had been merely on the fringes of sleep, aroused by the conversation which swirled around her head. Marriage!

She hoped that by marrying Percy, her father would welcome them back into the heart of the family. She missed her father so much; her heart broke whenever she thought about the fact that he had never seen his grandson, William, who had been named for him.

But that would all change once she and Percy became a respectable couple, taking their place in society, the world beginning to acknowledge his extraordinary talent.

She on his arm, his wife and fellow writer, the woman he deserved after all he had suffered with Harriet. He had once cried on her shoulder, saying that marriage to Harriet was like being shackled to a corpse.

She shivered, remembering that pitiful creature in the park.

All traces of slumber had dispersed and she felt alert. She felt for her pencil and the scrawled pages on the floor beneath her side of the bed. She kept them close at hand. Often, she awoke from her dreams with fresh ideas tumbling from her thoughts; clarity for her novel that was slowly coming into being.

She had begun writing it during their sojourn in Switzerland. Enflamed by the recklessness of Percy and Lord Byron and the strange summer storms that had split the night sky, its shadowy shape had been pressing at the sides of her mind ever since. Her progeny.

It was as yet, a faceless monster that dragged itself mercilessly across the pages but it grew daily.

Her ears caught the sounds of sleepy mutterings, a cough and then a tiny cry. She listened, poised to rush to his side should the dreams intensify. Poor Percy and his terrible night terrors. She had lain awake these past weeks, listening to his crazed ramblings, horrified to hear him moaning, 'Harriet', her name ending on a whimper. More than once.

People had begun to speak more openly about Harriet, now that she was dead. Apparently, she had been involved with a soldier named Ryan, based at the Hyde Park barracks. Others claimed she was the mistress of a groom at the barrack stables, commonly supposed to have been Smith. There had to be some reason she had left Chapel Street. It was obvious she had moved to be nearer her lover – whoever he might have been.

The rotten devil had not even come forward since her death, which had been reported in the Times. Not under her real name, of course. Mrs Smith. She'd been in the water for days. If she hadn't been wearing her ring, doubtless her family would not have recognised her. Maybe that would have been for the best.

It was ridiculous for Percy to feel responsible in any way. Harriet had been most amiable towards all his plans for her when she had followed him from her father's house, all those years ago. She had been lucky to have Percy to educate her, to prise open her blank mind. Transforming her. That's how he had described the process of loving Harriet.

And when the love had faded and he had seen her for the pathetic creature she really was beneath the bone, still he had offered her a place with them, a way for her to live her life. But always she had demanded more than Percy could give her.

Finally drifting off to sleep once more, she felt the tug of something at the edges of her consciousness and she shivered as she crossed the icy plains of her dreams.

Awake in the dead hours, hearing Mary muttering in her sleep as if she were about to wake, Percy held his breath. Not yet. Let him have the dawn to himself. Harriet danced in his mind, and burnt through his soul.

The cold earth slept below... He was writing a poem, setting her free.

When he had finally finished, he heaved a great sigh. He could say goodbye to Harriet but...Ianthe and Charles? All the odds were stacked against him. He knew beyond a doubt, that he would not gain his children back.

But still, he thought he must fight, even if simply for the fact that one day they may know how he had fought for them. Loved them. Loved them still...

He closed his eyes. At least his William was tucked up in the room next door. He wondered when Mary would give him the gift of a brother or a sister. He would not want for playmates in the meantime, with Claire due to give birth any day.

A new life. A different community.

He hoped Harriet would not rise from her watery grave to haunt him.

Volume Four
Matt

∽Twenty Five∾
Echoes

February 2017

Matt sighed and shifted in his seat. He felt drained. He'd been up until 1.30 that morning cramming and judging from the looks of his classmates they'd been doing the same. Exam revision had taken on a more serious cast once university offers had been received.

He still couldn't quite believe that anybody actually wanted him, but as long as he passed his 'A' levels with decent grades it looked as though he would be going to Sheffield to study Journalism.

'Some people think that Percy Shelley had a hand in writing *Frankenstein*, isn't that right, Miss?'

Matt stifled a grin. Jai Khatri, the class know-all, living up to his reputation again.

His smile died away as the lesson moved on. Everybody seemed to be fixated on the ghoulish side to Frankenstein's monster, whereas it seemed to him to be just plain sad. Perhaps it was the mood he was in, all the stuff going on with Henrietta, but the creature's abandonment resonated.

He was still half-resisting the idea of Gemma taking Henrietta to New Zealand. Gemma had rather unreasonably, he'd thought, pointed out that he was planning to be in a different part of the country himself, for most of the time. But at least he would be able to jump on a train and come home for weekends. It was the distance he couldn't get his head around, unable to imagine Henrietta being on the other side of the world.

He couldn't really understand the attraction of living in New Zealand, although it always looked to be an amazing holiday destination on those grass-is-always-greener type television programmes that his mother loved and that he watched with one eye; sombre-clothed Brits exchanging dreary suburban towns for the white light of a perfectly lush antipodean landscape.

What if Gemma found somebody out there and wanted to stay permanently? He was listed on the birth certificate and he thought that gave him parental rights.

At the thought of birth certificates his mind shifted. His aunt was due to arrive that evening for a short visit and she was going to bring the family research with her. She seemed to be getting on quite well with it, so she had told his mother. He rather fancied the idea of becoming more involved. Since Henrietta's birth, his ideas of family and belonging were widening.

He shut down his thoughts and tuned back into the class discussion.

'Yes, Jai, that's certainly a school of thought that has its followers. There have been detailed comparisons made between the *Frankenstein* text and Shelley's own lyrical poetry and I believe there are similarities. And of course, Mary was extraordinarily young and inexperienced as a writer to have produced such a piece, which adds weight to those thoughts that she might have done it in collaboration with her husband.

'Now, everyone, as we're discussing this, I'm reminded that on Wednesday we're going to watch a film which is a dramatization of the famous trip to Switzerland that Percy and Mary took in 1816. It's important that you attend as there are themes contained within that will enrich your final reading of the novel.'

At the end of the day, as he was rummaging through his locker, Rich caught up with him, twirling his fingers around a red fidget spinner that one of the Year Sevens had left on the bus that morning

'These stupid things are so addictive.'

He watched, mesmerised as the toy spun wildly. He wondered what kind of fads his daughter would indulge in; whenever he imagined her, with her pale blue eyes and mop of wavy hair, she was a serious girl, quietly reading or writing.

Although lately in his dreams, Henrietta had taken on a tanned complexion and was often on a beach waving at him from somewhere far away.

'Hey, why don't you come round to mine? We could do some chemistry revision together.'

Matt shook his head, thinking about the brown envelope that had arrived yesterday from Gemma, containing legal forms about the move to New Zealand.

'I've got stuff to do,' he muttered at Rich, 'and my aunt's arriving later.'

'Ok. See you tomorrow.'

When he arrived home, having raided the fridge and

dodged his mother's optimistic questions about his day, he placed the envelope at the back of his bookshelf and tried to forget about it.

His mother wasn't sure where to put Diana's boxes of files and her notebook of family research, so it lay in the narrow hallway during the first evening.

At the start of the weekend, Matt woke early and did a couple of hours of revision in his room before going downstairs. There was no sign of his mother but she had been busy; the dining table had been extended to its full capacity and now housed Di's laptop and research. The heater had been switched on in addition to the slender radiator, and a comfortable glow filled the room, belying the small wintry garden lying beyond with its skeletal trees and bare borders.

Matt sat down with a bowl of cereal and began to look through the papers. After a while Di surfaced.

'Where's your mother?'

'I'm not sure.'

'Maybe she's keeping her distance. I know she's not keen on the idea of this family tree.'

They were engrossed in names and dates when Matt looked up to find Polly standing behind them. She gave a cryptic smile.

'How's it going, Di?'

'Matt's offered to help input stuff into this program. We're just getting things into some kind of order which has been a bit time consuming.'

'Where have you been, Mum?'

'Well, I've been up in the attic to look in the old trunk that belonged to our mother. I wondered if it had any family stuff in it that would be useful. Unfortunately it seemed practically empty but I did find this.'

She was holding something wrapped up in a piece of cloth. She placed it on the table, pulled the cloth open and drew out a red leather jewellery box. Nestled on its bed of white satin was a turquoise and diamond brooch with a tail piece shaped like a feather.

The sisters looked at each other.

'It's exquisite.'

'Have you ever seen it before?'

'Never.'

'It's not something Mum would have bought for herself. She definitely wasn't a brooch sort of person. Maybe it was a present from our father and she didn't want to get rid of it in case she hurt his feelings.'

'Shall I take it out?'

It was tactile. Matt turned it over and over in his hand.

'Do you think it's meant to be an arrow? Maybe it was a gift from a soldier to his sweetheart?'

'It doesn't look military, though, does it?'

'It would have some kind of insignia on it, wouldn't it?.'

'Could it have belonged to our grandmother, Olive and it's been passed down? It looks so old though. Older even than Victorian times, don't you think?'

'It might be valuable.'

'I wouldn't have thought so.'

'It's quite heavy. I bet it's worth something.'

'I can't believe it's been up in the loft for all these years. Why did Mum never say anything? She left you all the photos and me this trunk and I never thought to look inside.'

Di was fingering the brooch. Polly had a thought.

'Why don't we go into Ealing, there's an independent jeweller there, and they always seem to have old stuff on display? There might be somebody who could have a look at it.'

'Oh, yes, let's do that. Matt, are you going to come along?'

'I need to revise.'

'If you've got a spare five minutes, maybe you could bring the trunk downstairs while we're out.'

Polly drove the short journey from the house in West Acton to Ealing Broadway and drove into the multi-storey car park. Saturdays were always busy and it took a while to find a space and when they did, they were up on the rooftop.

Di went and stood by the roof barrier, watching the busy streets below while Polly scrabbled around in the boot for a shopping bag.

'I thought we'd pick up a couple of pizzas for lunch. A treat for Matt. I'll get some garlic bread, and coleslaw too.'

'How is Matt? I mean, really?' Di turned with a look of concern on her face.

'Difficult to tell. He's really pleased with his university offers and he's working hard. He's on course to get the grades he needs. But the whole business with Henrietta, the uncertainty is dragging him down.' Her voice tailed off uncertainly. 'If they go to New Zealand I honestly can't decide if that's the best or worst outcome.'

'How do you feel about Henrietta?'

'She's a lovely little thing. I don't know, I suppose I'm not allowing myself to get too involved. The trouble is, we only see her in dribs and drabs; it's like being given the crumbs from the table.'

'Has Edward met her?'

'I haven't asked.'

Di winced at her own tactlessness.

'Well, let's get to the jeweller's shop anyway.'

They made their way down to ground level through the jungle of concrete pillars, glad to leave the heaviness of the conversation behind.

The jeweller's shop was away from the main precinct, in a small side road, closed to traffic. It had a reassuring, old fashioned look, with not a trace of twenty-first century glittery bling in its bow-fronted windows.

Like one of those Regency arcade windows, thought Di.

They were the only customers. A grey-haired lady wearing a navy skirt and jacket appeared at the sound of the discreet bell that had sounded when they pushed opened the door.

'Good afternoon. Can I help?'

'Hello, yes. You have a sign in your window that says you do valuations? I wondered if you could have a look at this?'

The leather box, hastily cleaned from its shrouds of dust by Polly before leaving home, was placed on the glass counter top and opened.

'Mm. Very pretty.' The jeweller pulled an eye glass from her pocket.

'18 carat gold...rose cut diamonds and turquoise in a closed setting. This is late Georgian, maybe into the Regency period, I would guess. The loops at the back were for a ribbon or a chain to be attached, so it could also have been worn as a pendant.

'What's nice about this piece is that it hasn't been remodelled like so many others of the same era. When some of the more flamboyant styles went out of fashion in the Victorian era they were often melted down. You also have the original box which is wonderful.'

She paused. 'Are you looking to sell it?'

'No.' The sisters spoke in unison.

A family heirloom, I'm guessing, from that reaction. Well,

value-wise you are looking at roughly £8,000. Maybe ten for insurance.'

Polly and Di looked at each in astonishment.

'That's insane.'

Di had taken possession of the brooch and was staring at it, lost in private thoughts.

Through the glass-fronted door, a familiar figure caught Polly's attention. She followed it with her eyes: Gemma pushing the buggy with its hood up against the light drizzle that showered the streets, Henrietta sheltered beneath it, a flash of pink and yellow blanket trailing out at the side, bulging bags of shopping beneath and Gemma's mother walking alongside. A perfect family snapshot.

For a moment, she felt Matt's pain as she watched her granddaughter go by.

'Come on Di. Time to go.'

She turned to the jeweller with a tight smile. 'Thank you so much, you've been very helpful.'

'You're very welcome. Now that you know something about it, I hope you will enjoy wearing your brooch.'

She chuckled as the sisters looked askance.

'It's far too beautiful to sit in a box, wouldn't you agree? It needs to be enjoyed.'

On their slow walk back to the car, Polly turned to Di.

'I feel awkward about this. Mum can't have had any idea about what the brooch was worth or else she would have left it to both of us.'

'It's not about the money, Polly, I know you'll never sell it. I have a hunch that this has been passed down the family. You at least, have somebody to pass it onto.'

Matt had been up in the loft and had laboured hard to bring

the heavy old trunk downstairs. The sisters stood regarding its filthy tanned hide, several of its studs missing, the brass clasp and hinges showing a greenish tint in the harsh overhead light.

Matt had been thinking. 'We could make it into a coffee table,' he said, 'we'd just need to get some glass fitted for the top.'

'Maybe,' said his mother wrinkling her nose.

'No seriously, think about it. It would be a nice way of preserving it. It looks really old. It could be worth quite a lot.'

His mother raised her eyebrows at yet another unexpected revelation.

'Let's see what's inside,' Di said kneeling beside it and undoing the clasp.

Anticipation, after the day's surprising revelations, was high. When Matt's mother had discovered the jewellery box containing the brooch, she had only given the rest of the trunk a cursory examination in the darkness of the attic. Now they craned their heads eagerly as Di extended the top upwards, into the light.

There were a few headscarves that Polly and Di recognized as having belonged to their mother. Underneath one of these was a headless Barbie doll, resplendent in hot pants and matching tank top, which had belonged to Polly before being handed down to Di.

'If we find the head we could keep it for Henrietta,' Polly said feebly.

Other than that, the trunk was empty.

They looked at each other sheepishly.

'Well,' said Polly, 'that was a let-down. I thought there might be something to help with the family tree. Sorry, Di.'

'Well, never mind,' Di said heading for the table. Sitting

down she began to sift through the piles of family research.

Matt closed the lid once more. 'I'll put this in the garage, shall I?'

'Good idea, it will be out of our way there.'

'Though I might clean it up a bit,' he said, the idea of turning it into a small table still in his mind. 'Would you mind?'

'Ok love,' his mother said absently, having lost interest. 'I'm going to put the pizzas in the oven.'

Later in the afternoon Matt brought mugs of foaming cappuccino, made in the coffee maker Di had bought them for Christmas, to the dining table where Di was explaining the tree to Polly.

'Let me show you how far I've got. We start with Henrietta, the latest edition to our family.'

Matt smiled with pride at Henrietta's name at the very bottom of the branch.

His mother traced the typed names, moving up the page.

'There's us, then Mum and Dad.'

Auntie Di, I didn't know your middle name was Charlotte.'

'What a shame he has to go on the branch,' muttered Polly at the sight of Matt's father's name.

Matt nudged her. 'You wouldn't have me, though without him.'

'Matt, there's your Granny and Granddad. And Olive and Henry, our Granny and Granddad and as you can see, I've managed to go up further and found the parents of our grandparents.'

'Oh, right,' said Polly, interested now, 'so our grandmother's mother was called Maude. Maybe she was the owner of the brooch?'

'She was born in 1906 so probably not early enough. Didn't

the woman in the jewellers say around the early nineteenth century, she thought?'

'Maybe the brooch was second-hand?'

'I suppose it could have been.'

Di pulled a folder towards the middle of the table.

'These are the births, marriages and death certificates I've collected. They're interesting because apart from recording the event, they provide us with snippets of information which opens up more lines of enquiry.'

Matt and his mother sifted through the papers, each one neatly filed in its own plastic wallet.

'On her marriage certificate it says that Olive Medley was a journalist.'

'She was. I did a little digging around and discovered she worked for the Bristol Morning Herald until our mother was born. I found a few of her articles in the online archives. Quite a talented writer from what I could tell.'

'How far back in time do you think you can go?' asked Matt's mother.

'I'm not sure. I found out that registration came into being in 1837 which would still give us a decent family tree.'

'But when you come to a halt with official registration documents, it's not really the end, is it?' Matt said 'I saw a programme about it. You can go and find old church records, and look around gravestones and that sort of stuff. I could help you, Di, I think it could be quite a fun thing to do.'

'That would be great. We'll do it over the summer once your exams are over.'

Later that evening, Di went upstairs and knocked on Matt's bedroom door. He had his books spread out across the floor and his laptop open on his desk.

'I just came up to see how you're getting on. In general.'

'I'm keeping my head down and working to get my grades. Art is heavy but I'm enjoying the photography element. Chemistry is hard. I enjoy the lab work. Some of the English Lit is boring but I'm really enjoying *Frankenstein.*'

'Really? I've read it and I can't say I particularly liked it.'

'I like the story.' He hesitated. 'There are bits of it that remind me of myself.'

Di looked surprised. 'How do you mean?'

'Victor Frankenstein creates something and when it doesn't turn out as he expects it to, he abandons it.'

'But why would that remind you of yourself?'

'Well...' He stopped. 'I mean when Gemma told me she was pregnant. I didn't really get it, you know? I wanted it to all go away. But now I feel bad for thinking of Henrietta in that way. I wasn't seeing her as anything more than an inconvenient problem that I'd created.'

'Matt,' said Diana gently, 'that was a perfectly normal reaction to have had when you weren't expecting something like that to happen. And look at you now, standing by and being supportive. Loving, even. You sound like the opposite of Victor; you created something but in the light of that, you're taking responsibility.'

'I guess you could be right.'

'Diana!' his mother called up the stairs, 'I've poured you a glass of wine.'

'I'll leave you to it.' She closed the door gently.

Matt sat back, wondering. Was Gemma acting responsibly in wanting to take Henrietta to New Zealand? Was he being responsible in wanting to stop her? He forced his mind back to his revision where at least, he could be sure of providing more straightforward answers.

⟿Twenty Six⟾
Trunk

…We come now to the part in the novel where Victor tracks the monster to the iciest region of the world, a place as cold and desolate as Victor's heart…

Matt typed rapidly…*Was that frozen wasteland a metaphor for Victor's conscience? Or was the monster a representation of Victor's conscience?*

He paused, staring at the computer screen, turning things over in his mind. If Victor Frankenstein had been trying to improve the lot of mankind, seeking cures for illnesses, he would have been better understood.

He wondered about the Shelleys; Percy, the radical poet and Mary, the perfect literary companion. Had they written the novel together? What secret darkness had they shared?

He typed some more and didn't stir for another hour until hunger pangs began to distract him and he shut down his laptop and headed downstairs.

His mother was in the kitchen, seated at the table reading

an email from Di.

'Your aunt is asking if you've begun work on the trunk.'

'Not yet. The thing is -' he paused and turned to look at his mother, who sighed.

'Yes, Matt?' She relented and managed a rueful smile.

'You need your father's help, I suppose? That's fine; I thought you would.'

'Really?'

'Just make sure I'm not here when he comes to collect it.'

'You don't mind if I take it over there?'

'As long as you bring it back again.'

'Of course I will. It's a family heirloom, I get that. Hey, did you sort out the brooch?'

'I've got an additional form to fill out for the insurance. I thought of something last night; that brooch will be yours one day and then I guess, as your first-born, it will eventually belong to Henrietta.'

'That's so cool.'

As he entered his bedroom he thought his mother seemed to have turned a corner at long last.

'Are you sure your mother's ok with this?'

'Yes. Totally. I checked.'

'Well anyway, we should sort this out as quickly as possible.'

'It's ok Dad, Mum's gone to meet a friend for brunch. She'll be gone for ages.'

'Even so, Jessie's cooking for us, so let's get a shift on.'

As Matt climbed the stairs to get his rucksack and phone, he turned to see his father fidgeting in the hallway. Edward had been relaxed in the garage, probably still feeling it was his domain, where nothing had changed since his departure except the spaces where his tool boxes had once stood. Polly had gone a little crazy after he left and had quickly redecorated the whole house in a style that Matt could only describe as loud; lots of colour and asymmetric shapes that he suspected she now regretted. He caught his father staring at a sequence of purple half circles leading the eye up the stairs, and realised he felt the same way.

'What's jessie making for lunch?'

'Lasagne, I think. Come on, let's get going.'

In the afternoon his father led him outside to the log cabin at the end of the garden, which he used as a workshop in his spare time. He was thinking about taking up pottery, he told Matt, Jessie had sourced a second-hand potter's wheel and was looking for someone who could come to the house and give him some lessons.

His father, had certainly changed. Matt could only remember him as a workaholic whom he only really saw at weekends. He recalled his father fixing things around the house, the usual domestic DIY but Matt was surprised to discover he had this creative side to him. It must be due to Jessie's influence. She had set up one of the spare bedrooms as a sewing room where she did embroidery, knitting and sewing, selling clothes and cushions and knitwear on her website and at local craft markets.

Jessie was, his mother had once described, dripping acid, 'arty'. He cringed, remembering how his mother also occasionally added a 't' in front of it, which was unfair, he thought. Hopefully his mother would change her opinion over time, maybe once the two of them had met, Imagining the meeting he realised how awkward it would be and put it firmly out of his mind.

The other bedroom in the house was his, supposedly. It had been newly decorated in neutral colours and contained a bed, a chest of drawers, and a hand painted wardrobe which Jessie had found in the market. He had never actually stayed overnight but he thought he might at some stage. Maybe with Henrietta, if Gemma allowed it.

'Now I come to think of it, I do remember this old thing,' said his father thoughtfully. 'It's a beauty underneath all the grime. It's bound to be valuable. Are you sure your mother said you could mess around with it?' He looked worried.

'She's cool about it.'

'Have you got time? Your 'A' level Art exam is weeks away.'

'I'm prepared for that. Almost. And anyway, this will be relaxing.'

'Ok, if you're sure. What did you have in mind?'

'I've seen demonstrations on the internet where people have turned these kinds of trunks into glass-topped coffee-tables which can also be used for storage. I was thinking it might be nice eventually, to keep Auntie Di's family research folders inside it.'

'Well, firstly it needs a good clean.'

'What about measuring it for the glass?'

'One step at a time. I need to look into how best to convert it first. As it seems so old I'm a bit worried that we'll damage it.'

They spent the afternoon cleaning the silk interior with a gentle solution of bicarbonate of soda mixed with water. Matt found the process eased his mind. After a while he felt able to bring up the subject contained within the envelope from Gemma.

'What do you think I should do, Dad? About allowing Henrietta to go to New Zealand?'

His father sat back and considered.

'How far is Gemma into the process? What exactly does

she want you to sign? We might need to get you some legal advice if it's not clear.'

'Basically, Gemma's Dad is going to work in New Zealand for two years with his firm. Her mum and younger brother are all sorted with visas and stuff but I think Gemma has to apply for her own visa because she's got a child of her own.' He sighed. 'She wants me to write a letter giving permission for her to take Henrietta to New Zealand, which has to accompany her application. She's sent me a copy of the form she needs to fill in. There's probably some information with it, I didn't really look at it.'

'But will she be allowed in? What plans does she have?'

'She's been looking at catering courses. She thinks her aunt, who owns a restaurant, can sponsor her.'

'I guess you're worried the two years may turn into a longer period. Forever, even?'

'Yep.'

'It's a tough decision, Matt. All I can say to you is that once you're a parent you mostly try to put your children's best interests before your own.'

'That sounds harsh. Like my own feelings don't matter.'

'Parenthood is tricky at the best of times but when you're a young parent it probably seems even more daunting. Next time I see you, bring the stuff Gemma's sent you and we'll look at it together. There must be some kind of deadline?'

Matt shrugged.

His father touched his shoulder.

'We can deal with this. Look Matt, if Henrietta does go to New Zealand there's nothing to stop you from visiting. I'll pay for your ticket.'

'Really?'

'Yes. But for now, let's just take it step by step.'

His father stood up.

'I'm going back into the house to have a nice cold beer and see what Jessie wants to do this evening. Come in when you're ready.'

'I'll tidy up. And thanks for helping, Dad.'

The tanned hide of the trunk looked creased and faded in the overhead spotlights of the workshop. Matt wondered if they would ever be able to get it looking smart again. He went to close the lid of the trunk and then thought better of it. The freshly cleaned silk needed to dry out. In one of its corners the silk was wearing and he fingered it absently. He would ask Jessie if she could put some invisible stitches in to hold it together. His mum would never know. He shunted away the guilty feeling that darted through him.

His finger traced the outline of something unexpected in the lid of the trunk. He felt around and managed to extract it carefully from behind the silken lining. A sheet of paper, folded down into a tiny square, lines of swirly handwriting. Without unfolding it he could just make out the faded date '1865' in the top right-hand corner.

He was about to run into the house and show his father and then he stopped. He would show his mother first. He rooted around the shelves and found an old envelope and he tucked it in there for safe keeping. He locked the door behind him, surprised to find he felt almost happy.

He had allowed himself to consider the prospect of Henrietta going away and he hadn't fallen apart.

After a bite to eat with his father and Jessie, he left to go home. They had wanted him to stay and watch a movie but he had a ton of revision to do and he also wanted to catch up with his mother and share his discovery so he didn't linger.

Walking up the pathway and out onto the street, he turned

left to walk to Chiswick Park tube station. It was a bitter evening and he zipped the front of his puffa jacket right up to his chin.

The streets had that forlorn, end-of-weekend feeling. A group of girls walked towards him, mid-teens, with high-rise heels and made-up faces. One of them was puffing inexpertly on a roll-up and the sweet smell of cannabis clung to them as they passed by, shrieking casually to each other.

'I just got a text from Jamie! You've been up to stuff with Nathan, haven't you, Mia?'

'I have not!'

'Everyone knows you have! Jamie said everyone heard the two of you on the bathroom floor at his party…'

'Jamie's talking out of his arse, you hear me…'

The girl that was being accused had ferocious looking feather-brows but her lip was quivering as the pack turned on her. Matt felt a vague sympathy towards her until she suddenly let out a raucous laugh and started bragging about the variously sized male genitalia she had encountered. Playing to the crowd now, she confided that Nathan's had disappointed.

Matt kept his eyes fixed to the pavement until he was safely past.

An image of a fifteen-year-old Henrietta, shouting her mouth off and swigging from a can, emerged. He shuddered, calling to mind her baby softness and the sweetness of her smile. Maybe New Zealand wasn't such a bad idea, after all.

He wondered if that was an example of what his father would call a parental attitude.

After he'd let himself into the house, the first thing he did was retrieve the copy of Gemma's visa application form in its typed envelope and place it squarely in the middle of his desk, where it could no longer be avoided.

∼Twenty Seven∽
Changes

During the first part of the Easter holidays, Matt decided to spend two days in Bristol with Di before finally settling into his revision programme. Polly had been unable to get time off from her job in the dental surgery, so he travelled alone.

He had come bearing gifts; a bottle of Di's favourite New Zealand Sauvignon Blanc, a copy of Henrietta's birth certificate and most importantly, the slip of paper he had found in the trunk. He had sent her an image but it had been difficult for her to decipher on her phone screen.

'I'll just put the supper in the oven to warm it through. Call your mother and let her know you've arrived.'

Speaking to his mother from his mobile, Matt thought she sounded more animated than normal. The surgery had been busy all day, she said, she was glad to be home, sitting with her feet up watching a boxset with a takeaway. Tomorrow she was going to the library to collect a book that she'd ordered for book club.

'Book club? When did that happen?'

'Recently. It's one organised by the library, they meet once a month on a Tuesday night.'

'Cool. Anyway, I'll be back Wednesday afternoon.'

'Well, have a good time. Take care. Give Di my love.'

'Bye, Mum.'

On Saturday Di took Matt shopping at Cribbs Causeway. She wanted to treat him and also buy Henrietta something but she wasn't sure what.

Matt said anything would be nice.

'I suppose she has everything already?'

'Yep. Gemma's parents are loaded.'

'Well, we'll look for something special then.'

'Kind of a going-away present.'

Matt's voice was casual. She looked at him but he turned away.

'Let's sit down for a bit. We've been wandering for a couple of hours and I could do with a break.'

They found a café and Di ordered soup and sandwiches and Matt chose an all-day breakfast with a round of toast.

'Your mother hasn't mentioned Henrietta for a while. I do ask, but she's always non-committal.'

'I don't always feel comfortable talking about Henrietta with Mum. She always sounds annoyed.'

'She's just trying not to get too attached to Henrietta and failing dismally, I might add. So what is the situation?'

Matt sliced the rind from the bacon. 'So, yesterday I signed the form and enclosed a letter stating I'm happy for Gemma to take Henrietta away. Gemma deserves the chance of something new. And as Dad said, if I stand in their way I'll forever be the bad guy; Gemma would hate me and Henrietta might hate me too.'

'Tough on you, though.'

'Yep. But at least this way, Henrietta will always think well of me.'

'How could anyone not think well of you?' his aunt scoffed.

He gave a rueful grin, failing to see the sudden tears in her eyes. She blew her nose.

'Let's get going then, if you've finally finished that massive plate of food. I'll buy you that expensive sweatshirt, you were eyeing up, earlier. And let's find something for your mother, too.'

Late in the afternoon as they were passing a gift and stationery store Di paused outside the window. 'I still haven't found anything for Henrietta.'

Matt squeezed her arm.

'Yes, you have.' He pointed at a leather-bound book.

'*Welcome to The Latest Bud on The Tree,*' she read, '*Baby's Family History. Wallet for documents included.*'

'Oh, that's perfect; that is most definitely special. I'll be able to chart all our findings for her to read when she's older. They do it in different colours. What colour do you think?'

Matt insisted on a pale shade of violet.

That evening, ensconced in the two armchairs in front of the wood burner, the pages of family research spread out on the rug. Matt handed over the sheet of paper from the trunk. Di carefully took it and scanned it with a magnifying glass.

'Such terrible handwriting,' she moaned, 'Matt, grab my notepad and a pen from the drawer, please.'

She wrote down the words that were legible: *guinea fowl, Norfolk, sister, venison, gooseberries.*

She put it down after a while. Matt could tell she was disappointed.

'I can't make head nor tail of it. It almost looks like some kind of shopping list, or menu. I was hoping for something more substantial.'

'When I looked at it I thought that as Norfolk is mentioned a couple of times, that might be a clue. The preceding word I can't make out at all.'

'Maybe our origins lie in Norfolk? Which is odd because all the certificates show our family as being from Bristol. I suppose it could be way back down the line that I haven't yet reached.'

'Auntie Di, did you never want to move? To London, I mean, like Mum did?'

'Not really. With your mother there, I've always had a place to stay whenever I fancied a visit to the capital but I've never been tempted. Too expensive, for a start.'

'I love being a Londoner. I can't imagine living anywhere else.'

His aunt returned her gaze to the paper and squinted some more.

'Let me look at this again. If I stare at the writing long enough, I may eventually start recognising more words.'

Matt left her to it and spent the next hour upstairs with his chemistry revision. He was ready for a break when Di called up to him in excitement. 'I might have found something.'

He came down, switched the kettle on and stood beside her.

'I almost gave up with this. The last bit is like a travelogue across Britain: Norfolk, Wales, Carlisle. I had no idea that people in that era travelled quite so extensively. But I think I've found a link. Look.' Di waved a death certificate at him. 'This arrived last week. He's the father of Maude. Your three-times great-grandfather.'

'Tobias Isles, died 1939, Bristol' he read.

Di passed him the magnifying glass. 'Now look at the piece of paper.'

'What am I supposed to be looking at?'

She pointed out a word near the end of the passage of writing on the paper. 'Look, there; that word, I'm sure is '*Toby*.'

He squinted for quite a while before finally agreeing with her.

'So, this person Toby who is mentioned here – you think it's this Tobias Isles?'

'It must be.'

'What does it say about Toby?'

'I'm not sure. I can't really make it out. A couple of words that I can't read and then it says, '*Toby looks like*' and then more smudged words and I can't get any further.'

'It still doesn't help with the Norfolk business though.'

'No, it doesn't but what it does is to link this trunk to our family.'

'Probably more exciting than finding we're descended from a load of turkey-farmers,' grinned Matt and Di laughed as she went to phone Polly and give her an update.

*

Gemma's visa process might take a while she had told Matt, she was awaiting confirmation of her place on the cookery course in Auckland. Although she tried to hide it she had been bubbling with anticipation, breaking off on occasion when the hurt in his eyes became unavoidable.

Pressing his advantage, he had asked if he could have Henrietta to stay for a weekend. It would be the last chance he could really spend time with her before his exams. She had only paused for a couple of beats before agreeing. She would spend the weekend with Kay, she said.

Matt's mother opened the door when Gemma arrived,

earlier than expected.

She looked at Henrietta and the buggy overloaded with bags.

'Hi Gemma. That's a lot of stuff, I'd forgotten how much you'd be bringing. I'm sorry, I would have come and picked you up instead of you having to walk all that way.'

'That's alright. We do a lot of walking and she had a sleep in the buggy so she'll be nice and lively for you.'

Gemma shuffled into the hall, avoiding eye contact. Matt's mother always made her feel ill at ease.

'Where's Matt?'

'I've just sent him out to get a few groceries'

Gemma's eye caught sight of the vacuum cleaner, hastily unplugged at the socket and a tin of polish standing on the shelf above the hall mirror.

'I guess I'm a bit early. Anyway, this is her changing bag and there's a small fold up mat inside as well. This bag has got her clothes and wash stuff, and there are clean bottles and milk formula in there. Matt knows how to prepare it. There are jars of baby food in there too. I'll come back in an hour with Henrietta's car seat and also her bedding and the travel cot. Kay's brother's giving me a lift.'

She paused, her throat thickening.

'Gemma,' said Polly, taking pity on her, 'why don't you come in and have a cup of coffee?'

Gemma, relieved to delay the parting from Henrietta nodded her agreement.

'I've never left her overnight before.' She unbuckled Henrietta from her buggy and carrying her in her arms, followed Polly through into the kitchen. Henrietta sat on her mother's knee and watched intently as Polly took lids off canisters, opened the fridge and lifted the kettle to pour boiling water into mugs. Henrietta made a little 'ooh' sound as the steam rose into the air.

Polly and Gemma looked at her fondly and then slowly began to reassess each other as they sat side by side.

'Granny time,' said Gemma placing Henrietta into Polly's lap.

'I'm sure she'd much rather be with you for a bit longer,' protested Polly who would have preferred her rusty maternal skills not to be on display.

Henrietta turned her head to stare at her and blew a stream of little bubbles from her rosebud mouth. Gemma handed her a clean pink muslin. Polly dabbed cautiously at Henrietta's mouth. The baby blew again. Polly smiled into her face and then across at Gemma. She looked at her more closely, noticing the dark circles under her eyes and a gauntness around her mouth.

'How are the family settling in New Zealand? It must feel a bit strange for you, being on your own.'

To her dismay Gemma's eyes began to water.

'You should spend more time with us,' said Polly briskly, 'how about next weekend for Sunday lunch?'

Gemma smiled.

'Thank you. I'd like that.'

'So, New Zealand?' Polly's tone was encouraging.

'Everything's going really well out there. My mum says the house in North Shore is amazing, it's even got a pool. My dad's enjoying the job. He commutes by ferry into the city and it only takes about twenty minutes. Davy will be starting school soon so I'm sure he'll make new friends. We Skype all the time; Mum really misses Henrietta –'She tailed off. 'I'm sorry. I shouldn't have said that. You'll be missing her when we've gone.'

'Don't worry about it.'

'It's so awkward. Me and Matt splitting up, I mean and Henrietta in the middle.'

'It happens,' sighed Polly and then she surprised herself. 'I know I'm Matt's mother but I do understand, you know. It's hard to have to share your child when every decision you make means someone is going to get hurt.'

They exchanged a glance.

'I'm back,' shouted Matt from the hallway and then gave an exclamation as he slammed into the unexpected handle of the buggy. The two women were laughing as he entered the kitchen, Henrietta too, carried along on the waves of amusement, gurgling companionably on her grandmother's knee.

*

With his exams finally finished, Matt found the time to finish work on the trunk, giving the wooden struts a final layer of varnish. After it had dried his father brought the finished item back in his car.

'Give us a hand, Matt. I'm parked opposite.'

After they'd carried it through the hallway into the sitting room Matt was surprised at the sight of his mother appearing beside them, holding a tray of drinks.

'Sit down,' she said to Matt's father, placing the loaded tray onto the glass.

'Thanks, Polly, that's thoughtful of you.'

Polly inspected the trunk from all angles, expecting not to like it.

'Well? What do you think, Mum?'

The leather was buttery soft, gleaming in the sunlight from the windows. Matt had settled on a simple design; plain wooden feet to give it some height and a thin layer of glass, its smooth edges held in place with clear suction caps.

Underneath the glass, discreetly placed in the bottom left-hand corner, Matt had mounted the mysterious sheet of paper filled with its myriad scribbles.

'It's wonderful…beautiful. Oh, you've done such a good job, Matt. I'm so glad you didn't spray patterns on it or change its colour. I love it. Much better than having it shut away.'

'I wonder what Gran would say?'

'She would admire your ingenuity. Thank you, Edward for helping,' Polly added.

'I enjoyed the experience. Matt had all the ideas and he did all the work. I just provided the tools.'

They sat sipping their drinks.

'I hear you've told Matt you'll buy him a plane ticket to New Zealand next year.'

The caustic tone from the past few years had gone; she was just a mother, grateful to her child's father for doing a good deed.

'I thought he could take a holiday over there once he's broken up from university', said his father.

Seeing his mother droop at the prospect of him going away to university and then abroad, Matt changed the subject.

'Henrietta will be here soon. Dad, will you stay and see her?'

'I'd love to. It's been a while since I last saw her.'

'You'll have to catch her first, she whizzes about the room like a spinning top, now.'

His mother got up and started to move the more hazardous things out of the way.

'Let's not move the new coffee table. The sides are so soft, I'm sure she'll be fine.'

'We'll have to watch her like a hawk though, with that

glass.'

Later that evening Matt was in his room listening to music when his mother knocked and entered.

'It's been a good day.'

He looked up and smiled. She wandered around, fiddling with picture frames, picking up books from his shelves, turning them over thoughtfully and putting them back in the wrong places. Finally she went over to the window and stared out into the dusk.

Matt watched her. Maybe she had been upset about his father's visit after all. But he thought it had gone really well. It had been great seeing Henrietta clambering over both her grandparents, his father tickling her until her giggles reached the ceiling, his mother rescuing her, protectively stroking her curls.

He'd taken a few photographs which he would upload later. He thought he'd frame one for each of his parents. The one he'd taken of them both together, Henrietta sat between them, he'd keep for himself.

'You all right, Mum?'

'Just feeling a bit emotional. Your dad being here, and then the reappearance of the trunk.'

'I'm glad you like it.'

'I love it. And Henrietta seemed fascinated by it. She must have crawled around it for ten minutes with that excited smile on her face, like she was on a whole journey of her own. Anyway, I'll let you get on.'

She paused. 'You're not worrying about anything? Stupid question, really. What with waiting for you exam results and Henrietta going.'

'I'm alright, Mum.'

'I suppose, I just wanted to say I was proud of you.'

She closed the door softly on his surprised face.

~Twenty Eight~
Contemplation

July 2017

Polly and Di had been to a matinee in Shaftesbury Avenue and were enjoying post-theatre drinks before catching the tube back to West Acton. The early summer evening was warm and they had been lucky to find a pavement table under an awning. They watched the crowd swelling as more and more people were disgorged onto the street from the bowels of the nearby underground station, spending a pleasurable half hour evaluating what the women passing by were wearing.

Taking another sip, Polly put into words something that had been playing on her mind.

'I'd like you to have the trunk. It would look nice in your house.'

'I thought you loved it – Matt's done a great job on it.'

'Matt thought it should house the family research. And it would be fitting, after all the trunk is as much an heirloom as the brooch.'

'Polly,' said Di gently, 'Mum left the trunk and its contents to you. And I don't have a problem with that. When I've finished the family tree – if I ever do – I think it's a lovely idea to put all the papers and certificates inside. It's a beautiful thing and we can all enjoy it, but it belongs to you.'

Polly slowly nodded agreement.

'By the way, we're having a party for Henrietta's birthday at the house next month. It will also be a goodbye bash for her and Gemma.'

'Will there be many people?'

'I haven't counted. There'll be some of Matt and Gemma's friends. You of course. I'll invite a couple of friends and the neighbours. And Edward and Jessie.'

The sisters exchanged a glance.

'Quite,' said Di after a while. 'Of course you have to invite them both. Better to be civil, for Matt's sake.'

'And my own,' said Polly, firmly. 'I'm quite alright now. I really am. It just took a while to accept the fact that he'd moved on and wanted a divorce. Not exactly a big deal in this day and age, is it?'

'I was very worried about you, for a while, Pol.'

'I know. I'm sorry.'

'There were times when I wondered...well, if you were safe to be on your own.'

'Oh really, Di. It would never had come to that. I always had Matt to consider. And when all's said and done, there's a big old world out there and I've got a right to it as much as anyone.'

They sat silently, finishing the remains of their wine.

'Edward has taken up pottery,' said Polly after a long pause, 'Matt has some unidentifiable clay thing sitting on his desk.'

Di spluttered into her glass.

'Come on, ' said Polly rising, 'time to get back.'

They were still laughing as they descended the stairs into the tube station.

They were sprawled on old deckchairs in the garden. From several streets away, a church bell signalled that it was midday. Delicious smells of roast lamb and thyme filled the air. Matt and Di listened fondly to Polly humming as she peeled potatoes and scrubbed carrots.

'Your mum seems a lot happier,' said Di quietly.

'I think she is. She's going out more. She's a lot more chilled about stuff in general.'

'And what about you, Matt?'

'What could I possibly have to worry about?'

His aunt shot him a look at his flippant tone. He relented.

'I'm alright, honestly. I've accepted that Henrietta's flying off at the end of summer. Gemma has promised to Skype regularly and keep in touch. Can't really say anything else.'

'You just need to get good results in your 'A' levels now.'

'Yep. And to be honest, that thought does keep my mind off missing Henrietta. There's a lot to think about. But I'm in a good place, at the moment.'

'I'm very glad to hear it.'

'Have you done anything with that book you bought for Henrietta? There's not much time left to complete it before she goes.'

'I'm almost finished. I'm just waiting to see whether I can find any further information before I give it to her. Also, I wondered if you could take a photo of the trunk and Polly's brooch which would be good to include.'

'I'll take some photos tomorrow. I really hope she likes

the brooch when I eventually give it to her. When she's old enough, obviously. I want it to mean something to her.'

'It will do.'

'I still think it's a shame we don't know more about it, seeing as it's a family heirloom.'

'Well, we think it is.'

Di spotted a novel lying alongside Matt's chair.

'*Frankenstein*? Haven't you had enough of that by now?' She picked it up and gazed at the cover.

'I wanted to re-read the novel one last time. While I was doing my assignment I had this nagging thought that the story was about something entirely different but I couldn't pinpoint it. I did my best but the ideas ran away from me like water.'

'I remember always being surprised by the conclusion. I mean, I always thought Mary Shelley could have given it an ending which at least hinted at the promise of redemption for the monster.'

'That's what I wrote in my course work. The creature could surely have made a new life somewhere for itself. It makes no sense for him to end his life like that.'

'Perhaps the suicide was a selfless act? To stop himself doing further harm to innocent people?'

'Matt!' called his mother, rapping on the kitchen window, 'could you pop round to the corner shop and get some ice-cream to go with the pudding?'

Matt stood up and stretched.

He walked down the road, his head a riot of thoughts. Henrietta. The brooch. *Frankenstein* and suicide. A thought struck him.

Did the creature actually die? What if he changed his mind and found the desire to go off somewhere to live a better life?

He suddenly remembered the beginning of the year when his mother had inexplicably started locking the bathroom cabinet. Every time he'd had a headache he'd had to ask her for paracetamol instead of being able to help himself. And she'd taken away his razors and bought him an electric shaver. He'd been furious at the time, wondering why he was suddenly being treated like a child.

He went cold. She couldn't have thought he'd been harbouring suicidal thoughts over losing Gemma and Henrietta?

He shook the thought away. He would never have done something that drastic; it was in his nature to find a way forward.

∼Twenty Nine∽
Celebration

'That's a very pink-looking cake,' said Matt. He was in the kitchen where his mother and Gemma were cutting crusts off slices of bread to create neat triangular sandwiches. Trays of mini-sausages, quiche and pizza were standing by ready to go into the oven alongside a cheesy pasta dish that was Henrietta's current favourite thing to eat.

The birthday cake, iced in a soft pastel shade with edible silver glitter scattered on the top and a large fairy, standing in the middle, holding a big number '1' had pride of place on the counter.

'You are a clever girl, Gemma,' Polly said 'to have made that yourself. It looks so professional. That catering college in New Zealand is lucky to have you coming through their doors.'

Gemma smiled and then looked round in sudden anxiety. 'Where's Henrietta?'

'I left Di playing with her upstairs, trying to keep her

occupied. Matt, have you put the gazebo up?' Polly asked.

'No, I thought I'd wait until Dad arrives and then he can give me a hand. He won't be long, he just texted they were on their way.'

'Right,' said his mother crisply, 'well, I'll just go and get ready. Are you alright in here, Gemma? Just the trays to go into the oven when its warmed up and then we're all done.'

Matt watched her hurrying upstairs to put on the new outfit she had purchased, the result of a long shopping day spent with Gemma, who Matt had to admit, had been incredibly patient.

The shopping spree had been a direct result of his mother, having generously invited his father and Jessie to the summer birthday party that was shortly about to start in the overcast grey garden, waking up to the dawning realisation that she didn't have anything suitable to wear.

As well as her own outfit she had bought Gemma a dress and of course, Henrietta, the birthday girl, who was resplendent in palest rosebud yellow with matching shoes.

A whole year, thought Matt, gathering a handful of pink balloons to tie in bunches along the fence. He'd been a father for twelve months. Although it seemed as if Henrietta had been in his life forever.

Gemma, kitchen duties having been completed, came out onto the patio to help with the balloons. She placed Henrietta, wriggling in her arms onto a patch of grass.

'I can't believe it's been a year already,' she said, echoing Matt's thoughts, as she cut up pieces of string.

He smiled at her sadly. 'And what a year it's been.'

'Yes.' She paused. 'Next year we'll have her party on the beach.' She punched him playfully on the arm. Like a sister would do, he acknowledged silently.

'You'll be there, right?' she said, 'your dad said you'd be able to fly out next summer.'

'Try and keep me away.' He smiled at her. 'A party on the beach puts West Acton well and truly in the shade.'

'Of course it doesn't! These are Henrietta's roots and they're important.' She gave him a big smile. 'You see, I do listen to you occasionally, I know you've been looking into your family tree.'

They carried on walking alongside the fence, attaching balloons at intervals.

'What plans do you have for tomorrow?' she asked.

Henrietta would be staying with Matt overnight after the party and then spending the following day with her; her last before flying out to New Zealand. He planned to make the most of it, to ensure he gave his daughter enough love to last the year, until he would see her next.

'I'm not sure. I think Mum's got an idea.'

They smiled as Henrietta, who had been sitting quietly playing on the lawn, toddled over to them. Gemma scooped her up and covered her with kisses. Matt gave her a balloon to hold and she went quiet in Gemma's arms, gazing up at it solemnly.

The door-bell rang. 'Dad's here,' Matt called. Upstairs he could hear his mother squealing anxiously for Di to come and help with her zip, nicely delaying her entrance downstairs and the moment when she would have to say hello and how-are-you, to her ex-husband and his new partner.

'Just breathe,' Matt heard Di say to his mother. He raised his eyebrows and grinned at Gemma as they answered the door together.

'Aha, it's the birthday girl!' exclaimed Matt's father.

Henrietta gave him a grin as he wafted her high above his

head, through the house and into the garden.

'We need to get the gazebo up, Dad!'

'Ready when you are.'

Matt and Edward departed to do battle in the garden leaving Jessie standing alone in the hall.

'We bought some fizz.' Jessie indicated a box at her feet. 'I'm not sure where…'

'Let me give you a hand,' said Gemma kindly, leading the way into Polly's kitchen.

Seeing Jessie looking around in trepidation, Gemma made a decision.

'Let's crack one open,' she said firmly. Pouring drinks into two disposable glasses they clinked them together.

'Cheers. To the birthday girl and her mother.'

'Did I hear the sound of a cork popping?'

Polly glided in. She was wearing a pair of silk cream wide-legged trousers and a ruffled top. She looked very glamorous.

'Hello,' she said graciously to Jessie, 'I'm Polly. So glad you could come.'

'Thank you for inviting me.' She gestured to Polly's blouse. 'That's a gorgeous brooch; stunning turquoise. It looks very old.'

'Thank you. It's a family heirloom, actually.'

There was a long pause.

'Polly, have a drink,' said Gemma finally.

'And one for me,' said Di, entering the kitchen in a mad rush with her shirt buttoned up the wrong way, the tension dispersing amid the ensuing laughter.

The rain held off and the garden grew crowded. Kay and Jo and an assortment of Gemma's friends huddled around her, tearful in a corner after a few drinks while Polly paraded Henrietta to her friends who had not yet met her grandchild.

Matt took Alex, Rich and James down to the end of the garden where it was calm.

Necking bottles of lager, the boys were discussing a film they wanted to see that was due out at the end of the month.

'I'm up for that,' said Matt.

The boys looked at each other. It had been a long while since Matt had shown signs of wanting to socialise.

'You doing alright then?' Rich asked Matt cautiously.

Matt took a long swig. 'I don't know. Probably not. Sorry that I've been so weird this year. Everything's felt a bit crazy. Not that I'm wishing Henrietta didn't exist. But I think I just need to get back to some kind of normality again now.'

'How do you think you did in your exams?'

'I think I did enough to get to Uni. I hope I did, otherwise my mum will kill me.'

The boys grinned, familiar with Polly's up-and-down temperament.

'Hey everyone, we're going to do the cake, now! Matt, where are you?'

Matt's father had his camera ready as Matt held Henrietta in his arms and Gemma brought the flickering candle flame close.

After the crowd had sung, Matt gently urged Henrietta. 'Blow, sweetie. Blow as hard as you can. Mind your fingers… do it like this.'

He pursed his lips. Henrietta laughed.

'Make a wish, baby,' said Gemma and Henrietta surprised them all with a sudden gust of wind from her perfect rosebud mouth.

The flame died instantly and everyone burst into applause.

The presents had all been opened and were strewn across the garden. Treading carefully through assorted soft toys, books and building blocks, Matt's mother and some of her friends were moving around the lawn, collecting up the piles of pink and purple wrapping paper into a bin bag.

The boys had found a playlist on Matt's phone but the music wasn't playing; James was fiddling with the speakers with Matt's father supervising. Gemma and her friends were listening to Jessie's news about her new vintage stall that was opening in Camden Market the following month.

Matt and Di were alone, sitting in the front room, an array of cans, bottles and paper plates spread across the glass top of the coffee table.

Henrietta had unexpectedly fallen asleep in Matt's arms.

'Too much excitement,' said Di, stroking Henrietta's curls.

'Did you give Gemma the present for Henrietta? The family tree book?'

'I did. She cried a bit and said she would keep it somewhere safe for when she's older.'

'Mum showed her the brooch. She cried over that, too.'

Henrietta sighed in her sleep.

'Well,' said Di, 'I'm looking forward to tomorrow.'

They had planned a visit to a nearby stately home that was holding a fete.

'I wonder what made Mum decide we should go there? We haven't been there for years.'

'Apparently, she's thinking of becoming a volunteer guide and she wants to check out the place before she applies.'

Matt and Di shared a look. Polly had changed so much. Matt's thoughts see-sawed as they had so often, since he had become a father.

'My last day with Henrietta.' His shoulders slumped.

'Well,' said Di, 'let's make sure it's a memorable one.'

～Thirty～
Old Shadows, New Light

Wilding House was a privately owned stately home, just outside Ealing. The sun was high in the sky as Polly purchased the tickets at a specially erected toll booth, bunting and pennants fluttering all around.

'Free entry for the little one. A fiver each for the adults which includes entry to the House today.'

The ticket attendant gave Henrietta a green balloon, with a large letter 'W' on each side.

'We don't need a balloon. We've got loads left over from the party.'

The attendant looked surprised as Matt took it roughly from Henrietta's hand and made as if to release it into the sky. Seeing his daughter's lip begin to tremble, he sighed, and tied it begrudgingly onto the handle of the buggy.

His mother and Di exchanged a troubled glance. Overwrought at the significance of this final day with Henrietta, Matt's mood was swinging wildly. Guarding

Henrietta like a lion, he had snapped at them each time they had asked if they could have a turn pushing Henrietta so instead, they focussed their attention on finding a shady spot where they could sit and eat their picnic lunch.

Matt conceded this was a good idea. Henrietta, tired of being strapped in, was making her displeasure apparent with a slow rhythmic kicking against the edge of the buggy.

On the main flank of the lawn was a magnificent cedar tree. His mother spread rugs beneath its lower branches while Di unwrapped the food. 'Special pasta for you, sweetheart,' she crooned in Henrietta's direction.

After she had been given her two spoonfuls which she promptly spat out, Matt gave her a few tiny pieces of cheese which seemed to appease her. Di unwrapped rolls, sausages and hardboiled eggs while his mother poured coffee from a thermos flask into plastic cups.

Matt realised first what was happening. He had taken his eye off her for just one second as he'd turned to take the ham roll that Di was offering him.

When he turned, Henrietta was hurtling down the hill, at top speed, half-running and half-bouncing in the direction of the ornamental lake that was directly in her path.

'Henrietta!' called Matt, springing to his feet.

She was quicker than he could have possibly imagined.

'Henrietta! Come back here, now!'

His mother and Di stood rooted to the spot in fear, shading their eyes, calling her back as Matt swiftly closed in on the little girl. As the waters came closer, he saw Henrietta's arms stretched towards the koi carp that were darting underneath the watery surface like floating jewels.

'ETTIE! Stop right now!'

He flung himself down on her in a rugby tackle, catching

her by the ankles. Fellow-picnickers laughed and applauded him as he held her aloft like a trophy.

She beamed as he swung her back down, pressing her close to his chest.

'-ter' she said muffled, 'w-a-ter'.

He turned her face towards him and stared at her. 'Did you just say your first word?'

Grinning, he carried her back and sat her down firmly on his knees. His mother and aunt clustered around.

'Water? Are you sure that's what she said?'

'Definitely. She's so clever, aren't you, sweetheart?'

'And why Ettie, all of a sudden?'

'There wasn't time to say Henrietta.'

'It suits her,' said his mother.

Henrietta, her gaze darting back and forth towards the water a few times, turned her attention back to the food and Matt finally began to relax, his inner pressure released at last.

After lunch they walked across the crowded lawns, packed with stalls and entertainers. They watched a troop of jugglers and Matt tried and failed to hook a duck to win a teddy bear. Henrietta had three rides on the merry-go-round, Matt watching proudly as she rode her chariot, one arm placed out in front, the other waving a plastic wand that Polly had bought her, like a fairy weaving a spell.

As Matt finally lifted her from the ride, his mother tapped him on the shoulder. 'I've just seen a Volunteers' Tent over there. I thought I'd wander over and have a chat.'

'What are you waiting for then?'

'Yes, Polly, go and make yourself known. Matt and I will go into the house now and maybe we'll see you in there when you've finished. Good luck.'

The old house was cool and quiet, most of the visitors

preferring to be out in the sunshine. Their footsteps echoed in the great marble hallway. They stopped to admire the gentle curves of the mantelpiece surrounding the rococo fireplace that was the focal point of the entrance hall. As she was grumbling a little, Matt strapped Henrietta back into her pushchair so that she could have a nap. Instantly she was asleep.

Ignoring the tour map, they chose to wander at random, content to discover rooms and passages wherever their steps took them.

'She doesn't seem too traumatised by the earlier incident,' murmured Di peering into the buggy as they took a turn down a panelled corridor.

'That's more than can be said for the parent,' Matt said indignantly, and then smiled. 'I sounded just like Dad.'

Di said, 'That's not a bad thing. I've always considered Edward to be one of the good guys. Even your mother would admit that, if she was really pushed. Speaking of your mother, I hope this volunteering works out for her, I think it's something she'd enjoy. Matt?'

He'd stopped in his tracks. They were entering a large exhibition space where a banner announced: FRANKENSTEIN - *ORIGINS OF A MONSTER: Reading Between the Lines on A Dark and Stormy Night.* A printed card informed them that various items were currently on display, loaned from various galleries.

'How amazing! Mum must have known this was here. She knew I'd be interested.'

'That's a good parent for you; they always have their children in mind. Even when they're grown up like you are.'

'Henrietta will always be in my mind.' He gazed protectively into the buggy. 'Let's see how much of this we can take in before she wakes.'

A dramatic model of the villa Diodati set the scene, lightning bolts poised over the roof and cardboard ruffled waves illustrating the storm across Lake Geneva.

Inside the house figures were posed huddled in one of the rooms in front of a fire, their arms in various storytelling poses. *The birth of the famous tale* read the caption, *Mary is seated in the centre of the circle, next to Percy Bysshe and opposite Lord Byron. Scientists have since put forward the theory that the violent storm was a consequence of The Year Without a Summer, with severe climate changes occurring in 1816.*

'Imagine if they'd gone in the spring,' said Di, caustically. Matt dug her in the ribs.

Matt pushed the buggy on, stopping for a while to stare at a collection of papers fanned out on a velvet cloth, Mary's scrawl boldly traversing the surfaces. Beside was a pen, one she had apparently used in her letter writing during her later years.

In the middle of the exhibition was a reproduction of the famous portrait of Mary, painted when she had reached middle-age. Her sombre gaze seemed to follow Matt around, reproving him in some way. He grimaced. Henrietta had woken up, he suddenly noticed, and was staring silently up at the portrait.

'You know what I always hated about the novel?' said Matt suddenly. 'The creature was never even considered worthy to be given a name. As if abandonment wasn't enough.'

'I guess Victor always felt that if he didn't put his name to it the world need never acknowledge his own errors of judgement.'

Matt walked slowly onwards into the section about Percy

Shelley. There was a picture and description of his birth place and family home, Field Place and references to his school days at the Syon Academy, Eton and Oxford.

Spread around were drafts of letters, pages of verse, copies of books, a map showing where he had drowned in his boat in the Gulf of Spezia and his guitar.

His portrait, a copy of the famous one in the National Portrait Gallery, by Amelia Curran, had been hung in the centre.

Matt stood and stared at it for a while. Amazing blue eyes, he noticed.

He looked down and saw Henrietta fidgeting violently in her seat, twisting her head around, emitting sounds of distress.

Di came up behind him. 'I didn't realise that Mary wasn't married to Percy when she started writing. Apparently she was his second wife.'

'Really?' said Matt, not really listening, his attention on Henrietta.

'What's wrong with Henrietta? She looks upset.'

'Something's spooked her. She's been on the verge of tears for the last ten minutes.'

Di laid her hand on Henrietta's blazing cheek. 'Hush now, sweetheart.'

Henrietta gazed up at her.

'I must say, Matt, I've enjoyed looking around here, I can understand your fascination a bit more.'

'It's such a shame this is the last day; the exhibition's being moved on tomorrow.'

'There's just one more exhibit that we haven't seen. Shall we go and have a quick look?'

Matt looked down at his daughter. Her face was creased.

He knew what was coming.

'If I don't get Henrietta out of here quickly she's going to scream the place down. I think we should go back outside.'

'We could go and get some ice-cream, couldn't we? Do you think she's allowed ice-cream?'

'I think that would be a good idea. As long as we don't tell Gemma.'

Relieved to leave the gloom they walked out, blinking in the bright shafts of sunlight as they headed across the tented lawns to find Polly.

If Henrietta had stayed quiet for just a moment longer, Matt would have turned the corner and come face to face with the final exhibit, almost hidden in the far corner. The smallest case in the exhibition, it contained a card with a few lines: *Harriet Westbrook, the poet's first wife.*

There was no grand portrait, nor exhibits of her writing; nothing save a map of the Serpentine in Hyde Park where she had drowned, and the unique turquoise betrothal ring that Percy had given her and which she had worn until the day she had died.

Recently a sheet of paper taken from an order book from Percy's jeweller had come to light, a coloured sketch of a commission for a brooch to match the ring, in turquoise and diamond with delicate feathering, giving the appearance of a quill.

There had been speculation that it had been a companion-piece to the ring and that perhaps Percy had presented it to Harriet, his muse during his blossoming years as a poet.

'*However*', read the accompanying notice, '*the existence of such a piece is hotly refuted. There was no sign of it in Harriet's remaining possessions after her death, and as it would have been something that, no doubt she would have wanted to pass on to her little daughter, Ianthe, one must assume that no such brooch ever existed.'*

～Thirty One～
Descendants

February 2018

From his room at the top of the student accommodation block, Matt had pulled back the blinds to reveal the night-time landscape outside. Restless, unable to sleep even though it was past midnight, he held his breath as he watched a bat flying beneath the crescent moon.

Since logging off from his Skype session with Gemma he'd been sat mainly staring at his blank-faced laptop. An hour ago he'd watched transfixed as Gemma had held Henrietta on her knee waving excitedly across the miles at him.

'Da-Da', she'd said over and over, showing a mouth full of teeth, most of which were new to his eyes.

His mobile phone purred softly. He looked at the screen and answered. 'Hello, Di. You're up late.'

'I wondered if you were still awake. I know you sometimes speak to Gemma at this time. How's the course going?'

'Hard work but I'm having fun.'

'Have you got time for a family update?'

He did have time and it would take his mind off his sadness.

'Remember Tobias? Also known as Toby? I've managed to find his father, Thomas and his grandparents, Catherine and Richard Isles.'

'Did you find out any details?'

'I looked them up on the 1841 census. They were all living in East Dean, in Gloucestershire.

'East Dean? Where exactly is that?'

'It's in the Forest of Dean. They were from somewhere called Cinderford. Richard was a school master, quite rare in those times. He must have just been teaching reading and writing, I suspect. Thomas is on the census as well, aged two.

'At the time of the census, Catherine is shown as being twenty, but apparently they used to round the ages down to the nearest five years. She would have been born somewhere between 1816 and 1820. Close to the period the jeweller mentioned. I bet the brooch was hers. Or her mother's.'

'1816,' said Matt, staring into the past, 'it seems so long ago.'

'But it's not really, not when you think about it. Count how many people are stretched in that line from you to Catherine – only eight.'

'Well, when you put it like that, I guess not.'

'On the 1871 census they all appear again, this time in Bristol. Tobias's father, Thomas is listed as being a bank clerk. Catherine is there too and her husband Richard, both aged around fifty.'

'Sounds like you're on to something.'

'Yes, I thought so. But according to Tobias's birth certificate,

Catherine's maiden name was Smith. Apparently, it's every genealogist's nightmare to be descended from a Smith. Especially as there would be no official documents that early on. So, on a whim, really, I took a trip out to Cinderford.

'I thought I might have been able to look through parish records for Catherine's parents but they've long since been transferred to the county archives. I did find, in a graveyard, a number of Smiths but a lot of headstones were starting to disintegrate and it was impossible to read most of them.'

She groaned. 'Smith. Of all things. I've made a few enquiries in Gloucester where any records would have been stored but they've come up with nothing relevant so far.'

Matt remembered the sheet of paper written in an unknown hand. *Toby looks like.* Who had Toby resembled? They would probably never know.

'You did your best, Di.'

'Yes. I'm not even sure how much it matters, I was just curious to see how far back I could take the search. I suppose it became a bit of an obsession for a while.'

She yawned. 'Perhaps I'll have another go at the paternal line, sometime. But my hunch is still that the brooch passed down the maternal line.'

They said goodnight. He was tired too but his mind was overflowing. He stared at his laptop screen. It was oppressively black.

To hell with it. He'd stay awake and finish his essay on media law. He had a free period in the morning.

He logged back on. Try as he might, thoughts of Henrietta crowded his mind like locked prisoners begging for escape. He remembered her at the fete riding the white swan, her sadness when the balloon had escaped into the sky, her glorious laugh as she had her first ever taste of ice-cream on the way home.

He thought again of the last time he'd seen her, at the airport, in her tiny pink leggings and matching cardigan, with a t-shirt he' given her that had 'Daddy's Girl' printed across the middle. At the sight of her baby waves from across the barrier, he'd had to turn away

He looked downwards. His fingers were flexing in an unusual way, almost pulsing with energy.

He wondered if he'd strained them playing too much guitar the other night in one of the student bars. He was part of a band now and much of his spare time was spent rehearsing. His fingers stroked the keyboard. Any minute now and he would start to get back into the essay.

He typed. Words filled the screen. '*Dispatches to a Distant Daughter.*' He stared at them in bewilderment.

After Henrietta had gone his mother had persuaded him to have a couple of sessions with a counsellor. He hadn't wanted to but she'd insisted and knowing how worried she'd been about him previously, he decided to go to put her mind at rest.

He had been told to write his feelings down, apparently it would be therapeutic for him to get into this habit when he was feeling down or emotional.

This didn't explain why he seemed to have plucked a random title from thin air.

Dispatches? He really didn't want to start writing long depressing pages about Henrietta. Or keep a diary about his thoughts. It had been suggested that he could perhaps, write a letter. He wouldn't have to send it to anyone.

He didn't think he'd ever written a letter in his life. He relaxed his shoulders, feeling the tension slip away. He let his mind go blank and closed his eyes for a moment.

Calmness. But still that tingle going down his arm, as if

he'd been given an injection.

He typed a few more words, experimentally, at first until suddenly he had a blinding sense of what he was meant to do. His fingers glided across the keyboard as he lifted each word from the depths of himself, giving them shape and form on the page.

It was four in the morning when he was finally satisfied. Overcome with weariness he sat back in his chair to contemplate the screen.

His first poem.

He felt there were more to come.

Volume Five

Ettie

∼Thirty Two∽
Revelations

1865 – Forest of Dean

In Resurrection Cottage, the last of the day's pale light ushers meekly in through the diamond panes of glass. Wrapped in a linen shawl, Ettie scarcely moves position on the bed they have made for her downstairs on the old couch; only her eyes flit restlessly around the room, chasing her daughter's wearied movements.

Cat is down on her knees, focussing her attention on the worn flag stones of the unlevelled floor, scrubbing away the day's dirt with a handmade brush of green twig. She is tired from looking after her grandchildren for the day and her movements are slow. Ettie prays that she herself will stay well tonight and not add to Cat's burden.

Ettie has been ill and suffering for weeks, but she thinks she has finally mastered the rhythm of the attacks. Underneath her covers she rises and falls with each wave of pain, riding the spasms like a horse galloping over jumps, until without warning the pain climbs to a higher level, cutting through her body like a blade.

Caught off guard she gives a smothered cry. Instantly Cat throws down her brush and rushes to her side.

'There now, Ma, you're alright. Doctor Marshall will be along soon. Let me fetch a cloth for your face, you're burning up.'

As the wave subsides, Ettie catches sight of her daughter's face, taut in the fading light, streaks of grey burnishing the pale tresses of hair through which she passes a weary hand as she moves into the scullery. Ettie feels the familiar sensation of guilt pulling like a knot around her heart.

When Cat returns, she reaches for her hand and indicates for her to sit beside her.

'Is Toby still here?'

Cat smiles. Ettie and her two-year-old great-grandson have always had a special bond.

'No Ma, he's gone back home. Maybe we'll see him tomorrow.'

'He looks so much like your father.' Her voice caught. 'It's uncanny.'

Cat takes a deep intake of breath. All these years her mother has said almost nothing about him. She stays deliberately quiet, hoping Ettie will say more.

'It's the eyes, you know. They're the exact same shade of pale blue.'

Cat hoards the information silently.

After a while Ettie says, 'You've been a good daughter Cat, more than I ever deserved. Were you happy to have been brought up here in Hydden? It hasn't been much of a life for you, I fear.'

323

'Don't be so daft. Life has been good to me.'

'You could have had so much more. You could have travelled. Been better educated. I took you away from all your chances.' Ettie pauses. 'And of course, I also took you away from having a chance to know *him*. I don't know if I did the right thing or not, Cat, and it worries me.'

Cat gives a gentle shake of her head and puts a finger to her lips, bidding her mother to lie quietly. It is all nonsense of course. She has lost count of the times she has heard this fantasy over the past months, listening to her mother tangled in the maze of words that make no sense, gradually soothing her out of delirium, watching protectively until the lashes fall and Ettie slips into sleep.

The next morning, for a while, Ettie is bright and free of pain. She asks Cat to sit with her. With no grandchildren to tend today, Cat gathers a bowl of blackberries, the first of the season, adds thick cream, and spoons a little into her mother's mouth.

'Ah, Cat.' She indicates the fruit. 'How quickly the seasons move; the end of summer already. I didn't think I would live to see another autumn.'

'Ma, don't be soft. Soon the apples will fall and I'll be feeding you up with blackberry and apple tart. Same as always.'

'No, Cat. I know I haven't got long left. The pain tells me that. But it's fine. I've had a good life here. I have been so happy. But I worry about you.'

'I'm happy too, Ma. I've got Richard and a wonderful family. I have never wanted more.'

'I've been trying to work things out...' Etttie lets her eyelids fall but she doesn't sleep. Images flash through her mind in random sequences and it takes her a while to put them together.

'Yes,' she murmurs, a while later, 'of course. That's how it happened.'

'Tell me Ma. Tell me our story.'

Ettie opens her eyes. Cat sits back and begins to listen to the tale her mother has been telling her since she was a child.

'I was still a young woman when I first came to the Forest of Dean; I must have been about twenty-one or twenty-two.'

Cat has fetched a pair of Toby's breeches from her sewing basket. Her daughter-in-law, not much of a seamstress, has asked her to mend a huge tear in the left leg. Toby and his sister Jane had been climbing trees in the wood and Toby had climbed too high and had been left dangling on a branch, awaiting rescue by his father. The trousers had been torn during the long climb down.

'Yes, Ma. You said you came here when Father went missing in the war.'

Ettie sighs, a sound that comes from the depths of her bones. 'I had no money. And you were about to be born. I had to do something. London was so very costly, you see.'

'And you had no family to help you.'

'I had no family to help me,' agrees Ettie. 'I'll tell you a secret, now, shall I? I hadn't planned to come here to the Forest. No, I was heading for Wales. When I got to the coaching inn in Fleet Street, I discovered I only had enough money to take me as far as Cheltenham. You were moving swiftly towards birth, buried underneath my heavy cloak and I had to go somewhere, so I purchased the ticket. I climbed inside, took my seat, placed my luggage around my feet for comfort and closed my eyes.'

Cat has put down her sewing. The story has deviated; it is the first time she has ever heard her mother mention Wales.

'Why Wales, Ma?'

Ettie closes her eyes She bats away the pain that she knows is coming. 'I thought it might be a nice, peaceful place. That's all.'

Cat looks at her mother sharply.

'The coach finally arrived in Cheltenham and deposited me at my journey's end. There I was, swaying on my feet, my trunk thrown down roughly onto the pavement. I could feel you coming. I sank down onto the trunk, right there in the middle of that genteel spa town; all the fine ladies and gentlemen scurrying to get home to their warm fires, to close the shutters against the dark, none of them caring enough to look down and notice me.'

'Except one, Ma.'

Cat, middle-aged, still loves to hear her mother's story, made more poignant as her mother slides inexorably towards the final fall of the curtain, when she will no longer be heard.

As if she has read her daughter's thoughts, Ettie mumbles. 'Sometimes, I feel as if I've been in a play, my entire life. And all those years ago, in that hopeless moment, I believed that the script had finally ended. That trunk of mine…that was the start of it all. My sister gave it to me…to be honest, I was never quite sure of her intentions…'

Cat makes an exclamation and bites her tongue. Ma has never mentioned having a sister. Hoping for further excursions into the unknown, she is disappointed when her mother takes up, once more, the well-trodden path of her tale.

'Reverend Appleton, turning a corner on his way home from the Poor Shelter where he had been helping out for the day, rushed to catch me as I fell. Called for the midwife who was over in the next town, found some lodgings where I could be delivered of my child. And an hour later, there you were, Cat. You were so alive, with your bawling mouth, your tiny fists that waved for my attention. I named you Catherine, after a dear friend of mine. And, all of a sudden, I wanted to live again.

'When Reverend Appleton came daily to see me, journeying through the forest on carter's wheels, bringing food and kind words, I was so grateful.'

'Dear old Appleby', says Cat, employing the pet-name she had always used.

'I don't know what would have become of us without him. He offered me a job and a home. I put aside all thoughts of Wales and resolved to become the best housekeeper I could possibly be.'

Ettie falls silent as her mind takes her into the trails of the past. When Reverend Appleton had first brought her to the village as his new housekeeper, she had stood on the fringes of the little village green, embracing the creeping sense that she had ended up exactly where she should have. Almost apologetically he had said, 'It's a small village, little more than a hamlet, really. But I think you might enjoy the peace here, Mrs Smith.'

She had looked around and spied the name of the village on the wooden board outside the church; Hyyden. Baby Catherine, already Cat, had looked up at her mother, reaching out from the safety of her mother's arms to trace the ghost of a smile on Ettie's lips.

Protected by two hills known as Sandstone and Blossom, the Saxon fields and dells of Hydden nestled comfortably into the Gloucestershire land, like a rug spread for a picnic. As well as the church there were two inns, a village school and a small shop. The locals, mostly made up of miners and agricultural workers who worked in nearby Cinderford, were friendly once they realised Ettie and Cat were there to stay.

And there had been no doubt that Ettie would stay. She fell in love with the forest and its surrounding countryside, enjoying the solitude and peace, walking for hours in her free time through meadows bejewelled with orchids, cradling Cat in the shelter of a blossoming wild cherry tree, listening to the splish-splash of the frogs through the murky pond water and the rise and fall of the nightjars' song in the falling dusk.

Ettie's wandering mind snaps into the present-day. 'Take me outside, Cat,' she whispers, 'I want to smell the air.'

Mother leans heavily on daughter as they head over to a cushioned wooden chair which has long been Ettie's spot in the centre of the garden, where she can observe at her leisure, the life of the Forest.

Once Ettie is settled with her shawl around her shoulders, her eyes drinking in the sights, Cat opens the kitchen door wide so that she can keep an eye on her mother from the window.

'Have you had enough to eat, Ma? You've barely touched that slice of ham.'

'I'm not feeling very hungry. But I would like something more to drink.'

Cat brings the jug of lemonade, freshly made that morning, and tops up her mother's glass.

'Cat; there is something I've always wanted to ask you. Did you mind not having siblings? Did you ever feel lonely growing up here in the Forest?'

As she has done so frequently in the preceding weeks, Cat looks at her mother as if she were a stranger. But she sees Ettie is serious, insistent on knowing her reply and so searches her mind as to her true feelings about her childhood.

She looks fondly around Resurrection Cottage. Set back from the path, it lay in the shadow of a small stone church, built to minister to the spiritual welfare of the ever-increasing number of cottagers and inhabitants in that area of the Forest of Dean.

The small but lively parish had been inherited by the new young vicar, Reverend Appleton who had been kept busy with increasing numbers as the population steadily grew, but he had still found time and a big enough heart to provide a new life for Ettie and baby Cat.

In Resurrection Cottage, Reverend Appleton had rearranged the first floor for himself; a small sitting room filled with books, a desk and armchairs for visitors, and a bedroom. Ettie and Cat slept comfortably at the top of the house in the newly white-washed attic room where Cat woke every morning to the cooing of the doves in the eaves and the sounds of her mother already at work downstairs.

The cast-iron range in the kitchen had been permanently lit as her mother cooked their meals, washed and dried their clothes, baked for the parishioners and kept the house clean and tidy.

Ettie had also worked in the church, sweeping it clean, polishing the brass, arranging the flowers and washing and mending the linens. After several months, Reverend Appleton had wondered how he had managed before she arrived, 'like an angel, fallen from above,' as he had been fond of saying.

Busy as she had been, Ettie always had time for her daughter. Cat remembered her as a gentle, encouraging mother, whether assisting her with unfathomable arithmetic problems, binding an ankle sprained during a fall from a tree or sewing a new dress for a dance on the village green.

She recalled her mother taking her into the church hall

one time, and playing songs on the old piano in the corner. She had been fond of taking her on long rambles, teaching her the names of insects and flowers. She could even speak and write in French and once, Cat had found a scrawl of unintelligible words in her mother's hand. Her mother had said it was a Greek translation of a poem and had put it away in a drawer.

She had been an attentive and loving mother, with scarcely a thought for her own self. Cat's childhood had been perfectly ordinary.

And yet.

Her mother had always been a closed-up soul, rarely discussing herself. Cat thinks of how her mother's face would sometimes cloud over, inexplicably, during a seemingly innocent conversation or at a stray remark, as if something deeply hurtful had been touched upon. When asked, she would never elaborate, just the slightest movement as if she were shouldering some private burden all on her own.

Cat casts her mind back to an odd occurrence, when she would have been about five or six years old. Her mother had been reading an item in a newspaper and had suddenly dropped it with a cry. When she timidly tugged at her mother's skirt, Ettie had looked down at her with a white face and said that somebody she had once known had been reported as having been drowned in the sea, in Italy. And she had drawn Cat onto her knee and rocked her for ages, as if it had been her loss, too.

At such times, she had thought she could see another woman peering out from behind her mother's calm eyes; someone less confident, less in command. Somebody less plain.

Cat shivers suddenly. Funny to think her mother had only

now mentioned that trunk. After all these years.

One cold winter's day, when her mother had been scrubbing the church steps free of mud, Cat, bored, had begun to poke around their rooms in the cottage, opening drawers and cupboards, growing increasingly disappointed to find nothing of interest. But then she had crawled underneath the iron bed-stead she shared with her mother and beneath a pile of hairy blankets had found a coaching trunk, with battered gold rivets and stretched calf skin.

In the uncomplicated modesty of Resurrection Cottage, the expensive trunk had seemed an object of mystery, out of place among their normal everyday belongings. Her heart had begun to race. Her child's eyes fixated on the small key in the lock which she knew she could turn and maybe open a host of secrets.

If she had possessed a sister they might have argued among themselves as to who would open the lid; a brother would have scornfully pushed past her doubts and rattled the key in the lock, like a pirate seeking treasure.

As she stared she thought she could see the faded outline of initials, 'H. W'. She traced them with an uncertain finger, wondering for the first time if Ettie was a shortened name.

Even as she had gazed at them, the initials seemed to lose clarity. Baffled, she had pulled the covering cloths back into place over the trunk and carefully replaced it under the bed.

Now, she looks across at Ettie, who meets her gaze with clear eyes. Cat realises, with a start, that she should have sought answers to these questions. Had her mother's family name begun with a 'W'? Maybe the trunk had been borrowed from the rarely-mentioned sister?

Questions that she knows she will never ask are left hanging in the air. Her mother looks at her expectantly.

'No, Ma,' she says slowly, 'I was never lonely. But perhaps it would have been nice to have had a sister.'

She hopes that in response to her reply, her mother may elaborate on her own shadowy sibling but Ettie stays silent. Only her eyes give her away; sliding into a furtive glance of regret.

*

∽Thirty Three∽
Fading

In the night hours, Ettie sloughs off the shrouds of sickness that cling to her in her waking moments and walks freely through her dreams, a young girl once again; one who brushes her hair dreamily in the looking glass, studies Latin verse by the light of a guttering candle, runs along a cobbled street distributing sheets of printed paper with a smile, picks her way across rock pools by the sea, searching for shells. Lying peacefully on a picnic blanket in a wooded valley by a stream, she is wishing for the moon and stars.

He never comes to her in these dreams. She wonders if he is forever trapped in the ocean waves that had eventually claimed him, trying to locate her in what he believed to be her own watery grave.

They would both go down in history as having drowned.

Strange.

She awakens suddenly, feeling her throat closing. She can't swallow. She can't breathe.

'Cat! Cat! Cat!'

'Hush, hush, now Ma. Everything's alright. You had a bad dream.'

'No, Cat it was a good dream...Cat, I need to tell you... there's something in the trunk...'

Cat stiffens. Again, her mother has acknowledged the presence of the trunk.

'The brooch...it's all I have left of your father. I had to hide it from him, you know. He would have sold it, otherwise.'

'But what brooch, Ma?'

'Don't get rid of it. I gave the ring away and now it's just the brooch that's left...'

'Ma. I understand, I'll keep it safe, I promise. But where...?'

Of course. It was in the trunk. Had been there for all these years.

'Pass it down to Toby. It's extremely valuable. He must keep it safe.'

'I will. Back to sleep now, Ma. It's not yet light.'

'Cat...' Ettie's voice is trailing away as she falls back into her slumber.

'I was wrong all those years ago. She did write a novel. When I read it, I saw myself...'

'Sleep tight, Ma. Sweet dreams.'

Resurrection Cottage is peaceful once more.

The weather has turned cool. Cat has been wearing a woollen shawl around her shoulders all day; even as she had baked batches of scones and cherry pies, the room growing hotter and hotter, she hadn't been able to throw off the chill that had spread over her.

When Richard, her husband arrives back from the new school room in town, late in the afternoon, bringing a fresh influx of chalk dust into the swept room, Ettie is already asleep in her makeshift bed in the corner of the room.

Cat rises to finish the evening meal and he follows her into the curtained recess of the scullery, kept permanently cool by the open back door through which blow the breezes from the Forest.

'A bad day?' he observes, briefly touching her shoulder.

'A disturbing sort of day. I can't stand to see Ma, wracked with pain as she is. And she's fading so fast I scarcely recognise her.' She pauses for breath. 'That's what I find so distressing; when she talks, she sounds like a stranger.'

Richard peeks into the room where Ettie is sleeping. 'Well, she shows no signs of talking now.'

He joins Cat at the pine table where she is scrubbing at a pile of freshly dug potatoes she had raised from the patch early that morning, ridding them of their claggy particles of earth.

'This morning' she continues 'I brought her a cup of tea. She was lightly dozing so I set it down beside her and made to tiptoe away but then her eyes unexpectedly snapped open, clear as day and she said to me quite firmly, for all the world as if she were ordering in an hotel, "Thank you, I would prefer coffee". I've never heard her speak like that. Her voice had changed; she sounded more refined.'

Richard raises his greying brows at her expression and swallows his amusement.

'And she carried on in that vein for a while longer. "I'd like it served in my special mug of pale pink porcelain, the one that my father keeps for me on the top shelf in the coffee house".

'Her father? Twenty-eight years I have been a part of this family and never have I heard your Ma speak of her family.

A coffee house sounds rather grand. She must have been reading something and grown confused.'

'No, Richard, I don't think she was imagining it. I will admit, I grew excited. Finally, some information about my grandfather after all these years! In my haste, my words tripped over my tongue as I rushed to ask more but even as I looked into her eyes it was as though the shutters had been drawn and once more she was out of reach. She fell back into sleep and that's the last I heard from her all morning.'

Richard takes the potatoes which she has put into a bowl and walks to the sink to run water over them before Cat puts them onto boil.

'There's something else odd that I haven't yet told you. Late last night, I heard her down here tossing restlessly and so I came down to settle her for the night only to find she had drawn the curtains wide open and had turned her face towards the lights which were blazing out from the Manor House across Farley's Meadow.

'She was smiling with pleasure and I was relieved to see her having a happy moment. She looked across at me and caught my wrist and said, "I see the Duke of Norfolk dines at Greystoke this evening. I wonder if he will be serving the venison tonight...how I should like to taste that dish again; the game mixed with the buttery potato pie spread across my golden plate". Cat pauses. 'She claims to have stayed with this Duke in his house for a week and everyone made a great fuss over her. A small house party, were the words she used. Imagine!'

'It sounds like a lot of nonsense if you ask me, Cat.'

'She sounded quite coherent.'

'If I'm not mistaken, the Greystoke estate is in the Lake District. Old Mr Roughwater's brother went to work in the gardens there, years back. Did your mother ever mention visiting the Lakes before?'

'She's been mentioning all kinds of places these past weeks; Bath, York, Wales and even Dublin. There were more places too. I've made a note of them somewhere. It's as if she has forgotten these past fifty years she has been here in the Forest of Dean.'

'Well, your Ma dining with the Duke of Norfolk sounds nothing more than a dream.'

'I'm sure you're right. How could the likes of Ma ever have been at a Duke's table! I'm sure Ma has never even been to the Lakes. She would have mentioned it, surely? None of it makes much sense; all I can do is write it all down as best I can and perhaps we can solve these puzzles in the future.'

'Just imagine your Ma eating venison from a plate of gold!'

Husband and wife laugh companionably together at the notion as they complete their simple meal with quiet content.

Later in the cooling dusk Cat chases the hens into the coop and latches it shut tight. She had found young Toby trying to entice a prowling fox up into his tree house den earlier in the day; when questioned he had said he wanted to see if he could teach it to dance.

Toby has such odd ideas and wild ways. Even though he is her grandson, sometimes she finds him ungovernable. But her son, Thomas, assures her he is as bright as a button. He can already write his name legibly. And read whole sentences. What to make of him? Her amusement at her grandson soon fades as once again her mother springs to the forefront of her mind.

Could Ettie have been to all those places in her youth? She knows so little of her mother's life. And her family, long dead she has always been told. Rarely had details been forthcoming.

Cat scarcely knows anything of her own father; only that he had met her mother in London where she had lived and that he had been a soldier who, before she was born had died out in India.

Now, when she picks apart this scant information she realises all her life she has accepted what was told, without truly believing it. She doesn't know why but she doesn't feel like a soldier's child. And she cannot imagine her mother married to one.

She draws in her breath to inhale the scents of early autumn in the Forest, her favourite time of the year; the lime, orange, yellow and red of the trees lambent in the final rays of the sinking sun, the lacework fronds of honeysuckle and wisteria weaving around the cottage walls, bestowing their final perfumed breath of the year.

She thinks of her mother, well spoken, almost a lady, as the villagers are oft to joke fondly of Ettie. Cat lingers on this last thought. Could she once have dined with a duke?

Upstairs she can see Richard in the bedroom, his moving shadow undressing against the shade. Overhead a barn owl stakes his claim to the night, screeching a warning over the top of the pines. It is time she went in.

Monday; wash day in Resurrection Cottage. Ettie, growing weaker each day has been carried out into the little patch of garden at the side of the cottage where a mild September breeze has scattered the clouds. She slumbers, wrapped in a red shawl upon a chair heaped with downy cushions, looking like the first fallen leaf of autumn.

Cat is pegging out the first wash load onto a hanging linen. It is bed linen, always cumbersome, billowing with life like pale phantoms flitting through the forest. She likes to give everything a blow-through before the cottage becomes festooned with lines of damp linen hanging from the ceiling like clouds.

Through the maze of sheets, she notices that Ettie is no longer asleep but is sitting up rigidly, moving her lips, her eyes glassy.

'Ma? Did you have a bad dream? Are you cold? I'll fetch a blanket from the box.'

'No! I must dress and pack my valise, for he is waiting for me. But you must not tell Mother or Father lest they stop me.'

Her voice is high pitched, girlish. Ettie gives a throaty giggle, staring into the distance at something a long way away. Cat feels a chill hearing her mother like this but a sudden instinct makes her run indoors. She has been diligently recording some of Ettie's outlandish utterances and she quickly retrieves the piece of paper with her assorted jottings and sits poised, pen at the ready.

Mother, Father,…at last, some family history.

She drops back down to the grass beside Ettie's chair and sits back on her haunches, listening, waiting.

'…the sun was setting as we finally rumbled into the city of Edinburgh. When we first set out on the journey we had no clue as to how to go about arranging the marriage but happily, we found ourselves travelling with a young lawyer who provided us with the information we needed. The day after we arrived we had to fabricate our story in order to gain a certificate, signed by two householders of the city and a member of the clergy, stating we were of legal age to marry, and the banns had been read in church.'

Ettie pauses for breath, her eyes still far away. 'I was not happy with this untruth, however, it did mean we could marry without delay. Two witnesses were pulled into the church from off the street. One of them, whose wife was waiting outside, presented me with a small posy which they had been taking as a gift for a relation; his wife had said a beautiful couple such as we were, deserved flowers on their special day. I wore a gown of violet silk that he was particularly fond of …'

That giggle rises from Ettie's throat again. Cat feels the hairs lifting on the back of her neck. Her parents had been married in Scotland! In her dying hours, her mother was laying a trail of discovery at her feet.

'As soon as we had been pronounced man and wife I remember my secret terror coming to the fore; we had lied in the face of God - were we committing a terrible sin? Ah, but when I looked deep into his blue eyes, nothing mattered. We would live a happy life as husband and wife, was the message contained therein. At the close of the ceremony we walked out assuredly to meet our future…'

On a whim, Cat pulls at Ettie's arm. Her mother's eyes, wandering wild, at last come to rest on her.

'Ma…tell me about my father.' Cat is suddenly desperate for crumbs of knowledge.

'All that is good about your father is contained in the pages of the notebook he once gave me. He was his truest and best self in those poems; the man I fell in love with as he was leaving his childhood behind but still trying to hold onto his dreams.'

'What notebook, Ma? Is it in the trunk?'

'I left it behind, for my beautiful girl.'

She falls back on her mound of pillows and Cat thinks she has fallen asleep but then Ettie's sunken eyes snap open and she sits bolt upright.

'He brought me to life and then he abandoned me.'

Her face crumples as tears leak down her waxy face. Cat

takes her frail form in her arms and gives what comfort she can, as questions fly through her mind.

Her mother's eyelids fall once more. Cat nestles her back in her chair but something is wrong. She can no longer sense any movement. She catches her breath, her eyes swimming, watching, waiting for the rise and fall of her mother's thin chest that fails to come.

Too late.

*

Cat sits quietly on the window seat in the bedroom. She has opened the curtains to stare out at the starry night and the garden that is bathed in moonlight.

She remembers Reverend Appleton turning over the vegetable patch in the corner, sowing rows of turnips and swedes in early summer, digging up frilled lettuces and bunches of pale orange carrots to present to Ettie with great pride, and herself as a child with a basket, stealing around in the hour before breakfast, plucking at the ripening strawberries, the stain on her lips giving her away each time.

Ten years ago, Reverend Appleton had been retired at the age of seventy-five. His congregation, dwindling year by year as families left the Forest to live in towns and cities, had been reassigned to a more central place of worship.

The little stone church was left to slowly crumble into dust but Resurrection Cottage had been generously signed over to him and he, upon his death, had left it to Ettie.

And now it belongs to Cat.

She and Richard are going to sell Resurrection Cottage. They are planning a move to Bristol with their son, Thomas, his wife Flora and the children, Toby and little Jane.

Thomas, a clever man, currently works as a clerk in an engineering company in Cinderford that supplies machine parts to the mining companies around the area, but he has confided to Cat how worried he is for the future of his children. Work opportunities in the Forest had been in decline for decades, since Cat had been a baby, with the loss of ancient rights to mining and grazing and the woods steadily enclosed.

Thomas intends to give his family a new start.

In the past, before her mother's ill-health, Cat and Richard had spent time in Gloucester, staying with an old school friend of Cat's with whom she regularly corresponded. Richard had spent his days down by the River Severn and the docks, sketching the ships, their masts and rigging stark against the summer skies, waves gently rolling into the port while she had enjoyed seeing the shops and taking the air in the newly-opened municipal park. In the evening they had attended a music festival in the cathedral.

She knows she will be happy in the city but she thinks there will be times when she might miss the trees and the open skies.

Her mother would have never envisaged leaving the Forest. Over the years, Cat has grown to realise that the place in which she had grown up had been much more than a home to her mother. It had been her sanctuary where beneath its sheltering gaze, Ettie had enjoyed a quiet peace.

The sky over the tangled tree line of the great forest is growing dim as day begins to trickle into the darkness. Before sleep finally claims her, she opens a drawer and takes out the sheet of paper containing the frenzied utterances she had scribed during Ettie's final days.

Since Ettie's death Cat has looked at it every day to see if the puzzle of her mother can be solved. A litany of place names. Who was Ettie's beautiful girl? And what poems?

Tomorrow, she decides, she will be brave and finally open her mother's trunk. When she finally turns the key in its lock, will she find a valuable brooch or indeed, any of the answers she seeks?

She climbs the stairs and clambers into bed beside the comforting form of Richard who is lightly snoring. She wraps herself in his warmth and his presence calms her racing thoughts and finally, she sleeps.

∼Epilogue∽

London, November 1816

She stood by the water's edge, dark in her cloak, darker still of mind. Night sounds came skimming like stones across the lake; a pair of water fowls flapping their wings as they bedded down in a nest of reeds, the shrill call of a fox to his vixen at the top of a grassy bank. A curricle drove by in the distance, its wheels rolling smoothly past on the way home from one of the pleasure gardens, the laughter of its occupants echoing faintly across the empty space of Hyde Park.

She lifted her head. She had been without companionship and laughter for so long she could acknowledge it in others without envy. She stood looking across the stretch of lake known as the Long Water, watching the wind blow and the water replying in gentle ripples, remembering a time when she herself could evoke a meaningful response. A child's affection. A sisterly kiss. The look of horror in her husband's eyes as she had lurched towards him one final time, arms outstretched. Begging.

The wind blew a harsh breath dispersing the memories, making the flesh on the tops of her un-gloved hands pucker into goose bumps. Her gold and turquoise engagement ring, bereft now of the sentiment it had once contained, rolled restlessly around her wedding finger.

She shivered. Thrusting her hands into the pockets of her cloak searching for warmth, she found instead several heavy stones that she could not remember placing there.

Staring with unseeing eyes across the body of water, she tried to divine the significance of her actions and realised that of course, she was about to drown herself.

A distant bell chimed the early morning hour. Breath streamed from her mouth in misty vapours and she watched it rise into the air, surprised by the reminder that she was still alive.

She took a step forward. The curving banks of the lake veered away sinuously, the blackness of the winter waters shining in the moonlight.

She was ready.

But as she made to step into the shivering blackness of the lake she saw a shadow move ahead. Instantly, she ducked back. She did not demand an audience for her final act.

Curiously she watched the shape take form in the dimness of the night and realised it was a young woman of about her own age, shivering in ragged clothes, standing a little further down the lake shore.

Seeing the woman about to wade into the water instinctively she cried out.

'Wait! Wait!'

Pulling her cloak tightly around her she ran clumsily with

her pockets full of stones towards the figure.

'Leave me please Madam, for pity's sake! You should be minding your own business as I'm minding mine.'

She was right of course. Even from a distance she discerned that the woman, gin-soaked and swaying, was endeavouring to cling on to her dignity. She saw that the woman was pregnant and ring-less and sighed at the inevitability.

She was struck by a thought. She twisted the ring on her own finger until it slid gently off. She had no further need of it. She hoped that perhaps it might bring a new owner more luck than it had ever brought her.

She held it out on her outstretched palm. It was too dark to see the pale icy blue of the turquoise but for a second the gold glinted under the stars.

'Take it' she said, coaxing the woman towards her like a frightened fawn 'It will fetch a good price. It will pay for a roof over your head and enough food to nourish yourself and the baby when it arrives.'

She expected to feel relieved when the ring was snatched greedily away. But she stood there emptily as if she had ceased to exist; her sole identity having been bound up in that circle of gold. She wondered if it would feel any different when the waters finally closed over her head.

She watched numbly as the woman put the ring on and pranced and preened, holding her ring finger up before her face, swaying by the water's edge, cackling uncontrollably.

With a start, she realised she had miscalculated. The woman was severely intoxicated and incapable of understanding the meaning of her gift. She hoped she would not lose the ring on her way home. She stepped forward to try and tuck the ring into one of the woman's pockets for safety.

But to her horror she found herself deserted on the water's

edge as with a drunken roar the woman took a running leap into the water.

Within moments the heavy folds of her skirts were soaked. The shock and cold of the water caused the woman's muscles to seize up. Caught in the grip of tangled water weed the woman began to be dragged under into the chilly depths of the lake.

'Come back!' Harriet screamed, 'there is no need for you to do this now!'

There was an answering cry of triumph from the centre of the lake. Clouds were closing in to extinguish the starlight as she listened in anguish to the final splashes and gurgles before they died away to an eerie silence.

She walked towards the water's edge as if it were now her turn but found she could go no further. She fingered the stones carefully, her mind working through the horrors of the night; tremors of energy running through her body as she realised she no longer had to be the same person who had left her lodgings all those hours before.

If she crept back and packed her belongings, she could disappear entirely. The landlady slept through thunder storms; she would not hear Harriet's final preparations. What of her children, Ianthe and Charles? They would have a better life free from the taint of her disgrace. She would have to do better with her next babe. But what about money? For a moment she mourned the loss of her engagement ring. But its discovery on the unknown woman's finger, would be vital.

And besides, if she found herself in dire straits, she still had Percy's brooch. She would have to force herself not to think about how he had given it to her with such love. Hopeless to try and fathom where that love had gone. She needed to put all her efforts into a new life. She would not willingly sell the brooch but it was comforting all the same, to know it was there.

It would be her talisman.

She threw the stones purposefully into the water before turning and walking briskly away into the darkness. Turning out of the park she hurried past the barracks, the restless horses snorting into the night air, and out into the streets beyond, colliding with somebody in her haste under the flickering light of the gas lamp on the corner of the street.

'I beg your pardon.'

It was Mr Alder.

'Pardon me, Madam, are you quite alright? It is late for you to be out on the streets alone.'

He stared closely at her and paled. 'Mrs Shelley!'

She clutched at him like the young girl she had been, not so long ago. 'Mr Alder, please do not be alarmed. I was so very tired of it all, you see and I thought…I don't know what I was thinking. Oh, Mr Alder, something terrible has occurred…'

She gestured in the direction of the park and the lake.

A sob wrenched from her lips.

'Can I do something for you, my dear Harriet?'

They stared at each other.

'Yes,' said Harriet after a long while, 'I think, perhaps you can.'

When she had finished speaking he nodded his acceptance slowly and with their heads touching, her tears mingled with his before she hurried away.

He watched her as she loped off into the distance to an unknown future, blending into the frozen darkness until he could no longer see her.

Author's Note

Harriet Shelley has been haunting me for thirty years. I first encountered her after a trip to a bookshop; when I came home, I discovered in my carrier bag along with my chosen novels, Shelley – The Pursuit by Richard Holmes. At that time, I was not a fan of biographies and I certainly didn't choose to bring this one home with me. How (or why) the book made its way to me, I will never know but I sat down to read it and there, in the early pages of Shelley's life, I met Harriet. The first thing I thought after I'd read about her was how sad that I had never heard of her before. But the thing that really excited me was the notion that here, in Harriet's story, undoubtedly, was the genesis of Frankenstein, Mary Shelley's most famous tale.

Although the novel is clearly a fictionalised telling of Harriet's tale I have stuck closely to her timeline. The facts of her life with Percy and the people she met have been well documented but naturally all scenes and dialogue in the novel have been entirely imagined. And of course, the rest is entirely the product of my creative inventiveness.

Some suggested reading to further your interest:
Frankenstein/Mary Shelley; *Shelley – The Pursuit*/Richard Holmes; *Harriet Shelley Five Long Years*/ Louise Schutz Boas; *In Defence of Harriet Shelley*/Mark Twain; *The Godwins and the Shelleys*/William St Clair; *Shelley's Lost Letters to Harriet*/ Leslie Hotson; *The Esdaile NoteBook*/Kenneth Neill Cameron; *Shelley and His Circle*/Kenneth Neill Cameron; *The Life of Percy Bysshe Shelley*/Thomas Medwin; *Harriet Shelley's Letters to Catherine Nugent*/ *Portrait of Shelley*/Newman Ivey White

Works by PB Shelley mentioned or quoted:
Prose:
St Irvyne or The Rosicrucian
The Necessity of Atheism
An Address to the Irish People
Declaration of Rights
Poetry:
To A Balloon, Laden with Knowledge
To Harriet
Queen Mab
Stanza Written at Bracknell
Alastor or the Spirit of Solitude
The Cold Earth Slept Below

Acknowledgements

I would like to thank all those who have read earlier drafts, given advice and continuous encouragement, especially Maurice Landsberger, Eloise Sinclair, Jo Sinclair, Diane Taylor, Harriet Blakeman, the Book Club girls, Chalfont Writers' Hub and my fellow volunteers at Chalfont St Peter Library. My thanks also to Antony Marr (www.chalfontresearch.co.uk) for genealogy advice - all errors and omissions are entirely my own. Grateful thanks to Jill Rennie for the beautiful artwork, and Hideaway Press for the typesetting and cover.

As ever, all my love and gratitude to Mike and Luke for their time and patience.

ABOUT THE AUTHOR

Sarah Roux was born and bred in North London but now resides in Buckinghamshire with her husband and son. *The Chronicles of Harriet Shelley* is her second novel. When she is not writing, researching or parenting, she can usually be found wandering the stacks of the community library, of which she is extremely fond.

Sarah's first novel, *A Painted Samovar*, is available on Amazon

For more information go to: www.sarahroux.co.uk

34977918R00211

Printed in Poland
by Amazon Fulfillment
Poland Sp. z o.o., Wrocław